To Aust

Valued friend and thanks for your excellent contribution to the Event.

DEADLY HUSH

Warm wishes

[signature]

March 2024

- Douglas Stewart -

WHAT'S THEY'VE SAID ABOUT THE RATSO SERIES

"Gripping, action-packed thriller."
   – Peter James – Voted the Best Crime Author of all time.

***** "A brilliant start to meeting Ratso. A story you can believe in and a gritty style of writing that works."

***** "Could not put it down!"

***** "Wow! A definite 5-star from me!"

***** "Fantastic read, great characters, gripping storyline. Roaring success Mr Stewart!"

***** " Engenders the same get-to-the-end compulsion as does a *Harlan Coben* crime suspense novel"

"People just love your books – you are getting an unusual percentage of high rankings."
   – M J Rose – New York Times best-selling author.

TABLE OF CONTENTS

What's they've said About the Ratso Series	ii
Geneva, Switzerland	1
London	5
London	9
Notting Hill, London	11
Putney	14
Putney	20
Mayfair, London	26
Mayfair, London	29
Mayfair, London	33
Mayfair	37
South Yorkshire	42
Hambledon, Surrey	46
Kirby Hill, North Yorkshire	48
Kirby Hill, North Yorkshire	50
Kirby Hill, North Yorkshire	53
Putney	55
North Yorkshire	57
South Yorkshire	60
M1 Motorway, Donington Park Service Area	64
Putney	68
Cricklewood	71
Bonnitor	77
Putney	82

Trafalgar Square, London	87
Putney	91
Bonnitor	94
Putney	98
Bonnitor	101
Putney	107
Bonnitor	111
Fulham High Street	114
New Scotland Yard	122
Battersea SW11	125
Hammersmith Grove, W6	127
Fitzrovia, London	129
North Yorkshire	138
Credenhill, Hereford	145
Ross-on-Wye	151
Bonnitor	155
Oxford	158
King's Lynn	167
Putney	174
Putney	176
Roehampton	180
Roehampton	182
Roehampton	184
Putney	187
Putney	191
Roehampton	196
The Shard – London SE1	200
Battersea SW11	205
The Shard – London SE1	207
Fulham SW6	210
New Scotland Yard SW1	214

Ravensworth - North Yorkshire	216
Putney	219
Putney	223
Piccadilly Circus	225
Putney	227
Heathrow Airport	234
Barbados	236
At Sea	242
Torrington, Bonnitor	245
Torrington, Bonnitor	247
Torrington, Bonnitor	250
King's Lynn	253
Torrington, Bonnitor	257
Kings Lynn	263
Torrington, Bonnitor	266
Torrington, Bonnitor	270
Torrington, Bonnitor	277
South End, Bonnitor	282
Torrington Marina	288
Grantchester Hotel, Bonnitor	292
Bridgetown, Barbados	294
Grantchester Hotel, Bonnitor	300
Grantchester Hotel, Bonnitor	304
Police HQ – Bonnitor	306
Police HQ – Bonnitor	310
Torrington, Bonnitor	315
Folkestone, Kent	319
Battersea SW11	327
Bonnitor	329
Battersea	332
Heathrow Airport	334

Heathrow Airport	336
Putney	341
Putney	346
New Scotland Yard	350
Putney	356
Putney	360
The Rogerson Hotel	365
The Bartlett Suite	368
The Rogerson Hotel	371
The Rogerson Hotel	373
The Rogerson Hotel	374
The Rogerson Hotel	380
Putney	384
Belmarsh Prison	390
The Connaught Hotel	394
Contacts	397
Books by Douglas Stewart	399
About Douglas Stewart	399

Geneva, Switzerland

19th June.

36 minutes to go.

It had been 36 days.

The planning.

Now, it was 36 minutes.

The journey across the border into Switzerland from the small French town of Coppet into Geneva's city centre was an easy seven minutes. The beauty of the distant towering shape of Mont Blanc rising beyond Lake Leman was of no interest. As the double-decker train sped beside the lake's silvery sheen, the killer's heart rate was steady, palms dry.

36 minutes.

No more, no less.

Swiss precision.

It felt good.

At Gare Cornavin, the killer joined the criss-cross of passages under the platforms. Of no interest were the tiny shops stuffed with cuckoo-clocks, tourist junk, cheap menswear or the busy convenience stores. After surfacing near the station entrance, the air outside was summer evening warm. Thanks to Google Maps, the scene was all so familiar – the red and white trams, the overhead cables, the long white bendy-buses and the line of taxis.

The clock above the entrance showed 7-35 pm. Perfect for the twenty-minute walk to the Rue du Puits-Saint Pierre in the heart of the Old Town. In London, there were thousands of CCTV cameras.

Not here. Not even one. The citizens of Geneva had not wanted them.

Privacy over Protection.

Within twenty-two minutes, one citizen was going to regret that.

After leaving Place Cornavin, there were fewer pedestrians scurrying from and to the station. In no hurry, taking a left here, a right there, this was just another forgettable figure going about anonymous business.

In the narrower back streets, there were drinkers and diners seated at outside tables. The restaurants were busy with prosperous Swiss lawyers, overweight bankers, unsmiling Russians and smart-suited diplomats on expenses, guzzling champagne with their shellfish or *filets de perches*. Barely pausing to admire the views from the bridge over the Rhone, the killer spotted the time on the clock.

Still on schedule.

Not good to loiter!

Fatal to be late.

Like Swiss railways and their clocks, meticulous planning had showed that Jules Quercy's routine was precise to the minute. With a staff of fifteen, he operated the Laterre-Quercy Private Family Office. As a bachelor, he lived a solitary life. For the pencil slim Quercy, life was about making money – dollars, euros and sterling. More, much more than he could ever spend. From his boutique premises, the team managed investments for a family of Ukrainian billionaires. Even before Russia's annexation of Crimea, let alone the February 2022 invasion, the Kovalenko family had flitted, butterfly-like, between homes in Paris, Cannes, Manhattan, London and Miami.

Home for Quercy was a discreet and high-ceilinged apartment, one floor up on the Rue du Puits-Saint Pierre. It was just 600 metres from his penthouse offices. Downstairs was an antique dealer displaying fine oil paintings and period furniture. The contents of Quercy's apartment were no less valuable. The killer knew that Quercy's street entrance was through oversized double wooden doors. Back in the day, a horse and carriage would have passed through with room to spare. Now, behind the doors, was an arched courtyard with matching high-security doors for accessing the two upstairs apartments.

At the end of the street with 48 seconds to spare, the killer paused as if admiring the water splashing from the floodlit and moss encrusted fountain.

Time to move on.

Beneath the now dark skies, every step was snail's pace slow. Outside a red-painted bistro, the drinkers were younger and mainly shirt-sleeved. Clutching their beers with condensation dripping down their glasses, there was laughter, probably about successful trades on Wall Street or the Zurich Bourse. From inside came the smell of woodsmoke, garlic and steak.

A few seconds later and right on cue, Quercy's dapper figure overtook the killer without a second look. He stood about five foot-eight but with his shoulders hunched, it looked less. His three-piece charcoal suit was tailored. His silk tie was yellow with blue spots. His shoes were tasselled black loafers. He walked, leaning slightly forward, his head lowered, deep in thought.

He had less than twenty seconds to plan his next millions.

Jules Quercy, aged sixty-one, was taking his last few steps.

Now, keeping pace behind the financier on the cobbled street, the killer removed gloved hands from the pockets of the dark grey cargo jacket. Quercy stopped by the heavy oak doors and tapped in a code. Instantly, one half creaked slowly open. It also closed slowly, ample time for the killer to follow Quercy through. As the financier stood by the door to his apartment, too late he realised that he was not alone. He swung round, his heavily lined face showing confusion.

Before he could utter a word, let alone scream, his mouth had been gripped and his scrawny neck clamped. Almost instantly, his neck was twisted in a sharp and deadly movement. Within seconds, his body became limp. The killer let him fall onto the cobbles, relishing the sight of the dead man lying on his back staring up at the arched ceiling.

I love killing.

London

Still angry after a mauling by a smart-arse King's Counsel down at the Old Bailey, newly promoted Det. Chief Insp. Todd "Ratso" Holtom hurried along Fleet Street. The throbbing rhythm of Iron Maiden's *Number of the Beast* filled his ears. The satanic undertones resonated with his feelings about British justice.

After yet another move, Ratso was now stationed in Jubilee House, just south of Putney Bridge in south-west London. Now, as the Met Police evolved, he was part of the Major Investigation Team. Thanks to the pen-pushers, London's Met Police was always evolving as one *brilliant* plan was discarded in favour of something even better. *Or so they said.* Ratso reckoned the big winners were political correctness, woke madness and alphabet spaghetti jargon.

In theory, he could walk to work from his apartment on Hammersmith Grove in under an hour. In reality, mostly, he no time for that. That was a plus. Mainly, he cycled, hating every dangerous diesel-fuelled minute of it. Today, though, he had gone straight to the Old Bailey. There, in the witness-box, he had crashed and burned – victim of a weak judge and a sneering but cunning pigeon-toed KC.

After two long hours, Ratso's truthful evidence had sounded as unconvincing as a car dealer's warranty. Ratso could now imagine the judge directing the jury that the murderer loved his Mum and was a good boy really. In his red robes, the old beak had seemed unconcerned about soaring knife crime. No doubt tonight the old fool would be in bed reading the Human Rights Act. He never would face reality – not until awoken by a masked burglar threatening his throat with a machete.

Now, as he passed yet another new nail-salon, Ratso saw an empty can. He imagined it as the judge's backside and let rip with a mighty swing of his leg. The can flew through the air before spinning and clattering along the gutter.

He felt better for that.

Through his headphones, Bruce Dickinson's scream fitted the moment.

After tubing it to Putney Bridge, he entered Jubilee House. "Rare seeing you suited, boss," prompted Det. Con. Nancy Petrie. She was one of the rising stars that Ratso had wanted in the team. "You look like a farmer who hasn't worn a suit since his wedding."

"Smell the mothballs, can you? If I never wore one again, it would be too soon."

Petrie saw the weariness on Ratso's face. "Went badly, did it, boss?"

"Don't go there. Anything exciting?" He saw the slight shake of her brunette hair with blonde streaks. He looked around the lines of desks. "Caldwell here?" He was referring to Det. Chief Superintendent "Smart" Alex Caldwell, his boss and the biggest *no-no* about his recent posting. Their turbulent history dated back to Ratso's days in Clapham at SCD 7. Neither had forgiven or forgotten.

To Ratso, Caldwell was oily, dislikeable, homophobic, devious and with ambition beyond his capability. Even picturing him in his designer suits made Ratso's flesh creep. To Caldwell, Ratso was ruthless, ambitious, devious and a dangerous maverick.

Petrie pushed aside her bowl of tofu, hemp and chia seeds. "Smart said he was off to the Yard. Don't know why."

"Licking backsides as usual then." Ratso ran his fingers through his brown hair, still combed Caesar's style. He sounded sour and his mouth twitched. "So nothing new?"

"The usual bollocks." She paused debating whether to make his day worse. "Tosh phoned." She was referring to Det. Sgt. Watson.

"And?" Ratso perched his tall, angular body against the corner of her desk. His slate-grey eyes showed impatience.

"Not good. The doc has signed him off again. Reckons it's Long Covid."

Ratso looked up sharply, his hooded eyes full of concern. "Poor sod! What's it mean? For him personally? Not gonna finish him off, is it?" He tugged at a droopy ear lobe, not one of his best features.

"Nah! Tosh says give it a few weeks." She raised an eyebrow before continuing. "Wikipedia reckons Covid picks on fat guys." Petrie shrugged, thinking of the bulk that Watson took everywhere. "Nuff said, eh? I was reading. Covid can cause chest pains, fatigue … or confused thinking." Petrie's cheeky glance said it all. Watson was brave and dedicated but his brain rarely functioned faster than bottom gear.

"I'll take him grapes but he'd prefer a double-whopper with cheese and fries." Ratso's face got close to a smile.

"Yeah!" Petrie patted her own trim stomach and grinned. "Till then, we'll still be one light."

Though he rarely smiled, his designer-stubbled face was friendly and always expressive. "Thank God I got Jock Strang posted here." Having heard that Strang had been bored to his boots on white-collar crime "with papers stacked higher than Ben Nevis," Ratso had put in a word. Within weeks, the big no-nonsense Glaswegian, now nearly fifty, had been promoted and transferred as Det. Insp. Strang. Ratso glanced at a new message on his phone. He turned away to head for his office.

Moments later, courtesy of Teams, Ratso could see Kirsty-Ann

Webber in Florida. She was seated at a large but empty desk. Until she had just quit, K.A. had been a detective with the Fort Lauderdale Police Department. Their relationship had grown from a shared crime investigation into something way beyond attraction. That was until Covid and three thousand miles of ocean had kept them apart. "Hey K.A! That's some picture you just sent. I bet you're proud."

"Sure am. Like my new shingle?" She was referring to the sign displayed outside her office.

"Terrific." Ratso was looking at the photo of her new office with a sign outside – *Webber Associates – Investigators.*

"It's strange not moseying on down to HQ. But the Chief wished me well."

Ratso had a bunch of regard for her former boss, Bucky Buchanan, the pugnacious yet friendly Chief at FLPD. "Mutual respect, no doubt." He took in the sparse surroundings as she circled her new office. "Still an empty desk?"

"Pretty much. But there's gonna be plenty of work." Ratso saw a guy appear, dodging around a packing-case. "Sorry, Todd. I must go. I'm fixing insurance cover. Great hooking up. See you soonest."

"Cheers to that. It's been a sod of a day." He blew her a kiss and received one back. "Let's talk later." He glanced at the Apple watch she had given him. It had so many functions, he guessed it played God Save the King if you pressed the right button. He sat down at his desk to check the day's events.

Petrie had been right. Nothing new. But there would be. There always was.

London

Three weeks after Quercy's murder, throughout Switzerland, it was no longer big news. Plenty enough had speculated on-line about Quercy's bachelor lifestyle. Others favoured theories of a hitman from Russia, Belarus, the Ukraine and all stations east. Stories circulated that Quercy had recently called in a billion-euro loan provided to a Kazakhstan commodity trader. Murders of bankers and financiers always made international news and Ratso had skim-read the headlines. There had been no request for help from Geneva and so he had given the story no more thought. Compared to a double-murder in Chiswick High Street, the execution of a Swiss gnome was only of passing interest.

Ever since European capitals had become home to countless oligarchs with their billions, murder squads had been kept busy. Ratso knew only too well that it was not just oligarchs who died mysteriously. Tainted by working for or against them, bankers, lawyers, journalists and accountants had been murdered or had *apparently* committed suicide, jumping from roofs or falling from high windows or drowning in the bath.

Lawyers and bankers in London, Frankfurt, Zurich and Geneva had received warnings or stark death threats from Eastern Europe. Some had ignored the warning and paid the price. In the Swiss banking community, Quercy's death had been no surprise. Sudden death was the price for mixing with a world of laundered money and long-running vendettas.

Now, a ninety-minute flight away from Geneva, in a pub off the

Old Kent Road in south-east London, a solitary figure was seated in a corner. On the beer-stained table there was a bottle of sparkling water and a grated carrot salad. The football, tennis and golf on the screens lining the walls were of no interest.

I've ticked every box.
I've dotted every i and crossed every t.

Dermot Doyle, the UK's most loved TV presenter, would soon be dead. By reading Doyle's banal Twitter-feed and Facebook pages, his tastes, social life and TV schedule were an open-book. Since Geneva, there had been no rush to murder the bouffant-haired and boyish faced Doyle.

Careful groundwork was more important.

In varying disguises, West End casinos had been cased, mainly watching but sometimes playing the occasional few hands of blackjack. Early evenings had involved mingling with drinkers in the LGBT bars in the crowded streets near Piccadilly Circus. Today's research had involved a high-vis jacket, hard-hat and a clipboard for crossing London to Ladbroke Grove. By pounding pavements and with help from Google maps, the streets surrounding Doyle's magnificent home were now familiar territory.

Just three days to go.

Notting Hill, London

At 3-25 a.m. Ladbroke Grove was silent and almost deserted. It was three miles from the late-nighters and their whoops and shouts around the clubs, fast-food takeaways and casinos near Leicester Square. The street was lined with large properties suitable for CEOs of international corporations, oligarchs, merchant bankers, celebrities and politicians. It felt spacious because the pavements were wide and the imposing houses were mainly set back behind walled and tree-lined gardens.

Dawn was still a while away as the figure in dark clothing, hair almost invisible beneath a black cap, entered Ladbroke Grove from the east. Head bowed to avoid security-cameras, the lone individual turned northwards towards the distant Tube Station. A passing taxi purred by. If the occupants had looked, they would have noticed nothing memorable. More likely, their focus would have been on an urban fox, scurrying across the road and disappearing into the shadows.

The figure never paused beside Doyle's mansion. The destination was the derelict property immediately beyond. It had a planning notice pinned to the entrance. Soon, a giant makeover would be under way. Tonight, there was no moon and the silent shape of the mansion stood darkened and unloved, its doors and windows shuttered. After slipping between the tall brick entrance pillars, every step across the cracked concrete drive was familiar.

The intruder slipped deep between the abundant fragrant shrubs until beside Dermot Doyle's immaculate front garden. The low boundary wall presented no problem. With an easy movement, the shapeless figure straddled that and was hidden in the bushes and rowan trees that lined Doyle's side of the boundary.

The shadowy silhouette of Doyle's palatial Regency house was set back about twenty-five metres from Ladbroke Grove. At night, the glossy paintwork of the front-door, with its prominent brass fittings, was invisible. Lawful visitors, after being seen and quizzed using the entry-phone, entered his property through a solid arched gate set in a wall, topped with razor-wire.

When Dermot Doyle had bought Vortex House for close on twelve million pounds, privacy had been a high priority – that plus the convenience for getting to the White City TV studios just a few minutes away. As the UK's highest profile and best paid Breakfast Show presenter, he wanted to enjoy summer drinks on his west-facing patio undisturbed by prying fans. Even so, his address had been leaked onto social media. Now, the white stucco wall was plastered with scrawled hearts and loving messages from his army of followers, most of them men.

From a previous discreet visit, the intruder knew it was fourteen slow paces over the damp earth, every small step tucked in behind the foliage. One false move into the lawned area and the floodlights would be triggered and alarms would sound.

Eleven, twelve, thirteen, fourteen.

No alarms, no light.

It was 03-27 a.m. Outside on Ladbroke Grove, a sleek grey executive limo pulled up to take Doyle to the studio. Almost at once, the front-door opened and a downstairs light revealed a chandelier hanging in a spacious hall before Doyle closed the door behind him. Immediately, overhead lights illuminated every corner of the weed-free lawns and colourful flower-beds. Swinging a laptop-bag onto his shoulder, the celebrated presenter leaped down the three steps from the patio. He was wearing a sloganned light yellow T-shirt and dark yellow Bermuda shorts, so unlike his screen image of a hand-stitched Savile Row suit and silk ties.

Full of energy, the thirty-four-year-old bounded along the paved path towards the gate. As he stretched out to activate the security lock, from the shadows behind the trees and shrubs, two hands grasped his mouth and neck. With fingers carefully positioned, his carotid artery was squeezed hard so that his knees started to sag. Then, the killer gave his neck a sudden and violent twist. Death was silent and almost instantaneous. Having eased the slim figure to the ground, the murderer tucked a playing-card, the Jack of Spades, into the neckline of the yellow T-shirt.

Uncertain how long before the limo driver would investigate, the killer moved fast, tracking back out of sight back into the neighbouring property. Exiting to Ladbroke Grove was now impossible but scurrying through the overgrown wilderness next door, the rear boundary was close. There, with impressive agility, the intruder escaped was over the wooden fence and into the public gardens behind.

03-31 a.m.
Right on schedule.

The route back to the car involved dodging the cameras, crisscrossing the backstreet, hooded head lowered. The getaway car, with illegible number-plates, was one of several parked three streets distant from Doyle's body. By now, on Ladbroke Grove, the limo driver had given up calling Doyle's phone. He could hear it ringing, just the other side of the gate. Instead, he dialled 999.

DCI Todd Holtom was going to have a short night.

Putney

Ratso got the call at 4-20 a.m. After burning off a ton of calories at cricket practice, he had put a fair few back on by sinking pints of Guinness with his mates. Later, in his apartment, after grilled bacon and tinned tomatoes on toast, he had zoomed Kirsty-Ann. In her tank-top and red shorts, as she tilted back in her chair, her appearance was quite a turn-on. As usual with his late-night calls, the conversation had turned to when they could meet up. As always, it had been inconclusive.

"Todd, it's real difficult. My Mom's doing okay but she's getting older. She's still not recovered from her heart operation. Leon is a handful for her – and for anybody come to that. I can't step away for too long. I'd say come here but you may see so little of me."

Ratso said that he understood. What's more, with her new business, he thought it was true. "Let's hope something works out soon."

"I do too. Truly I do."

Ratso thought he believed her.

After the call was over, at long gone midnight Ratso had hit the sack. The phone's intrusion had not been welcome. "Dermot Doyle? *The* Dermot Doyle? Oh okay. I'll be there. Twenty minutes, maybe thirty." He was still getting used to the thought of becoming increasingly deskbound. With promotion had come mountains of paperwork and less time at the sharp end. But being at a crime scene during the golden hours, was vital – at least that's the way he saw it.

Some eight hours later, at shortly, after midday, Ratso was in the ancient cellars of his favourite wine-bar on the Upper Richmond Road. With him, were Jock Strang and Nancy Petrie. They were surrounded by dusty wine bottles and black-and-white photos from historic moments in London's history. After ducking under the low, curved and blackened brickwork, Ratso had treated them to a bottle of red and a massive cheese-board. Petrie though was only drinking water.

"I mean Dermot Doyle. It's sort of like ... oh shit, some nutter's murdered John Lennon," prompted Petrie. "Not that I was alive in 1980," she added hastily.

"I was thinking more of Jill Dando, the BBC presenter," Ratso volunteered. "She was a national treasure before the expression became hackneyed."

"Remind me boss," said Jock. He cocked his head as he spoke. This made it even more obvious that his right eye was lower than his left – a legacy of policing the neds in Anderston, one of Glasgow's toughest areas.

"She was professionally executed just off the Fulham Palace Road. Not far from here and not far from Ladbroke Grove. That killer is still on the loose. Dando had also been a presenter on Breakfast TV but was more remembered for Crimewatch."

"Aye. I remember now. Terrible, just terrible," Strang agreed, his rasping Glaswegian accent adding emphasis to the words. "Ye think the same guy murdered Doyle? Jill Dando was a wee while back. 2004?"

"Before then, Jock. 1999. Murdered on her doorstep in Gowan Avenue. Different cause of death. Single bullet to her head. Doyle looks a pro-job too. Getting access via the neighbouring property showed good planning. "

"So not far from Ladbroke Grove," Petrie murmured, sipping her sparkling water.

"Under four miles, Nancy," Ratso nodded. "But with the White City TV studios close by, that area is filled with media celebs. "I met Jill on Crimewatch. I was appealing for help with a murder in South Croydon."

"Jill Dando had enemies then?"

"Crimewatch stirred up a hornet's nest of dangerous villains. Which brings us to Doyle."

Jock looked longingly at the bottle of Malbec and then topped up his glass to the very brim. "Nothing like Crimewatch in his CV?"

"Apparently not." Ratso selected a chunk of Stilton. "I'm no expert about Breakfast TV. Or on Dermot Doyle come to that. Nancy?"

She helped herself to a low-fat cheese and water-biscuit. "I liked him. He was never an in-your-face interviewer. His style was relaxed, sitting on a sofa. He was your good friend chatting *just to you*." Petrie's voice showed more emotion that either listener had expected. "I felt he was almost sitting with me, sharing my muesli."

"You couldna help but like him," Strang agreed.

"Someone didn't." Ratso looked at each in turn. "Okay. Public image. Doyle was a regular guy. Why would a professional killer take him out? Unlikely to be bad debts – not on what these so-called celebs get paid. But it needs checking out. Nancy?"

"Boss, he was a gay icon, so ..."

"I saw the graffiti on his wall. This doesn't feel like a gay-hate crime. Far too professional."

"Okay. Let's think jealousy. Lovers falling out?"

Ratso flicked a crumb from his brown leather jacket below which he was wearing an open-neck striped shirt. "Doesn't look that way either. Not a crime of passion. Someone wanted Doyle dead and no messing. Someone paid big money for a job well done."

"Espionage?" said Petrie. "A James Bond assassin type would kill with bare hands."

"Can't rule that out. Maybe a trained professional. But how does that fit with Dermot Doyle?"

"Ye're right, boss. This smacks of hitman." Strang rubbed what was left of his receding iron-grey hair. "I shut off the surrounding streets but the guy would have been long gone."

"Time of death?"

"Nothing official but it had to be 03-30 a.m. Not much traffic around then. Jock – get someone onto NAS and view the ANPR from say two till four. Cameras on buses. Domestic security cameras."

"Looking for?"

"In a two-mile radius, the same vehicle arriving and departing. There are footprints for forensics to get their teeth into." Ratso grinned. "Footprints and teeth! I like that image. They'll maybe also get fibres from the overgrown garden next door. It's a wilderness – thorns, nettles and unkempt grass. Forensics are all over it." Ratso took the last tranche of Brie. "The limo driver saw no pedestrians or parked cars on Ladbroke Grove. Nancy, what did you find out about Doyle's personal life?"

Petrie popped a grape into her rounded mouth. "I googled him. There's a ton of stuff. He lived alone. Never married. A past live-in boyfriend had left on good terms and is now living in Marbella. DeeDee, as the tabloids called him, often played tennis at the Hurlingham Club. Though well known in the gay community, he hung out with heteros as well – many were politicians or media celebs."

"Or thought they were," Ratso said.

"He threw iconic dinner-parties. Eclectic mix."

"Looking for a new partner?"

"Seemingly not. Only last week, he said he was in no hurry."

"I'll check that," Strang offered, before suggesting another bottle which Ratso forbade.

"Smart Alex wants me to report." Ratso's brow briefly furrowed and his chewed lip showed his displeasure at the prospect.

"That louse! He'll kick your arse round the room if ye let him," Strang sympathised. "Come back DCI Tennant, all is forgiven. Right enough, Tennant was a lazy piece of shite but he wasna' reptilian like Caldwell."

Ratso's eyes did his laughing as he recalled Tennant, their unloved boss at SCD7. "Anything else I should know about Doyle because if I don't, sure as hell, Smart will."

"Casinos. Doyle played the tables. Maybe unpaid debts, money troubles after all?"

Ratso's sniff showed disinterest. "I don't see him getting into debt with moneylenders, gambling or crossing the Triads at a West End casino. But Jock, get someone to visit the casinos. Check how often he played. Where he played. Check out the crowd he hung out with. Was he a high-roller? How much did he risk? His parents, siblings. You'll need to get them interviewed." Like a mole tunnelling up into daylight, Ratso stood at the top of the stairs, blinking in the sunshine. Then he led them across at the lights, surrounded by Putney's polluted air from the endless traffic on the High Street. Overhead, the noise from a Boeing 747 on its final approach to Heathrow added to the noise and the fumes.

"The playing-card in his T-Shirt?" Nancy's eyes showed her eagerness for Ratso's take. "Linked to casinos? Blackjack?"

"The Jack of Spades?" Though the shrug was non-committal, the listeners knew Ratso better. Sure enough, he continued. "Significant. Chosen for a reason."

"Which is?"

A foxy look crossed Ratso's face, quickly to be replaced by his eyes closing and a head-shake. "If I knew that, I'd have more foresight than Mystic Meg. I'd know the winner of the 3-30 at Ascot. But it is significant." He paused to face them. "If it had been gay-hate, I'd have expected a Queen."

Putney

Det. Chief Superintendent Caldwell was looking at his phone and standing beside a grimy window. He never slouched and so looked his full beanpole six-foot-two. He seemed as pleased to see Ratso as if he had trodden in dog-shit. With disdain, he took in Ratso's open-neck striped shirt beneath his ageing jacket and black jeans. The trainers also had too many miles on the clock. The contrast with Caldwell's navy hopsack suit with razor-sharp creases could not have been greater. The sleeves of his monogrammed pale blue shirt revealed chunky gold cufflinks. The Windsor-knotted tie was in three shades of blue. His black loafers were so highly polished he could have used them for up-skirting.

Ratso wondered if perhaps he did.

What Caldwell did in his down-time was an unknown and a matter for canteen speculation. Ratso despised the Beau Brummel elegance and, as usual, wondered how Smart could afford to look like a model out of GQ magazine. What really made him want to puke was the look on Smart's face. The smirk showed arrogance and contempt for everyone, inferiors and superiors alike.

Ratso clenched his fist and imagined planting it on that receding apology for a chin. Without any invitation, he perched on Caldwell's desk and made no attempt at a friendly greeting. The air was heavy with expensive after-shave that Caldwell always dabbed on his eggshell smooth cheeks. Ratso sniffed loudly and wrinkled his beaky nose. "Smells like the Duty-Free maze at Gatwick Airport."

Deadly Hush

"Doyle?" Caldwell's raised eyebrow was dagger sharp, his practised trademark.

"Everything in hand." He could not bring himself to say sir, guv or boss. *Dickhead* was the word that surfaced but he kept it to himself. It was that or a four-letter word.

"There's a media shit-storm."

If the comment was meant to provoke a reassuring reply, Caldwell was to be disappointed. "I'll get back to work then." Ratso rose to leave. "Can't have a shit-storm, can we?"

"You may be the SIO on this investigation but with such intense media interest, I want to be kept in the loop. Got it?" Ratso shrugged and let Caldwell continue. "I don't give a toss about the occasional dead faggot. You know my views on them. This is different. Doyle was famous. The media are howling for news and expect action. So do the top brass at the Yard. So do I."

Ratso snorted. "Your homophobia is unacceptable and out of order. We protect all lives, all equally valuable."

Caldwell continued as if nothing had been said. "*My* concern is we don't get lambasted in the media."

"You mean like the Stephen Port horror story?" Ratso saw Smart flinch at the reminder of the outcry at the Met's failure to arrest Port after the first gay had been murdered. Port had gone on to kill three more. The media and the public had blamed the cops for indifference to investigating a few dead gays.

Caldwell's face darkened. "My personal views about bloody poofters don't come into this." Smart shot his sleeves to display his cufflinks even more prominently. "*My reputation* does. Get me Doyle's killer and PDQ."

Ratso said nothing about Caldwell's reputation, although he wanted to do so. Neither did he mention the playing-card. The Jack of Spades pointed to a serial killer. Caldwell could find that out for himself on Holmes 2. Reading that, would blow off Caldwell's mauve socks. "Catching killers?" Ratso paused to add insolence. "Yes. That's in my job description as the Senior Investigating Officer on Doyle's murder. As to your blatant gay hatred, Baroness Casey's report made clear there's no room in the Met Police for your attitude."

"My personal views are irrelevant. I'll be watching you. Any stepping out of line, and your career will end long before mine." Caldwell spun round to look away. "Theory about Doyle?" he said without turning.

"Yes?"

"And?"

"I'm working on formalised hypotheses. Why develop a theory without the autopsy, forensics, ANPR, local CCTV? If my middle name was Lieutenant Colombo of the LAPD, I'd probably make an arrest in twenty minutes. As it is, I have no theory."

Caldwell was never going to backtrack. He swivelled again, menace in his eyes and his words clipped. "Insolence does not work in here." The piggy eyes glared across the narrow divide.

Ratso never flinched and said nothing, just grabbed the handle to the door.

Caldwell took a step closer. "Gay or celeb-bashing? Or both? That's your focus. Or should be."

Ratso stroked his forehead in a theatrical Colombo move. "I'd never thought of that. I'll bear it in mind, sir."

Caldwell looked down at his shoes as Ratso exited. He eased himself onto his chair and popped a Polo into his thin-lipped mouth. He could hear Ratso whistling tunelessly as he sauntered away. Back in his corner office, with upstream views of the Thames towards Hammersmith, Ratso called in Strang, Petrie and DC Carole Viment. The sun was streaming in the compact but efficient room.

On his desk were only the usual laptops and gadgetry. The white walls were uncluttered, except for a photo of him at Windsor Castle after receiving the Queen's Police Medal.

"How's Caldwell?" Petrie asked.

"Smarting." Though Ratso's face was not designed for huge grins, he gave a satisfied smile. He was rewarded with laughter. "Caldwell warned me about a media shit-storm and, oh don't forget this crime could be both gay and celeb bashing."

"Valuable. Positively smart, I'd say," commented Viment who was grazing on a mixed-leaf salad with quinoa. Ratso rated her. With her ambition, she'd quickly be catching Petrie. Because of her strong features, Viment reminded Ratso of a woman in a Cezanne painting. Only the chestnut-coloured fringe softened her image. Nothing could conceal the strength of her cheekbones and jawline. Viment played men well, sometimes teasing with a wide smile. At other times, she was not afraid to use a raised eyebrow or a wink with a frisky come-hither look to make her point. Water-cooler gossip was that she lived with an insatiable and well-hung computer nerd in Merton. To Ratso, this sounded like the usual crap. Viment was not one to discuss her private life.

"Boss. The Jack of Spades? What did Smart make of that?" Strang leaned forward expectantly.

"I didn't tell him. I despise him for what he did to me over Boris Zandro."

"Aye! He was a right shitbag back then."

"I didn't tell him because with him, I'm an awkward sod." Ratso took in the watchful faces. "I'll mention the Jack in my report. If he reads it." He stroked his chin, deep in thought. "Why a Jack? Why any card?" He paused before answering his own questions. "It was a calling-card from a serial killer. There'll be another death. Maybe a Queen of Spades."

"Then a King and an Ace?" Petrie's tone combined concern and respect. "Now you say it, that's so bleeding obvious."

Ratso clamped his hands behind his head. "That would be four. Why only four? Why start with a Jack? Get the full team together for a briefing. The playing-card we keep tight as a clam. Nothing about that must reach the media or we'll get copycats." Ratso saw the nodded heads.

"More late nights if you're right, boss," Jock said.

"More than enough overtime for Nancy to treat us at the Drum & Flute." He answered an incoming call and played with a coffee-cup while listening. He ended the call after a few moments. "Doyle died from fractures to his first and second vertebrae. Probably starved his brain of oxygen by pressure on the carotid artery and then a violent twist to the neck."

"Quickly over then." Petrie watched Ratso's hooded eyes close as he nodded his head.

"We're looking for someone with that knowhow. A professional. Maybe a doctor. Carole. Check out killers with this *modus operandi*. Get the civvies to check that out on Holmes 2." This national computerised database was a prime source for cross-fertilisation. It helped linking past crimes to the present facts. "There won't be many like this. Most neck deaths involve slow strangulation by hand or a ligature like a belt or scarf. Professionals might use a garotte."

"And your plan boss?"

Ratso shrugged. "The first meeting of *Operation Footstool* Team will be in the morning. We'll assess how each line of enquiry is shaping. Thanks and get to it." For him, it was a time for thinking, for prioritising hypotheses. Time to prevent the killer playing the Queen of Spades. He was just about to settle down to summarise the lines of enquiry when his phone rang. It was Assistant Commissioner Wensley Hughes calling from Scotland Yard.

"How can I help, sir?"

"We're short-staffed here. I'm doubling up with some Commander duties. Your help would be most welcome but that's impossible. Enough of my problems. Unfortunately, Todd that's not why I'm calling."

"Sir?"

"Bad news. Or it may be."

When Ratso ended the call, he sat in silence before standing by the window. There he stared down at the white vans, buses and cars but without seeing them.

I always expected this.
Overdue really.
Now it was reality.
Or seemed to be.

Concentrating on *Operation Footstool* was impossible. He flung on his jacket and within minutes was walking beside the Thames in the bright sunlight past the boat-houses. He put on his earphones and selected a Dave Brubeck album. It was no time for anything heavy. The tinkling piano and captivating rhythm were soothing as he strolled along the towpath, head lowered and deep in thought.

Boris Zandro.
Bad news?
Too bloody right it is.

Mayfair, London

For the killer, besides the thrill of delivering sudden death, the best part was always the planning. Investigating Logan Goldie's lifestyle had been easy. Facebook and Instagram had plenty about him. His hair was straw-coloured but shaved high above his ears, almost like a Mohican. His narrow moustache was slightly darker. He favoured faded jeans, torn at the knee with ornate cowboy-style boots. There had been a photo of him leaving a casino, cuddling up to a youth less than half his age. There were stories and pictures of him glugging vintage champagne while cruising gay hang-outs like the Ku Bar or Village.

A city slicker, aged 36, Goldie had made his fortune by publishing a share-dealing tip sheet called *Saints & Skeletons*. The guy relished tabloid interest. Photos of his £750,000 McLaren Senna had been splashed across them. Sometimes, he was standing beside it but in one, he had been provocatively sprawled across the bonnet, his pert buttocks prominent.

Goldie's office was on Dowgate Hill, in the heart of the City, not far from St Paul's Cathedral. For the killer, researching the area and the office block had been invaluable. Murdering him in his office had been a preference. After trawling the area, that plan had been abandoned. Goldie's two-roomed suite was glass-fronted on a long upstairs corridor. The new building, designed like an oversized goldfish bowl, housed dozens of businesses, large and small. There was no privacy. City-types had been scurrying around the corridors like demented ants. The location was useless. Besides that, there had been no pattern to Goldie's working day.

Nothing in Goldie's life was predictable.

Except it was going to end.

Soon.

Instead of Dowgate Hill, the killer had chosen his fifth-floor Mayfair apartment. Now, in there, Logan Goldie was lying dead. After exiting the building, a sharp left turn on the forecourt ensured that the killer was well distant from the Night Porter. At the junction with Curzon Street, a camera captured a rear-view of a woman walking east and away from busy Park Lane. There, she waved down an approaching cab and the driver did a tight U-turn. "Leicester Square."

The cab pulled away, passing the splendour of the Saudi Embassy protected by armed police. By sitting directly behind the driver, the woman avoided eye contact and said nothing. In a few swift moves, she slipped on a lightweight dark coat, concealing her summery dress.

Progress in mid-evening traffic was slow but the killer was relaxed. The body was unlikely to be found tonight. After the usual tailbacks on Piccadilly, the cab eventually crawled the last few hundred metres along Coventry Street. After she had paid and climbed out, the driver watched the woman's swaying walk as she crossed the pavement before disappearing among the teeming hordes who were laughing, shouting and applauding the street-entertainers near the Swiss clock.

Standing in the middle of the huge crowd who were being entertained by a fast-talking juggler, the woman pushed her way into a group of tall Swedish youngsters. She crouched slightly to remove her cap and replaced it with another. Then, remaining slightly stooped, she zigzagged among the noisy crowd. There were young and old of every nationality. As she headed towards Charing Cross Road, she remained anonymous in a sea of bobbing heads, all dodging, weaving and jostling in every direction. Then, the woman stopped at a spot where the throng was particularly thick. They were singing along to a talented rock-singer in a purple jacket He was belting out YMCA. Everywhere there was movement with the listeners waving their arms and singing along to the lyrics. Still with her knees slightly bent, the woman reversed her coat to fawn before moving away to disappear into the night.

Mayfair, London

As Ratso was driven to Logan Goldie's apartment, he was thinking of the call from the Assistant Commissioner. Given the difference in ranks, their relationship had been one of trust and mutual respect. That dated back to when Boris Zandro had mixed with London's high society, despite being an Albanian drug baron. Wensley Hughes had stood by Ratso then, despite Alex Caldwell swinging a wrecking-ball at Ratso's career.

In his usual no-nonsense style, at the meeting, Hughes had revealed that, from his jail cell, Boris Zandro had ordered Ratso's death. "He's appointed his nephew in Albania, Hysen Kola. He lives in Tirana. An NCA source working out there stumbled on this evidence."

"Kola? What's known?"

"He's a hitman with a serious reputation. Six or seven victims. He's so powerful, he's never been arrested or charged."

"And?"

"Now, he's dropped out of sight."

"Your take? What's happening?"

"We're trying to pick up his scent."

"You mean keep him out of the UK?"

"That's the plan."

As Ratso was dropped off in Chesterton Gardens, he immediately spotted an orange McLaren parked outside the imposing red-brick mansion block. Chesterton Gardens was a short side-street in what Americans would describe as a *tony area* of London's

Mayfair. He showed his ID, ducked under the cordon and put on his protective gear. The elevators were out of use while forensics were at work, so he walked up to the 5th Floor. Only slightly breathless, he entered the hall and was met by Strang.

"The Queen of Spades, right enough." Det. Insp. Jock Strang's weathered face showed respect for the gaffer's prediction as he led him to the body. After speaking to the Scenes of Crime Officer, Ratso was satisfied everything was under control. Strang led him to the victim where Ratso took in the scene. The slim figure lay on his side, sprawled across a black rug with gold motifs. On his right cheek lay the playing-card. There was a chunky diamond-studded ring on one finger and a stud in the visible ear.

The photographer had finished but the forensic crew were still busily poring over anything that might prove to be breakthrough evidence. Strang turned to Ratso. "Likely time of death was yesterday evening. No sign of forced entry. Similar cause of death to Doyle."

"Who found the body?"

"Logan Goldie's cleaner. She arrived at 8-15 this morning. She's being comforted in the admin office. She arrived expecting an empty apartment. Says the guy normally leaves for the City by 6 a.m. Anything known about Goldie, boss?"

Ratso shook his head. "Name means nothing to me. But looking round, you get the vibes." He was referring to the butterfly colours on the walls and the large black and white erotic photos of male cheesecake displayed on three walls of the sitting-room. "Comfortably off or even stinking rich."

"Right enough. The porter said visitor must use the entry-phone to get up here. I've made sure that it's been checked already for dabs. There are eighty apartments in four different wings, average value upwards of three million." Through the window, Strang pointed to a doorway across the forecourt. "The porter sits in the next wing. DC Petrie is down there. That flashy orange car at the front was Goldie's."

"Hardly a shrinking violet, was he?"

"No forced entry. Goldie must have expected a visitor."

Ratso rubbed his curving nose thoughtfully. "The killer at Dermot Doyle's wore size nine ribbed soled footwear. Distinctive but common as muck. Maybe forensic will find them here too."

Strang said. "Gays falling out? Back to a jealous lover scenario?"

"Put DC Viment on that. See if Doyle and Goldie knew each other or had shared friends." Strang followed Ratso into what had been Goldie's office. Most owners would have used it as a spare bedroom. There was a smoked-glass desk, three office-chairs, a locked safe and a 4-drawer maple filing-cabinet. On the desk were a laptop and two large monitors. A smartphone was lying on a small stack of papers. Ratso studied the confined space with its small window looking onto a brick wall. "No sign of theft. The safe is untouched. I don't see a diary so I guess that'll be on his phone or laptop. Getting into the diary and his contacts is top, top priority." Ratso tapped his foot. "Was Goldie expecting a lover or was it business?"

Petrie appeared. Her default image was smiling but even by her standards, her perky features looked flushed and animated. "The porter, that's Eric Hollaby, said Goldie was a flash city type, not the traditional three-piece and rolled umbrella. Apparently, he provided financial advice." She almost quivered as she continued. Ratso could tell she was bursting to say something. "Unusually for him, he had a woman visitor. Mid-evening. Hollaby's view across the forecourt is around forty metres. It was dusk. He saw the woman leave, on foot, heading for Curzon Street. Couldn't describe her face."

"A woman? He was sure?"

"Positive." Petrie, in her lightweight navy suit, was brimming with nervous energy – all movement from her feet to manicured fingernails. "Eric said Goldie had occasional male visitors, sometimes overnight. Not any permanent live-ins. He couldn't remember any other women."

"How long was she up here?"

"Ten minutes max."

As Ratso was listening to Petrie, he spotted print-outs on the desk by the photocopier and crossed the room to take a look. Ratso glanced at them. "Interesting. Maybe very interesting."

Mayfair, London

Ratso continued flicking through the pages. "This was printed at 8-40 p.m. yesterday evening." He saw he had full attention. "It's the latest Annual Return for Rolstern Genomics Ltd, a business in North London." He shook his head. "Never 'erd of them!"

"Homework before his meeting?"

"My thoughts too, Jock." He put down the documents. "Nancy, this'll be one for you to check out."

"Maybe wait for his diary? His appointments?" Petrie's lowered her prominent eyelashes so as not to appear too challenging.

"Yup. You're right. Anyway, Nancy. Explain this. How does the porter know which buzzer she used? There are twenty apartments in this wing."

Petrie's broadening smile showed she knew the answer. "Pressing the apartment number at the front-entrance flashes up on a console on the Porter's desk."

"No photo though?"

"Not a still. I've seen the CCTV."

"Built like a Russian shot-putter, was she? Huge hairy hands?" Ratso was not joking.

Petrie shook her head. "Check the footage for yourself. The front view was never closer than twenty-five metres before she went out of camera-shot. Medium height, medium build in a flower-patterned print summery dress, quite full length and flowing. Long white gloves. The sort of pic you see in old family albums. From the way she walked, I'd say she was wearing wedgies. She had a dark shoulder-bag. No full facial view. Her hair looked darkish beneath a distinctive red cap. Age indeterminate. Not old, not judging by the way she walked."

Ratso and Jock shared a look as both had a similar thought. "Transvestite, boss?"

Ratso said nothing, shuffling the few known facts. He led them back to door to the spacious luxury of the kitchen-sitting-room-diner where the body had yet to be moved. There was no sign that Goldie might have been offering dinner. Not even drinks, just one nearly empty glass by a bottle of sparkling water. At last he spoke. "No sign of a struggle. I'd say Goldie let her in and was immediately attacked from behind as he led her in here."

Strang leaned against the door-frame. "For business, he'd have taken her into his office. But seemingly, he didn't. Not with that Rolstern stuff still in there. He'd bring a social visitor in here."

"Or the bedroom," prompted Petrie.

The trio crossed the windowless hallway and checked the spacious bedroom. The crisp linen on the Californian king-sized showed it had not been used since the maid had left it the previous morning. There was a pleasant scent of wood smoke from a still burning Dyptique candle on a dressing-table. More murals of nude males. The heavy grey drapes were closed and a single bed-lamp provided soft lighting. "Romantic. Well ... kind of." Petrie sounded impressed. "Perhaps he was expecting to bed his guest later?"

"Open mind, Nancy. Jock – get me the full nine yards on what this guy did for his money. And the sooner the IT guys open up his diary and phone, the better." Ratso knew that there would be delays getting back electronic data. Understaffed and underfunded, Ratso resented that the Met was expected to deliver results but with third-world resources.

He spotted several low stacks of pink, green and black casino chips on the dressing-table. "These are cash chips. At a guess, I'd say they're worth over twenty thousand." He read the name in the centres. "Carleton Casino. That's off Baker Street."

Strang's face broke into a smile, accelerating into a huge grin, the wrinkles on his face creasing together. "There's the first link. Dermot Doyle played there too. The Carleton's a high-end joint, boss. Assuming Goldie was gay, there's a second link." From the bedroom window, Jock Strang stared down to the street below. It was all cordoned off, flashing lights everywhere. "Third – they were both pretty damned rich. The Jack, now a Queen… follow the trail."

Petrie seemed gripped; her green eyes wide with her usual enthusiasm. "A King of Spades could point to a love triangle." After a slight frown, she checked herself. "But if there's then an Ace, we'd be talking foursomes gone wrong. That's unlikely. So back to homophobic crime, boss?"

"Bullshit and bollocks." Ratso's tone was gruff – unusually sharp and dismissive. Her reminder of Smart Alex Caldwell's theory had raised his hackles. Both listeners flinched, their faces showing puzzled surprise. Normally, their boss was even-tempered and treated his team with respect. Ratso saw their discomfort and immediately regretted his edginess. "Sorry. There's a lot going on."

Hysen Kola.
Something he had just been told.
Something top-secret.
Something that nagged away like raging toothache.
Something I go to bed with.
Something I wake up with.

At least tomorrow, Ratso knew he would be escaping London for his annual cricket trip to Yorkshire – his first weekend away in months. Even so, he could anticipate Caldwell's sneering tone about him effing off in the midst of a double murder investigation. *Only working part-time, are you, Todd?*

"If there's a King and an Ace and we're no closer," Ratso continued after putting his concerns to one side, "all hell really will break loose. The media are already comparing this to Stephen Port."

Strang nodded. "Aye. It makes me puke what these reporters stir up. I'm no anti-gay." He laughed. "And I'm no racist either. Reading the crap in the papers, you'd certainly think we were all bigots. Me? I'm tolerant to a fault. Sometimes I even like you English." His throaty laugh was rewarded with an old-fashioned look from Ratso.

"*All* lives matter. No feet off the pedal because the victims were gay. We give *all* murders maximum effort. Of course, the journalists from red-top papers don't want to believe that." He turned to Strang to pose a question, yet almost sure of the answer. "Jock, let me ask you this."

Mayfair

"Good question, boss." Jock Strang was searching his memory. "Do I think a woman could kill like this? Just bare hands. Quickly, silently? With no sign that Goldie resisted?" He turned away from a painting of a nude male on horseback. "Possible in theory, if trained. We're talking spies, foreign agents, assassins." He saw both his boss and Petrie agreed. "Anyroads, we may have a man in drag."

They returned to look at the body which was about to be removed. Ratso looked down at the contorted body in a scarlet shirt, yellow slacks and cowboy boots. "Height? What you reckon?"

Strang looked the corpse up and down before replying. "Not tall. In old money, maybe five foot seven."

"So was Dermot Doyle," said Petrie.

"And you reckoned his visitor was medium height too."

Knowing that Ratso had been counting down the days till his Yorkshire trip, Strang continued. "Doyle was murdered early on Saturday 17th July." He raised one grey bushy eyebrow to add impact. "Logan Goldie was ten days later on a Wednesday. Maybe we've time to prevent the King of Spades. If I'm right, nothing will happen while you're poncing around Yorkshire with your wee bat and wearing your daft white breeks."

Ratso nodded but was on autopilot. His mind had moved on to tomorrow's headlines. "After the Media Briefing today, the gay community is going to be …"

"Shit-scared," Petrie intervened.

"That too but I was going to say noisy, angry. Demanding answers. Wanting action. Quite rightly, too." Ratso waved an arm around the comfortable opulence. "And yes – bloody terrified too. Both victims are … well …were wealthy. Probably influential."

"No theft. No mutilation." Strang paused before continuing. "I investigated a gay-hate in Broomielaw. That's Glasgow city centre. Two young kids, nineteen. Throats cut and their genitals removed. We found their todgers stuffed up their backsides. That *was* gay-hate."

Everyone fell silent for a moment at the graphic image. It was Ratso who spoke, his eyes emerging from beneath the heavy lids to flash irritation. "This is not gay-bashing." Each word was separated to add force. "We're not dealing with a bunch of drunken thugs kicking a gay to death on Hungerford Bridge. Nothing close. We don't even know it's about sexuality. So far, we've no motive. We need meat on the bone. Jock – get someone scouring the gay social media. See if there's anything useful among the wild rumours and crap speculation."

Ratso took in again the thickness of the rugs, the matching pale pink sofa and chairs, the elaborate coffee-table and the array of interesting North African artefacts. Bottles of wine, whisky, Campari, Aperol and Fynoderee Gin were racked up behind the marble-topped cocktail bar. In a chiller, were over a dozen bottles of champagne. Everything was so different from his own booze-stained carpet and Ikea flat-pack furniture. "I doubt there'll be any fingerprints here. The team got nothing bankable at Doyle's except the trainers and clothing fibres from the shrubs. Even they may not have been the killer's."

"Boss, suppose the visitor was business but also social."

Ratso said. "Or so Goldie thought?" He see-sawed his hand.

Deadly Hush

"No drinks on offer. No nuts or crisps. Why was he interested in this geriatrics company?"

"Genomics, boss" suggested Petrie with a big grin.

"Managed by Geronimo, I suppose." Jock, we need to increase the team. We're one body short of a serial killer." He looked at Nancy. "Are uniforms checking the area and cameras?"

"Yup! We should get something from this area. We've still got sod-all useful about how Doyle's killer fled."

"The killer got lucky round Ladbroke Grove," Strang suggested.

Ratso's eyes narrowed, his firm jawline jutting forward. "Not luck," he snapped. "Careful planning. He, or maybe she, *knew* how to get away unobserved. The Ladbroke Grove trail never got warm. All those trees and shadows in the roads round the back. The street lighting was piss-poor. But he or she must have parked close by."

Taken aback at Ratso's continued sharpness, Petrie offered round her peppermints. "Or how about living nearby? We've that sighting by a taxi driver on Ladbroke Grove. Almost certainly, he saw the killer. But just a back view of someone in dark clothing. Not tall, not short. He assumed it was a man."

"You mean *we* assumed it was a man."

"Boss, I'll get him questioned again about that."

"Sorry, Nancy. I'm being a bit ... ratty this morning!" They welcomed his joke against himself. "Truth is I'm knackered."

True but untrue.
Not the full story.
Omerta.
Tell nobody.

Ratso walked to the door, tugging at his protective overalls. "The crimes are linked – that's the killer's message. Door-to-door? Who's in charge?"

"DC Willison organised that, boss."

Ratso did not look enthused but said nothing. "So ... is this what I tell the media about this murder? We are looking for a woman ... or maybe a man, not tall, not short, darkish hair, flowery dress?"

"What about adding hairy feet?" Strang laughed at his own joke. The lighter moment was quickly gone as Ratso motioned them towards the elevator. "Here's the big thing! If I appeal for witnesses for a woman in a summery dress, the next questions will be why and how are we linking the two crimes? I can't mention playing-cards because of copy-cat shysters." He groaned, his face creasing up as did so. "Before I face the press hordes, I'll have to lick Caldwell's loafers first."

"Tell him we've now got a *double*-shit-storm," suggested Petrie with a grin.

"And tell him we haven't got an effing clue, boss," Strang suggested.

"I will ... but maybe dressed up just a little." Ratso's usually agile brain was running on empty. His instinct was to tell the media as little as possible. Today he had no choice. Put one wrong foot, and Caldwell would hang him out to dry.

Petrie started reading from her phone. "Boss, we have this advantage. Round here there are far more cameras. There are four casinos just a short step away. Several big hotels, the Saudi Embassy, in fact probably a dozen embassies. They'll all have CCTV. We should get plenty of footage of this woman arriving and leaving. There may be a car involved. We need to match it with any possible getaway car on the move after Dermot Doyle."

"Ladbroke Grove? What getaway car?" The Scot laughed dismissively. "Despite hours of time going through footage, the lads have found nothing. A Vauxhall Invisible, mebbe? A Rolls-Royce Silver Ghost?" Then his face turned hangdog. "Mid-evening in Mayfair? I'm tellin' ye boss, there'll be thousands of cars."

"If we see the killer get into a car, maybe we're in business." Ratso pulled at his ear. "Yes. That's what I'll tell the media. *Useful lines of enquiry. Interesting lines of enquiry.* Maybe even *promising lines of enquiry.*"

South Yorkshire

As he sped along the motorway in South Yorkshire, Ratso's knuckles were still white as he gripped the wheel. In murky drizzle, spray from big trucks was making visibility and conditions difficult and progress was slow. After three hours, his Scotch Corner junction was still an hour away. His concerns about being stalked by Kola had been left behind. But not his seething anger about Caldwell. Even Bonnie Tyler's pounding beat about needing a hero barely soothed the recollection of his recent meeting.

It had been less of a meeting and more of a confrontation. With no progress on Doyle's murder, Goldie's death had been his platform for another tirade. Ratso had no illusions. Given the slightest chance, Caldwell would end his career. The meeting had started badly before heading further downhill. "Think this is a part-time job, do you? I cop the flak from the top brass at the Yard while you pratt about Yorkshire chasing a red ball and scoffing sandwiches and home-made cakes."

At the Doncaster Service Area, over coffee and a chicken wrap, he had checked in with Strang. Jock told him he too had just gone "ten rounds with Caldwell and I'm away for a pint."

Ratso pushed his coffee to one side. "When I saw him, his face was puce. Spit was flying like tracer bullets. I barely got a word in. Even by his standards, he was in a foul mood. He even *ordered* me to cancel my leave."

"What?" Strang's shock reverberated down the line.

"I gave it to him straight. I reminded him this long weekend would be my first break for fifty-three weeks. He'd also heard that the judge at the Old Bailey had thrown out the prosecution. It never even got to the jury."

"What? That murderer filmed with the bloodied knife in his hand, walked free?"

"No doubt grinning from ear to ear and planning his next heist. Smart blamed me." Ratso lowered his voice because the couple at the next table were now more interested in what he was saying than talking to each other. "That's when I blew up. I told Caldwell straight. It was *you* instructed me on the line to take when cross-examined. He walked free because of *you*."

"Aye, I mind that fine."

"With that oily smirk that makes me want to punch his mouth, he denied it. Told me I'd screwed up *because mavericks like you always do*."

"That's Caldwell. Terrible." The Scottish accent seemed even stronger on the phone "The bastard seems to be Teflon-coated." After a pause, he added. "At least for now he is. He bollocked me because no vehicle's been linked to Doyle's murder. Then he was on about you buggering off to Yorkshire. I told him straight. You have a phone. You're always in contact."

"Not if I'm batting, Jock. Not then." They both chuckled.

"Sport doesn't turn him on."

"Yeah. He gets his rocks off listening to Wagner or being measured up for tailored suits. Right now, he's playing me to fail." Ratso dumped the debris from his tray to return to his grey Volvo, 83,000 on the clock. "Trust me, Jock. I have no intention of giving him that pleasure. As I stormed out, at least I got in the last word – told him he'd kept his suntan after his three weeks in Mykonos."

Strang chuckled. "This isn't going to end well."

"He won't rest till he's got me nailed to a cross." Ratso fired up the engine and eased away. "Back to Op Footstool. Any new leads? CCTV? The casino? The gay community? Goldie's business? That company in north London?"

"We know the woman grabbed a taxi. We have its number. DC Viment is tracing the driver. Petrie's working on Rolstern." The Scot exhaled noisily. "I'm tellin' ye, this Logan Goldie. He was some guy."

"Go on."

By the time Strang had finished, Ratso had covered another twelve miles. He was still thinking about what a shit Logan Goldie was when he entered the winding lanes over the rolling moorland of North Yorkshire. Now, as he approached the hilltop hamlet of Kirby Hill, the rain had stopped. In every direction were cows and sheep grazing on vast swathes of hardy grasslands. Through the trees, he glimpsed the 12th century church. He opened the window and the sounds of bleating and the smell of new mown grass filled the car.

He parked outside Sprog Booth's tiny cottage that dated back two-hundred ghostly years. Rumours still circulated of an old woman in a milking smock stoking the fire. Neither Ratso, nor his old pal Sprog had ever seen her – not even after a skinful. For a quiet moment, he looked down the sloping field where hundreds of sheep were grazing. From beyond the graveyard behind him, came the sound of bell-ringers practising. The peals drifted over the pub and the scattering of stone homes.

Ratso sat in silence. Perhaps his old mate had got it right. After his wife had died of cancer, Det. Sgt Keith "Sprog" Booth had quit the Met and moved north. With no children, he now lived for his sport – playing cricket in the summer and following Newcastle United in winter. He sighed as he removed his overnight bag and cricket kit. At moments like this, Ratso also felt like quitting

– chucking in the long hours, the endless bureaucratic crap and dumping Caldwell in a box marked history.

As he walked along the flagged path, memories of times shared with Sprog flooded back – they'd had some great years working together. He reached the familiar unlocked wooden door with no knocker or bell and shouted his arrival.

Hambledon, Surrey

Two-hundred and seventy miles south of Kirby Hill, the killer parked down a track leading into dense forest about 30 yards off a country lane. Probably England's wealthiest county and certainly its leafiest, this part of rural Surrey near Hambledon was still sleepy. It was just gone 5 a.m. on Saturday 31st July and the sun was fighting to break through the foliage on a bright Saturday morning. It would be another hour before the first golfers would be leaving their *desirable residences* with manicured lawns.

The overnight drizzle had stopped and the dawn-chorus was in full cry, everything serene. The smell of damp undergrowth and the sound of rain still dripping from the trees was soothing after the journey. Following a pit-stop on the M25, the killer bit into a tasteless sausage-roll and sipped a nearly cold and forgettable coffee.

After painstaking research, the killer knew that Lord Ernest Ongerton was an early bird. There should not be long to wait, not unless unusually he wanted a lie-in. In a recent Observer interview, the Labour peer, now sixty-eight, had helpfully mentioned that he rarely missed his dawn walk on the forest paths with his two Labradors. After leaving his Belgravia home the evening before, Ongerton's weekends were generally in the Surrey hills where he lived alone in his Lutyens country mansion, one of many of these stylish buildings designed by Sir Edwin, who had once lived nearby.

In a camouflage jacket and a green balaclava, the killer was now concealed among the pines. In the car, the escape route using back lanes was marked on a map. A scribbled note was a reminder to change and dump the tyres, along with the camouflage gear and trainers.

Within fifteen minutes, the tall figure came into view. Lord Ongerton was wearing bottle-green cord trousers, a burgundy windcheater and a tweed cap. Bose headphones on, his Labradors were off the lead and sniffing excitedly either side of the path. For his age, the peer looked pretty fit as he walked briskly enough, no sign of advancing arthritis. The killer watched the swinging arms and the head swaying in time with whatever he was listening to. After waiting till the dogs had lolloped on, the killer moved slowly and silently to fall in step a few paces behind the unsuspecting target.

Kirby Hill, North Yorkshire

As the killer was waiting for Lord Ongerton, Ratso had not long got to sleep in Kirby Hill. His brain had been fired up by the best evening since last year's visit. Up here, surrounded by cricketing mates, Wensley Hughes's warning-shot about Hysen Kola seemed like a distant bad dream. Even so, despite the Guinness, plentiful Rioja, a shared bottle of port and Sprog's array of cheeses, sleep had been impossible.

The strange bed had played its part but above all, his late-night brain had been like a tumble-dryer, churning for links between Doyle and Logan Goldie. By dawn, as a distant cockerel started to crow and the smell of new mown hay drifted in the window, he had nothing worthwhile to show but tired confusion.

Since they had first met at Hendon Police College, Ratso's bond with Sprog had remained unshakeable. On Ratso's arrival, it was as if they had never been apart. As always, there had been the short stroll to the ivy-clad Shoulder of Mutton. Perching on the red-topped bar-stools, they enjoyed sinking a couple of pints.

The simple room was everything you could want from your local – Stan, a landlord with a fistful of stories; a blackboard full of specials, low ceilings and beer served at its best. Immediately, on seeing Ratso, Stan knew to start lining up a Guinness. For him, Sprog's annual cricket weekend was like Christmas come early.

Inevitably, pub banter with a couple of locals had been about cricket, football, and the great North-South-Divide. To them, Ratso was a soft southerner who knew nothing of real life. They still regarded Sprog as a newcomer despite him now being a familiar figure in the local community. He was a couple of years older than Ratso but still looked under forty. His twinkly eyes and plentiful sandy hair had never changed. Though not as tall as Ratso, he still looked as fit as a butcher's dog. His biceps showed why he could challenge all-comers at arm-wrestling. Despite his ability to sink copious quantities of real ale, somehow, he had remained slim and lithe, still jogging several miles most days. His cricketing pals always joked that he still ran between the wickets like a whippet with its arse on fire.

Back in the cottage, after pie and mash at the teak table, Booth had produced the cheese and port. "No point decanting it," he laughed. "let's just sink it before we hit the sack."

"So tell me about tomorrow. You got your usual team?" Sprog annually pulled in a group of mates to play against an eleven raised by Alfie Blyth, a drinking pal from Ravensworth. Rivalry was fierce. Bragging rights would linger long into the evening.

"We play at Barningham. I'll bowl you down the slope. It's known locally as a lively pitch. For quickies like you, the ball can spit up like a cobra. I'm banking on you to pick up a few wickets." He saw the enthusiasm in Ratso's eyes and grinned. "Sunday, we head the other way to play near Scotch Corner. Good batting wicket. A graveyard for bowlers."

"Yeah. I remember last year. That ex-Durham player carted me all over Yorkshire. And you, you bastard kept me bowling. 0 for 48 off 6 overs."

Sprog's head rocked back at the memory. "Nobody else wanted to bowl. Not Rolf, Wilfie or Terry."

"How are they?"

Sprog loved cricket banter and gossip. He rolled his eyes and passed the port. "You'll love this story."

Kirby Hill, North Yorkshire

"**B**efore I get to the story, here's the team news. Rolf's opening the bowling with you. Terry has torn his Achilles tendon. He's wearing a surgical boot. Limping and hobbling. Wilfie's put on so much weight, we could use him to roll the pitch!" They clinked glasses at the image. "Terry's limping in for the booze-up tomorrow night. All the others are raring to go. Chicken and chips and the usual sing-song."

"Didn't Terry do something on the ships?"

"Made his money in ship-security. Y'know – all that piracy around the Red Sea and Nigeria. He's not at the sharp end now. We reckon these days, he's too busy counting the cash. You should see his place – quite something."

"And you? How's your job going?" Ratso knew Sprog worked for an engineering company in Darlington.

"Good employers. Pay's okay. No excitement. HR's pretty bloody boring. I really miss Saturday nights in the nick at Lewisham. Drug raids. Shootings on the Lee High Road. Facing down a thug with a blade."

Ratso topped up their tumblers with the cheapo Late-Bottled. "London's changing. The Met too. What *hasn't* changed is needing more guys like you. Traditional policing, no bloody woke crap and political correctness from pimply-faced kids."

"Cheers, mate. We had some great times. *You're* still having great times." Sprog's eyes looked wistful as he recalled the old days but then they watered at memories of his young wife, now in Bromley Hill Cemetery. "I saw you on the BBC News. "Serial killer, is it?"

Ratso nodded. "Only two so far but if I'm right, there's more to come. Hopefully not while I'm up here."

"Sod them. You're on holiday. Turn your phone off!"

Ratso shook his head, knowing he could never bring himself to do that. "Come on Sprog! You had some gossip."

"It's one of Stan's stories," Sprog enthused. "A while back, Rolf and Terry were propping the bar. Both rat-arsed downing pints with whisky chasers. They both live alone, never married but there's nothing gay about them. Far from it! Terry often disappears clubbing to Whitby, Scarborough, Newcastle or even Edinburgh. Occasionally, they go on-the-pull together, using Terry's big motorhome. When the clubs shut, they bring the little ravers back to it. Nights like that, Rolf reckons the van rocks and sways like a ferry on the North Sea."

"Christ, they're both older than us," Ratso grinned.

Sprog gave a lopsided smile. "Friday night in Newcastle's pretty wild. Been up myself a couple of times. So get this. Stan reckoned that Terry must have fallen in love with some little raver up there. Emma, that was her name."

"Goes with the job. Landlords listening to drunks."

"By closing-time, Terry and Rolf, they were burbling in their booze, almost crying on each other's shoulders. Terry kept repeating *bloody Emma. Cost me a fucking fortune. Fucking millions.* Stan had to laugh 'cos Rolf was barely listening. He was too busy cussing some bit called Madge. He'd picked up a dose of the clap. Rolf was crying in his beer, telling Terry that every time he pissed, it was like his dick was on fire. By closing-time, the pair of them couldn't walk, let alone drive. Stan paid for their taxi home. Next time he saw them, he asked whether it was worse to lose millions or to have a flaming dick."

"Tough call," Ratso agreed.

"They both denied everything. Said Stan must have misheard. Anyway, next home game, when Rolf walked into the dressing-room, everyone stood and applauded. The skipper said he reckoned *Rolf would appreciate a clap*. I tell you! Seeing his face! But Rolf and Terry, they still denied everything."

"Terry had made millions, had he?"

"Before Emma saw him off?" Sprog paused, his port glass nearing empty. "Yeah! Easy I'd say."

"What happened in Newcastle, should have stayed in Newcastle."

Sprog nodded. "You still chasing that woman in Florida?"

"Not exactly chasing," Ratso laughed. "Apart from distance, we'd be an item. For now, we're ... well ... freelance. But I'm not up for bedding the local totty in Terry's motorhome."

"Slowing down are you, Ratso. Anyway, its gone two. Time to hit the sack." They drained the last of the port and climbed the creaking stairs to bed. In no time, Ratso heard the snores from the next room but he was far from sleep. Thinking of the two murders and tomorrow's lively wicket saw to that.

Kirby Hill, North Yorkshire

Ratso rolled over again. He was restless, tossing and turning as he tried to get into the killer's mind. On his journey north, Jock Strang's summary had said it all. Dermot Doyle had used his celebrity to fund-raise for charities. He had no known enemies, no money problems, no drug habit and no known connections to criminals. Yet someone had wanted him dead.

Logan Goldie was very different. With his fast-lane lifestyle, Goldie had rubbed up against drug-dealers and probably the rent-boy crowd. Several bags of cocaine had been found in his apartment and in his Dowgate Hill office. "Boss, credit to the guy," Strang had explained. "He was self-made. Ten years back, he started a share tip-sheet called *Saints & Skeletons*. Hugely successful. Thousands of subscribers. Shady city contacts were feeding him insider information about shares. He was dealing for himself – big sums but just below the radar. Then he published the tips, pushing shares up or down."

"Easy money. Bent as hell."

"You got it, boss. He made enemies by revealing dirt from the boardrooms – enough to crash shares and trash reputations. He wasn't always right but he was fearless."

"Upset powerful people?"

"Right enough."

"Strong motive to silence him."

"Goldie fought and exposed corruption."

"Yet he was corrupt," Ratso interrupted.

"That never stopped him attacking anything smelling of stinking fish. He exposed big name directors – knights, lords, captains of industry. Thanks to him, crooked directors have been jailed or barred from holding directorships."

"On a good day, a kind of Robin Hood. On a bad day, the Sheriff of Nottingham."

" But my informant reckons Goldie had become reckless."

"A loose cannon?"

"Aye! Maybe the drugs had got to him. Or just too cocky! Not cross-checking carefully enough – sometimes damaging honest directors."

"Meaning?"

"He treated death threats and warnings from solicitors as a badge of honour."

"Links with Doyle?"

"Yes and no. Both members of the Carleton Casino but never seen together."

"Check whether Dermot Doyle was a subscriber to *Saints & Skeletons*. The guy had plenty of millions to invest."

"Checked already. He wasn't."

"Anything from Goldie's electronic diary?"

"Imminent."

"Meaning sometime this year?"

Putney

In Jubilee House, at shortly before noon on Saturday, as Sprog drove Ratso in his ageing VW to Barningham's lively wicket, Jock Strang was just finishing a ham and cheese toastie and debating whether to back a couple of horses at Lingfield, when he saw breaking news from Surrey. A man's body had been found in woodland earlier that morning. After a short debate with himself, he decided to track down the officer in charge. Within ten minutes, he was talking to Det. Insp Ahmed Iqbal who was at the scene.

"Det. Insp. Jock Strang in Putney. I'm interested in the body found this morning." Realising that Iqbal sounded harassed, he explained in headlines why he had called. "I bet there's a King of Spades with the body." Strang could almost sense the jaw-dropping moment down in the Surrey hills. There was an over-long pause.

"On his chest. Yes."

"Murdered by a neck injury, I assume?" Again Jock heard the intake of breath and a muttered yes. "We have a serial killer. We were expecting this. Let me explain." Strang had Iqbal's full attention. He was a good listener and intrigued. When he had heard enough, he suggested Strang get down ASAP.

"Victim?"

"Lord Ernest Ongerton. Murdered about a mile from his country home near Hambledon."

"A Lord, eh? I'll put on my plus-fours and deerstalker."

"I don't believe his Lordship will insist on any dress-code." Iqbal gave a snorting laugh. "I'm told he's a multi-millionaire from the dotcom boom twenty-five years ago. Anyway, here's the directions. It's not easy to find. From Jubilee House, it should take you about fifty minutes."

"Any obvious clues at the scene?"

"I'll know more when you arrive."

North Yorkshire

As usual in Kirby Hill, it had been a hard weekend. Playing cricket in unseasonably hot weather had rolled into rounds of Guinness and wide-ranging drinking songs like Sweet Caroline, the Lambton Worm and Blaydon Races. Monday had been different. With the drive home ahead, it had been alcohol-free. At just after 9 p.m. Ratso waved Sprog goodbye and deftly reversed the Volvo.

To keep him alert, he phoned DC Viment, hoping it was not too late to return her missed call. He could phone Jock Strang much later as time meant nothing to him. Since Strang's messy divorce and his forlorn attempt to date Nancy Petrie, the Glaswegian now lived a quiet life – just fish suppers and Irn Bru with his feet up. Or so he said.

As the headlights pierced the darkness at a steady 70mph, from the Volvo's speakers, Carole Viment's voice, sounded so close. She sounded delighted, even eager, to be called at home. *Perhaps life with her apparently well-hung geek wasn't so great after all.*

The junction to Catterick flashed by as she updated him. "Boss, we traced the cabbie who picked up the woman in Curzon Street. He lives in Essex."

"Don't they all?"

"He remembered the fare but little else. He dropped her off beside Leicester Square. When he picked her up, she was wearing a red jockey-cap and a white dress with flower patterns. When she left, she was wearing a dark coat over it. She paid cash and disappeared into the crowds. Then the trail went cold."

"You said she?"

"Driver never gave it a thought. Said her bum had a good wiggle. *Leicester Square* were the only two words she spoke. Might have been English or foreign. He had no idea."

"And once in Leicester Square?"

Viment faltered. She knew her answer would be disappointing. "There's six of us working on the cameras, boss. The place was packed. Evenings it always is. Hundreds, thousands all milling about and moving like a giant kaleidoscope."

Ratso could imagine it only too well. As one of London's busiest locations, it was ideal for gangs of pickpockets – and for disappearing. "From around Leicester Square, she could grab another taxi or a bus. Close by, there's the Bakerloo, Northern and Piccadilly lines. Or she could even walk. We're dealing with one clever cookie."

"Considering there are more than a half-million cameras in London, she seems to have avoided too many of them and too damned well."

"You're right, Carole. This killer is cunning."

Are we dealing with a copper gone rogue?

"Anything else, guv?"

"Thanks. No. See you tomorrow."

From Viment's tone as the call ended, Ratso sensed she wanted to keep talking.

Was that because of boredom at home?
Enthusiasm for her job?
Or did she enjoy chatting to me?

He had wondered a couple of times before whether she had been flirting with him but had played dumb. No point dwelling on that. He decided to call Strang who was leaving a chippie with a supersized portion laden with vinegar and ketchup. Ratso wished he could smell it. Between mouthfuls, the Scot promised to update him on the Ongerton murder. "First, get this, boss. About Logan Goldie. Could be the break we needed."

South Yorkshire

"Tell me more Jock." Ratso moved to the motorway's inner lane while he listened.

"Logan Goldie had an appointment that evening with Jenny Fort of Rolstern Genomics." He paused to wipe ketchup from his lips before continuing. "His diary was on his phone."

"You've more! I can tell from your voice."

"The techies got into his laptop too. Goldie had a wee note on it. This Fort woman had promised *information to blow Rolstern out of the water. Corruption. Covid 19. Will bring evidence.*"

"Goldie got rich on tips like that," Ratso agreed.

"Tomorrow, Nancy Petrie's going to Rolstern's in Cricklewood."

"I'm listening. And?"

"Goldie's incoming calls-log showed nothing involving Rolstern or Jenny Fort."

"Whoever called used a burner. That's my take. Most criminals do. Using an unregistered phone stops us from tracing the caller. They're cheap and anybody can buy one. The Thames must be littered with dumped burners."

"Aye! Whether it's burners or using VPN to trawl the web or using the dark web, modern science and technology keeps making our job harder."

"Not always, Jock! Though it feels like that." Ratso was thinking of the advantages of ever more powerful DNA and cameras on buses and doorbells.

"Willison and the uniforms got nothing from door-to-door

in Goldie's block. Most apartments are investments for foreign owners. The majority were empty. Those at home saw or heard nothing unusual. Most didna' know Goldie except for owning the McLaren."

"News about the Surrey murder?"

"We've mainly taken over from Iqbal now. I've left them crawling all over ANPR for the M25. The tyre tread pointed to a 4 x 4 with badly worn heavy duty tyres."

"Those tyres? Inconsistent with a small saloon car?"

"Right enough but not impossible."

"About Lord Ongerton?"

Still chomping on his chips as he dawdled along the darkened streets of south London heading for Wandsworth, Strang finished a giant mouthful. "His Lordship lived in a palatial house. Eaton Square in Belgravia. The lads found membership cards for a casino in Berkeley Street and for the Carleton but so far nothing else connecting him with Goldie." He paused to pop a couple of chips into his mouth. "Doyle, I'll come to. The casino managers both said Ongerton came alone. He always played low stakes blackjack and never dined. Sometimes he sank a couple of large gins, always on his own."

"Anything else?"

"Plenty, boss. He gave the appearance of wealth but his weekend place in Surrey was an inheritance, for use in his life only. It wasn't his to sell. I think he's called a tenant-for-life. In Eaton Square, he lived rent-free."

"Give."

"Ernest Ongerton shared this mansion with a slightly older man called Patrick Marney. I interviewed him. Twelve years ago, they had met at the Turkish Baths in Edinburgh. Within a few days, Ongerton had moved in. Marney's family company had been bought out for over twenty million, some forty years ago. The lucky sod has never had to lift a finger again."

"An item, were they?"

"For several years, yes. Then they lived apart on separate floors. The place has eight bedrooms. Ongerton had an entire floor to himself. Marney described their present relationship as *good chums*."

"How spiffingly top-hole, old bean." Ratso mimicked a toff accent before continuing. "If he murdered Ongerton, he would say that, wouldn't he. *Good chums*! Believe him?"

Strang tossed the empty carton into a waste-bin. "Unsure. He could suggest no motive. But get this. Marney reckoned Ongerton had no real enemies but plenty of lovers. The old boy was highly promiscuous. He bedded younger men – guardsmen a speciality. They came from Wellington Barracks in Knightsbridge. All casual, sometimes under-twenties."

"Paedo was he? Rent-boys?"

"Not that Marney was volunteering. Ongerton used to boast he never needed to pay for sex."

"Reckon Marney was jealous?"

"He denied that. The guy's seventy, pig-ugly, overweight and creepy. His arse sags to his knees. He didna' even smell too great – like a chicken gone past its sell-by date. He described Ongerton as a handsome fella, haughty and aristocratic. Oozed charm apparently. Raffish. Marney had a photo of him by his bed. He showed me. Botoxed forehead, boyish looking mane of hair and silky-smooth face. He looked twenty years younger than Marney."

"And Marney?"

"Told me he was currently celibate."

"You believed him?"

"Yes." The Scot's answer was blunt. "I mean with that face and a smelly body, he was scarcely God's gift to the gay community."

"Or to any community by the sound of it." Ratso heard a can being opened and knew his inspector would now be swilling down an Irn-Bru. "Can't rule out jealousy. Plus he knew where Ongerton would be." Ratso accelerated past a giant truck with an Estonian number-plate.

"His lordship was church-mouse poor because he had to live up to his image as a peer. In the last year, he picked up just over thirty thousand for attending the House of Lords. He had only a modest annual income from a family trust. Otherwise he sponged off Marney."

"Try this for size, Jock. Ongerton wanted a posh home. He's short of the readies. For a few years, he ignored the smell and the pig-ugly face. Then Ongerton started rogering the entire regiment of the King's loyal guardsmen. Marney, meantime, let him stay on, dreaming of them being an item again."

"Right enough. When I asked him, Marney confessed to still being in love with Ongerton. He broke down. Inconsolable, blubbing like a bairn – that's baby to you. His huge spotted hankie was soaked."

"I'm just pulling in for a break. I could slaughter a chicken and cheese pasty. I'll ring back. Then tell me about Ongerton's apartment."

M1 Motorway, Donington Park Service Area

"No pasties left, luv!"

Ratso had to settle for a heated meat pie and a large coffee. He moved between the tables filled with the usual late-night crowd of students, truckers or nondescripts discussing deals or problems back home. He sat down by a window with nobody close. He felt more at ease like that. He rang Strang. "Ongerton's London suite?"

"Fully self-contained with a home movie theatre. A large library of gay porno movies. He wrote up a daily diary. Intended to publish it next year. DC Broadbent is reading it. Must be full of stuff. I warned him not to get a stiffie."

"Political gossip? Stuff that gets serialised in Sunday papers?"

"Marney said it was dynamite. Y'know – about Honourable Members of the House of Commons behaving dishonourably. The diary linked a number of Scots Guards to several household names in the Commons and Lords. Ongerton had even fessed up to Marney about the occasional blow-job in the parliamentary lavvie with a noble earl. You know – queer peers."

"Can't say that these days, Jock." Ratso sounded stern before laughing. "Perhaps it was the Earl of Wankerton." They both chuckled before Ratso continued. "Fifteen years back, I had to investigate a House of Commons scandal involving a well-known politician. He's dead now. Suicide. My boss ordered me to read Tom Driberg's book *Ruling Passions*. He said never underestimate the vile depravity of our MPs. Driberg was a top guy in the Labour Party. That book opened my eyes. I've never considered politicians the same way again. I could believe anything that Ongerton was about to publish."

"Right enough, Westminster's still a cesspit. If Cabinet Ministers were worried about Ongerton's diary, there's a motive."

"Only if they knew he had been jotting down every grope, kiss or threesome. Check out what was known at Westminster."

Strang sucked the last drops from his can. "Last week, Marney had booked dinner at Osteria Romano in Knightsbridge for tomorrow evening. Table for two. Him and Ongerton. That checked out."

"Doesn't prove his innocence, Jock. Links to Dermot Doyle?"

"Marney and Ongerton both knew Doyle and thought him delightful. They both considered Doyle a tad too camp."

"How did they know him?"

"Don't laugh boss but his prissy answer was *we met him at a party in The Boltons. Where else darling!* Marney even gave my arm a wee squeeze as he told me."

"Your lucky day, Jock. You don't get many offers." Ratso laughed, imagining the scowl on the Scot's face and was rewarded with a derisive snort.

"They had dinner with Doyle in Ladbroke Grove a few times. Dined with some of his slightly boho friends. Media types mainly, one or two of them up from Brighton for overnighters."

"Women guests?" Ratso walked briskly to the exit.

"When I asked Marney that, he gave me a *you foolish boy* look."

"Any one of these boho guests special to Doyle?"

"Not so Marney could tell. Doyle was always the queen-bee, the centre of attention. These young men willingly shared his bed, sometimes two at a time."

"And Logan Goldie?"

"Marney and Ongerton had read of his murder. His name meant nothing. Since then, Marney had been asking around. He got the impression that Goldie was not popular."

"In the gay clubs or City finance circles?"

"Marney reckoned both. Pure gossip though. People who'd come across him considered him flash, brash – always boasting of his wealth and laughing at the death-threats."

"He's not laughing now." Under the clear skies and starry night when Ratso went out, the air was decidedly chilly but still heavy with traffic pollution. "I'm heading back to the car." As he speeded up, Ratso shivered in his T-shirt and wished he had worn his jacket. "Go on."

"People considered Goldie was a bore. Interesting the first time only. You understand – *come and look at my McLaren. I keep the Ferrari in a lock-up in Chelsea.* His conversation was me, me and more me. As if nobody else had ever done anything. Oh, aye! Marney did mention that Goldie reputedly had once a bit of a thing with Ambrose Alban."

"What?" Ratso's surprise was genuine. "The American crooner? He's sold millions of albums. Fills the Royal Albert Hall."

"Right enough. Alban's married wi' two kids. Apparently, he has an industrial scale drug habit and will bend over for anyone. Young DC Myerson checked Goldie's phone contacts. There were two numbers listed for Alban."

"Follow that up." Ratso slipped into the car-seat and slammed out the night air. "It's a long-shot. Even if Goldie tried blackmailing Alban, why would Alban want the others silenced."

"Oh, boss before you go. DC Bonkale checked back-numbers of *Saints & Skeletons*. Goldie boasted of mebbe twenty death threats."

"I'm not hot on death threats." Ratso's shiver was involuntary as he thought of Hysen Kola closing in on him. "They're best in crime fiction. Real professionals don't piss about giving warnings. They don't play damn-fool games with playing-cards either. For them, a quick kill and escape – that's what counts. Let's speak in the morning." Ratso ended the call wondering where Hysen Kola now was.

He decided to drop by Jubilee House. He had some ideas to check out.

Putney

Ratso had parked up and was at his desk by just gone 2 a.m. Before entering the underground car-park, he had looked in his mirror for anything suspicious. Nothing behind or ahead. Upstairs, it was obvious that the King of Spades had ramped up the dial to *serial killer on the loose*. The Major Incident Room was now devoted to *Operation Footstool*. There was a scattering of civilians and a couple of officers at their work-stations, rattling in the large room. Ratso gave some a wave and others a passing greeting.

Spooning a takeaway porridge as he worked his way through the developments, thirty minutes later, he felt up to speed. Not that Smart Alex would see it like that. Questions had tumbled around his head the entire journey. Why had the killer selected these three? No thefts. No inheritance prospects. Pig-face Marney had no apparent motive to kill Doyle or Goldie. They all played the casinos. They had similar sexual preferences.

Could there be vengeance from way back? Schooldays even? He messaged DC Viment to check all three back to University and before. With Ongerton so much older, it was a long-shot. "It's gay-bashing." Caldwell's latest barb about Ratso *not pursuing the bleeding obvious* had just made him more determined to prove the shit wrong. But … God forbid … had Caldwell been right all along? That the killer actually was a gay-basher?

In Ladbroke Grove, the footprints had been sized nine. At Hambledon, the prints had been sized eleven. The thick carpet in Goldie's apartment had been inconclusive. The Mayfair pictures confirmed the woman did not have size eleven feet. Did women ever have size eleven feet? He guessed the answer was yes – but not many. Someone with size nine feet could wear elevens. But the reverse? *Well maybe.*

As a distant clock struck three, Ratso read updates from Holmes 2. The search he had asked for on Friday was there. A trawl of London and the Home Counties had identified a number of unsolved murders or very suspicious deaths. Most outstanding murders had involved hitmen or suspicious suicides. None involved a female killer. Three murders with bare hands had to be a pointer.

After a few moments reading, he stopped in mid-track. There was another line to investigate. He jotted down two words before leaving his office to visit the whiteboard. Ratso knew some of the younger guys regarded him as a dinosaur for still preferring a whiteboard. Occasionally, to humour them, he projected PowerPoint slides onto the wall.

Doesn't beat the dramatic impact of adding a red arrow to link a couple of suspects.

He studied the photos of the victims and the multi-coloured loops and arrows. So far, they pointed to nothing at all. With a final shrug of the head, he decided to head home.

Why would the serial killer stop with an Ace?

When will the killer play his Ace?

With unerring accuracy, he lobbed his empty carton into a bin several feet away. Then, he studied the blow-up photo of Goldie's killer and compared Jenny Fort's website photo as Company Secretary of Rolstern.

Jenny Fort would never use her own name to meet and then murder Goldie.

That made no sense.

Was there another visitor that the porter had missed?

Had the visitor been a man?

Yawning, he returned to his desk and logged out of Holmes 2. Would a psychological profiler assist? On his SIO course, he had learned this had to be considered but he was sceptical.

Don't give Caldwell an open goal.
Play it by the book.
Involve a profiler.

Yawning again as he stretched before leaving, he watched a refuse vehicle stop close to the church followed by the clatter of waste being hurled into the rear. A few minutes later, thoughts of Dermot Doyle surfaced as he drove home along the Fulham Palace Road. He spotted Gowan Avenue. Impulsively, as if it would give him inspiration, he turned right and drove slowly past number 29. Doyle and Jill Dando had both been admired, respected, even loved and her killer was still on the loose.

Am I missing a link?

Besides the letter D and their TV careers, there was nothing obvious. That didn't mean there was no link. With nothing yet making sense, the Dando murder needed to be looked at more closely.

Nah!
Where did Logan Goldie and Lord Ongerton fit in to that.
Makes no sense.

Next morning, it was nearly ten when he was awoken by the phone. It was DC Petrie. "Good break, boss?"

He tried to sound alert but Petrie was not fooled. "Oh ... oh yes, Nancy." His mind flashed back to his bowling success of 4 for 28 at Barningham. "Yes. But I only got to bed at dawn." He propped himself on one elbow, his bare chest protruding above the bedclothes. "You been to Rolstern yet? How's Jenny Fort? Was she wearing a flowery dress?"

"That's why I'm calling."

Cricklewood

DC Petrie had arrived at Rolstern Genomics at 08-30 a.m. The company's premises were in a drab flat-roofed brick building, probably dating back to the seventies. A wide metal gate slid across after she had announced herself. In the yard were about a dozen family style cars, a couple of motor-bikes and one maroon Jaguar F-Pace. "I'm Tara," she was greeted in the well-lit and functional reception. Around the walls were Awards Certificates. "You must be DC Petrie?"

"Correct and I'm meeting Mr Will Morgan."

"I'm his PA. I'll take you through." As she spoke, she was already walking down a corridor that could have been in any NHS hospital – cheap prints of rivers and castles on the walls and easy-to-clean grey flooring. From one of the side-rooms, Petrie heard the distinctive sound of Amy Winehouse singing *Back to Black*. In the next office, a man of medium height in an open-neck red and black checked shirt rose to greet her. The room smelled of furniture polish or maybe carpet spray.

Morgan had a face like a full-moon and his hair was beyond receding, barely tufting at the sides. Petrie put him at early fifties. "I'm Will Morgan, the CEO. Tara – fix us some drinks, please. Tea, coffee?"

"Green or Jasmine. Anything herbal."

"And I'll have my usual." He pointed his visitor to an expensive black leather chair and he returned to his swivel recliner where he sat, swinging his short legs. "I hope we can help. You said this is a murder investigation. I'm intrigued."

"Nothing to alarm you. Just routine enquiries. Firstly, what does Rolstern do?"

"We're in the biotech sector. As a detective, you'll be familiar with DNA from its value in forensics. We're a giant leap on from that."

"For the benefit of a colleague who suggested that Genomics meant you made garden gnomes, perhaps a bit more detail?" She was thinking of Jock Strang who may not have been joking.

"Genomics is the study of all of a person's genes – that's the *genome* bit. It includes the interactions of those genes with each other and with a person's environment."

"I won't pretend to understand," Petrie laughed after she had finished scribbling. "You've been busy for some while with Covid 19? Maybe Monkeypox too?"

Morgan looked puzzled. "Why does that interest you? Yes … of course, Covid was right up our alley."

"I'm not even sure it does interest me." Petrie stared across the desk trying to assess whether mentioning Covid was touching some kind of raw nerve.

"We got involved in a project assessing large numbers of people, thousands. Our aim was to discover why some people who caught Covid had mild to non-existent symptoms while others died or nearly died." He paused and waved a hairy hand. "Our early conclusions pointed to obesity, deprivation or ethnicity."

"I'm intrigued."

"It's a bit like you hunting down a murderer. It's detective work. We're tracking down something elusive. We believe there may be some other factor in our bodies that may dictate the life-or-death difference. So we study the DNA and by comparing genome sequences, we intend to find the mysterious X-factor or factors that made Covid so hard to understand."

Petrie thought of Tosh Watson, her obese colleague who was still absent from work with Long Covid. "Valuable work." She laughed to lighten what lay ahead. "So we're both detectives."

Tara reappeared with drinks and biscuits as Morgan continued. "So what are you here for?"

"Jenny Fort. Does she work here?"

"Jenny? In a murder investigation?" Morgan blinked and ruffled one side of his remaining hair. "Yes. She's our Company Secretary."

"Is she in today?"

"Saw her ten minutes ago."

"Would she know about the company business?"

"If you mean the finances, the corporate stuff, yes. On the bio side, she wouldn't know a genome from a gnome either." He grinned at his explanation.

"I'll need to see her."

"Of course. But I'd like to know why?"

"Logan Goldie. That name mean anything?"

"It does, yes. He was murdered last week. He was a share tipster-come-Robin Hood. Exposing corporate misdeeds. I never came across him. I saw some detective on TV waffling about him."

Petrie imagined Ratso's hoot of derisive laughter at his Press Conference being described as waffle. "Goldie soaked up gossip about companies quoted on the stock exchange. Are you listed?"

"Yes. We're on what is called the AIM market. We're a public company with shareholders."

Petrie studied his body language and reckoned he was shifting uneasily as she continued. "Goldie published an on-line tip-sheet called *Saints & Skeletons*. At the precise time he was murdered, he had an appointment with Jenny Fort who was visiting him – apparently to blow the whistle on corruption in your company."

"Jenny? Jenny? Corruption? Us?" He placed both elbows on his desk which was empty of all paperwork. "She's my daughter-in-law. Sort of. They're not married but she and Carl have been together for two years. My son is a micro-biologist working here. Is it likely? Draw your own conclusions. To me it's utter bollocks, if you'll excuse my plain speaking."

"As I said, just routine enquiries. Can you get her in please?" Petrie watched as he dialled her number and almost at once, she appeared. She was around thirty, average height, rather on the thin side, short dark hair with pleasant but unremarkable features. *Did she match the photos taken around Chesterton Gardens?*

"Jenny. This is Detective Constable Petrie. She's investigating the murder of that guy Logan Goldie."

Fort sat down beside Petrie, a puzzled look on her face. "Killed in Mayfair, correct?" Her voice was Home Counties and probably privately educated. The smell of Imperial Leather soap drifted towards Petrie.

"Have you ever met or communicated with Mr Goldie?"

Fort shook her head, at first saying nothing, just twisting her hands together. "I'm aware of his nasty reputation. He can, well he could, influence share prices. AIM is geared to start-ups or higher-risk companies with zero to hero profiles. We're quoted on it. Share prices on AIM are driven by gossip, often untrue, and by herd mentality. It's sometimes described as a casino. Goldie played on that sentiment."

"Not that we were complaining, mind you," Morgan chipped in.

Petrie ignored the comment, her focus nailed on Jenny Fort. "Did Goldie ever write up your company? Name it as a winner or loser?"

"Not that I knew. We never subscribed to *Saints and Sinners*."

Petrie corrected her gently. "*Saints and Skeletons*."

Fort ran her fingers across the sleeve of her lime-green blouse.

"If he had hammered us, we'd have heard from our shareholders." The words were spoken slowly as if carefully judged. "We were lucky. Covid was good for us. Big contracts and fairly won. Our shares rose sharply. End of."

"His diary showed a Jenny Fort from Rolstern Genomics was due at his apartment at 21-30 p.m. That's the night he was murdered." Petrie stared heard at Fort and saw the shock on her face. She produced a screenshot of Goldie's note "Take a look: *Could blow the company out of the water. Corruption. Covid 19. Bringing evidence to prove.*"

Fort raised her hands to cover her face, letting out a yelp of surprise. Morgan walked round the table to put an arm across her shoulders. After a heavy silence, Fort continued. "Unbelievable. It wasn't me." She spread out her hands and looked pleadingly at Will Morgan and Petrie in turn "Why would I destroy Will's business? Why did someone pick on me?"

"Get this straight!" Morgan had sat down again but his face had reddened with indignation. "There's nothing corrupt here. No skeletons about Covid." He thumped the table for emphasis.

"Jenny, where were you last Wednesday evening?"

"I'll get my diary." Petrie took in the size of her feet in her white trainers as she returned with a smartphone. "These are my movements that day. Board Meeting till lunch. A session with our auditors till five. Carl, my partner and I, then we went into the West End. Six of us had dinner at Bentley's in Swallow Street."

"That's Mayfair, then?"

"Yes, I suppose it is."

"There all evening? Both you and Carl?"

"I was. Yes. Both of us. From eight until around ten-thirty."

"And you, Mr Morgan? Where were you that evening?" Not that it made any sense but Petrie wondered absurdly whether he was a cross-dresser and could have worn a flowery dress.

His podgy fingers turned to his desk-top computer. "Quiet evening at home in Bayswater."

Petrie wasn't sure why the thought came to her but on impulse she continued. "And last weekend?"

"Was Goldie murdered twice?" Morgan's joke fell flat as Petrie watched him scratch his elbow. Then, she waited, saying nothing while he tapped away on his phone. She reckoned this was a charade. He had no need to check.

Morgan is playing for time.

But why?

"At home in Inverness Terrace on Friday evening. Golfing on Saturday morning."

"Where?"

"Nice little club in Surrey. Chiddingfold. A foursome with some old pals."

Petrie played dumb. "Where is that near? Remind me."

"Beautiful spot. Say ten miles south of Guildford."

"What time did you tee-off?"

"I don't recall exactly but around half-past-eight."

"And you left home when?"

"At around seven, I guess. Perhaps a bit after."

"Can someone confirm that? Your wife maybe?"

"I'm divorced. Live alone. Anyway, I'm not sure why you're quizzing me."

Petrie shrugged saying it was just routine and rose to leave. As she did, she paused by the grimy window. "Is that your tasty looking Jag?"

"Bought it three weeks back. My pride and joy. You like it?"

"I'd love one. I can dream. The Lottery maybe."

Back in her battered red Mini, she made sure nobody spotted her sneaking a pic of Morgan's car.

Bonnitor

The Caribbean island of Bonnitor lies rather more than four thousand miles from London. Though Ratso was aware of it, like most Brits, he had never been there because there were no direct flights. The travel industry had begged for a longer runway but in keeping with most things involving corruption and local politics, somehow it had never happened.

Being part of the British Commonwealth, Bonnitor's laws and its Parliament were modelled on Westminster and the English legal system. Most of the population were black but with a history of English, Dutch and Spanish settlers, some were white or of mixed-race. Sixteen years ago, a devastating hurricane had destroyed the poorest parts of Torrington, its capital and main port. Several thousand of Bonnitor's 180,000 population had been swept away in an eighteen-metre tidal surge that had smashed and trashed the yellow, green and purple wooden shacks with their corrugated iron roofs.

For survivors, life had been about scavenging for scraps and queuing at food kitchens amid the squalid filth, smashed furniture and battered cooking utensils. Survivors had hunkered down to survive and part of Torrington was still a dangerous no-go area for strangers. Sixteen years on, in the ramshackle huts and pot-holed streets, even those who wanted to work had little chance. As always, local politicians had made bold promises but achieved little. Now, they had the excuse of the lingering ravages of Covid for the poverty and soaring crime rates.

Until 2020, giant cruise-ships had unleashed an army of

shoppers to buy bling or luxury fashion goods or to chomp fast-food. They had yet to return. Many hotels had closed, waiting and hoping for better days that were yet to happen. Unemployment, always a problem, had soared bringing with it home invasions, muggings, rapes, murder and turf-wars over drugs.

Kendall Campbell KC had been raised in Windylea, an area of Torrington most definitely on the wrong side of the tracks. Whereas most kids down his street, if they ever got a job at all, had drifted into working as kitchen porters or fishermen, with his clever tongue and determination, Campbell had gone on to read law at Manchester University and had obtained a pupillage in a fashionable barrister's chambers in London's Gray's Inn Square.

When the hurricane had struck, Campbell had still been in London. Back home though, his parents and three sisters had been swept away in the thundering power of the tidal surge. They had never been found. His former two-room shack had been turned into matchwood. Shortly afterwards, scarred by the tragedy and weary of life in London, Campbell, his wife, Brenda and their twin daughters, had returned to Bonnitor.

In no time, he had acquired a reputation of being the *go-to* attorney. His home was now a four-million-dollar bungalow in the guard-gated community of Robinson Cove. Campbell though, had never forgotten his roots. Now, he had folk-hero status – a champion of the underdogs, fearless of Government and ready to fight injustice, often on a *pro-bono* basis. In contrast, he was often hired at eye-watering fees by the super-rich or multi-national corporations to sue each other or more often to challenge the corrupt and manipulative politicians who ruled the island.

After a big victory in court that afternoon, Campbell was feeling exhilarated, singing along to Jimmy Buffet's *Margaritaville* that played from his headphones. Darkness had fallen two hours before. Seated in the stern of his small dinghy, the outboard motor was chugging him back to his private mooring after an evening's fishing. Other than sex with Brenda and savouring his taste for fine red Burgundy, he could think of no better way than fishing to unwind after a full-on day in the dry, dusty surroundings of the Bonnitor Supreme Court.

He was proud of his reputation as a champion of life's losers. But his lavish lifestyle needed days like today when the judge had awarded him his fees of 1.8 million dollars, payable by the Government. A crony of the Prime Minister had paid a hefty bribe to secure a new power-station contract. Campbell's client, who should have been awarded the contract, had been *royally stitched-up,* as Campbell had told the judge.

Greed and corruption in Bonnitor ensured that no heads would roll. The Prime Minister would not resign. Campbell liked it that way. Fearless of the risks, it kept his fees rolling in. Because of victories like today, Campbell could fight for the underprivileged victims of injustice without charge.

As he drew close to his private jetty, Campbell saw the black emptiness of land beyond the promontory to the left of his property. To his right, he could see the lanterns in the gardens of neighbouring properties. They were swaying in the gentle balmy breeze. From his right came the smell of someone's barbecue and the rhythm of reggae from a pool-party.

Like the British Virgin Islands, the Caymans and the Bahamas, Bonnitor had become a favoured tax haven. The KC guessed that many of these palatial homes had been financed by untaxed wealth or narcotics. In Robinson Cove, his neighbours were silver-spoon kids, corporate tycoons, white-collar criminals and a sprinkling of celebs. Being guard-gated was essential but even that guaranteed nothing. Back in February, a wealthy

Brazilian couple had been robbed, mutilated and murdered, their killers never caught.

Campbell switched off the outboard. His jetty was in darkness as his dinghy glided to a stop. He waved both arms high above his pepper-and-salt hair. Instantly, the security lights were triggered. He saw the patio beyond the kidney-shaped pool and hot-tub. Behind that, Campbell could see the yellow walls, picture-windows and pale-blue roof of his sprawling single-storey home. For a few moments, Campbell took in the pleasures of the evening air, scented by the abundant hibiscus, frangipani and royal-poinciana.

Normally, on his return, Brenda would have been on a recliner, having fixed them a couple of Bombay Sapphire gins and a conch and lime salad. However, this week she was just a short hop across the water in Barbados on a shopping-spree. With their daughters studying in Miami, Campbell was alone. Once in a while, that suited him just fine. Tonight, after savouring a bottle of Grand Cru La Tâche 2009, he had a stack of reading for his next big case.

As the dinghy bumped against the timbered jetty, a smirk still played on his weathered face, his large brown eyes still crinkling with pleasure at today's victory. He imagined the Prime Minister, scowling on his veranda, seething at Campbell's success. No doubt, he would be invoking the black arts of Obeah and sticking pins into the KC's image. Like everyone on Bonnitor, Campbell had been brought up to respect the sinister powers of voodoo, Obeah and the black arts. Now, after his years in London, he laughed that he had ever believed a word of it.

He tied the boat to the bollard and shifted his bulky, muscled frame onto the jetty. Stiff, after being seated for three hours, he wiggled some circulation into his knees before attempting to walk. Puffing slightly at the exertion, he leaned into the boat and removed his rod and cool-box containing a couple of striped-bass. His breathing still laboured, he set off up the crazy-paved path towards his patio. Behind him, were the dark skies and smooth Caribbean waters. Ahead, and beyond the large cluster of pink-flowering azaleas, was the welcoming sight of the sliding-doors to the coolness of the air-conditioning and that bottle of La Tâche adjusting to room-temperature.

Putney

Smart Alex had left the session in the MIR and returned to his office, leaving the brainstorming to Ratso. However, before going, he had commented that it was good of DCI Holtom to find time to be present rather than prancing round Yorkshire in his white cricket flannels. Coming from a good mate, Ratso would have laughed. Coming from Smart, he was furious but short of provoking WW3, he had laughed and played an exaggerated forward-defensive cricket shot. Some wag shouted *Owzat* to general laughter.

Caldwell's main contribution had been that *gay-bashing is still my odds-on favourite but maybe DC Petrie is onto something with Will Morgan and Jenny Fort. Morgan was so close to where Lord Ongerton was throttled. Keep digging. Check out his golfing mates too.*

Ratso was underwhelmed. "Walk us through your meeting again," Ratso invited Petrie as he stood in front of the now large team, coffee in hand. Over thirty pairs of eyes turned towards her. A year ago, she would have blushed and spoken hesitantly, Now, she stood, head erect.

"The cameras on the A3 southbound are being checked for sightings of Morgan's 4 x 4 Jag. I'm not hopeful we'll get much on the lesser roads to Godalming and Hambledon. Other than admiring it, I never hinted any interest in his car. I gave Surrey the registration. D.I. Iqbal said the tyre treads were suggestive of a 4x4." She pointed to the photo, now pinned to the board. "I sneaked this shot in the car-park."

Ratso looked hesitant. "Ignoring Morgan's Jag, the wheelbase will tell us whether we're dealing with a big 4 x4, the so-called Chelsea tractor, or a family saloon. That's not rocket-science."

"How far was the murder from the golf-course?" enquired Strang.

Petrie looked at her small feet and then back towards the Scot. "Just over three miles. Pretty handy, eh?" As usual when she was fired-up, her nostrils flared.

"Why would Morgan murder Lord Ernest Ongerton," Strang continued as he tilted back in his chair.

"Agreed Jock," Ratso chimed in. "Don't waste much time on Jenny Fort or Will Morgan. Frankly, this Rolstern link is utter crap. The killer set it up. Okay, we do need to check out the Jag's wheelbase. I'll wager Morgan will then be in the clear." Ratso pointed to the photo of the Jag. "It's a new car. Those tyres are not worn – unlike the ones at the scene."

"Why did the killer pick on Jenny Fort and Rolstern?" It was DC Viment who had asked.

Ratso strolled across in front to the team, hand on chin. "My take, Carole? The killer picked the company because it had won lucrative Covid contracts. That was sure to attract Goldie's interest."

"So maybe we are looking for a woman."

"Go on."

"If Rolstern was random, why not pick another company with a male whistleblower?"

"Makes sense." Ratso was not yet done. "Look – has the short and fat-arsed Will Morgan the profile of a professional killer? Totally wrong shape to have been Goldie's visitor. Was he even tall enough to throttle Ongerton? Nancy, would this guy have the balls to kill like a pro?"

"Put like that, boss," Petrie blushed.

"Don't worry Nancy. DCS Caldwell thinks you're onto something." Ratso milked the laughter before raising his hands. "Let's move on."

Viment though had not yet finished. "Boss, I'm checking camera footage on Inverness Terrace for the night Dermot Doyle was murdered. That's where Will Morgan lived. We've not traced a car used to escape yet but Morgan could walk to Ladbroke Grove in under thirty minutes."

"Move on, Carole. I'm done with Morgan murdering anybody." Ratso's tone was sharper now. "But listen up. Trawling on Holmes uncovered that Will Morgan had been identified for closer scrutiny in *Operation Grange*." Ratso saw jaws drop everywhere and he heard a few shocked expletives.

"Portugal? The search for Madeleine McCann?" It was Petrie who gave Ratso a hard look.

"It's not relevant to us, least I don't think so. He was in Praia da Luz in Portugal the night Maddie disappeared in May 2007. He had an apartment about sixty metres away from the Ocean Club where Maddie was last seen. His name had been linked to a paedo-ring that had prowled the Algarve. Morgan's alibi just about held up. He was about three kilometres away in a Lagos restaurant and was not directly involved. But someone might have abducted her to his order. That's about when his marriage broke up."

"He seemed a decent regular guy," Petrie's tone and flapped arms said it all.

Ratso shrugged dismissively. "There was no solid evidence he was a paedo anyway. Nor were our three victims. Not on what we know, so far. For now, Morgan and little Maddie are not in focus. But don't forget this. It might fit in somewhere. Personally, I doubt it."

"I was involved in *Operation Grange* for a while," volunteered

DC Helen Briscoe. "During the golden hours, the Portuguese police were obsessed with the McCanns and their friends at the Ocean Club."

"Yeah," Ratso nodded. "That's why we need to concentrate on the facts yet never dismissing the improbable." In a few languid steps, he moved to the other side of the audience. "No *failure of imagination*. Follow the ABC principles – *Accept Nothing, Believe Nobody and Check Everything*. This killer may have picked random victims."

"Someone who just likes killing," Strang muttered thoughtfully.

"Perhaps Jock, but I don't think so. For now, we rule nothing in or out." Ratso rapped his knuckles on a desk. "Jock – I want you and DC Bonkale to drill down into Goldie's business life. Go big on this." He refrained from using the *Bonkers* nickname though he knew the young and razor-sharp West African lapped it up, always joking along with the rest of them. "Y'know, the *Saints and Skeletons* stuff. Go through every company Goldie attacked in the last two years. Names of directors picked on. Directors jailed. Check on the death-threats. From the front-runners, see what damage Goldie did to the share price. Check out who got arrested. Who might be pissed off with him? Goldie had no staff. It was just him and his flaming hot keyboard. Got it? Everything about Goldie's *modus operandi*."

From somewhere, a voice in a camp style muttered, *get you boss* but it was Strang who continued. "Good call. Bonkers is a whizz on ferreting." He turned to look at the enthusiastic Ghanian who beamed, all wide-eyed and flashing white teeth.

Ratso saw that Willison was tapping on his phone. "Willison? Are you with us but watching porn? With us and playing with yourself down there – or just with us in body only?"

Looking guilty, DC Danny Willison rubbed his freckled cheek as he looked up. "All ears, boss. Just waiting for instructions."

"Gay forums, chatter. Visit the gay clubs. Everything on Patrick Marney, Lord Ongerton, Doyle and Goldie. Report in forty-eight hours. Any linkage between these four. Got it?"

"Yes, sir."

"Try not to enjoy it too much!" Ratso's comment attracted hoots and howls of laughter. Willison was a Lay Preacher and nobody's favourite person. People avoided him in the canteen because he wanted to encourage repentance from sin or quote verses from the bible. Ratso turned to DC Viment. "Carole – concentrate on the casinos. Maybe the killer selected victims in a casino. Check when they were last playing and see who took any interest in them. Who followed them out?"

Ratso checked the message that had just arrived on his phone.

Position Amber.

Poker-faced, he looked round his audience, absorbing their eagerness to perform. "Okay," he concluded. "We need to prevent this bastard playing his Ace of Spades. Except for Danny who will be cruising round Soho, everybody else, same time tomorrow. Thanks."

With none of the usual niceties for the closest members of the team, Ratso was gone.

Position Amber was the accelerant.

Trafalgar Square, London

Assistant Commissioner Wensley Hughes was already sipping a Latte when Ratso entered Caffè Nero on Trafalgar Square. The place was packed with tourists who had been taking in the sights of Whitehall or dodging pigeons around the foot of Nelson's Column. "Can I get you anything, sir?"

"I'm good, thanks, Todd." Hughes patted his slim waistline. "These days, I resist chocolate brownies and Danish pastries. But you go ahead." Ratso had never seen Hughes look anything other than trim but let it pass. He returned with a decaff and a Brie & Bacon Panini. Hughes had selected a back-corner table distanced from crying babies and lively toddlers. "Sorry to meet here, Todd, but this was urgent and I've a lunch meeting in the City."

Ratso had good reason to be grateful to the man opposite him. He viewed Hughes as a fair-minded officer with a reputation that had seen him advance quickly through the ranks. With his experience in homicide, Hughes spoke his language.

Hughes placed his elbows on the table as he leaned forward. "*Operation Footstool?*"

"So far, we're poking around with white sticks. Nothing makes sense." Ratso saw Hughes weighing up what to say. "Yet," he added hastily.

"Settled okay in Jubilee House? Good team?"

Now it was Ratso's turn to pick his words. "Not quite true. But I think you know why."

Hughes adjusted his half-glasses before a knowing smile

played around his mouth. "I spent a few minutes checking. You got the Queen's Medal for bravery for that night in Enfield," Hughes continued. "Saved a fellow officer's life. Well deserved."

"Nothing you wouldn't have done, sir." Ratso nodded, uncertain how to play it. This was no time to bleat that he could face down a gunman but couldn't cope with Smart Alex Caldwell. As he looked at this gaunt and austere looking man with his waxy skin, he glimpsed sympathy. Ratso recalled once describing Hughes as *having the body of a stick-insect, the balls of a stallion and the courage of a lion.* Nothing ever seemed to faze him. But sometimes, as Ratso knew only too well, the bigger dangers on the Met's greasy pole, were internal politics rather than villains.

"Todd, I know you and Detective Chief Superintendent Caldwell have more history than I learned for GCE. I'm backing you to use your QM grit to handle him. At least for now." He drained his coffee and when he looked across the table, Ratso picked up the steel in his eyes. "Now, to business. You know why we're meeting."

"Sir. *Position Amber*. Rising stakes involving Hysen Kola."

"You been coping okay?"

"Burying myself in *Footstool*. Trying not to drink myself to sleep."

Hughes blinked over his half-glasses at an admission that Ratso would never have made to anybody else. "An empty bottle is never the solution. You'll let me know if that becomes an issue. Keep your mind on *Footstool*."

"You're not taking me off it?" Ratso's rising voice and raised eyebrows showed surprise and relief.

Hughes shook his head. "Best therapy you can have. Keeping you busy."

"So why now upgraded to *Amber*?"

"Today, it's just got worse. We're not yet *Position Red* but ... " Hughes let the flourish of his arm say the rest.

"I understand, sir. How reliable was the original intelligence?"

"I wanted to be sure. It checks out at both ends. More loose chat in Tirana." Hughes saw Ratso flinch at mention of the Albanian capital. "You went there, didn't you?"

"A few years back. I narrowly avoided being hacked to death."

"These Albanians don't pussyfoot. That's why the present position is so serious."

"Sir?"

"The undercover NCA officer was investigating a gang smuggling migrants into the UK. By chance, she picked up about Hysen Kola. Now, it's been doubly corroborated."

Ratso froze for a moment. It had been three years since he had watched Boris Zandro get sentenced to thirty years at the Old Bailey for conspiracy to murder and operating the largest drug empire in the UK. "You have more on Hysen Kola?"

Hughes showed Ratso a photo of a fit-looking man, aged about thirty. He had dark curly hair, a tanned face with pinched features. Wearing a well-cut grey suit, he was getting into the back of a black Mercedes with tinted windows.

"So why upgraded to *Position Amber*?"

"We had a watch on all ports and airports."

"But?"

"Hysen Kola has now entered the UK." Hughes produced his phone and showed Ratso a picture. "That's Kola getting out of a VW near a beach between Dunkirk and Calais. He crossed the Channel in an inflatable with maybe six or seven other illegals – probably all Albanian. They landed on the Kent coast at Dungeness thirty-six hours ago. Five were caught by Border Force near Lydd. During interrogation, they identified Hysen Kola. We now know he was picked up by a small dark-coloured saloon car. We must assume he's now in London."

Ratso lowered his head and eyes and pushed aside the remains of his Panini. His appetite had gone. "Not good. Your plan?"

"Tell nobody. Kola must not be tipped-off we know he's here. That's our best chance."

"We always feared someone in the Government or the Met was leaking to Zandro. Even up to Cabinet level. He was too well informed."

"I've set up a discreet team under Detective Inspector Reg Gastrell. He's in the Anti-Corruption and Abuse Command. A good man."

"Their brief?"

Hughes shrugged dismissively. "To find Kola before he finds you."

Putney

As Kendall Campbell KC was looking forward to his Grand Cru Burgundy, Ratso and Jock Strang were sinking the cheapest Metaxa brandy on offer. Although Ratso would have preferred to share the Hysen Kola threat with Strang and Petrie, he could say nothing. He wondered who he could trust. Who might be leaking to Zandro or Kola? Who would brief Kola on where to find him?

In the Greek Taverna across from Putney Station, Ratso was unsure whether he was drowning sorrows or hoping for inspiration from the bottom of a glass. Probably both, he decided as he called for the bill. "We're still chasing shadows."

Nancy Petrie, today not drinking, was clutching a solid-looking coffee. "The dots are as far apart as ever," she agreed.

Jock looked wistfully at his empty glass and slowly cocked his head in agreement. "It's not that bad. Paedo or not, Will Morgan did not murder his Lordship. His Jag went straight from the M25 to the golf-club. Jenny Fort was scoffing in Bentleys. Everything checked out. Rolstern is out of the loop."

Ratso sank his fiery brandy with a swift toss of the head before fixing each in turn. "Maybe there are no dots to join." He saw he now had their full attention.

"Meaning?" Nancy frowned and slurped her coffee, heavy with sediment.

"Either we have a killer who targets well-known names but

randomly selected." He see-sawed his hands as he often did. "Or maybe this trio is like an oyster with a pearl inside?"

Strang got the drift before Petrie. "There'll be four victims but only one was the real target?"

Ratso's heavy lids opened and closed in acknowledgement. "Just a thought."

"So which one?" Petrie was tapping on her phone as she spoke. "Willison picked up nothing useful from the gay joints. Waste of time, that was."

The Scot laughed. "Hold your horses, Nancy. Not wasted. He told me he had an offer of a blowjob and had his bum pinched."

"I bet that turned his face as red as his hair," Nancy retorted as they all laughed at the image of Willison coping with unwelcome offers.

Ratso's face showed he was going to add another dig. "After being pinched, I expect he wanted to turn the other cheek." The laugher matched the lateness of the hour. "I chose Danny boy because he doesn't look like a copper. In fairness, he picked up plenty of gossip about the murders. I don't blame him for uncovering nothing of value."

"And Carole Viment has still found no casino link," Petrie added, patting down her short brown hair, the highlights now removed.

"That's my point, Nancy." Ratso studied the bill and suggested spoofing for it. Jock lost and reached for his wallet. "First time that's seen daylight since the Battle of Bannockburn, Jock." After the banter had died, Ratso turned serious. "The feet sizes point us nowhere."

"The three victims were all at Royal Ascot the same day," prompted Nancy. "But not together. Not even close." She saw Ratso was uninterested and so returned to scrolling on her phone.

It was nearly 1-30 a.m. Wanting to get home, the waiter scowled as Jock ordered two glasses of ouzo. "To get over the shock of the bill, " he added. Moments later the two glasses landed on the table with a thud. Jock asked the sullen-looking waiter if they served breakfast and was rewarded with a piss-off look.

Ratso added water and watched his ouzo change to a milky texture. "Rolstern – there's nothing to move the dial unless ..."

Jock's eyebrows met in a frown like two fighting badgers. "They paid someone? A woman?" He shook his head. "I'm not buying that. If they had a motive it had to involve Logan Goldie. But they said they'd never been fingered by him. They had no motive for the others."

Ratso chopped his hand across the table in an *end-of* way. His eyes rolled. "You think Rolstern hired a professional dumb enough to use the name Jenny Fort?"

"Put like that ..." Strang faltered. "But anyroads, whoever did it walked like a woman. Shapely legs too."

Bonnitor

Having removed his headphones but now humming *Yellow Bird*, Kendall Campbell continued his rolling gait up the path from his jetty. In front and from the trees, the lights shone down and he looked wistfully at the empty recliner where normally Brenda would be laid back seductively in a glitzy top, bare midriff and skimpy shorts. He had just passed a bank of azaleas and bottle-brush trees when, unseen, a figure emerged from their protection to walk behind him. The first awareness of an intruder was when Campbell felt something hard pressed against the back of his skull.

"Freeze," the voice commanded in a hissed quiet tone. "Is Brenda at home?" Campbell's normally astute brain was numbed. His fluent silvery tongue was silenced. He said nothing, trying to make sense of what was happening. "Tell me or I kill you right now." The words were accompanied by a jab into the hairline. "Count of three. Give. One ... two."

"I'm alone" The baritone voice, normally so commanding in courtrooms was throaty and reflected utter terror.

"Walk. Your safe and other valuables. Move."

Campbell knew better than to resist. You were lucky if drug-crazed intruders didn't trash the place and crap on your bed just for the hell of it. You were even luckier if not made to kneel to be executed. "Okay, okay. Take anything. Everything. Brenda's jewellery," he simpered, wondering how much the intruder knew. "Afterwards ... leave me alone, don't kill me."

The KC reached the louvred double-doors that gave access to

the rear of the bungalow. For a moment, he considered entering the panic-code to set off the alarm.

Pointless.

Those lazy bums at security would arrive too late.

They'd just reach my corpse quicker.

His long fingers shaking, somehow, he managed to enter the six numbers correctly and opened the doors. The jabbed knee into the lawyer's spine jettisoned him into the sitting-room. The lighted room was silent except for the swish of two overhead fans. The far wall was purple, the others magnolia. The furnishings were oversized wicker chairs in brown and white, a glass-topped coffee-table and a couple of goatskin rugs. On one wall was a recent painting of Campbell and Brenda standing under a colourful floral arch.

"The safe. Don't turn round." The air smelled of bamboo and lemon as the duo crossed the lobby. Campbell dumped the cool-box and the fish tumbled out onto the tiled floor. He led the intruder into his business-like office. Behind the well-ordered desk and several stacks of legal documents tied in pink ribbon, the internal wall was lined with law-books.

Campbell pressed a concealed button. The shelves divided to reveal a two-metre safe built into the wall. Despite the cool air, Campbell's body was now glistening with sweat. He could feel it running down from his neck towards his buttocks. Squatting slightly, he positioned himself for iris-recognition and was rewarded with a small green light. His fingers trembled as he turned his attention to the keypad. For a moment, he struggled to recall the pass-code 8 3 6 1 9 5 3. In his first clumsy attempt, he tapped the two instead of five. "No messing," came the deep-voiced command. At the second attempt, Campbell got it right and the heavy door swung open. On the top shelf were title-deeds, share certificates and a binder of banking records. The bottom tier contained bundles of US dollars, wrapped in cellophane.

"The cash." The intruder produced a sturdy black bin-liner bag. "In here." Before the intruder spoke again, Campbell had dumped over twenty thousand into the bag. "The jewellery."

Sweating profusely, his T-shirt saturated, Campbell stumbled across the high-ceilinged hall and into the over-sized bedroom with floor-to-ceiling windows. It overlooked the lawn down towards the jetty. The room was dominated by a heart-shaped bed and contained little else besides small bedside units. Campbell led the way into the en-suite with lavish *his and hers* marble vanity units, each with gold taps.

Side-by-side, were walk-in closets. In Campbell's, there hung an abundance of expensive suits for court appearances. Brenda's even larger walk-in was lined with haute-couture clothes and the air was heavy with a lingering smell of her musky perfume. It was still cluttered – her shoes, dirty clothes and sports-socks littering the floor. In pride of place though, on a white and gilt vanity unit, was a large crocodile-leather casket with a golden clasp. It had no lock. After a momentary fumble, Campbell had it open. The intruder sounded disappointed. "The diamond necklace? Where's her necklace?"

"Brenda," he faltered while trying to think straight. "I … I guess, she took it to Barbados. But there's plenty good-stuff here." He shuffled the contents revealing pearls, diamond brooches, bracelets and rings stuffed with rubies or emeralds. "Take them and go," he pleaded.

"Look again you fat shit." The tone was sharp. "There's a lower-deck. And you know it."

"No, no I didn't," the KC whimpered, his voice cracking. Feverishly, his fingers now scrabbled for the gap to lift the false floor of the box. Then it tilted upwards.

The intruder grunted in satisfaction as he recognised the

Pomellato gold and diamond Tango Chain worth around $80,000. "Campbell, don't go fucking with me again." The words were accompanied by a jab to the nape of Campbell's neck that made him wince and lurch forward. "In the bag."

Sweat now dripping into his eyes and making him blink, now it was his stomach that was churning, painfully so. As Campbell felt the weapon prod the back of his neck, he tried to sound calm but his throat was parched and croaky. "You have ... what you ... wanted. Now go. Please go."

Putney

After leaving the taverna, and having checked up and down Putney High Street, Ratso pulled up his collar. If Hysen Kola was around, he was well-hidden. In the drizzle, and still wary, he crossed towards the station.

Kola's here – plotting where and how to kill me.
And how to get away with it.

Now, in the near-empty street, he could hear a distant wailing siren heading west towards Barnes. Outside Putney Station, he saw a familiar figure, lying on sheets of cardboard. The man stirred and raised an eye before wiping the rain from his stubbled chin. Ratso had known the vagrant for years – ever since his pitch had been by Clapham North Station. "Hi Jonno!" Ratso crouched down beside him. "No night to be lying out here."

The man eased up to one elbow, wincing as he adjusted the bag of bones that was his fifty-six-year-old body. "Well, if it ain't Mr Todd! Hi guv!"

"What's up with your usual shelter in Putney Park Lane?"

Jonno ignored the question. "No night for you be prowling the streets neither, guv. The cops nick folk like you because you look so bleedin' shifty." He laughed with a coughing wheeze thrown in. His Yorkshire accent lingered but now with a strong dose of Cockney. "Nah! I did me good knee in, guv. Couldn't be arsed to walk there. Mind I didn't expect this effin' rain."

Years before, Jonno had volunteered how his life had been shattered. When mining for iron ore in Africa, he had been in a rail-crash that had taken his wife and baby daughter. With residual brain damage and losing a leg, Jonno was unemployable. For the feeble figure in grubby trainers, old flannels and a grey parka, begging was a necessity. No way was he conning the public. "What happened to your mutt, Jonno?"

"Smokey snuffed it a few weeks back. Okay, you got a dog, more folk chuck you brass. But I ain't replacing him. Picking up dog-shit in poly-bags? I'd had enough of that!" He grinned with too few front teeth and put on a refined accent that could have graced any royal palace. "Mr Todd, me being the Squire of Putney Hill and a gentleman of the road, I do have my standards."

"Sure you do, pal, sure you do. No consolation to you but in Jubilee House, I spend most days shovelling shit too." He reached over and tucked a tenner under the cardboard. "Get yourself a good breakfast. See you, Jonno."

"Cheers, guv."

Again, he checked the near deserted street before continuing past the shuttered shops and closed fast-food outlets. Back at his desk, disposable cup of coffee in hand, he studied the pathology reports. All three neck injuries were consistent with a right-handed person. Hand-size suggested a male of around average height or a female of slightly above average height. He sipped the coffee and stared at the photos of the killer leaving Goldie's apartment. The techies had reduced blur and pixilation and had zoomed in on the distant view of the face but despite this, the only person who could be sure of the sex was the killer.

At Petrie's suggestion, the entire Major Incident Team had pitched in a fiver for the closest to the date of birth and sex. "If the person is genuinely transgender, then all bets are off," Strang had commented as he tossed his note into a bowl. So far, sixty-six percent had voted male. Ratso was now looking at a woman in her flowery dress but murder stats suggested a male. His bet had been a fiver on a male aged thirty-nine.

He then spotted a cryptic post-it from Caldwell. "Need report in the morning." He enjoyed leaving his response on the emptiness of Caldwell's desk. He timed it at 2-35 a.m. "Sorry to miss you."

On leaving Jubilee House, Ratso's focus returned to Kola. He doubted he would try anything by Jubilee House with so many cameras. Far more likely would be the shadows of late-night Hammersmith Grove. After cycling round the Broadway, he changed his route and instead approached by Agate Road. Whistling tunelessly as he cycled the empty and darkened street, he recalled Zandro being sentenced and his parting shot. *Holtom! You'll die horribly.* No doubt, ever since, Zandro's anger had gnawed at his stomach every waking hour in Wakefield Jail. But Kola? He doubted a professional like him would be ready yet. He would need to plan to avoid arrest *and* escape the UK,

But would Kla know where he lived?

Ratso did not own his apartment. There would be nothing on title records. As a tenant, tracking down his home address would not be easy.

Not without a leak from a bent copper.

Ratso swung round the corner into the silence of Hammersmith Grove. There were just three-hundred metres to go. Not even a dog was barking. The lingering smell of someone's barbecue drifted from a back yard. He looked down the street. In the shadows from the line of trees, it was hard to tell if he was alone.

Bonnitor

Det. Insp. Bastien Alleyne of the Royal Bonnitor Police stared at the wide frontage to Kendall Campbell's home. The bungalow was set back seventy metres and protected only by a low stone wall. Nearly every other residence in Robinson Cove was shielded by high walls with entry-phones. Alleyne was on the gravelled drive talking to a security guard. Beyond them, in the street were four police vehicles, two motorcycles and a waiting ambulance.

Alleyne had never trusted security guards as far as he could spit. They were as trustworthy as the size of the brown envelope. Now, in the supposedly top-security Robinson Cove, this was the third murder in just a few months. "I'm not satisfied." Alleyne closed in on the guard's pockmarked face. "The murderers got in. How much were you paid to look the other way?" He saw the sullen look. "My sergeant will take your statement at HQ."

The detective turned on his heel and went back inside to talk to Det. Sgt Venables, a youthful thirty-two with wide-set eyes that gave him a quizzical look. "I want statements from every guard."

"Boss, remember the murdered Brazilians up the street? The guards told us they always checked with the home-owner before handing over a visitor-pass. That was the theory. In practice, it was bullshit. In theory, CCTV cameras at their post captured every vehicle and visitor. More bullshit!" He spat out a piece of gum into a trash-can.

Alleyne shrugged a *so-what* gesture before studying the

splintered front-door. The lock and a bolt dangled free. "Crowbar mebbe. But the alarm never sounded. Campbell musta not had it switched on. He had no personal CCTV neither."

"He trusted the guys at the front-gates."

"What?" Alleyne sounded incredulous. Nine years older than his sergeant, his short-cropped hair was fast receding, giving his long face and pointed chin a horsey look. "Venny, I know a bit about this big-shot lawyer." He motioned his head towards the room where the corpse still lay.

"Tell me."

"Guy had plenty enemies. But PC Yonge, he reckoned that around Windylea, he was a god. Campbell had no fear of them bastards from that part of town." Alleyne led Venables into what had been the sumptuous designer kitchen. Slabs of steak, sausages, tomatoes, carrots, ice-cream and milk had been thrown around. The debris lay mixed with smashed goblets and broken plates. Bottles of wine had been ripped from racks and smashed against the walls, leaving shards of glass lying in puddles of wine. "Situation normal. Drug-crazed thugs." Alleyne stroked his chin thoughtfully. "Crapped on the bed, did they? The usual?"

"No sir. Mebbe they were constipated." They both laughed.

"Two of them at least. Encouraging each other. Causing all this." Alleyne's downturned lip and unflinching eyes added emphasis.

Venables chose his words carefully. Ever since his boss had returned from training with the Met Police in London, Alleyne had become increasingly arrogant and intolerant. He was rarely receptive to contrary opinions. "I expect you're right, boss, but here's no *evidence* of how many were here. No sign they drank the wine, ate any food."

He heard Alleyne grunt but there was no put-down. "These guys, they now got cash, jewels. You wait, Venny. We'll soon hear of these dumb crackheads splashing the cash."

"Agreed boss," Venables lied, thinking just the opposite. To him, something about the entire scene did not add up. "But plenty big-shot politicos will dance on his grave."

"Venny, I don't have cloth-ears."

"So boss, his wife Brenda? You heard the stories?"

Alleyne had not but pretended otherwise. "I've heard tales. Tittle-tattle. What have you got?"

"She's been hanging out with Morry Rolle, y'know the head honcho in the Cabinet Office."

Alleyne's eyes narrowed as he bluffed. "That's what I heard. Is it true?"

"She wasn't here. She told her neighbour she was flying to Barbados for a few days. She's now been informed. "

"And Mr Rolle?"

The sergeant's grin was infectious. "Attending a four-day symposium," he paused for effect "in Barbados."

"I heard that Campbell knew nothing of this affair," Alleyne bluffed, one highly polished shoe scuffing the tiled floor.

"Mr Rolle has a motive."

"Venny, Brenda is a damned fine attractive woman." His hands waved to emphasise her generous curves. He was thinking of the smashed framed photo of her that he had spotted on the bedroom floor. "If this affair was more than Rolle just giving Brenda the old porker, then mebbe yes. Rolle could have hired someone. Plenty of killers round Windylea."

"We play down this Rolle connection?"

"For now, agreed. We don't need him getting as mad as a bug with us. He's too damned powerful." Alleyne opened a packet of mints and took one but did not share.

"Them guards, boss, they would know Mrs Campbell had jewels. I knew. Everybody knew. Always drippin' in expensive glitter as she drove round town in her open-top." They turned into the sitting-room. "I've been in smaller airport hangars," Venables continued as he looked round the wide-open space of the room. Then he looked down at the bizarre sight in front of them. "No positive time of death but the pathologist gave a preliminary guess of mid-evening yesterday."

Alleyne circled the body. "At least we know the cause of death." The body, face down, lay beside the overturned coffee-table. The KC's skull had been battered with a blunt instrument. "Crowbar again mebbe," muttered Alleyne. "But what do you make of this?" He pointed to Campbell's upturned bare buttocks. "You can almost hear these thugs cackling and teeheeing as they did that."

"I never seen anything like that. It's a first for me, boss. I hope it was after he was dead."

"No sign of any other weapon?"

"On a quick look-see – nothing."

"Here's what happened, Venny. They forced entry through the front door. A neighbour saw it smashed this morning and called security."

"Looks like he had just returned from fishing. There are fish on the floor."

"Did they piss in his Doc Martens, another favourite."

Venables laughed. "Like I said, boss. None of their usual pranks. You reckon the killers entered Robinson Cove mebbe hidden in the back of a truck?"

"Makes sense," agreed Alleyne "except how did they leave?"

"I'll check the CCTV at the gates for anything unusual." The sergeant paused and rubbed the back of his head. "Mebbe arrive by boat?"

"Venny, since when did guys who trash and murder ever use a boat?"

"You're right, boss. So mebbe a guard smuggled them in and out."

"I've listened to worse ideas. Make sure Mrs Campbell is back in town today. His daughters?"

"The Miami cops are telling them."

Stepping over a fishing-rod and the fish that were starting to stink, they stood outside the patio doors, looking down to the jetty Alleyne wiped his finger round the inside of his open-neck white shirt. "Boss, except though the property, you can't get from front to back. The high wall at the side is topped with razor-wire."

Alleyne glanced at the outside keypad. "Campbell and the fish entered here. He never reached the kitchen. The killers must have waited for him to switch off the alarm here. Or it was never on. Then they smashed in the front-door."

Sergeant Venables twisted his goatee beard and tried to look impressed. "Boss, I checked. Any activity by the front-door triggers all the outside lights, front and back. Campbell would have seen that."

Alleyne shook his head. "Okay, so they arrived when he was at sea. They triggered the lights then but then waited by the front door in the dark."

"I don't see bums from Windylea waiting quietly ... or not moving. They'd be smokin' drinkin', scratchin'. The lights, they'd be non-stop on and off." Venables went back inside. "I'm going back to HQ."

Bastien Alleyne, alone now, looked down the lawned backyard. There was nothing unusual – the chatter of excited birds, a pelican diving for fish and the scent of flowering shrubs. He took a couple of paces, immediately triggering six powerful lights. In the mid-morning sun, they were barely noticeable. He ambled to the jetty, mopping his brow and scratching his generous greying sideboards.

The air smelled of fuel from the outboard motor as the inflatable bobbed at its mooring. He crouched and stayed motionless for a few moments. As soon as he stood up, the floodlights were activated.

Muttering *just as I thought*, he headed back, passing the Scenes of Crime Team who were engrossed with the front-door. Satisfied, he clambered into his aged dusty Subaru for the twenty-minute drive to HQ. There he munched a crab sandwich and swilled a cold root-beer. On the TV fixed to the wall, the murder had made big news. Already, tributes from friends and clients were being read out. A small crowd was gathering on a street corner in Windylea, many of them sobbing and wailing, some of them beyond consolation.

"Since New Year's Day," the TV journalist reported "there have been eighteen murders and twenty-nine home invasions. The Prime Minister warned that without a major uptick to the economy, no Government can pretend there's a quick fix."

Alleyne had heard enough and switched off angrily. "More money on policing would help, you lying pompous prick." Moments later, he answered his internal phone. "Mrs Brenda Campbell has arrived."

Putney

At 5 a.m. Ratso's first waking thought had been of Hysen Kola. Then, as he lay back, rehearsing what he would say to get up Caldwell's nose, George Ezra was on the radio singing about green, green grass. He stretched out to silence him.

Mate, you're not thinking of Hammersmith's concrete jungle.

After six minutes of bending and stretching exercises, he hurried from the bedroom to the front-room. He inched back the curtain to peep at the street below. His mind returned to his comment to Jock Strang. *I'm not hot on death threats. Carrying out murder – that's what counts. The best professionals don't piss about giving warnings.* The words rang so true. Kola would give no warning.

Between the swaying branches of an overcast dawn, everything looked the same as every other morning at just gone 5 a.m.

And it was.

Arriving at Jubilee House before six, his cycle ride had been wet, miserable but uneventful. Promptly at 10 a.m., he went straight to Caldwell's room. "Will Morgan may be a suspected kiddie-fiddler but he did not kill Lord Ongerton." Deliberately, Ratso was munching a toasted muffin as he opened his update to Caldwell. He knew Caldwell hated people eating in his presence but then his boss had no doubt breakfasted at home before cruising to work in his Mercedes, arriving nearly three hours later. Caldwell said nothing, so he continued. "His Jag was never at the murder scene. There's no suggestion that any of the victims had paedo instincts.

There's nothing linking Morgan to any of the victims. Jenny Fort did not kill Goldie. Her alibi is solid."

Looking relaxed to the point of contempt as he wiped a crumb from his mouth, Ratso gazed towards the tinted-glass window where Alex Caldwell was standing, back against it. Even from three metres, he could smell Caldwell's sickly after-shave. On a shelf beside Ratso was a geranium plant that Caldwell was carefully nurturing. It didn't smell much better. Head down and hands in pockets, Caldwell still gave no clue what he was thinking. "As to the playing-cards, they sell in thousands and are not used in any casino linked to our enquiries."

Caldwell stretched out a long arm and flourished his hand, his slender fingers pointing at Ratso's face. "You've made no casino connection. You've got nothing from Willison's time in the gay hang-outs." He wagged his fingers even closer. "In fact, you've achieved fuck-all in solid connection between any of the victims."

Ratso smiled back. He had no intention of volunteering that he thought there was no connection. Instead he replied. "Except Dermot Doyle was friendly with Lord Ongerton and his housemate Patrick Marney."

Caldwell shifted from foot to foot. "Build a scenario around the unattractive Patrick Marney being jealous of Ongerton's charm and conveyor-belt of young guardsmen."

"But no link to Logan Goldie."

Ratso's contemptuous tone was close to insolent, "So you still think we're looking for a gay-basher." He enjoyed watching Caldwell fighting back an instinct to slam a fist into Ratso's teeth.

After a long silence while he jangled some coins in his left pocket, he tried a new tack. "The top-brass are chasing me like angry hornets. Stephen Port's name keeps coming up. Until you give me something solid, gay-bashing cannot be ignored." Caldwell's voice showed his irritation. "Are you any closer to identifying the vehicle after Dermot Doyle's murder?" He saw Ratso's shake of the head. "I thought not. And Goldie? You're still uncertain whether the killer was male or female?"

"The killer looked and wiggled like woman but the psychological profiler has pointed us to an intelligent male, possibly linked to security but eager to be a household name when caught. Clever enough to wear different shoe sizes."

"So," Caldwell's tone was disdainful, his eyes flashing contempt. "Right. No more pissing me about. What's your theory?"

"I'm now going to follow gut-instinct. Put my bollocks on the line."

"Meaning?"

"One of these three was the real target. The other two are to send those stupid enough to rush like demented ants down blind alleys about gay-bashing ..."

Ratso never got any further. Caldwell pointed to the door. His growl came from deep down "Get out. Get out and prove it. Make sure the killer never uses the Ace." His lip jutted out. "Your career is on the line."

"If I were a more sensitive soul, sir, I'd say that was bullying and harassment." Ratso paused by the door. "Luckily for you, I'm not."

"Not bullying. Not harassment. Not even a warning. Take it as a prediction."

Moments later, Ratso summoned Strang and Bonkale. They grabbed chairs beside him. "*Saints & Skeletons*. Update me."

Bonkale's face broke into a broad grin, all fresh-faced enthusiasm. The young Ghanian was a graduate from Oxford Brookes University and was big on corporate affairs and finance. He checked his watch. "Boss, give me till mid-afternoon. I have a short-list of eleven companies attacked by Goldie. I'm checking out his recent rant about an illegal arms deal. That must have upset the Government, the Israelis and certain directors. The media, social media and Reddit followers have been all over it."

"We're aiming to get a top-three," added Jock Strang.

"Go for it. Restorp? Will Morgan and Jenny Fort?"

"Boss, they didn't even make the eleven."

"Good work." Ratso watched the burly Scot and the much smaller figure of Bonkale leave. They were talking animatedly. Though chalk and cheese, they made a good team. Ratso's attention turned to the SCAS – the team at Serious Crime Analysis Section, a part of the National Crime Agency. Tasked with collating every scrap of data on serial killers, their analyst had found no link to any previous killings. Ratso knew the experienced woman had also scoured VICLAS, the computerised database delivering joined-up national thinking.

He took an Abbey Crunch from his drawer and then doodled on his notepad. After ten minutes of lines, loops and squiggles, he had his thoughts summarised. *It's bollocks on the line time.* His mind made up, he completed his paperwork:

- Dermot Doyle – selected to grab headlines.
- Ongerton – selected for newsworthiness and politics.
- Goldie – selected because he had trashed at least eleven companies.

He ringed the name Goldie.

But

The Ace is the issue.

- Who would be chosen and why?

The Bigger Issue

- Suppose the three deaths are all red herrings and the Ace is the real target.

Bonnitor

Det. Insp. Bastien Alleyne and Sgt. Venables looked down over the HQ's car-park. They watched as Brenda Campbell walked briskly to her Z4 convertible in her beige lace-up sneakers. Tall and elegant, her back ramrod straight, her curves were amply emphasised in her white cotton blouse and an above-knee tight tartan skirt. "Not exactly dressed for mourning," Venables volunteered.

"Two interviews and we've got nothing."

"Just the pong of her expensive perfume," Venables agreed.

"I don't get no buzz that she gives a dime for her husband's death." Alleyne paused. "She don't fool me none. She dabs her eyes, shakes her shoulders. I reckon she sees life insurance and a big inheritance."

"And later, she then goes legit with Morry Rolle." They heard the throb as Brenda started the engine. "Lucky man," the sergeant added as the Z4 accelerated away, the driver's hair being blown around as she did so.

"Sure. If she doesn't have him murdered too."

"You reckon...?"

Alleyne returned to his seat. "No. Not yet. Now she's admitted her affair with Morry Rolle, we gotta get him in."

Venables looked doubtful. "I agree but he's a big cheese." Then his face brightened. "He's a married man and a top honcho to the Prime Minister Assume he's got no part in a murder. Morry will be worried about the scandal. He'll want confidentiality."

Alleyne paused to help himself to a jerk chicken snack and then nodded. "You still heard nothing round Windylea?"

Venables shook his head. "No idle talk. No buzz from them drugged up scum. Nobody splashing cash. No necklace being offered. Oh and still nothing to nail the security guards."

"Except suspicion. Guilty till proved innocent with them guys." They both laughed. "Brenda reckoned there was over eighty thousand bucks in the safe."

Venables looked doubtful, mouth curling up. "Exaggerating for insurance, mebbe?" The sergeant paused, tapping his teeth. "I'm thinking maybe a Cabinet Minister might be behind this. Plenty must have motives. Campbell was always mocking them on TV."

"The kinky-stuff with Campbell, the whole joint beat-up – that's not a pro-job, Venny."

"A hitman wanting us to think it was amateurs?" His eyes showed his enthusiasm for the suggestion.

Alleyne sniffed the still perfumed air. "Okay, Venny. Check flights and ferries. Find out if any known hitmen from Barbados paid Bonnitor a visit."

"Wouldn't Brenda have given the killer the alarm code? Save smashing her door."

Alleyne's famous hooted laugh bounced off the walls. "That's why you're a sergeant and I'm an inspector. If the killer knew the code, dead giveaway." He stood to emphasise his status, preening himself like a strutting cockerel. "See, that training course with the Met. They said eliminate the most likely person first. That's Brenda." He pushed back his shoulders. "Trouble is – I still can't."

Venables wanted to suggest that the smashed door was to cover for someone knowing the code. He decided to let it pass and moved on. "Did the Met teach you how a killer gets into a secure compound, murders someone and leaves stashed with cash and jewels and nobody sees nothing." Venables knew at once that he'd gone in too strong. He lowered his eyes and waited.

Alleyne's face hardened, his eyes flashing a warning. "Accomplice. One of the guards."

Venables scratched his polished bald head and again forced himself to stay silent.

"How about this, Venny? Before going to Barbados, Brenda picked up a hitman somewhere downtown. Concealed him in the Z4's trunk. She then hid the killer in the house."

"Okay boss," Venables smiled. "So he battered in the guy's head just like a local. Then to fool us, though I ain't so stupid, he smashes the front-door so we think he forced his way in." He sucked his teeth and changed his tone. "With Brenda and Morry in Barbados goin' at it, four legs in a bed, how did your hired hitman escape Robinson Cove?"

Go figure that, boss.

Alleyne snorted but said nothing, so Venables continued. "Mebbe the killer was a resident of Robinson Cove." He was pleased to see a light-bulb moment cross his boss's face.

Fulham High Street

The evening air was still warm as Ratso's team sat around an outside table at the Eight Bells. The pub, on the north side of Putney Bridge, was not one Caldwell was known to frequent and the few tables were far enough apart for quiet conversation.

Ratso put down his half-empty Guinness. "Iqbal has come good. We now have a guy buys coffee and a sausage roll at Cobham Motorway Services on the M25. They're checking where he joined the motorway. He leaves in what seems to be a black or dark Audi saloon. The timing's good. Not many people stopped for a snack around 4-30 a.m. He could reach Lord Ongerton's murder scene just after five."

"Countless vehicles thunder round the M25. Plenty will have turned off towards Guildford and Hambledon." Ratso recognised Nancy's scepticism.

"Anyroads," Strang chipped in, "Wasn't it a 4 x4 at the scene?"

Ratso enjoyed the moment. "No. It was not. News just in. Wrong wheelbase. The tyres were typical for a 4 x4 but the wheelbase matched an Audi saloon."

"Number-plate?" Petrie was now less challenging.

"The plates were false." Ratso raised his glass to clink all round. "Nuff said."

"Mugshot at the cash-till?" Strang asked.

"Male. Medium build. Not tall. Bearded with tinted glasses and a hoodie. Age uncertain but not old."

"A woman dressed as a man?" Strang was being serious but everybody laughed.

"Similar build to a woman in a flowery dress?" Nancy had chosen a spritzer which she was sipping thoughtfully.

Ratso see-sawed his hand. "His walking style is being compared to the shots from the Mayfair cameras." He turned to Bonkale who had been silent. "Your turn, Bonkers. Take it slowly. Jock warned me. It's heavy stuff."

The Ghanaian pushed aside his scotch egg and spoke without notes, something that Ratso admired. "My top three for murdering Logan Goldie. Number one is Fergus Edwards. Goldie named him for timeshare fraud. Over five thousand owners lost their money in Tenerife and Morocco. Goldie revealed that their contracts were worthless. They had no remedy."

"This Fergus Edwards? Now disqualified from being a director, is he?"

"Not yet. That could take years. Proceedings under the Companies Act grind slowly." Bonkers sipped his Diet Coke. "Edwards has other holiday ventures in the Caribbean." Bonkale waited while a tube train trundled by. "The trolls on social media really went for Edwards – death-threats, bricks through his office window. His Bentley was sprayed with graffiti. That was eighteen months back." Bonkers looked at each in turn. "Eighteen months ago was when a blog-poster calling himself *LongMemory* issued death threats."

"Pause there." Ratso said. He ordered another round. "Fergus Edwards's background?"

"Not a man to cross. Born 1985 and brought up in Deptford, south-east London."

"I remember Deptford from my time in Lewisham. Now, it's

more gentrified. Back then, Deptford was full-on trouble. Got form, has he?"

"Aged twenty-two, he rammed a broken bottle into a rival market-trader's throat. He was charged with attempted murder but plea-bargained GBH. Nothing known since then." There were headshakes and murmurs all round as Bonkers produced a recent picture of Edwards. He was leaning against a Ferrari, his face tanned and wrinkle-free, his lips thin. Round his neck was a gold medallion. He sported designer stubble and black wavy hair. His cocky look and penetrating stare broadcast a *don't mess* image.

"Good start. Number two?"

"Crypto." Bonkale paused. "You're aware of Bitcoin but don't really understand it – am I right?" He laughed as he saw their reactions. "Almost nobody does. Okay. Forget Bitcoin and think WPCoin – the same but different. Millions made a fortune in Bitcoin and WPCoin. Then the crypto sector crashed. Millions then lost their wad. WPCoin was the brainchild of a Hungarian woman called Hanna Farkas. WP stood for Women Power. Using social media, she marketed her cryptocurrency especially to women. She toured Europe and then the UK. She filled halls and conference centres. Her message was about empowering women to become millionaires."

"I remember that," Petrie leaped in. "I was tempted by her pitch but decided against. You're saying she *impoverished* women."

"Correct!" exclaimed Bonkale. "It was a scam. Unlike say the blockchain corporations or better cryptos, there was nothing underpinning WPCoin. Hanna Farkas was running a giant Ponzi-scheme."

"Better cryptos?" Ratso rolled his eyes. "Do they even exist? Okay – let's not debate that now." Ratso gave Carole Viment a wry look. She had sat silent and poker-faced and Ratso knew why. Her partner worked on crypto technology. "Logan Goldie spotted this?" Ratso now leaned forward, elbows cupping his chin.

"Correct, boss. Farkas had previously swatted away critics as peddling fake news. Goldie's tip-sheet had a cartoon of Hanna Farkas, on horseback and as naked as Lady Godiva. He burst the bubble. Soon, so-called crypto experts from Hong Kong through to California were boasting they'd been warning about WPCoin all along."

"What happened next?"

Bonkers was in his element. "The auditors couldn't unravel the accounts. There were none. Just empty bank accounts and layers of companies in obscure places hidden behind trusts. WPCoin was her personal piggy-bank. All three billion of it. Disappeared like a magician's white rabbit."

Jock Strang peered over his glass. "Aye, Bonkers but give them the beef."

"A big loser was the daughter of an Albanian crime boss. He's massive in the drug scene around Manchester. Her name is Valbona Jakupi. She lives near here in Roehampton. She lost over ten million. I spoke to a pal in Manchester. The word up there is that Valbona wanted both Goldie and Farkas dead."

Ratso lowered his eyes and frowned. "And?"

"Farkas is missing, presumed dead. Perhaps murdered."

"Why would Valbona blame Goldie? He exposed the scam." Ratso asked.

Bonkers hesitated to pick the right words. He didn't want to rub the boss's face in it. "But for Goldie, the scam would have continued. Valbona could have cashed out."

The furrowed brow and twitch of Ratso's beaky nose suggested he was not persuaded. "And your third candidate?"

"Sorry, boss," Petrie intervened. "I've something more. I was just reading about a woman in Wales who lost thousands on crypto. She was so angry, she took a machete to a public meeting about what had gone wrong. It wasn't WPCoin. She said she wouldn't have used it but the magistrates convicted her for carrying a bladed article."

"Okay! I'm sure feelings can run high," Ratso agreed.

"Number three then," prompted Bonkale. "You could fill Wembley Stadium with angry investors in a company called Energy Management. It was an oil explorer. Goldie's torpedo pretty much sank the company."

"Keep it simple."

Jock Strang laughed. "Aye, spoon-feed me too."

"The shares were expected to rocket on an oil-strike. Without an oil strike, they had little value. As drilling drew closer, the shares were trading on AIM at 6p each. With an oil strike, they were expected to reach 70p or even 120p almost overnight."

Ratso clasped the youngster's arm in a friendly way. "Right, Bonkers. Bring in Goldie. Which fan from Wembley Stadium killed him – and why."

"Goldie published that the company was running out of cash. Printed that it couldn't afford to drill without raising money." Bonkale grinned, obviously in his element. "He warned it would have to do a Placing – issuing more shares at only 2p per share, far lower than the current price of 6p."

"True or false?" Ratso enquired.

"False. The directors *were* about to do a Placing but at 5p. That was top-secret ... or meant to be. His story crashed the share price to *below* 2p – down to 1.7p."

Ratso looked thoughtful. "So the directors couldn't raise money at 5p when shareholders could buy on AIM for 1.7p."

"Correct, boss. This meant that the cost of fund-raising became crippling. The company needed several more million to fund drilling." Bonkers looked at the listeners. "Still with me? There's worse to come."

Petrie stuck out her neck. "I get it. Goldie's false rumour showed how risky the shares were."

Bonkale waved a tick with his right hand. "Logan Goldie created a vicious downward spiral. The directors were forced to do a Placing at 1.2p per share, having to issue over four times as many shares as they had planned."

"So if I'm in Wembley, watching Scotland beating England, why do I kill Goldie?" Strang asked.

"In your dreams, Jock," Ratso replied.

"Your shares have crashed. You've lost your shirt. Your one-hundred pounds invested is suddenly only worth around eight quid. Big investors got their backsides burned."

"Especially the directors?" said Nancy Petrie.

Bonkale nodded. "The directors owned millions of shares. They were outraged but it gets worse." He paused to ensure he had their attention. "Green activists appeared wanting oil exploration banned. Like that was the final nail. Investor confidence was shot. Blue-chip lenders disappeared."

Ratso looked thoughtful as he stroked his chin. "Was Goldie just careless?"

Despite his open and honest rounded face, Bonkale somehow managed to look mysterious. "I'll come back to that."

"I'm getting it," Strang wiped brown ale from his mouth. "Death threats from angry investors?"

"Plenty. By now, with drilling close, the company was running on fumes. The directors were forced to raise more money. It was shit-or-bust desperation. Shareholders called it *death spiral borrowing*. The shark ate the directors for breakfast."

"And now?"

"The company needs a sugar-daddy *and* a fairy-godmother."

"Combine the two? Call in the Sugar-Plum Fairy?" Ratso's face was deadpan.

After the chuckles died down, Bonkale's face turned serious. "Here's the nugget. City gossip is that someone paid Goldie to trash the shares. In turn, it seems Goldie had tipped off his mates in the City that he was about to crash the share price down to 2p. So they then *shorted* the shares. That means *selling shares they didn't even own* for 6p. After the share price fell to under 2p, they then made a killing by buying the shares at 2p."

Ratso looked at his team in the gathering darkness. "If you sell a car you don't own and vanish with the cash, that's a crime. You mean these spivs in the City can sell shares they don't even own? Dirty, dirty business. More bent than Yuri Geller's spoons!" He fixed Bonkers with an appreciative nod. "Good work! "We have three interesting situations. Why isn't this oil company your number one?"

"Because there was no obvious loser. So many thousands were cleaned out."

"We could start with the directors." prompted Nancy. "But I'd go for Fergus Edwards and the timeshare scam. Valbona Jakupi and the crypto thing? To me, that's a leap too far."

"Unless Farkas is dead in a ditch." Ratso turned to the Scot. "Jock?"

"Right enough, I'd go for the oil. Punters and directors with a real grievance."

"Bonkers, earlier, you enthused about an arms-dealing scandal. That sounded like a *numero uno*."

"Non-starter, boss. *Saints and Skeletons* only broke the story the day Goldie was murdered. The timing is wrong. Sorry."

"I wouldn't go that far, Bonkers. Maybe Goldie was warned

that if he did publish, he'd be dead. Retribution was swift. The same day."

Viment now broke her silence, waving a well-manicured finger to make her point. "Looking at these three ideas makes sense." For a moment she looked hesitant. "But…"

"Go on Carole," Ratso said.

"Why would Goldie's killer make a threat? Makes no sense to me. That's for lonely and disgruntled wankers letting off steam from their lonely bedsits."

"I'm with you there." Ratso fell silent and his jaw-line firmed as Hysen Kola gate-crashed his thoughts. He finished chewing slowly on his ribeye. "Bonkers – you go big on oil exploration. Jock, dig into WPCoin and Valbona. Carole, you start with Fergus Edwards and his timeshares. He had a violent past and has a motive but he'd be too canny to do it himself. Nancy and I will …" Ratso was interrupted by his vibrating phone. It was a message from Wensley Hughes.

New Scotland Yard

Being called to a meeting at the Met Police's new HQ on Victoria Embankment was infrequent. Previous bollockings had been at 55 Broadway, no great distance away. In his gunmetal grey jacket and chinos, Ratso walked briskly from Westminster Underground. As he entered the glass-fronted building, he was feeling uneasy. Had Smart Alex pulled a trigger?

Am I in for the high-jump?

He swallowed nervously as he waited to be called into the meeting. If Smart Alex Caldwell had his way, the Assistant Commissioner could make him jump higher than the current Olympic champion.

"Take a seat," Hughes pointed to a chair in front of his desk. There was no offer of coffee, not a good sign. "I've no news on Hysen Kola. D.I Gastrell's team have staked out known addresses for contacts of Boris Zandro. They've checked all Central London 4 and 5-star hotels."

"Not expecting him to use his real name, I hope?"

"Photo, name and nationality," Hughes replied. "They're still tracking the car that picked him up at Dungeness. It certainly reached Ashford, Kent." He ran his hand down his cheek. "But today is not about Kola."

"Sir?"

Hughes rose and stood by the window looking across the Thames to the London Eye. "There is no place for mavericks in the Met." Ratso looked at Hughes's profile and could gain no insight about what was coming. He decided to say nothing. Suddenly

Hughes turned and gave him a direct look. "We discussed this when you were bringing down those match-fixers."

"You did raise it, sir."

"But looking at your records, Todd, I've found no reports of *maverick* in your behaviour – except from Superintendent Caldwell." He pointed to the monitor as he sat down. "Your record is of solid and sometimes inspired police work. Someone who sticks out his neck rather than covering his arse."

"Sir?"

"Superintendent Caldwell views you as a loose cannon – more likely to miss than hit. He believes you are costing the Met a fortune – chasing wild ideas." He touched the screen. "In his report, he used the word maverick twice – particularly over your approach to these serial killings."

"Superintendents are entitled to a viewpoint." He paused to show his most sincere unflinching look. "But whoever stationed me under Caldwell was playing the joker. Alex Caldwell and I see policing and detection differently, sir."

"Caldwell wants you off the case."

"Sir, he's fixated about the Stephen Port fiasco. He's far too sensitive to media comment that we're not trying because *it's only gays*."

Caldwell peered over his gold-rimmed glasses. "Well?"

"Caldwell *is* a homophobe. That's what's bugging him. He's worried he'll be fingered by the media – exposed for what he is."

"Go on."

"Me and the team, we need a breakthrough. Caldwell says we should focus on gay-bashing. Sir, with respect, that's crap. These are cold, calculated crimes, well executed." Ratso maintained an unflinching look, wondering if he had gone a step too far.

"The Superintendent has a strong record."

"I understand, sir, but ever since that murder in Hammersmith, he's wanted to bring me down. With your support back then, I got a result." Ratso wanted to say that, back then, he had virtually rubbed Caldwell's nose in dogshit but he refrained. "After we've caught this killer, maybe I should move elsewhere."

A near-smile hovered on Hughes's lips. "Moving you may not be the only solution. Leave that with me. For now, your marriage made in hell must continue."

"Sir, you mean?"

"I agree with you continuing." The Assistant Commissioner swivelled his chair and looked towards the ceiling. "You've got five minutes to explain why Caldwell's theory is wrong."

Battersea SW11

While Ratso was with Wensley Hughes, just four miles away, Hysen Kola entered the wrought-iron gates of the White House, a large apartment block in Vicarage Crescent, Battersea. He had just walked the short distance from Asda with a carrier-bag of food and essentials for which he had paid cash.

This quiet residential area lies just south of the Thames and under three miles from Jubilee House. The two-bedroom apartment belonged to Colette Lafleur, Kola's former French girlfriend who worked in real estate. When they had met in 2017, she had been living in Belleville, not far from the centre of Paris. Despite being Albanian, he had been free to visit her with minimal formalities but even before Covid, the tempestuous passion in their relationship had been cooling, although their friendship had continued.

Since Covid, Colette's employers had transferred her to their head office in Portman Square, London. Currently, she was on a six-week secondment to their branch in Brussels. Now, Kola was living rent-free and alone in her London home.

Until his illegal landing at Dungeness, Kola had never been to England. He spoke some broken English, picked up in Tirana, by watching CNN, old movies and Sky TV News. The young woman who had picked up Kola close to Dungeness beach had then driven him to London having collected the keys from the Portman Square offices.

In the tight secrecy surrounding Kola's trip, she had not even been told the apartment's address. When dropping him off outside

Clapham Junction station, she had handed over a rucksack containing fifteen thousand pounds in cash, maps of London, three burner phones, a fake passport with a UK entry stamp, a loaded laptop, two photos of DCI Todd Holtom and a loaded Glock 19 handgun.

After making sure she could not follow him, Kola had walked to the White House in about twenty minutes. He had been pleased. Only Colette knew where he was staying but even she had no idea why he was in England, how to contact him or of the double-life that he led. Since his arrival, Kola had communicated with nobody, though he assumed Uncle Boris in Wakefield Jail had been informed.

In the rather tired and dated kitchen, he heated a chicken pie for two and poured himself a glass of Hungarian red wine. On the wall, he had pinned the two photos of his target – taken full face and profile. Also on the wall was the map. On it, he had ringed his present location, Holtom's home in Hammersmith Grove and Jubilee House.

After devouring the entire pie, he sat at the kitchen table, thoughtfully sipping his wine. He then booted up the laptop and using street-views on Google Maps, he assessed the possibilities. Already, he had seen Jubilee House from the upper-deck of a bus. He had walked the entirety of Hammersmith Grove in both directions but, so far, had avoided walking near Jubilee House. Instead, he had pored over street views, hoping to keep his time in Putney as brief as possible. From what he had seen so far, neither location was ideal. Close to Holtom's apartment seemed preferable but the next move was to change his appearance. He poured a second glass.

I have four advantages.
He doesn't know I am in England.
He doesn't know why I am in England.
Nobody, not even me, knows when I will strike.
Nobody, not even me, knows where I will strike.

Hammersmith Grove, W6

It was nearly 11p.m. as Ratso cycled the last quarter-mile to his Ikea-filled apartment. Tonight, he had changed his route again, avoiding the Fulham Palace Road by using the alphabet streets nearer the Thames. The fish-supper he had picked up on King Street was still hot as he chained the bike inside the tiled front entrance. In the hallway, the smell of his chips mingled with stale odours of cooking-fat, curry, garlic and London dust. He paused at the foot of the stairs listening for any sound of someone awaiting his arrival.

All quiet.

He entered his apartment and out of habit, checked each room. Everything was just as he had left it – the porridge bowl waiting to be washed; yesterday's evening paper lying beside a couple of empty cans of Guinness and a pair of socks on a chair waiting to be washed. After putting on his headphones to listen to an Eric Clapton album, he flopped onto his easy-chair and tucked into the haddock, sprinkled with salt and oodles of vinegar.

When he had finished, and after pushing aside the empty carton and ketchup, he went to the fridge to grab another Guinness. He was planning to catch up with Kirsty-Ann later. First though, all he could think of were Bonkale's top three targets. As he walked back to the sagging chair, jerking the ring-pull, a moment of inspiration hit him. He punched the air with a long hissed *ye-e-e-s* before necking a copious swig.

Why hadn't I spotted it before?

Hidden in plain sight!
Game-changer or blind alley?
Okay, it's a long-shot.
So what to do?

Fitzrovia, London

Ratso was seated at a corner table for two in a Brazilian restaurant. He was now into his second Caipirinha. As the lime sharpened his palate, he could feel a third coming on as he watched and waited for the restaurant's studded oak door to open. He checked his watch and sucked in his breath. The combination of arriving early and Sprog's train being delayed was boosting sales of the cachaça, a Brazilian liquor. He ordered another with a plate of olives and a portion of sliced spicy sausage.

For a moment, he imagined Kirsty-Ann entering, swinging her handbag, her swaying blonde hair, radiant smile and long legs attracting the attention of every hot-blooded male in the room. *Dream on!* That would have to wait. Neither could diary-up any plans. Yesterday evening, she had told him that business was booming and she was flying to Montreal to track down a secretive billionaire.

He bit into the warm sausage, the hopes and anticipation of the evening ahead making his nerve-ends tingle. It had been five days since his late-night Eureka moment and tonight, over a vegetarian's idea of a nightmare feast, it was dot-joining time.

Or might be.

Depending what Sprog had achieved.

In the cosy ambiance, with the smell of wood-smoke and barbecued meat drifting towards him, Ratso turned his attention to the *passadore* who was flitting from table to table, holding a long skewer. This was filled with offerings of finest cuts of beef, lamb and pork. With mounting hunger, Ratso watched as slice after slice was deftly carved to customers showing their coasters, green side up. He had not eaten for nine hours and lunch had only been a cheese and pickle sandwich. Now, his stomach was growling with discontent.

Where are you Sprog?

In fact, it was another Caipirinha later before the door swung open and his closest friend appeared, pulling a small wheeled-suitcase. Instantly, Ratso was on his feet to exchange back-slaps. "Sorry, mate!" Sprog gasped. "Points failure just outside King's Cross."

Ratso summoned a round of drinks as the two fell into an immediate conversation about the Test Match between England and the West Indies. The close of play score from the Oval had been dismal. Much as he loved talking cricket, right now, Ratso's heart was not in it. He was bursting to ask the million-dollar question. Instead though, he waited till the cocktails had been sunk and he had filled large glasses of South African cabernet sauvignon. Only then, after they had upturned their coasters from red to green, did Ratso raise a quizzical eye which asked the question. He had thought of almost nothing else all day. "Good news?"

After receiving succulent cuts of lamb, Sprog reached down and from a zipped pocket on his suitcase produced a flash-drive and a signed statement. "The video says it all."

Ratso turned their coasters back to red to stop any more meat arriving. "Sorry, Sprog. I can't wait. I'll view and chew." He fired up his laptop and moments later had the video on screen. "Amazing! Astounding. How did you film this?"

"You're forty-one yet you're still an impatient git!" Sprog replied. "Read my statement. I was hidden in a clump of trees on the hill. Maybe seventy metres away. Unobstructed view."

Ratso skimmed the three typed pages. He looked up, his eyes

already fired by alcohol, were now even wilder with excitement. "We'll have quite a party tonight." He leaned across and gave Sprog a friendly punch. "Sambucas here and port at my place." He replayed the two-minute video. "Let's go green again and get stuck into some of their finest *picanha*. I'm almost lost for words. This evidence is extraordinary!"

For a moment Ratso's mind zapped back to a lively exchange with DC Carole Viment. She had really shown her claws, ripping into Ratso's new theory, pulling no punches. "Cart before the horse, boss. On what we know and putting it politely, I'd say it's pie-in-the-sky."

"You mean its bollocks," Ratso said. "Carole, no offence taken. I value all opinions. You may be right. I've no monopoly on wisdom. I do though have experience. Hunches may be bollocks. But," here he had paused and waved his arm across the entire team, "now we've decided on a plan, I expect total commitment."

Sprog shaking his head in disbelief brought him back to the moment. "You really think?"

"Gut instinct, hunch – for now."

"But Terry? A person of interest? Terry Yates who shags away his nights in his motorhome?"

"Or who is a serial killer." The silence hung over them like a low cloud as the enormity of Ratso's words sank in.

"What triggered this? You wouldn't tell me over the phone."

"Hare-brained idea, Jock Strang called it. Well, words to that effect." He piled a colourful mixed salad onto his plate. "Remember your story about Terry and Rolf. The publican heard them mumbling their woes."

"Pissed as rats, Stan reckoned. Yeah! I remember! Rolf had picked up a dose from some slapper."

"And Terry was on about losing millions."

The conversation stopped as they accepted picanha, chicken and sausage. Ratso savaged a lump of chicken with the heavy knife. "Who did Terry blame?"

Sprog shrugged. "I forget now. Elsie? Edith? Something like that."

"Emma. He said Emma had cost him millions."

"Oh yes! Then he denied saying anything like that. So?"

"Thanks to Guinness and some quality time, I had a Eureka moment. We're in-depthing on the murder of Logan Goldie who published stuff in his tip-sheet, *Saints & Skeletons*. We were role-playing – who might want to kill him. Plenty enough had threatened him. Social media was full of stuff."

"And you found threats from Terry Yates of North Yorkshire?"

Ratso shook his head. "Quite the reverse."

"So?" Sprog flourished his fork eager for Ratso to get to the point.

"If I'm right, we're dealing with a cold, calculating killer who just gets on with it. No messages from a hot keyboard."

"Okay. I get that Goldie was a pain in the butt. Why Terry? Your Eureka moment?"

"In the Incident Room, we'd been talking about an oil explorer called Energy Management. Logan Goldie had attacked it, crashing the shares." Ratso gave a wolfish smile. "The other evening. I was sinking Guinness quicker than the brewers can ship it. The company's full name is Energy Management Associates. On AIM, its ticker is EMA. That took me to EMMA and to Stan's pub story about Terry Yates. Emma had cost Terry millions. Light-bulbs flashed. Eureka!"

Ratso could almost see and hear Sprog's brain accelerating through the gears as both men resumed attacking the remaining reds, yellows and greens of the salad. Sprog put down his cutlery for a moment and slugged a generous quantity of the wine. "The lads assumed he was talking of some Geordie bint with a skirt barely covering her arse. We thought maybe she was pregnant or under-age."

"Right now, Terry may be an outsider but I'm going to flog this horse till its dead."

"If he lost millions. Sure, that could spoil his breakfast. But murder? He was a shareholder then?"

Ratso's look was sheepish as he admitted he didn't know. "But I soon will." Ratso ignored Sprog's astonished raised eyebrow. "Why did Terry deny the conversation? Suspicious or what?"

"So did Rolf. Denied he'd caught the clap." Sprog topped up their glasses before savouring the spicy sausage. "So to sum up, the other night, through a can darkly, your Guinness guessed that EMA linked Terry." He paused to laugh. "Except you don't even know he's a shareholder." There was disbelief in every word. "Sounds a big ask. Wacky, I'd say."

Ratso flourished his sharp-pointed knife across the table. "Don't you start. We've already begun seeking Court Orders – banks, the company's Registrars who handle the share register, even the Company Secretary. We'll follow a virtual paper trail."

"Let's assume that pigs fly and you're right. On TV, you've said this is a serial killer. Why kill the simpering Lord Ongerton and that smarmy TV presenter?"

"No connection as yet." Ratso flipped the coaster to green and moments later the waiter was offering chicken hearts and kidneys which Ratso accepted as he ordered another bottle of red. "Did you know Terry had been SAS?"

Sprog's eyes narrowed and then widened at the news. He spoke slowly as if grappling with the new situation. "No. When he moved north, Terry never spoke much about his early life. Or maybe he did say he'd been in the Army. I can't recall. When he joined the cricket club, we all assumed he was stinking rich from his ship protection empire."

"A real whizz on my team uncovered the SAS bit this morning. That's a big tick in a big box. I'll be heading for Hereford."

"To the SAS HQ?"

Ratso nodded yes as he exited full-screen. "This video is dynamite. It bolsters my confidence even more." Sprog's filming had shown Terry sprinting like Usain Bolt with no surgical boot. "That proves he's a fraud and a liar. I want to know why." Ratso clinked glasses.

"Yeah!" Sprog exhaled noisily. "Just last week, the sneaky sod said he'd need the boot for another three months."

"Whoever murdered Goldie walked without a limp. The deep footprints in Dermot Doyle's garden showed no sign of a limp either. The same down in Surrey."

Sprog's usual toothy grin excelled itself. "Here's how I got the evidence. Besides his huge pad, there's a small hill where sheep graze. From up there, I could see over his high hedges. Like you asked, I filmed him walking around. I got lucky. He went to his motorhome. He wasn't wearing his boot, so I rang his landline as an unidentified caller. Christ! He ran back into the house, all of thirty metres. The cunning bugger couldn't have run quicker if some little darling had just dropped her thong for him." Sprog ran his hands through his crinkly hair. "Last night the lads went for a pie and pint at the Fox Hall. Terry arrived, hobbling like a cripple who'd lost his crutch."

"Smart work, Sprog. Ever thought of becoming a detective." Both men high-fived. "Terry's height? I'd guess five foot-eight." Ratso was thinking of the hooded figure in Cobham Services and the Mayfair images.

Deadly Hush

For answer, Sprog scrolled through the photos on his phone. "Club Christmas party last year. I'm five foot-seven."

Ratso compared Terry Yates to Sprog. "That makes Terry about five-foot nine." Ratso allowed himself a fleeting smile as another box was ticked. The height and build might be similar to Goldie's killer and the driver at Cobham Services. He turned to the second page of Sprog's statement. "Your paragraph 12. You're right about that? Quite sure?"

Sprog groaned as an answer, his eyes rolling with disdain.

"Sorry, Sprog. But this is vital." He pointed to the date in Sprog's statement. "You're sure that was when he cried off cricket because of his ruptured Achilles tendon?"

"Positive."

"That was three days before Dermot Doyle was murdered."

"Last night, Terry reckoned he won't be able to play again this season."

"How did you keep a straight face?"

Sprog looked deadpan across the table. "Listening to your jokes or maybe those late-night poker sessions back in the Lewisham days."

Ratso's face turned serious as he leaned forward. "Any idea where he was on the days of the murders?"

Sprog shook his head. "If I drop into The Bay Horse for a pint after work, I drive past his place. He's got a big hedge around the front. I've never checked whether his Rapido motorhome is there. His run-around car is a white Aston Martin. Otherwise he cycles. Check with Rolf. He might know."

"No. Far too soon to quiz him. Do nothing to alert Terry. Just keep eyes and ears open. If he goes away on his own, give me a bell." Ratso's fixed stare and clenched jaw suggested this was an order, not an invite. "Please."

"Terry Yates has never missed a game until all this. Cricket was his thing. I can see why the surgical boot gave him cover to be down south murdering when he should have been playing." He stretched out and clasped Ratso's arm. Sleuthing. I loved helping. It was like the old days. I really miss that life, the mates, the laughs."

An image of Alex Caldwell flitted through Ratso's mind. "Keep your rose-tinted specs for those good old days. Now, mostly, it's just shit and slog. Lining up for arse-kickings, form-filling, diversity training and waiting for more budget cuts."

Sprog looked down, avoiding eye-contact. "Seriously, I don't want to piss on your parade but Terry's a top guy, one of the best. Very popular. Your motive is piss-poor thin." He looked up and grabbed his glass. "Or maybe I just haven't drunk enough."

Ratso scowled at the inference, his eyes flashing anger. There was an overlong silence while Ratso let this pass. "Sprog, you know I value your friendship – and experience." He looked sheepish. "I guess your comment pissed me off because my head tells me you're right. On what *you* know. But there's more I haven't told you."

"And?"

"I shouldn't be telling you but all three were killed by someone who knew what they were doing – a quick and violent neck injury."

"His SAS training?" Sprog saw Ratso agree. "That fits your jigsaw." He wiped the last drop of dressing from his plate. "At the murder scenes, are you looking for his Fiat Rapido 4-Berth camper or his Aston Martin?" Sprog laughed at the notion.

"Point taken. Nothing so bloody obvious. I wish. We've a lead but, nah, not a Rapido. An Audi saloon."

"Rolf drives a yellow Audi. Reckon he knows more? Maybe he lost money in this company too."

"Good shout," Ratso was quick to agree. "But not a yellow one."

"Rolf's not been missing cricket, not even to drop by the clap-clinic."

"Nobody's ever mentioned Terry driving any other vehicle Maybe rented?" He saw Sprog shake his head. In a decisive move, Ratso pushed his plate aside. "Gotta 7um room for the Crème de Papaya topped with cassis liqueur. Tried it?"

"Our local mobile-chippie doesn't go beyond apple pie or deep-fried Mars Bars, so no."

Ratso ordered. "If I'm right, Terry must have hired a car."

"Or borrowed one," added Sprog. "But not from Rolf."

"Come to that, he might have had a lift. An accomplice."

"You must have other lines of enquiry?"

"Nothing better. Hours on Holmes 2 have led to dead-ends. Several of the team have been tracking down and identifying keyboard warriors. Lonely wankers – brave as hell anonymously pumping out defamatory shit. By day, they're probably bought-ledger clerks or sharpening pencils in Social Services."

"You get cooperation from, y'know, Facebook and Twitter?"

"They're getting better." Ratso's answer was said with indifference. His mind was racing ahead. The evening had sparked some new ideas.

North Yorkshire

As Nancy Petrie drove Ratso north-westward on the M40, destination Hereford, Detective-Sergeant Wansdyke from t North Yorkshire Police was driving to Ravensworth from Northallerton. His brief from a Det. Chief Inspector Todd Holtom from London had been sparse. All he had was the name of Mr Terry Yates, a house called Arcadia Heights and a few simple questions that needed answering. As he sped north on the A1-M, he imagined the London detective in his snappy suit, immaculate shirt, silk tie and shooting his cuffs as he commanded a room. The reality, around two-hundred miles away, was Ratso in a black open-neck shirt and a brown leather jacket, spooning instant porridge from a Tesco pot.

Wansdyke entered the pretty hamlet. Ravensworth was less of a village and more a scattering of pretty stone houses and a pub. The road to Richmond ran through it. Finding the address was easy. Arcadia Heights was on the very edge of the community. He turned between a pair of pillars with stone eagles on the top. He pressed the buzzer and the gates eased their way apart. He drove across the spacious gravelled drive and parked up close to a large Rapido motorhome. The triple garage doors were closed and there was no sign of any other vehicle.

Unlike most of Ravensworth's stone cottages dating back over the centuries, Arcadia Heights, though built with local grey stone was elegant yet ultra-modern. Set substantially back from the road and out of noise range from the Bay Horse pub, the long

Deadly Hush

low building was sheltered from the road, tucked way back behind a three-metre hedge. Beside the property was a steeply rising field, full of sheep and a scattering of trees.

Wansdyke took in the long line of upstairs windows. They seemed endless. Did Arcadia Heights have eight, ten or even a dozen bedrooms? Captivated by the grandeur, Wansdyke stood for a few moments, collar up against the keen north-easterly wind. *Four-million quid if it's a penny* he thought as he approached the stout front-door.

Yates had probably paid cash and never even missed it.

A sweet smell of silage was blowing across the courtyard as Yates appeared in a surgical boot, swaying from side to side as he crunched across the gravel. "Right on time, officer. No trouble finding me then?" He extended a hand. "Terry Yates. You must be Detective Sergeant Wansdyke. Let's sit in the conservatory. Get the sun but avoid that bloody north-easterly."

Wansdyke followed Yates inside. "Leg trouble by the look of it, sir?" His voice was deep and the accent was broad Yorkshire.

"I'm sick to death of it," Yates replied from over his shoulder. "I haven't played cricket for weeks now. Did my Achilles tendon playing squash. Worse still, I'm a slow healer."

"Operated on, were you sir?"

Yates shook his head and led his visitor across the wide-open space of the hall. Wansdyke took a sharp intake of breath. The vaulted hall alone was bigger than the entire ground-floor of his home in Thirsk. "The doc reckoned the tear was near complete. This damned boot makes my foot sweat something rotten. Thank God, I'm still allowed to drive."

They settled into Rattan chairs with tiger-striped patterned cushions. Yates shook a bell. "You're lucky. My housekeeper is here this morning and she'll have tea and coffee brewed." Moments later, an elderly woman shuffled in, looking nervous. With a rattle of cups, she lowered the tray to the large circular table before offering both men an array of chocolate biscuits. "Thanks, Nelly." They both had coffee poured by the host.

"Lovely place you have here, sir," Wansdyke commented as he looked out at the immaculate lawn and flowering shrubs.

"I rattle here most of the time but when I have cricketing celebs visiting or my employees meet here for a bash at Christmas, I fill every room." If Yates had been gargling with iron-filings before breakfast, Wansdyke would not have been surprised His voice was rough-edged, a touch Ray Winstone, part Rod Stewart. Wansdyke guessed the accent was from around London, maybe Essex. Yates's grin was infectious. "I need a big place because I love a party. There's a piano and a karaoke machine in my Jungle Room. I modelled it on the one in Graceland."

"You're not from round here, sir?"

"Dad was a Petty Officer in the Royal Navy. We lived in the toughest part of Portsmouth. Mean streets and then some. *Talking with fists*, we called it. Fights every Saturday. Loved it." His eyes lit up with obvious pride. "Since then, I've got lucky, done well. My business was brisk and so I bought Arcadia Heights nearly five years ago. Anyway, how can I help?"

Wansdyke put down his delicate porcelain cup. "Like I said on the phone, sir, this is very discreet. I don't know the whole story. My instructions came from London. We're, I mean London, is investigating a Greek shipowner. A tycoon."

"In the trade, we call them shipping magnates. Carry on."

Wansdyke checked his notes. "Yiannis Bakirtzis. You know him?"

"Know Baccy? Sure. We protect several of his fleet. His cargo-ships are often destined for Nigeria. Y'know the Gulf of Guinea?"

"Not familiar with it, sir. Scarborough to Whitby – that's about my limit."

"No pirates round there. Not like the thugs off West Africa. Mbesa Security, that's my company, we provide security against kidnapping and ransom. Or worse. Calling them pirates makes them sound glamourous. To me they're scum. Vermin." He pushed forward the plate of biscuits. "Anyway, Baccy? He's not in trouble, is he?"

"Can't say, sir. This is just a preliminary chat. A possible fraud. But please keep this to yourself. Okay?"

"Sealed lips, officer. Happy to help. Some of the Piraeus shipping crowd are pretty shifty – well thieving bastards to be blunt. But Baccy? I doubt it. Maybe I can help clear his name."

"Through a web of faceless companies, someone, and perhaps Mr Bakirtzis, made a large insurance claim against Lloyd's underwriters. It followed an attack on a container vessel in a possible attempted hijacking off Yemen. The ship's bridge and accommodation were attacked with grenades and rocket-launchers. Underwriters think it's a put-up job. The plan may have been to con underwriters into paying up."

"And?"

"Mbesa Security was mentioned. Maybe you were at meetings at the London office when things were discussed? In Albemarle Street."

Yates's eyes became slits and he pulled his legs tighter towards him in a defensive pose. "Me?" Wansdyke sensed prevarication. "Get real. Who said that?" His voice rose several notches. His hair seemed to bristle and his grey cheeks reddened. He put up both his palms in a stop signal. "I warned Baccy to hire us but he reckoned he didn't need security on that voyage." Yates shook his head. "I said the Gulf of Aden round Yemen, you need Mbesa. He said it would be okay."

Wansdyke threw up his hands. "Don't get me wrong, sir. You were not named in any conspiracy. But him not wanting security …"

"Point taken." Yates frowned but spoke without sounding concerned. "Doesn't look too good for Baccy, does it? Declines my services and his vessel then gets attacked in what underwriters think was a put-up job."

"The guys in London hoped you might have been at a meeting or one of Mr Bakirtzis's lunch parties. Heard something. Seen something."

"Ah! Got you. I see Baccy every so often. He throws a good lunch or dinner but I never heard of any scams." He laughed. "Once the bouzouki music starts, he's flying! Smashing hundred quid plates. God's gift to the crockery industry, he is."

"You keep a diary?"

"Old-fashioned paper one, yes."

"We're checking when Mr Bakirtzis is believed to have been in town. Last year and this year if I can trouble you."

Yates eased himself from the chair with a grunt and a grimace before hobbling out of sight. He returned with two red diaries. During his absence, the sergeant had scribbled notes describing the house and the opulent furnishings. He had placed Yates at around forty, close-cropped hair and good-looking in a weathered way. It was a face that had seen a fair share of life. "You worked on the ships yourself?"

"I did. Still could – my leg apart. With so much piracy, thefts and violence, Mbesa grew like crazy. As it grew, I had to stay ashore to run the business. Bloody admin! But these past couple of years, the attacks have dropped right off. If you had time, wanted to stay for a bite of lunch, I could tell you a few tales of pirates around the South China Sea and the Red Sea."

"Another time, sir. It sounds more exciting than kids nicking traffic cones."

"Mbesa has an office in London – they do the hiring. I mainly look after the owners. Today we've got twenty-seven guys out there protecting vessels. Five years back, we had six times as many."

As he leaned forward, the young detective's eyes and open-mouthed look revealed his enthusiasm. "I've always loved this piracy stuff. That movie about Captain Phillips. Terrific. Hard to believe it was a true story." He put down his cup. "But I'd better not get side-tracked." He flipped over his notepad. "I'm here to check four dates last year and three since then when you might have met up. The most recent was just last week the 9th." He read out the dates, one by one. "Just confirm also where you were, if you can."

Yates checked each date in a diary as he answered. "No. Vienna. No. Liverpool. No. London but not with Baccy. No. Here at home. No. Newcastle. No. King's Lynn. No. Oxford." He waved a dismissive arm, all rippling muscle. "I've met Baccy this year on 14th March and 29th June."

"Most helpful. Thank you, sir." Wansdyke rose to leave. "That big beast outside must burn a load of fuel."

"Yeah! For business in London, I train it from Darlington. I've got a tasty Aston Martin for day trips. For overnighters, I often kip in the wagon." He gave an unsubtle wink. "I'm single. The Rapido's my passion wagon."

"Plenty of room in there for a huge bed, if I may say so."

Yates thumped his knees as he hooted with laughter. "Say away. It's true. You want any more about when I was with Baccy? Like who was there? I can check."

Wansdyke had already closed his notebook and was rising to his feet. "I don't think so. The dates were specific. If there was a loop, you were outside it. If I get it in the neck from London for not getting more, I'll call you."

"Any time. I like Baccy. I hope he's straight. He's a valued customer."

Wansdyke's feet scuffed the gravel. "Sorry to waste your time. And Mum's the word. Probably, those smart-arses up in London have the wrong guy."

Credenhill, Hereford

Within minutes of leaving Ravensworth, Det. Sgt Wansdyke had phoned. "How did it go?" Ratso asked as Nancy manoeuvred a roundabout on the outskirts of Hereford.

"No issues, sir. He's very crippled. He wears a surgical boot."

Ratso smirked at how Terry Yates was fooling the world. "Dates?"

"Yes, sir, he produced diaries for both years."

"Give me a moment." Ratso checked his notes. "Was he with Yiannis Bakirtzis on any of the dates I gave you?"

"Negative. He volunteered some dates when they were together."

Ratso had no interest but played along. "Yes please." He listened and jotted down the detail. "And on those dates, I gave you, where was he if not with Bakirtzis?"

"In date order, sir – Vienna, Liverpool, London, at home, Newcastle, King's Lynn and Oxford. He stayed in his motorhome when he was in Newcastle, King's Lynn and Liverpool."

"Did you believe him?"

"I did, sir. I saw the entries."

"Was he shocked by allegations against Bakirtzis?"

"Possibly but not astonished. Like you told me, I played down there was anything definite against him. He was more concerned about losing a big client."

"You think he'll keep stumm?"

"Can't be sure. Y'know human nature."

"Good answer. Thanks for your help." Ratso ended the call.

Petrie pulled into a lay-by. "Helpful, boss?" She knew that Ratso had taken a gamble by making even vague allegations against the Greek shipping tycoon. Ratso's calls to a top shipping lawyer had helped. As the lawyer had told him, you could name any number of Greek ship-owners operating out of Piraeus and there'd be stories about fraud, scuttling ships or stolen cargo. Rumours about Bakirtzis had circulated for years.

Petrie knew there had only been one date Ratso had been interested in. The rest had been red herrings. "Boss, where was he when Dermot Doyle was murdered on 17th July?"

"King's Lynn." Ratso's lips pursed as he shook his head. "Maybe I should have gone for the jugular and asked about all three dates. Or at least two."

"Surely, Yates would have been suspicious." She turned towards his strong profile. "Nail him for one date. The playing-cards do the rest."

Ratso sighed, his disappointment obvious. "King's Lynn is way outside London. After the MoD confirmed he had been SAS, I was sure we had our man. Someone trained to kill."

Petrie checked her watch. "We ought to be moving. Our appointment is in ten minutes."

"Drive on." Ratso started tapping away on his phone. "According to Google Maps, at King's Lynn, his motorhome was around 100 miles from Ladbroke Grove. No good roads until you reach the M11 or M1. Let's say a six-hour round-trip."

"We need to check out where he might've been staying? Maybe a caravan park?"

"I'll get Jock onto it. Sure as hell, he didn't drive to Ladbroke Grove in his giant Rapido."

"And you still don't know if he lost millions in Energy Management."

Ratso sounded irritated at the reminder and replied sharply. "We'll know soon enough. Maybe tomorrow."

The red and white barriers appeared as Nancy drove between the solid brick pillars at the entrance to Stirling Lines, the ultra-secure HQ of the SAS – otherwise known as the 22nd Special Air Service at Credenhill. The place was named after David Stirling, the legend who had created the idea of elite troops, operating at the highest risks behind enemy lines in 1941. They had been called the Special Air Service to fool the Germans into thinking the SAS was an airborne unit. Instead, Stirling's men caused havoc by invading German air-bases and destroying their aircraft.

Petrie pulled up at the guardhouse of the former RAF base and after meticulous checking, they were escorted to the meeting-room. On the way, Ratso studied the lines of drab, symmetrical and anonymous-looking quarters. As he took it all in, he was enjoying the edginess of the top secrecy – just as he had felt when visiting MI6 at Vauxhall Cross.

Moments later, they were shown into a utilitarian office. An austere figure, with a slender jet-black moustache and *café au lait* colouring, rose from behind the desk. "Major David Tang. I'm Commanding Officer of B Squadron." Ratso introduced them both and they seated themselves as coffee or tea was offered. "How can I assist?" Ratso placed him as aged forty-six, Singaporean and with an English public-school education.

"Some background about the SAS first would be useful."

"Who Dares Wins," Petrie chimed in.

Tang's face remained impassive with no hint that he had been listening. "To be part of the Special Air Service, applicants must already be members of the Armed Forces. Many come from the

3rd Para Regiment. Those fellas are tough but even some of them don't make the grade here. Applicants first attend a short Special Forces Briefing Course. Following that, those that look promising and who want to take it further, do a six-month course. The vast majority, about 90% fail or give up and return to their regiments."

"Why?" Ratso sounded as surprised as he was.

"After intense trekking through the rain, snow and gales of the Brecon Beacons, the remaining wannabees go to Belize for jungle training." For a split second, Tang's eyes glazed over as if reliving a hellish time. "A couple of the last lot encountered a nine-metre anaconda. You could end up inside one that size. Venomous coral snakes, vipers, Black Widow spiders and bullet-ants. You name it, they're somewhere close to you in the jungle at night. If you can cope with that, then on return, there's training in evasion and escape techniques." Tang gave an unfunny smile. "Because our operations can be high-risk, the applicants must pass tests involving resistance to intense disorienting interrogation."

"Hmm. I get the drift. Impressive. The surviving ten percent – what do they learn?"

There was a long pause, the silence broken only by the ticking of a clock on the wall. "I can't discuss details. Operational reasons, you'll understand. You can assume they are trained in parachuting, weaponry, detonation, close-combat, marine training, covert operations. That's apart from surviving conditions that would turn most people into gibbering wrecks."

"Trained to kill?"

"An incidental necessity." His already narrow eyes threw out a defiant challenge. "But not a sport like shooting rabbits."

"Kill or be killed," murmured Petrie who was still troubled by an image of a giant anaconda slithering along her thigh at dead of night.

"Major Tang, we need to know about Mr Terry Yates."

"Yes. I have Sergeant Yates's records on screen. What do you need?"

"You talk please. We'll listen and take notes."

"Why do you want to know, may I ask?"

"For operational reasons, I can't say anything more, major." Ratso enjoyed throwing back that remark. "Would that answer get a pass in your intensive interrogation training?"

Tang laughed for the first time, showing immaculate white teeth and a single gold crown. "With distinction." He looked Ratso up and down. "Your height would have been against you for signing up. Our ideal height is five foot eight, neither too big nor too small. You're about six feet?"

"Just over but close enough, major. I'm shocked. I assumed your men were built like gorillas."

Tang wrinkled his nose as he checked the screen. "Yates was five foot nine. That's typical. He served in Iraq and Afghanistan. Lots of places doing other covert operations. Well liked. Well regarded. He left the forces nine years back. I hear he became successful in ship security."

"Skills?"

"Assume what I mentioned earlier."

"You've been very helpful, major." Ratso was less than sincere but remained polite. "From Yates's records, can you please dig out the top ten names of guys he worked with. His best mates."

"Still serving?"

"Retirees for now."

"Will do."

As the officer rose to his feet, Ratso noticed how small Tang now seemed. Maybe just under the ideal height. "Nothing unusual on Yates's records? Indiscipline? Bar brawls? Violence? Quitting the SAS suddenly?"

"Sorry to disappoint you – but no." The words were accompanied by a rather bored and dismissive wave of his arm.

After leaving Credenhill, Ratso and Nancy travelled in silence through several roundabouts outside Hereford. It was Nancy who spoke first. "I'd have freaked out in the equatorial jungle. Spiders, snakes. Ugh!"

"Being interrogated under duress too. Tang called it *resistance to intense disorienting interrogation*. That sounded like waterboarding. Makes our job seem like tea with scones at Buck House. Except for dealing with our own reptilian Caldwell." He saw a sign ahead for The Chequers. "Let's stop for a quick lunch. Jock just messaged me."

Ross-on-Wye

Ratso plonked Nancy's lemon and lime and his pint of Guinness on the table. A pizza was on its way. Nancy yawned loudly. "I'm not looking forward to driving back. It's been a long day."

"I'll drive if you want," volunteered Ratso, putting down his barely touched Guinness.

"I'll be fine but maybe a ten-minute nap after the pizza?"

"No problem. You nap. I'll talk to Jock. Stretch my legs by the river." In fact, after lunch, with rain suddenly sheeting down, walking was not an option. They both returned to the car. After their 5 a.m. start, the pizza and Guinness, Ratso's eyes were also drooping and they both tilted back the seats for a snooze. On awakening ten-minutes later, he joked that he would tell Jock they'd just slept together.

"Not sure Jock would appreciate that, boss. Not if you recall ..."

"Oh God! You're right! How could I forget!" He remembered how Jock, on the rebound from his divorce, had dreamed of whisking Nancy away on a romantic cruise. Nancy had no such intention.

"I'd never meant to raise his hopes. To me, we were just colleagues. I really liked him – but not in the way he wanted. I still feel bad about it."

"Forget it. He misread the situation. Jock's son in Glasgow is almost your age." He dialled Strang's number. "Jock. It sounded important."

"Iqbal from Surrey police called. The Audi is almost certainly an A3 saloon. 5-door. Since 2015, there have been more than 250,000 sold in England. They've spent over one thousand hours looking at footage from cameras. Just after 4 am, the Audi joined the M25 at junction 9 coming from the south."

"The Leatherhead junction. Is Iqbal still sure the plates were false?"

"Seems so, boss. It's the same Audi."

"This has to be our man who stopped at Cobham for his coffee and sausage roll. How did he reach Junction 9?"

"Before joining the motorway? They traced him only about 5 miles. He must have been using Surrey's minor roads, avoiding cameras."

"And after the murder?"

"Vanished. The guy's no fool. Done his homework. Iqbal reckons the driver either lives in the area or he again avoided cameras on main roads and larger towns."

"Dumb move him joining the M25 at all. He must've been hungry. There's a ton of minor roads he could have used instead."

"Right enough. Update on pig-face Marney?"

"What's news?"

"At 6-05 a.m. Marney used his bank debit-card at his local newsagent in Belgravia. He didn't kill Lord Ongerton."

"I never thought he did. Murder with bare hands? Laughable. Anyway, he was rich enough to hire a killer. But I don't think he did that either. Anything else?"

"Logan Goldie's bank records were interesting." As he spoke, the Scot could imagine Ratso's face now on full alert, mouth sucked in, jawline prominent. "The guy was making regular payments to about thirty-something companies. One-hundred quid each time. Bonkers suspects Goldie was paying them to attack targets on blog-sites and bulletin-boards."

"Timing-wise, linked to Energy Management?"

"Aye and there was another flurry about the time he exposed WPCoin."

"You're checking the recipient companies?"

"A couple of the youngsters are onto it."

"My news now. I want you and Bonkers to head north. King's Lynn."

"Tea with King Charles at Sandringham?"

"No royals where you're going. I don't see the King and Queen roughing it at a wet campsite."

Ratso heard the melodious chuckle "Aye! Standing in the rain queuing for the communal lavvies."

"Check if Terry Yates parked his Rapido at any caravan park when Dermot Doyle was murdered. If he was, check if he had an alibi."

"Yates still a suspect?" The Scot's voice had risen an octave in making his point.

"Until I find someone better. Here's the registration for his Rapido." Ratso guessed Jock was scribbling down the number but the silence was too long for that. "Jock? Still there?"

"Sorry, boss. I was just thinking."

"Give."

" Mebbe check Audi saloon car-rentals? Around King's Lynn."

"Go for it. Anything else?"

"Fergus Edwards, the timeshare guy. He abandoned Deptford long ago. Now, he spends most of the year in Barbados and he's never left there when any of the murders occurred."

"We can't rule him out, not with his London heavies. WPCoin? The crypto scam? Progress? I forget her name – something Jakupi."

"Aye. Valbona Jakupi. DC Willison has been checking. It's

hard to get close to these Albanian mobsters. They're secretive and suspicious."

"If Willison's getting nowhere, get someone else on it."

"You back here later?"

"Negative. Evening cricket. Tomorrow, it's Oxford to meet Energy Management Associates."

Bonnitor

Overhead, the electric fan swished while the outdated air-conditioning fought to beat the humidity. The smell of cheese and chorizo from Bastien Alleyne's wrap filled the room. The inspector put down the print-out. As he glanced at it, his brow crinkled and his mouth showed his disappointment. "That's it? That's all we know about every resident of Robinson Cove."

"Boss, not one resident has a criminal record for violence. I've run the names through the Feds in the USA and with Scotland Yard. Nothing known. Plenty of suspicion about fraud and money-laundering."

"And no bad blood between Campbell and any neighbours?"

"Not according to his missus."

"I thought my idea of the killer being a neighbour was a winner."

Venables bit his lip at Alleyne hijacking his idea. "If there ain't no other way, then mebbe the killers musta come by sea? There's CCTV at Torrington Marina. I can check."

Alleyne's shoulder shrug was dismissive. "If you must."

Venables sipped coffee from his colourful Manchester United mug and handed over another spreadsheet. "Here are the guests at the party in Robinson Cove that night. Y'know, thrown by the couple three-hundred metres down the street. Twenty-nine guests had champagne cocktails and a five-course feast. The usual chattering clique – all bling and Botox. Local politicians. Bankers. A baseball star from the Miami Marlins. Some Brits doing business here. A couple of South American diplomats that we'd love to nab for money-laundering. All guests left around midnight. We tracked down most. Nobody saw or heard anything."

Alleyne's eyes lit up. He banged a fist into the palm of his other hand. "Rich guys. Several must have known Campbell. May have had reasons to kill him. Just slip away from the party. Or mebbe a chauffeur."

Venables tried not to groan. "No guest slipped away using the front entrance. We've checked their CCTV." He paused to give Alleyne a chance to make his next illuminating remark but instead, his boss just poured Red Bull from a can. "Drivers, chauffeurs," Venables continued. "Sure, they did wait around, laughing, smoking, chowing down takeaways on the host's driveway. They do say none of them left."

"Chauffeurs. They're just taxi-drivers in peaked caps. Giving each other alibis. Thieves the lot of them."

"So you reckon one or more of them murder Campbell and return to the driveway with the money and jewels?" Venables was enjoying taunting his boss.

Alleyne knew he was under pressure. He picked up and took an intense interest in the porcelain dog on his desk. "Maybe a guest slipped away by sea? By boat?"

"Good idea boss but the only boat was the host's twenty-metre yacht. That never moved. The killer could hardly swim to Campbell's place and return to the party, dripping wet."

"He could say he fell in the pool."

"And hid the jewels and cash in the deep-end." Venables turned away to hide his smirk.

Alleyne did a double-take but said nothing at the sarcasm. "Run every owner's name by Brenda Campbell again. You said seventy percent were off-island, so that makes it easier."

"Sure."

"That bitch is in this up to here." Alleyne's hand rose above his head. "She claims insurance for stolen cash and jewels. She inherits his wealth. She collects life insurance. The merry widow then enjoys her enormous wealth and endless rumpy with Morry Rolle."

"If you say so, boss. The flaw is evidence. There's none."

"None yet. None yet, *sergeant*." Alleyne emphasised the lower rank as he turned away.

Oxford

"We should have stopped here last night. We were only five miles away yesterday." In a line of slow-moving traffic Nancy Petrie was driving through suburban Oxford. On both sides of the road were Headington's small shops and ethnic takeaways.

"On the upside, I got to my cricket." Ratso was responding absent-mindedly, his thoughts more on his questions for Jamie Fargher at Energy Management.

Petrie checked the satnav. "Bit of a mess this city. They've been blocking off streets to discourage driving. Going from A to B involves passing through X, Y and Z. To get to St Aldgate's, we've got to drive in the opposite direction."

"I was reading about it. The council here hates cars and car drivers. They've made Hampton Court Maze seem a doddle." He shut his notepad. "No rush anyway. Fargher offered us a sandwich lunch. Sounded friendly enough but curious."

"Well you would be," she replied dodging yet another student on a bike. "Ever wish you'd gone to Uni?"

Ratso shook his head. "I always struggled with exams. But since then? Maybe a little. Not being at Uni for the degree. More for the horizons that might have opened up." He ran his fingers across his hair. "My vision never extended beyond Fulham. Now, look at me! I still live and work just a couple of miles from my first school. You?"

"I'd just started at Leeds Uni when my mum got cancer. I

dropped out to nurse her. Two years later, she died. That's when I joined the Met."

"I'm sorry. I never knew that."

Petrie's head-shake was almost imperceptible. "I love my job. I'm ambitious. I might try an online degree course." She slowed the car. "There." She pointed to a tired looking three-storey office block. "Thank God they've got parking. Nightmare otherwise round here. EMA is on the second-floor."

After using the stairs, they pressed a buzzer on a very secure looking door. It was opened by a bulky figure, about Ratso's height but carrying more weight, too little of it muscle. "Come in. I'm Jamie Fargher and you will be DCI Holtom and Detective Constable Petrie?" Nancy placed the man at mid-thirties with dark hair receding at the temples. Fargher had a three-day stubble look. He looked friendly enough despite the strength of his features. His wide-set brown eyes showed no sign of wariness. He extended a hairy hand with a fierce handshake.

Ratso looked round the Reception area. The surroundings were sparse. The air smelled stale, as if no window had ever been opened. The grey-tiled floor was shabby and needed replacing. Mopping down would never cut it. There was a desk and chair for a receptionist but it looked unloved and unused. In a side office, he saw a couple of figures and sensed a third. Another door led to a tiny kitchen and there were WCs at the end of a short corridor.

Fargher showed them into his spartan office. "This is my office but it doubles for meetings." It was almost an apology for the surroundings. "Like I said, seeing as it's nearly lunchtime, I got pasties sent in. I'll get them heated now and we can talk and eat. "Soft drink, tea, coffee?"

They both volunteered for water and he poured three glasses of sparkling before heading for the kitchen. "Not what I expected," prompted Petrie keeping her voice down. "A company quoted on the AIM market. Thousands of shareholders. I sort of imagined something glitzy. A place with a buzz to it. Glam-looking PAs with the latest hi-tech kit and rows of dashing young men looking at their monitors."

"They don't waste money, that's for sure," said Ratso looking at the table-top, stained with rings from hot cups. The seats of the dozen hard-backed chairs were shiny from too many years of use. "Dunno whether that's good or bad."

"As a shareholder, I'd hate thick carpets, expensive works of art on the walls, y'know all the bells and whistles, a reception area like a stately home. I would …" Nancy never got to finish as Fargher breezed in with a tray bulging with mini-pasties and sandwiches. As he sat down opposite them, he waved his hairy mitt over the food. "Tuck in while they're hot. There's chicken and mushroom, beef and ale or diced mixed veg."

"Nancy: you prefer veggie?" Ratso was rewarded with a broad smile as she put three of them onto a disposable plate.

"So what's this all about?" There was a touch of Scouse in Fargher's accent.

"You're a Liverpudlian? I love placing accents."

"Correct, Mr Holtom. Born in Fazakerley. Been away over ten years."

"Great city. I did a sting there once. It was an attempt to smuggle smelted gold to the Isle of Man. We reckoned it was originally stolen from Brinks-Mat back in 1983." He flipped open a notepad. "Business. We're interested in your share price crash and who were the big losers."

"Besides me?" The comment was accompanied by a rueful look and then a grin. "I had share options. I was hoping to trouser several million. Right now? My shares might as well be confetti."

"Jamie, you're a director and company secretary?"

"Correct. As a trained accountant, I do the finances. As company secretary, I am general dogsbody doing all the admin shit." Petrie put down her pasty. "And the other directors?"

"You mean the Olly and Molly Show," he laughed. "Oliver Young as CEO and Molly Bishop. She's a geologist."

"If we need to speak to them, are they around?"

"Not today. They lost their investment and share options too. They're on our site in Morocco. You might get them on Zoom but the internet in the Atlas Mountains is definitely Third World."

"I may need to speak to them."

"So Olly and Molly? Why are they out there?" Ratso took up the questions.

"We're into gas production. Right now, it's just a cottage industry."

"So tell us more about Energy Management."

"We explore and exploit oil and gas. We have an income stream from the Moroccan gas. It's daily volume just about pays for your pasties and the electrics." His laugh was self-deprecating but infectious. He stretched to help himself to a tuna sandwich. "In the Caribbean, we drilled for oil. The experts reckoned we might find a billion barrels. Wrong! We had a duster – no oil." His eyes hardened, suddenly cold, adding a sinister look to his previously sunny appearance. "But it wasn't that simple."

"The shares crashed?"

Fargher nodded. "If we'd struck oil then the shares would have rocketed. As it was, they went even further south. Like Antarctic south."

"I'm new to all this," Petrie intervened. "Can you flesh out?"

"Sure." Fargher's smile flashed across the table. He then rested his hands on his ample stomach. "Typically, once a drilling date is announced, oil explorer shares on AIM rise sharply each day. Speculators pile in. In the run-up to drilling, suppose you can buy shares at 8p on Monday. On Tuesday, drilling is announced to start in six weeks. By the date the drill bit starts turning – we call that spudding – the shares could easily have risen to 30p or even more. That's speculators gambling on a big oil-strike being announced a few weeks later. An oil-strike could race the shares up to a quid, maybe even two quid. Meantime, as speculators pile in pre-drill, long-term investors who had bought years before for peanuts, will be taking mega-profits without risk of a duster."

Ratso jotted down de-risking. "But maybe keeping some shares?"

"Correct, Mr Holtom. Many would sell 80 %. They'd lose no sleep by writing off 20%. If there's an oil-strike, then their 20% will also rocket."

"Nice work if you can get it." Petrie sounded impressed and was. "But its shit-or-bust." In her black trouser-suit with a dark green blouse and a Cuban chain choker, she was dressed to impress.

"You're a fast learner. What you call shit-or-bust we call a binary situation." Fargher's smile showed admiration for more than her brain.

Ratso played with his egg sandwich for a moment and then raised his eyes. Keen to watch Fargher's reaction, he paused to focus on his eyes. "Typically. You said typically. Why?"

The answer came quickly with no hint of evasion. "Because what happened to us was not typical – not nearly."

It was the answer Ratso wanted. "The name Logan Goldie. Mean anything?"

"Goldie! That lying dishonest scumbag. Somebody gave him what he had coming." He pushed his plate aside. "Is that why you're here? I wish him nothing better than burning in hell."

"We are interested in Goldie, yes," said Petrie.

"That bastard. I've often felt like beating the shit out of him. On sleepless nights as he crashed our share price, I cheered myself by planning his murder in different ways. Boiling him in oil was a favourite." Suddenly, he fell silent as if regretting his outburst. His cheeks coloured and his hands clenched and unclenched. "Hey! You don't think it was me, do you?" He looked at each listener in turn but neither said anything. "I mean ... Christ! You don't think *I* killed him. I only felt like it. With good reason. Plenty did."

"Relax, Mr Fargher." Ratso flourished his arm. "Routine enquiries. We've nothing to suggest you were involved. But check your diary for 28th July."

Fargher rose slowly and padded, bear-like, to his Army-surplus metal desk by the window. He returned with his phone. "28th July, you said." He flicked through the screens. "I thought the date was familiar. I was best man at a wedding in Cornwall. Stayed there from the 26th to 29th July."

"Tell us about Goldie."

Fargher clasped his hands together. "His subscribers get a tip-sheet."

"*Saints and Skeletons*?"

Fargher smiled at Petrie. "Correct." For the next few minutes, Fargher explained the Placing debacle and the savage cost to the company. "Goldie's fraudulent lies cost the company millions. Goldie's crooked mates in the City creamed off big profits at the expense of our shareholders." He offered round a bowl of apples, bananas and grapes. "But there's more. Something worse, maybe."

Beyond Logan Goldie, Ratso was not much interested in more detail. "Tell me about your shareholders – the big ones."

"Any company or individual holding 3% of our shares must notify us. That's the law." As he spoke, he returned to the keyboard and monitor. Deftly, he opened the data. "This is public information, you understand." Petrie followed Ratso to look at the screen. "There are four institutional investors. Between them, they own over 35% of the issued shares There's a handful of others owning 3% through their own companies. One individual invested in his own name. That's Frederico Sorrentini. Nice guy. Flies in from Milan for our meetings."

"What was his holding then? Just to give us an idea." Ratso's mind was already racing with images of an Italian Mafioso.

"Forty million shares. He told me his plan was to dump 85% just before spud and make ten million minimum, probably double that. He had planned to buy a penthouse overlooking the Thames. Not now. Despite the well-known algorithm for explorers rising until spud, mainly because of Goldie, the shares never rose at all."

"So Sorrentini never sold?"

"Correct! Like most shareholders, he had no chance to de-risk."

"Pretty angry, was he?"

"Angry is not the word I'd use Mr Holtom. It was way beyond that. Manic fury wouldn't even be close. We all felt like that – Logan Goldie's dirty tricks had given him a huge win. Our investors were destroyed." He pushed aside his plate and, as if throttling Goldie, screwed his paper napkin into a ball. "Striking oil is like that game – *Pin the Tail on the Donkey*. Even if there are billions of barrels down there, you can miss them by a just a few metres. By industry standards, our prospects of success were pretty damned good."

"So instead of making ten million, what are Sorrentini's shares worth today?"

Fargher shrugged. "Right now? He could buy a wheelbarrow, a few bricks and a sack of cement towards building his penthouse." Ratso could tell Fargher was going to add something more. His

Deadly Hush

body language had broadcast a clear message. But unexpectedly, he stopped, mouth half-open like a goldfish and saying nothing He closed his mouth, shrugging his shoulders. Wanting an uncomfortable moment of silence to push Fargher to continue, Ratso also said nothing. Unfortunately, Petrie chipped in.

"Does Sorrentini blame Logan Goldie?"

"Not just him but ..."

"Who do *you* blame?"

"Not just Goldie." He repeated the answer.

"Jamie – you'd better explain," prompted Nancy.

"It'll take a while. You in a hurry?"

"Carry on," Ratso nodded. "But first print out the details of everyone holding at least 3%. Then maybe that coffee? Herbal tea for DC Petrie."

"You won't need coffee to stay awake," Fargher laughed, his confidence returning. "Not unless you normally nod off in horror movies." Fargher headed to the kitchen.

While Fargher was fixing the drinks, Petrie read out names of the big shareholders. Mbesa Security did not feature.

Ratso swatted the setback aside. "Terry Yates would have bought using a different company. I'm not giving up yet. Even without owning 3%, you could still lose millions." They sat in silence, locked in their own thoughts until Fargher returned with a pot of coffee and a peppermint tea for Petrie. Ratso handed over a document. "Here's our authority to go behind the public info. Terry Yates or Terence Yates. Is he or was he a shareholder?"

"Not something I am able to answer, nor could our Registrar."

Ratso looked surprised and wondered if Fargher was being evasive.

"You assume we know the I.D of every small shareholder. Wrong."

"Who does then?"

"Most shareholders buy through their bank or a big trading platform like Hargreaves Lansdown. Under KYC laws, they must know the identity of their customer and the names behind a company. Sorry. I can't help."

"How many shareholders do you have?"

Fargher scratched his ear and drummed the fingers of his other hand on the table. "At a guess, perhaps twenty thousand, many of them day-traders, y'know in and out trying to make a quick buck."

Ratso did not let his disappointment show. "Time now for your horror story."

King's Lynn

The ancient town of King's Lynn in Norfolk had become an overflow township from London. As they drove through the centre, Jock Strang reckoned the mix of ancient and modern was as uncomfortable as in his beloved Glasgow. Not that anywhere looked its best on a summer's day like this. The rain was beating down on the roof of his Vauxhall Corsa. Strang turned from the driver's seat to look at Lumo Bonkale. "Makes me feel at home. This is Scottish weather, son."

Bonkers laughed. "You call this rain? Just visit Ghana in the rainy season." They peered through the windscreen and spotted the sign for The Merry Harriers Leisure Park. Today, it was not looking merry. This was the third site visited. The previous two had no record of Yates or his Rapido.

"Better luck here, eh, son. This is our last chance. If Yates didna' stay here, then he invented King's Lynn. But why would he?" He swung the car off the winding rough-stone drive into the car-park. "That's as close to Reception as I can get. We'll still get drowned."

Bonkers pointed. "At least we're not putting up a tent – like them two over there." He pointed to an elderly couple, dripping wet, battling to pitch a green ridge-tent against the easterly wind and horizontal rain.

"I went camping once near Loch Lomond in weather like this. I was seventeen. I never even put the tent up. Instead, I caught the next train home from Balloch to Glasgow. I wasn't even away the night. I was home for my tea. Give me a warm room and a dry bed." He laughed a deep chuckle at the memory. "Ready to run?"

Once inside the spacious Reception, at least the welcome was warm from one of two young women at the front-desk. "Checking in?" The brunette was skimming her finger down a list of bookings. Her name-badge identified her as Zoe.

"Sorry to disappoint you, Zoe." Jock wiped away the rain that was dripping from his hair and down his florid cheeks. "Detective Inspector Jock Strang and DC Lumo Bonkale." They showed their IDs.

"How can we help? P'raps a pot of tea while you dry off? The café's open over there." Zoe nodded to a colourful room with steamed-up picture-windows.

Strang's face lit up. "Hard to refuse. Thanks."

The slightly older of the two women now spoke. "I'll join you. I'm the Duty Manager. Jess Perkins. Hot buttered tea-cakes as well?" The roll of Strang's eyes was answer enough. "Sort that with the kitchen, Zoe."

They crossed the navy-blue cord carpet, removing their weatherproof jackets as they walked. The air smelled of lemon freshener mixed with the chips from the lunch menu. Mid-afternoon, there were plenty of spare tables. Only a scattering of campers had abandoned the cosy comforts of their vans to dash to the main building. They chose a table for four. Bonkers wiped down the window and pointed as he watched the couple still battling with their tent. The woman was finger-wagging the man as he wrestled with a guy rope. "Recipe for divorce I'd say."

The Duty Manager joined them. Strang put Jess as being late-twenties. She was wearing a Merry Harriers tank-top, torn jeans and flip-flops. Her face was friendly and attractive enough to have won her plenty of welcome and unwelcome suggestions. Only the ring on her finger may have slowed the aspirations of chancers like Terry Yates. "We don't get detectives visiting. I'm intrigued."

"Nothing to worry you, anyroads, Jess," Strang reassured her. "We're just fact-finding." After the two previous interviews, he had his approach off-pat. He showed her a picture of a Rapido van. "No doubt you get plenty of these?" He saw Jess shrug and continued. "I guess you keep details?"

"All arrivals give us name, address, vehicle reg and sort out payment arrangements."

"You had a bookings diary at the front-desk?"

"Yes. That's just for meet-and-greet. Y'know, a friendly welcome. Everything is computerised as well. In the season, any day we have upwards of eighty overnighters. Some glamping, some in our static mobile-homes, a few in shepherd's huts but most in their own vans." She saw the couple struggling with the tent. "Not so many of those, these days."

A young Indian boy delivered the tea and tea-cakes as Bonkers spoke. "You get to know the visitors – some of them?"

"The regulars." For the first time, Perkins looked uneasy as if wondering where this was leading. She knew they turned a blind-eye to occasional drug dealers who visited the bar. Besides, them, she remembered the young woman from Salford who used her van as a mobile brothel.

Jock showed her the number of Yates's Rapido. "Please check this one, can you?"

"Easy."

"All dates in the last 18 months." The two detectives watched her stride confidently between the colourful tables. Here and there, she stopped for a word or gave a friendly nod. From the sound-system, Freddie Mercury was belting out that *We are the Champions*.

"Seems straight-up to me, gov."

Strang's head and hands movements suggested the jury was out. He returned the photo of the Rapido to his folder. He could see Jess Perkins in Reception, chatting as Zoe's fingers raced over the keyboard. When she returned, Jess was clutching a single sheet of A4 paper. "Terry Yates. You interested in him?"

"Your system works." Strang glanced at the dates and knew at once that Yates had been here on 17th July, the night when the TV presenter had been murdered. "I see he stayed three nights."

"Correct. I know Terry. *Everyone* knows Terry. He visits at least once every year. He loves playing darts. That's over there in the bar. Usually, if there's a few others like him, they'll maybe play cricket or football. Y'know a kickaround, just for fun like. He's always in the middle of everything." She faltered in mid-tracks. "No. I tell a lie. Not so much this year. He was wearing a strange boot thingie."

Strang's glance at Bonkers warned him to say nothing. "How well did you know him?"

"I mean like, Terry was fun. He drank in the bar. Told stories about piracy. Held the stage if you get me." Jess put down her cup. "Terry's not in trouble, is he?"

"Just routine enquiries. Those three nights. Was he in the bar? Darts?"

For her reply, she stood up and motioned them to follow. The barman looked pleased to see some life. A solitary pensioner was sat in the corner staring into space, his half-pint glass empty. "Billy, pass me the album." He handed over a hefty red tome and they seated themselves. "Visitors mainly take photos with their phones but we take these for our Memory Lane evenings." She pointed to the enlarged pics that filled every page. "We take a few most evenings. Y'know bingo winners, best karaoke singer, competition winners. We then display them on the *Wall of Fame* for a few days."

Deadly Hush

She pointed. "See? Over there. People like their names and pics on display." As she spoke, she was riffling through more pages. "There he is. That's Terry. His team had won the darts match."

Yates was seated with seven men of mixed ages standing around him. A fake gold-medal hung from his neck and his surgical boot was prominent. In front of him was a jug of beer. Strang adjusted his specs and saw the date. It was the 16th July. Dermot Doyle had been murdered in London at around 03-30 a.m. on the 17th. He maintained a poker-face. "Time?"

"Usually, darts ends between 10 and 11."

"Would they stay on drinking late?"

"We shut the bar at midnight. Opening later just gave the boss trouble. Drunks. Assaults. Groping. You get the drift?"

"Did Terry have anybody with him?"

"He always came alone. I don't want to speak out of turn but, well, like – sometimes, he got lucky. Y'know, after the band finished at weekends."

"Tell us about the morning after the darts." Bonkale prompted.

"I wouldn't be there mornings. Maybe Tomasz would know. He does mornings as Duty Manager."

"We may need to speak to him."

"Wait one!" Jess stood up suddenly. "That was a Saturday morning. Let me check something." She returned from Reception with a pink exercise-book marked Bookings. Her manicured fingers flipped through page after page of scribbles. "There you are. Terry had booked the TV room from nine-thirty for breakfast and lunch. Ten people. Sky Sports channel reserved." She saw the puzzled looks. "Before this booking system, we'd had trouble. Londoners wanting to watch Arsenal play Chelsea clashing with petrolheads wanting a Formula One Grand Prix. Now? If you want the big screen, you hire the room."

"And Yates had the room booked."

"I expect it was a one-day cricket match. They had the TV room booked all day."

Bonkers gave her a winning smile. "You know the guys in the photo?"

Jess looked at the photo. "A couple. First names only" She pointed to two of the men, both over sixty. "That's Pat and the other's Damian."

Jock clapped his hands on his hefty knees and eased himself up. "We'll be away. We'll have a wee talk to Tomasz in the morning."

"But a list of everybody staying on those July dates. A takeaway – that would help," Bonkers added. Jess nodded yes as she left the bar.

"Ratso's hunch isn't looking good, gov."

Strang tried not to sound patronising. "He wouldn't see it like that. He'd say Yates had plenty of time to be in London and back."

"But he needed a motor. An Audi preferably."

"Homework for this evening. Car rental agencies and other overnight guests."

With another pleasing smile directed at Bonkers, Jess appeared and handed over several printed pages.

"Jess, where we came in from the road, is that the only entrance?" Bonkers was rubbing a finger down his smooth-skinned cheek.

"Yes. The CCTV records all movements in and out."

"Would you have that?"

"For back then? No chance. It's wiped every week."

Strang glanced at the print-out and saw that every visitor's make and model of car was listed. "You've done us proud, Jess." He eased himself up to leave but in Reception, he stopped by the desk. "Now, both of you. Mind and not tell anybody of our visit.

Understood?" He waited for both Jess and Zoe to agree. "Good. I'm serious about that. Thanks." Once outside, they saw the ridge-tent was now erected. The man, head bowed against the wind, was carrying his rucksack towards it but the woman had disappeared.

"The joys of camping, eh? Come on, son. Let's get to the B&B. Hot bath and few bevvies for me."

"And if I can find an Audi owner stayed the night ..."

"Aye! Better still if the owner was a darts player too."

Putney

Armed with the data from The Merry Harriers, Ratso was ready to brief DC Viment. "Carole, I need you to cross-check every name from the Merry Harriers against Yates's SAS mates. They've all moved on from the military. See what all his SAS mates are now doing."

"Judging by the bestseller lists, writing daredevil books about their exploits."

"That's for you to find out. Some may work for Mbesa Security – y'know protecting ships from piracy. See if any drive an Audi saloon. Don't do anything that might tip off Yates. Okay?"

Viment flicked her hair back from her brow. A moment of respect crossed her face the boss had moved away. Then, still seated at her desk, she slumped till her chin was cupped by both hands. She let out a slow, long sigh as she stared at her monitor. *Terry Yates? Never. Waste of bloody time*, she muttered under her breath. *Ratso's on an ego trip.* Of the three targets, she rated Valbona Jakupi as a WPCoin victim but now Ratso wanted that dimwit Danny Willison to investigate her.

Asking damn-fool Willison?
Can a blind person admire the Mona Lisa?
I'm stuck here just analysing ... stuff.
Cunning bastard!
The boss knows my opinion.
Now, I'm bloody here tasked with proving him right.
And me wrong.
He plays us all like pawns on a chess-board.

But my God what a man he is!
I know what I want, what I really really want.
For a moment her imagination had him caressing her cheeks, fondling her breasts and pressing her back to the wall while he kissed her with lingering intensity.
I bet he does that to Nancy.
I bet that's what happened on the way back from Hereford.
I bet the sneaky bitch overnighted with him at his place.
Sod her.
Why doesn't he take somewhere?
She sighed again and reluctantly turned to her screen. An hour later, she had identified three Audis at the Merry Harriers when Yates was there. One owner from Holland was in a left-hand-drive and nothing close to an A3 saloon. The other two couples were friends from Abergavenny, staying in adjacent huts. Facebook searches confirmed this jolly looking foursome were all in their seventies. She ruled them out.

Bonkers had told her he had contacted every car-rental company within forty miles of King's Lynn. Not one Audi saloon had been hired by a Mr Yates or Mbesa or by anyone wearing a surgical boot.

Boss, with Yates, you're piling improbability upon delusion. The bits of this jigsaw don't fit.
Pretty damned pointless.
The motorhome never left King's Lynn.
There was no mate there with an Audi.
Meantime, Willison is probably still working out how to spell Valbona.
While I'm shovelling this shit.
She glared at the pile of bumf from Credenhill.
Waste of bloody time.
Chasing wild geese would be more useful.

Putney

Ratso's warning to DC Danny Willison about investigating Albanians had been reinforced by Jock Strang. "Let your fingers do the walkin', son. Dinna give the bastards a chance to identify you. They damned near killed Tosh Watson. Hit and Run. Dinna you go near Sigwell House. You get me Valbona Jakupi's connections. Use TOR. Visit the dark web. Identify her contacts. See if her contacts match the woman outside Logan Goldie's Mayfair pad. Check on her Daddy's enforcers. They'll keep lower profiles than a snake's arsehole. Get what you can from Holmes 2."

"Jakupi? Could she be the person caught on camera?"

Strang's scoff had been answer enough. Even so, his bushy eyebrows had shot up towards the remains of his greying close-cropped hairline. "Even if she were a dead ringer for the killer, I'd never believe it was her. There's a better chance of the Pope supporting Glasgow Rangers than her getting close to a murder scene. Sonny, she would have been quaffing champagne in a five-star restaurant or having a lover drop grapes into her mouth while relaxing in her spa."

"Not her then?"

This time, Jock's withering glare silenced Willison. "Check with Australia. They used their TOLA legislation to destroy an encrypted cellphone network that criminals believed was secure."

Willison looked puzzled, his face and mind blank. "Can you explain, boss?"

"Ye've been living under a stone, have ye? Swot up on

Enchrochat. Specially designed handsets were sold in Holland – like a phone but no GPS or normal phoning. Thousands of international criminals, maybe 60,000, thought their texting was 100% secure. They chatted freely about buying or selling guns, drug deals and contract killings." Strang saw the bewildered look on Willison's face. "Son, I realise you're quite new to the team but you should have known about the UK's *Operation Venetic* and *Operation Eternal.* They led to a hundreds of arrests – drug barons and other real hard bastards."

"You mean somebody was reading their messages – like I mean *everything*?" Willison's surprise was like a kid being told there was no tooth-fairy.

"Aye. The judges love *Enchrochat.* These thugs and dealers are bang to rights. They are crucified by their own admissions."

"If it was so secure, how come we got to know?"

"The French police hacked it. The *Enchrochat* network suddenly closed down in June 2020. They admitted it had been compromised." Strang's chuckle came from deep down." The guys who had made millions running the network had to disappear."

"Hiding from angry subscribers?"

"Right enough, son. I wouldn't give them life insurance."

"So I can't buy one in a Vodaphone store?"

"No. You had to be trusted to obtain one. Then you used a nickname. But they still gave themselves away. Easy meat."

"What about the Jakupi gang from Manchester?"

Strang looked disappointed. "The boss reckoned they never used it. Our cyber team believe Valbona Jakupi's old man used another secret network, run from Rumania."

"She lives not far away. Right? In Roehampton."

Strang nodded. "Sigwell House. In Santona Close. But don't go near it. That's an order."

Ever since the previous day, Willison had spent hours staring at a screen, poking round on the dark web – digging, researching, collating and digging some more. From Google maps, he could see that Santona Close was three-hundred metres long with a turning-circle at the end. But there were no street views. What lay down Santona Close was a mystery. Intrigued, Willison had phoned the local postmaster. He provided the names of the three properties in this short cul-de-sac: Godwyn House, Hillview and Sigwell House.

At quiet moments in his New Malden bedsit, Willison often seethed at the lack of respect he got from the MIT in Jubilee House. Shit was thrown at him because he loved and followed Jesus, his best friend. *Okay, I'm not as smart as Ratso or this whiz kid Bonkers but given a chance I could match Strang and Watson any day.*

Well, I'm going to show them.

Willison's route home passed close to Roehampton. With Strang and Holtom away brainstorming with Surrey police, it was a chance to do some detective work – real detective work. His mind was made up. He would check out Valbona's place. Afterwards, he'd pick up a Lucozade with sausage and chips from the local takeaway.

No harm in that, was there?

It could do me a shitload of good.

I'll show them I'm as good as those stuck-up bitches Petrie and Viment.

What might I learn?

No idea.

It was mid-evening when he parked his Fiat Uno in Ranbury Crescent. The menacing black clouds scudding overhead obscured the lights of aircraft rumbling towards Heathrow. Despite being an area for the mega-rich, barely a few hundred metres away was a big council estate. From the crime stats, Willison knew there were regular muggings, so he emptied his pockets and left the car-keys on the front-offside tyre. All he took was his Canon camera.

In the gloom, and wearing his olive-green beanie, a donkey-jacket and black jeans, he felt fired up and invisible. The narrow street was empty, no cars and only some old git walking his spaniel. The park on his left was silent and almost invisible in the blackness. The trees surrounding it swayed in the chilly breeze. As he neared the junction with Santona Close, his heart rate quickened.

Now I'm a real detective.
Not just slumming it in sleazy Soho dives.

Roehampton

This is real detective work.

The words in his head, spurred him on. Coming from the park, Willison now heard the clanking of swings in the kids' playground but otherwise all was quiet. He stopped at the junction with Santona Close to his left. The postmaster had said that Sigwell House was the last property near the turnaround. Guessing there would be security cameras, he decided to avoid the street and instead skirted through the edge of the park.

Good move, Danny!

Subtle.

Between two trees, Willison clambered over the post-and-wire fence into the rough grass. Dodging behind the shrubs and bushes, and sheltered by them, it was over two-hundred metres before he had passed the first two properties. Of them, there was little to be seen except for the red lights on the cameras beside their entrances. Then, through the darkness, he saw the outline of the gates to Sigwell House. Having pushed his way deeper into a flowering bush right opposite, he was now surrounded and obscured by abundant greenery.

Then, just moments later, from along the street to his right, he saw the lights of an approaching car. A dark Range-Rover appeared. Overhead floodlights came on and illuminated the street as the gates swung open. As he peered between the branches, he glimpsed the large home inside the compound. Willison fumbled for his camera but was too slow. The gates slammed shut and any chance of getting the number-plate had gone. A minute later, everything turned black as the floodlights went out. By then, he had seen that a high boundary wall, topped with razor-wire, stretched to the turnround to his left. Until the gates opened again, there would be no view of anything of value.

He felt deflated. It was an anti-climax. Nothing to see. Nothing to photo. Perhaps the Range-Rover would leave or something different arrive. He decided to wait. With its wide aperture lens, the Canon's fish-eye needed no flash. Next time, he would be ready.

Maybe he'd spot the elusive Audi A3.
Now wouldn't that be just something.
Knowledge is power, Danny.
Great view of vehicles coming or going.
Give it an hour.
Till 11-30.
I'm invisible.

Except that he *had* been spotted.

Roehampton

A military-grade drone had been in hovering mode six metres above the entrance to Santona Close. It was silent and so tiny as to be almost invisible, even in daylight. Weighing in at only eighteen grams and easily held on a cupped palm, it was equipped with a thermal camera to send back live stream video. Ever since spotting movement, the tiny drone had followed Willison as he had skulked between the shrubs in the park. After he had pushed his way into the flowering bush opposite the gates, it had soared silently over his head. There it had remained, circling just metres above Willison as he chewed noisily on his gum.

Inside Sigwell House, in a high-tech security room, six monitors displayed various shots around the property. One of them was picking up the high-quality feed from the drone, operated by one of two squat but swarthy men. In black T-shirts, their arm muscles on display, they could have passed for all-in wrestlers.

The man controlling the drone had grown increasingly interested in transmitted pictures as a tall figure had scurried ever closer to Sigwell House. Now, both officers were pointing at the monitor, muttering cryptic comments. When the figure had stopped moving, one of them disappeared and returned with a third man. Matching the Albanian flag, he was dressed a red shirt with a black double-headed eagle across the front. He looked at the screen. With a nod of his head, he beckoned one of the men to follow him. The drone-controller continued to circle the drone just above Willison. Before leaving the room, the guy in charge said something and lifted his leather jacket to show his shoulder holster. The other man removed a gun from a drawer and tucked it into the top of his jeans.

Satisfied, the boss led the way.

Roehampton

The first Willison became aware of anyone near him was too late. Startled by movement behind him, he looked round. Almost in touching distance, were two figures. Their faces, concealed by balaclavas, scared him shitless. He yelped and found himself frozen to the spot. "Come out." The accented voice was deep and guttural. "Hands on your head."

For a moment, Willison was tempted to run but as quickly realised that would be hopeless. Even if his legs had not been shaking, he doubted he could escape. Slowly, he pushed his way between the branches, until he was close enough to see faceless men with guns trained at his chest. Then his foot caught in the undergrowth and with his hands clasped on his beanie, he overbalanced and unable to save himself, fell at their feet.

"Get up." The words were accompanied by a swing of a booted foot which caught him on his right cheek and eye. He howled in pain as he started to push himself up. He took another couple of violent kicks into his chest. The pain was instant but, panicked now, he scrambled to his feet, trying to ignore the sharp stabbing pains from chest and head.

His camera was wrenched from his shoulder and next moment, he was being patted down in a swift and professional manner but none too gently. Willison was then part pushed and part jettisoned in a direction away from the safety of his Fiat. With each step, Strang's Scottish accent rang out the warning.

Dinna you go near Sigwell House.

Too late now, Danny.

Occasionally, a gun jabbed into his spine until, after stumbling along the darkened unmade footpath in the park, he was led across the turnaround and pushed through a side-entrance. The door in the wall slammed shut behind him. His captors forced him into a single-storey building that maybe once had been a stable. When the lights came on, Willison saw that he was in a derelict room, stone floor and walls all bare. It smelled damp and unused. Head lowered, he had no wish to stare at the guns and the concealed faces. Only the men's eyes were visible. "Why you here? Why watching? You police?"

"No." His mouth was parched, his throat dry. He struggled even to get the single word out. His legs were quivering, his heart racing.

"So who? Why?" The accent was eastern European. They were barked out and guttural. Willison assumed, and rightly, they were Albanian. That meant… he didn't care to think what that meant. *Dinna give the bastards a chance to identify you. Dinna you go near Sigwell House.* He grappled with what to say that might save his life.

With death staring him in the face, he struggled for a plausible explanation. A thought, any coherent thought would have been welcome. The sight of the brutes with their Lugers had made his throat dry and his brain was in deep-freeze mode...

Deny being a cop.
Deny.
Deny.
Otherwise you're dead.
Which lie was best?
What might save me from a bullet?
I was sent by a rival drug dealer.
Nah! Too risky.

Just a curious snooper?
Laughable, Danny.
Peeping Tom?
Not credible.

He saw the bigger figure swing his Canon on its strap so that it crashed and smashed into a dozen pieces against the bare concrete wall. "Your turn next," the voice rasped from behind the balaclava. "Explain. Now." The last word was barked out just millimetres from the salty blood that was running down Willison's cheek and reaching his lips.

"It's about the new Home Cinema you ordered," Willison improvised. He struggled to get out the words. "My boss wanted to me to check out the customer. Like can the customer afford a fifty thousand installation. Y'know – before extending credit. Is the owner for real or bullshitting?" Willison was amazed where the idea had come from. The words came out as gasps between sharp intakes of breath.

"You're lying." The words were accompanied by a stinging slap across his bloodied cheek. "The boss has a Home Cinema."

Willison swallowed hard as he tried to think on the hoof. He could feel the lid of his right eye closing. His entire face was throbbing. The slightest move caused a sharp pain from his ribs that ripped across his chest.

What had the postmaster said?
Think Danny!
The name!

"The boss said check out Mr Anatoli Federov at Godwyn House." He waited as the men conversed rapidly in their own language. Then he heard a laugh. Was it mocking or taunting? He was unsure. The answer came quickly enough.

"On your knees." Willison saw the bigger man flourish his Luger. "Down. Now."

Putney

It was 8-30 a.m. Standing at the centre of the Incident Room, Ratso was surrounded by generally eager faces, some listeners sitting, some standing. Clutching a large coffee, he walked back and forward as he addressed them. "This is today's update on *Operation Footstool*. Firstly, I put my hands up. My mistake. I was too cautious when I got the detective in Yorkshire to question Terry Yates on a pretext. My concern was about tipping him off. If I'd included all three murder dates, I reckoned he would have smelled stinking fish." To general laughter, a wag called out that *this room stinks like that every evening*.

"Yes – I'd noticed," Ratso said. "Anyway, looking back, maybe I could have got away with selecting a second night." He paused. "Now, I wish I had."

"Is Yates still a front-runner then, guv? The alibi from King's Lynn looks strong." Carole Viment tried, none too well, to keep scepticism from her face and voice.

"In racing lingo, yes by a short head. That's because none of you has given me anything better on Fergus Edwards and his time-shares or on Valbona Jakupi. That includes you, Danny Willison." Ratso looked round for the familiar gingery head and beard.

Viment chimed in. "He's not due in today. He has a day's leave to visit his brother in Southampton. They're going to some religious festival."

"A well-deserved break, I'm sure." A ripple of laughter spread quickly. "We'll need to wait till tomorrow to read the tablets he's brought down from the mountain." He turned to Nancy Petrie. "Your update."

"Do we still assume Goldie was the target and Doyle and Lord Ongerton were just to confuse us?"

"Collateral damage? Yes. That's still my thinking. The Super thinks not. He still believes there's someone out there enjoying murdering gays."

"Has the Super any idea who might be next? Who might end up with the Ace?"

"He suggested it would be some well-known gay."

Strang growled from his seat. "Bigger than Dermot Doyle? You dinna' get much higher."

Ratso was dismissive. "Yes, there is! There's so-called pop royalty. A Premier League footballer. The Royal family. A Cabinet Minister. We can't protect every well-known gay."

"We could warn a short list," Petrie said.

Strang's voice boomed across the room. "Maybe the top-twenty." He grinned around the room. "Total waste of time but we could do it."

"Agreed, Jock. Every gay in Britain is already on red alert." He pointed to Viment. "Carole, you have something?"

"Yesterday afternoon, I interviewed Dermot Doyle's Croatian maid. She lived-in at Ladbroke Grove."

" And…?"

"I showed her a dozen photos of different men. Six were guys we knew visited Dermot Doyle. Six were random."

Not for the first time, Ratso was impressed by her direct and no-nonsense style. Without doubt, she was a rising star. *There'll be trouble if she rises quicker than Nancy Petrie.* "Go on."

"She identified every visitor correctly. The random ones, not." She played to the gallery with a teasing smile and a toss of her hair.

"We knew Ongerton and Patrick Marney had been there to dinner." The broadening smile on Viment's face promised a revelation. "But get this. Ongerton had twice weekended with Doyle ... but not when Marney was around. Once down in Hambleton and once in Ladbroke Grove.

"Homo and Away love-in," prompted DC Searby, a comment prompting a mix of laughs, groans and some disapproving looks. Then the room fell silent as the implications of a motive sunk in. Everyone waited for Ratso's take. He sucked in his narrowed cheeks, then exhaled noisily. "Let's recap. Marney denied he was jealous of Ongerton's looks and charm. He also told us that he didn't care about the young guardsmen."

Strang intervened. "Marney denied that Doyle and Ongerton ever had something going on."

"He would, wouldn't he?" said Bonkale.

Viment laughed. "After leaving the maid, I dropped in on Marney in Eaton Square. I gotta say he gives me the creeps. Those soft sweaty hands and blubbery lips don't help. He said he was shocked at what the maid had told me. Said he didn't believe it."

"Do you believe him?"

"Not yet, boss."

From all of four metres, Ratso lobbed his oversized coffee-cup into the trash-bin. "Marney denied wanting to kill Doyle or Ongerton. Now we have a motive. Not a big one but if he knew Doyle and Ongerton were getting serious? Just maybe ..." He let the words hang in the air.

"Killing two lovebirds with one stone," prompted Strang to more groans and laughs. "But then where does Goldie fit in?"

Ratso acknowledged the valid point with a nod. "Observations anyone?"

"Maybe Goldie was the red herring." Viment had no intention of letting the boss off the hook.

"We know Marney had an alibi for the Ongerton murder," said Petrie.

"Try this" continued Viment. "Marney hired Mr Audi to kill Doyle and Ongerton. Maybe there is a link between Marney and Goldie. We just haven't found it yet."

Ratso did a 360 spin-turn to attract attention. "Thanks, Carole – that was good work but useless for briefing me on Terry Yates's SAS mates. That's still what I want." Those in the audience who knew Ratso well could see this was a serious dig at Viment – about as far as he ever went to a public bollocking. He could smile but still spit bullets.

"Did you hear about Tosh Watson? There's a rumour?"

"More than a rumour. There's some good news. Det. Sgt Tosh Watson has thrown off Covid and is back tomorrow." Happy murmurs spread round the room. Among his peers, Tosh was respected as a guy who would always have your back. His uneasy relationship with the top-brass, for whom he had no respect, endeared him to most but not all. "Jock, get Tosh to go in-depth on social media, blogs. Willison found nothing but revisiting them may be worthwhile." Ratso was tempted to add that *Willison couldn't find the elephant in the room until it trod on his foot* but forced himself to say nothing. "Nancy – dig much deeper into Marney's bank accounts and cash withdrawals. Let's see if he paid a hitman. Or hit-woman."

"Boss, can I discuss Mr Audi?" It was Viment again.

Ratso was already turning away to his office. He was due an update on Hysen Kola. "I've a call to make. Let's reconvene in 20 minutes."

Putney

"Carole, you wanted to talk about Mr Audi. Surrey police are working gradually south-east. The driver never rejoined the M25. He never reached the Dartford Tunnel. That leaves a large sector from Kent to Surrey and West Sussex. If he used a devious route to return to London, we're in trouble. There are insufficient resources to study every major road entering London – until we know which one."

"So Surrey are looking to the south-east?"

"Correct. With Inspector Strang, I met Iqbal." Ratso displayed a map showing Surrey, Kent and Sussex. "There are these six major roads from London to the coast." He used a pointer. "To Worthing, Brighton, Eastbourne, Hastings, Folkestone and finally the A2 to Dover. They're reviewing footage at every junction where Mr Audi had to cross one of them if heading south-east. That's a lot of junctions. So far zilch."

"If he headed west?"

"Time for that team to be given wet towels round heads and double scotches. When they've done the south-east, they'd have to start looking west and then up north." Ratso milked the moment. "Don't look at me! I'm not volunteering to instruct those guys to start over." He laughed yet deadly serious. "Those guys looking at screens, for most of time it's like being blindfolded and asked to search in a dark room for a black cat that isn't there."

"Yup! I did it just for a couple of hours," said DC Angie Riley.

"I felt brain-dead. Numbed. You can see why they make occasional mistakes and don't spot a vital vehicle."

Viment waved her hand, still persistent and eager to contribute. Most of all, she wanted Ratso's attention.

Wanted him to look at me.
Wanted him to see my beauty.
To value my strength of purpose.
Wanted him to want me.
To be with me and not arse-licking Nancy bloody Petrie.

At times like this, as he commanded the room, she found it hard not to lust after the tight curve of his buttocks and the unspoken air of authority that oozed from him.

Why the hell doesn't he admire my buttocks?
My breasts?
My breasts and buttocks are all perfectly formed.
What does he see in Nancy Petrie?
Fawning around her.
Sweeping her away to Hereford and Oxford.
Shagging her something rotten.

"I'm listening, Carole."

"Boss, Terry Yates lives in Yorkshire. Mr Audi, if he's the guy who killed Lord Ongerton, came from the south-east. There's nothing linking Mr Audi to a cricketer in North Yorkshire with a fake gammy leg." She saw several people looking uneasy at her challenge but she continued. "If, alternatively, Mr Audi was hired by Marney, why are we still in-depthing on Yates?"

If Ratso was irritated, he managed to conceal it well. "Okay, Carole. You're correct. Mr Audi could have headed north after murdering Ongerton – using any one of dozens of minor roads without cameras. As to Terry Yates I'm not ready to give up on him. Not till *you've* finished checking his SAS contacts. How is that progressing?"

Ratso was still fuming that she had gone off-piste to interview the Croatian maid. True, she'd got a great result but her orders had been to track down the mates from the SAS. He watched her nervously shuffle her dainty feet before answering. "Not easy boss. These guys, they've scattered all over. But boss, I don't get the importance."

After sensing her discomfort, Ratso continued. "What is *important* is whatever I say is *important* – whether I am right or wrong. Everybody? Listen up." He looked round the group who sensed that Ratso was furious. "The playing-cards point to one serial killer." He waved his right arm at the white-board. "But did the same person leave each card?" He saw jaws drop, eyes widen and pennies drop all round him as the message sank in. He pointed now directly at Viment. "That, Carole, is why I urgently need your input on Terry Yates's SAS contacts."

Face flushed and oozing even more sex appeal than ever, Viment tossed her head and hair before continuing. With every word, her eyes showed defiance. "I'm onto it boss," but she tilted her head and curled her mouth in disdain. "I'm onto it because you say so. But the fact is there's still no evidence Yates lost even one penny, let alone millions in Energy Management."

Viment looked round the rows of listeners and saw a variety of reactions.

Sod it!

I'll go on.

Her shrug was both defiant and dismissive as she threw down the gauntlet, her mocking laugh showing her contempt for Ratso's theory. "There's no evidence he was even a shareholder. You've given me no evidence he was a loser from EMA. On the *evidence*,

Emma was a Geordie slapper with a skirt that barely covered her arse who conned millions from the randy old sod. So boss, here's my question. Why am I wasting time checking out his old SAS chums if we don't know he was a loser and had no motive to kill Goldie. Premature, don't you think?"

The listeners were stunned. The room fell silent, broken only by the occasional horn being sounded in the rush-hour traffic. Nobody had ever before confronted the boss at a full team meeting. But Ratso's reaction was an anti-climax, just firm and in point. "Just get it done and pretty damned smartish." Ratso's eyes emerged from beneath the lids to skewer her. He was ready to play a trump card. "You'll know why after Nancy has updated everybody." He looked to where Petrie was eating her health-kick breakfast of sunflower, pumpkin and chai seeds mixed with oat-milk, banana and stewed apple.

Petrie laid down her spoon. "The boss and I met Jamie Fargher, the Company Secretary of Energy Management. There was no surviving record of Yates ever signing in as an attendee at any AGMs He didn't know and couldn't tell us if Terry Yates was even a shareholder. That much was true but we were sure, he was holding something back."

Ratso smiled a bullet in Viment's direction "But get this. Fargher thought the face was familiar. True, that's not enough to arrest him. Not yet." Ratso closed in on the white-board and pointed to each line of enquiry in turn. Earlier, I said Yates was in front by a short head. I haven't changed my view. But the rest of you – keep the foot to the pedal on all lines of enquiry."

Petrie nodded agreement. "All three directors had a bigger motive to murder Goldie than anyone. One director is Molly Bishop. Maybe she wore the flowery dress."

"Nancy, tell them what you asked Jamie Fargher at EMA."

Deadly Hush

"Being pig-ignorant ..."

"But not pig-ugly like Marney," someone chipped in.

"Pig-ignorant," repeated Petrie. "I asked whether investors always obeyed the law about disclosing if they owned 3% of public company shares." She spread her arms wide. "The answer is no. Maybe Terry Yates bought shares using different companies. None of them over 3%. Using just three companies, he could have owned nearly 9% and nobody would have known."

Ratso clapped his hands for attention. "Okay. We're going to prove Terry Yates was a big loser in EMA and wanted revenge against Goldie. By obtaining court orders against banks and brokers, you're going to help me prove it."

"And Mr Audi?" Viment's demure smile and unusual little-girl-lost tone was lost on nobody but had been aimed at Ratso.

"So for now, Mr Audi remains our focus. Linking him to smarmy Marney or Terry Yates is essential." He paused for effect. "Although we can't discount what goodies DC Willison will have discovered about Valbona Jakupi."

Petrie waited till the laughter had died down before waving her hand for attention. "There's a shareholder meeting in London next month. Yates may be there."

"Thanks, Nancy. Hopefully we'll have an arrest long before then. Thanks everyone." As the attendees disappeared in different directions, Ratso summoned Nancy, Carole, Jock and Bonkale to his office. "With Tosh coming back tomorrow and my birthday the next day, be my guests that evening at The Shard. 7pm. He'll join us."

Amidst the smiles and thanks, Ratso spotted a flicker of concern cross Bonkale's face but all agreed to be there. "Excellent. No shop-talk. Deal?"

They all nodded.

It was not going to be quite like that.

Roehampton

Ten hours previously, as one of the captors had spat out the command for him to kneel down, Danny Willison had done so. His knees trembling and hands shaking, the order was almost welcome. As he eased himself down, wincing from the pain in his ribs, the flagstone floor felt cold and hard. The blood was still trickling down and his lips tasted salty. Yet again, he cursed himself for ignoring the warnings.

This is how it all ends, Danny.
One mistake.
Now curtains.
Nearer to Jesus and eternal life.
Please God!
Not what I wanted so soon.

He started whimpering. Knees close together and sitting on his haunches, he shut his eyes as if that would help. With difficulty, he raised his hands in front of his face in silent prayer. He heard one of the gunmen move to stand behind him. The metal of the Luger was unmistakable. It felt so cold pressed just above the nape of his hot and throbbing neck.

"Don't," Willison simpered. "I'm nothing to you. Please don't." His voice now rose to sound shrill and strident. "I was just … only doing my job. Checking credit."

"Shut it."

Silence fell except for Willison's laboured breathing.

"On the count of three."

Again a long pause. Then Willison heard "One... Two... Three." The trigger clicked and then nothing. The magazine had been removed. The captors both roared with laughter at their joke. "Next time, fucker, you get the right house. Now get up!"

Willison felt a boot slam into his buttocks. Only his outstretched hands saved him from toppling over as he struggled to stand. From his wet hands, he realised that the dusty floor had now been soaked by his freefall piss. With slow movements, he eased himself to a stooped position. Then, as he tried to straighten, a searing, burning pain ripped across his ribs.

"Move. Now!" Like it or not, another prod of the gun propelled him on his journey, this time towards the main gates. Willison realised that his right eye was now completely closed. Every step was painful and his whole body was shrieking at him to stop. *Fat chance of that.*

As they crossed the eighty metres to the gates, they swung open. The entire area was bathed in light. To Willison's left, he saw Valbona Jakupi's home. Short of Buckingham Palace, it was the grandest place he had ever seen. All that was missing was a platoon of soldiers in their busbies and a marching band.

Heroin and cocaine had bought every brick.

"Go! Next time, find the right house you stupid fucker." In guttural broken English the words still carried menace. A boot lashed into his left thigh. He stumbled and tottered into the darkened street like a drunk at chucking-out-time. It took him nearly twenty agonising minutes to reach his car. Stooping to retrieve the keys made him wince but somehow, he made it. Panting, he sat motionless in the car for several minutes before firing up the engine. Home was a fifteen-minute journey. There, hungry with no take-away, mentally and physically drained and stinking of stale sweat and piss, he showered till the water ran cold.

It didn't help the pain.

Afterwards, in the muted colours of his bedsit, he gulped down three Ibuprofen. Through a tormented night, with just occasional moments of dozing, he stared at the ceiling, playing and replaying the count to three. Eventually, exhausted, he fell asleep as commuters started their crawl to work.

When he awoke at 9-40 a.m. he felt as if he had never slept at all. The bloodied sheets wrapped round him were soaked. Fearful of moving and concerned he must look like a boxer after ten bruising rounds, he lay still, his mind in turmoil. Very gently, he raised his hand to feel his eye but was forced to stop as a searing pain ripped through his chest. But he had to reach the phone. No choice. He sent a text to his brother cancelling his trip to the Beach and Bible-Reading Barbecue.

At least I'm not due at Jubilee House.

It was gone eleven before he struggled to the bathroom. A glance in the mirror proved his worst fears. Under his slit of an eye, the swollen skin was yellow and deep purple. He downed more Ibuprofen wishing it could kill the memory of kneeling on the floor, expecting to die.

Forget that, Danny.
Tomorrow
That's your biggest worry.
Explaining your beaten-up face to Jock Strang.
Admit I defied orders.
Admit that?
Impossible.
Don't tell him.

Deadly Hush

Lie to him?
Invent something.
Against all my beliefs?
No choice, Danny!
Needs must!
Forgive me, God.

The Shard – London SE1

The team, now including Det. Sgt. Tosh Watson, met at the foot of the elevators that were going to speed them to the top of The Shard, the UK's tallest building. While they waited, Ratso mentioned that he had been up before with Kirsty-Ann. "72 floors. Over one thousand feet."

"Our tour-guide, are you? Expect a tip?" Strang laughed as they piled inside. Only Bonkers seemed hesitant. As the elevator raced skywards, Ratso saw his eyes were tight shut and his fists were clenched. In their excitement, nobody else noticed. After the elevator glided to a halt, Ratso held back to put an arm round Bonkers' shoulder. With a nod of the head he motioned Jock to take charge. "You lot go on. Take in the view. We'll join you in a mo."

Ratso shepherded Bonkers in a different direction until they were distanced from the throng of visitors. "Problem? Tell me."

For answer the youngster turned and buried his head on Ratso's chest, his shoulders now heaving as he sobbed.

"Take it easy, lad. No rush. Tell me what you want – if you want."

Maybe a minute had passed before Bonkers raised his glistening wet face and looked Ratso in the eye. "I'm sorry, boss. I'm spoiling your birthday."

"Nonsense. Something big is troubling you."

Bonkers took a step away but never looked down. He spoke slowly as if every word was being dragged from him. "I've never been up this high in a building. I'm not scared, boss. But your invitation. I was so proud to be asked. I was determined to enjoy it and to put aside ..." He faltered as his eyes started to well up again. Then he bit his lip.

As he fought for control, he dabbed his face with a red hankie. "My father worked in international finance. He flew from Ghana to New York for a three-day visit. On 11th September 2001, he was in a breakfast meeting on top of the World Trade Center. He ... he never came back." Struggling to avoid a further meltdown, he paused before forcing himself to carry on. "They say ... he jumped." He dabbed his eyes again and then produced his wallet with a photo of a fine-looking man, aged barely thirty. His face radiated happiness and a young Lumo Bonkale was at his feet.

"I'm so, so sorry. He looked like he was a great dad, a fun dad."

"I was only young when he died. But yes. I remember playing in the park. Riding on his shoulders, y'know."

"You did well to come. It can't have been easy. I can't imagine what every 9-11 anniversary must mean to you – let alone being up here. Would you like to go home. I'll pick up your cab fare."

"Thanks but I want to stay. I must get through this."

"Do you want me to say anything? Say nothing?"

"Will you please? But not with me there. I'll go to the Gents. When I join you, I won't spoil your party."

Ratso gave him a huge hug.

By the time Bonkers reappeared, Ratso had explained everything. Jock and Tosh said nothing. Both simply grasped his shoulders in solidarity. After the two women had given him loving hugs, Ratso suggested they head for Gŏng, where he had a reservation. In there, as they absorbed the view, normality returned but only slowly.

"The Tour Guide bit again," Ratso chipped in. "We're now in the highest bar in Europe." They all looked around at the cossetting colours of reds, browns, grey and charcoal that created an immediate warm and friendly ambience. "Glad to be back then, Tosh?"

"*You'll* be glad I'm back. I've a very special birthday present, guv."

"Not pork scratchings then."

"Them were the days. Down at the Swan & Duck in Clapham. This is a bit posher than piss-ups in them days. I remember celebrating your birthday with a few pints, watching pole-dancers with huge, implanted knockers. Then we'd treat ourselves to a couple of bags of Cheese & Onion crisps."

Ratso's eyes acknowledged the old days. For a moment, he was back in the sleazy pub on the Balham High Road. "The best thing about those Clapham days was bringing down Boris Zandro." But even as he said the name, the pleasure of the recollection was lost. Hysen Kola was still somewhere in London.

"This joint?" Tosh continued as two bottles of Perrier Jouet champagne served in elegant ice-buckets appeared beside them. "Must be your huge salary after promotion." He grinned like a schoolkid. "Mind I'm not complaining." He looked round the plush surroundings and then pointed to the menu. "Spiced Nori? Chicken Gyoza? You reckon they can do me jellied eels followed by pie and mash served on a chipped plate like the Swan & Duck?"

"For you, Tosh. Just for you."

"Nah! I'm kidding. I'm eating less junk these days. Bloody Covid really did for me."

Ratso looked around the team. They were seated by a window looking across the lights now appearing all over Central London. "Listen up! Raise your glasses. When you were in Intensive Care, you had us worried. The toast is welcome back."

"Aye but can I add this," Strang grinned. "There's a lot less to like about you."

Watson grinned. "Three stone and four pounds to be precise."

"I only saw you run once," Ratso nodded "and that was to get into the King's Head at closing-time."

"That's fat-shaming, boss but I'll ignore it. Remember when the Met wanted to sort out, er …fatties like me?" He laughed, head rocking back. "Without Covid, I'd never have done it."

Strang leaned in close. "I'm missing your turkey-neck but ye must like seeing your knob again without a mirror. That must've been like meeting an old friend after twenty years." Strang was rewarded with a playful punch and a loud laugh.

"How's your lovely wife Patsy?" enquired Ratso, thinking quite the reverse. He rated her the most poisonous woman he had ever met – and then some.

"When I was in Intensive, my daughter said that Patsy had checked the life-insurance and had been singing *Oh Happy Day*."

Strang raised his glass. "And changed to Michael's Jackson's *Beat It* when you came home."

"There were no yellow ribbons round the door, that's for sure."

"You all heard about Danny?" Petrie was eager to move on.

Ratso's face showed a wary and tumbling cascade of emotions. "Go on."

"He pulled a sickie."

" What's up? Man Flu?" prompted Viment.

"Watch it, Carole," Ratso teased. "That's sexist. Take a look at the *Equality, Diversity and Inclusivity Guidelines*."

"Danny tripped on a kerb," Nancy continued. "Badly bruised face and ribs. He hopes to come in tomorrow. He told me nobody must make him laugh. Not till his ribs are better."

"More likely he'll make us weep as usual," muttered Strang.

"Boss, can I break your rule about no shop-talk?" Tosh leaned forward looking intent. "It's my birthday present to you."

"I'm intrigued."

"You wanted me to bring a clear head, to the investigation."

"I reckon the boss meant your empty head," Strang joked with a friendly punch.

"Ignore this Scottish haggis-murderer! Guv, you wanted me to trawl the web about Energy Management. Right?"

"Yes. Willison had found nothing. I wanted a second bite." Ratso wagged a stern finger across the table. "Promise me your present is better than those wind-up-and-go chattering false-teeth you gave me three years ago."

"Trust me, guv. This is a game-changer."

Battersea SW11

Reckoning that he needed to look like most other Londoners wandering the streets south of the river, Hysen Kola was heading for Borough Market. His route took him close to The Shard. Unknown to him, his target was sipping champagne nearly 1,000 feet above him.

It was early evening, a time when back in Tirana, he would be downing beers outside a street café with the rest of the gang. They might be talking girls or whether to drop by Club Mexico or L'Arena. More often, though, the discussions were of the latest drug deal or plotting to teach a lesson to any chancers daring to enter their turf.

The previous day, Kola had taken a bus to a fancy-dress shop on Kensington High Street. He had bought sideburns, a wig and two styles of beard in different shades of brown and grey. His plan was to be as quickly forgotten as he was seen. Now, after walking several miles along drab and nondescript streets south of the river, he saw what he needed. He had not found what he wanted in Borough Market. Eventually, he spotted a pop-up charity shop off the New Kent Road. Although he was more used to buying silk ties, finest cotton shirts and lightweight suits, he enjoyed rummaging through much-used jackets, windcheaters, thick woollen shirts, T-Shirts, overalls and dozens of pairs of faded jeans.

From them, he selected a variety. He avoided the used beanies in the colours of London's Premier League teams. *Too likely to start a conversation or be remembered.* He opted instead for a forgettable grey one and another in dark blue. He also selected a black cap with a curved peak. Satisfied, he left in a rather worn denim jacket and stuffed the rest into his rucksack.

Tomorrow it would be Putney High Street.

The Shard – London SE1

Tosh saw that he had everybody's attention. "I found a blogsite where shareholders in any company can rant – usually effing and blinding about the directors. Mainly it's a load of bollocks – vile garbage. So I was reading that Goldie had screwed up a Placing."

"Correct. He crashed the price. To survive and drill, the directors had to raise money on *death spiral* terms."

"I traced back. That new finance came from Geneva." He pulled a slip of paper from his jacket-pocket. "The finance was from a business called Laterre-Quercy Private Family Office."

"Okay."

"The boss, Jules Quercy was murdered." Tosh enjoyed seeing the jaw-dropping looks. For a moment there was total silence, almost a deadly hush, as everybody absorbed the game-changer.

At last, Petrie broke the silence. "Holy shit."

Ratso's jaw stiffened and his eyes narrowed, his face suddenly wolfish as if his prey was in sight. "Why in hell didn't Willison spot this? When did it happen?"

"Several weeks back."

"Was there a playing-card?"

"Pass!" Tosh raised his glass and emptied it with gusto and held it out for a refill.

"Why murder him?"

"He was a hate-figure on this blogsite. Shareholders called him Shylock. Extremist anti-oil activists threatened him for helping out the directors. He then promised to end the loan. That caused more outrage and more death threats."

"It's coming back to me." Ratso rubbed his hand across his mouth, deep in thought. "I read about a Swiss financier being murdered. The media linked it to criminals from Russia or Belarus."

"They got it wrong then," said Carole Viment.

"Some of these extremists are … well… extreme," Petrie agreed. "So we have angry shareholders and angry activists."

Tosh motioned to silence her. "There's more. I haven't finished."

"More?"

"Guv, The same blogsite mentioned that anti-oil activists had started a lawsuit against EMA to stop drilling. That really buggered the share price. That was the last nail in the company's coffin."

"Not quite accurate but go on."

"The wealthy oil protesters hired a lawyer to stop the drilling- Kendall Campbell KC. He was a local."

Ratso jumped on the word. "*Was*? You said *was*?"

"Yes, guv. Campbell has also been murdered."

Ratso reached for the second bottle and topped up all round. "If I get my hands on him, Willison will be next. How in hell's name did he not spot this!"

"Where did this happen?" enquired Viment.

"Bonnitor. Out in the Caribbean." Watson gave a knowing look to Jock and Ratso. "Remember those guys from the Royal Bonnitor Constabulary. We had to teach them Met Policing techniques – DNA, scenes of crime protection and the rest."

"Aye! I mind it fine! Dinna bet on them solving anything. They were more interested in the Soho girlie-dens and playing blackjack at the Hippodrome Casino."

"Strange that Jamie Fargher never mentioned either of these deaths," Viment said.

Ratso offered round some savoury snacks and helped himself. "Agreed." Ratso's frown was etched deep. "Maybe this is what Fargher was holding back." He placed both hands on the table and leaned forward. "His silence means the directors must join Terry Yates in the frame."

Viment's nose wrinkled as she fought to look apologetic. It did not come easily. "Boss, I owe you an apology. Seems you've been right about Goldie and Yates. EMA is the link."

Ratso's face broke into a conciliatory smile. "About Goldie? Yes. About Yates? There's a way to go. He was in King's Lynn when Dermot Doyle was murdered. But no apology needed. It's not healthy everyone singing in unison." He rose from the table. "Time to eat. Time to celebrate. And no more shop." He clapped Watson on the back. "Great job, Tosh. One helluva birthday present."

Strang's hefty figure blocked out the sunset as he rose to his full height. "Right enough," he grinned. "But how about a late birthday present tomorrow? Kicking Willison's arse so hard he lands in Bonnitor."

"Willison has lost us days – well, nearly two weeks." Ratso looked grim for a moment before brightening. "Come on. Let's forget that twerp. I feel a good bottle of red coming on."

Fulham SW6

Ratso had changed his route to work yet again. He descended the worn wooden stairs at Putney Bridge Tube Station having detoured via Earl's Court. As he exited, a stiff breeze from the Thames was swirling round the enclave of small shops and food outlets. Almost at once he saw Jonno. With his arms clasped round his knees, he was sitting on a torn blue sleeping-bag with a grey blanket for cover. In front of him was a small box for any loose change.

"You've crossed the river, Jonno. Moving up in the world, are you? Posher clientele?"

"Mr Todd. I ain't ever seen you tubing it to here."

"Change of air for us both."

"This is a good pitch mornings. Putney Hill is better afternoons. The shoppers."

Ratso looked at the few bits of small change in the box. "Had a bite yet?"

"I can't move from here till after rush-hour."

"I'll fix that." Ratso crossed the road to the welcoming warmth of a greasy spoon café. He returned with a bacon bap and a dark brown tea. From his wallet, he slipped Jonno a tenner which was quickly stuffed into a pocket of his thin green shirt. "Since Covid, not many of us carry cash. Buy yourself something warmer. It'll soon be autumn."

Jonno raised his gnarled fingers in something between a wave and a salute. "Cheers. God bless you squire."

"See you soon, pal." Ratso hurried away, his thoughts immediately turning to meeting Caldwell. His mind went back to something Bonkale had asked him at The Shard. It was a puzzle and he had been unable to answer. "Bonkers, the truth is that Caldwell never mentions his private life. He wants to feel he has control. Letting down his guard about anything personal, he would see as weakness."

"So married? Kids? Bachelor? He has a flash car. Big inheritance?"

Ratso had shrugged. "Never mentioned. Almost nobody has ever probed. He has no small talk. I did hear that a sergeant once asked about his personal life."

"And?"

"He was told to mind his own effing business." With a familiar shoulder shrug, Ratso had ended the conversation. "I don't recommend you asking." There had been laughter all round when Jock Strang had suggested that Danny Willison be encouraged to ask.

Later, that morning, after leaving Caldwell spluttering over his Earl Grey tea, Ratso updated his inner circle when they gathered in his room. "First time I've had Caldwell even close to silenced. When I told him of the murder of the Swiss banker and the Bonnitor lawyer, he sat stunned. He never said sorry. Never admitted it wasn't gay-bashing. Never acknowledged that I was right. After he'd got over the shock, he gave me a bollocking for not discovering these other murders sooner."

"What next?" asked Tosh Watson,

"I explained that neither murder had been solved and I could now join the dots. It was grudging but he's approved my Geneva trip but not Bonnitor. He told me I could use Microsoft Teams for that."

"As if," Petrie agreed. "Mind you, the SIO is normally chained to his desk. Filling in reports, not jetting off."

"Sod that! I'd already decided. I'm going to Bonnitor at my own expense. I've told Bastien Venables I'm coming. He promised me red-carpet treatment – repaying me for his training with us."

"Stopping in Florida, are you guv?" Jock maintained a poker face.

"You could say that Florida is coming to me. Kirsty-Ann will join me in Bonnitor for a day or two." He turned to Watson. "Anything else?"

"Bad news. No playing-cards in Geneva or Bonnitor. The KC was clubbed to death. The banker had a violent neck injury."

"Whatever way the KC was murdered, I don't believe in coincidence."

"Maybe you could meet Fergus Edwards in Barbados?"

Ratso made a note. "Won't do any harm but Olly, Molly and Jamie Fargher are tops."

"Maybe Fergus was a shareholder?" suggested Bonkale.

"I'll ask. Good idea."

"But still no Ace played." Watson looked round for comments but there were no takers.

"Other updates for me?"

Nancy nodded. "Boss, the Olly and Molly Show has moved on from Morocco. Jamie Fargher phoned me. They are in ... Bonnitor."

"Perfect but bye-bye to another day of my R&R."

Strang leaned his bulk against the window. "I got this yesterday. An ex-SAS sergeant told me. Close-combat training includes how to deliver instant death."

"Thanks, Jock. Nancy? Anything more?"

"Boss, Campbell KC was extreme marmite. The have-nots loved him. The people close to Government found him as welcoming as an angry hornet. He had plenty of enemies, so his murder might be coincidence."

Ratso's chopped hand dismissed coincidence. "I'll find out what Detective Inspector Bastien Alleyne knows. He's been promoted since he was here in London."

"Good luck with that," Strang's laugh was dismissive. "Nice guy but he couldna find his arse with a torch and map."

New Scotland Yard SW1

"This is DCI Todd Holtom." Wensley Hughes introduced Ratso to Det. Insp Reg Gastrell as he poured coffees.

"Sorry, Todd," said Gastrell. "There's still no trace of Kola. At least with you off travelling, he'll be wasting his time."

"Nab him before my return then." Ratso eyed each listener in turn. "Reg, I know this isn't easy. The guy's a lone operator."

"Which makes him a danger," Gastrell agreed. "Nobody is gonna snitch."

"What pisses me off are these precautions – y'know changing my route, my routines. Time-wasting."

Gastrell's eyes met Ratso's. "We're looking for one man in a city of nine-million." With his flat Midlands accent, Gastrell did not radiate enthusiasm or confidence. Ratso nodded. He knew that Wensley Hughes rated Gastrell but on first impressions, Ratso reckoned he would have been well-suited to using a loud-hailer shouting *we're all doomed, we're all doomed – the end of the world is nigh.*

"We were sure Zandro had a mole. Either somewhere in the Met or the Home Office. Uncle Boris Zandro will have briefed Kola that I am based at Jubilee House. Kola probably has my home address and the size of my shirts, socks and underwear. These are your clues on where to arrest him." He made sure that Hughes was still with him before adding. "Your nine million can drop to just one professional hitman."

"We will maintain surveillance. You're away. Kola doesn't know that."

Ratso's eyes showed he was unconvinced. "Maybe he knows exactly where I'm going. That's if Zandro's mole is still operating."

Hughes leaned across the table. "I'm with Todd on this. Kola may know Todd's away. That depends on where Mr Mole is tunnelling."

Gastrell continued as if nothing had been said. "Kola will be watching, trying to work out where to make the hit."

"The hit is easy. Getting away isn't," Ratso interrupted.

"We've watched Jubilee House and Putney High Street every day."

Ratso's tone softened. "Your team has done well. I've never spotted them."

Ravensworth - North Yorkshire

"Zoe! Great to hear from you." Terry Yates sounded more enthusiastic than he felt.

I hope she's not pregnant.
Or a MeToo money-grabber.
About to drag me through the Sunday tabloids.
Heh! How did she get my number?

Yates never shared his phone-number with women he had bedded. Then he remembered. Since Covid, the Merry Harriers Leisure Park insisted on a number – a legacy of *Track & Trace*. "How are you doing? All well?"

"Doing just great Terry. When you coming to see me?"

"Zoe darling, King's Lynn? I'm so busy with my business. But, for you, I could be tempted. We had great times." *If she's not pregnant, why the call*? He fought back the urge to ask but she was straight into her message anyway.

"Like we had a couple of cops here the other day. Detectives they was. Asking about when you was here."

"They think I nicked some spoons?" Yates tried to sound flippant but his brain was racing in other directions.

"It was Jess who spoke to them. Nearly an hour, it was."

"About me? That's strange." Yates tried not to sound that interested.

"Jess said they wanted to know what you did while staying here. Who you hung out with. Y'know the scene."

"Me? I'm confused. With my leg trouble, I didn't do much. I wasn't even able to use the dance-floor."

"There was one particular night they was asking Jess about." Zoe's voice showed her tension. "Not that first night when you ... well us, ... when we went to your motor-home. Jess doesn't know about that ... not anything about us. But ..."

Terry remembered that night very well. Zoe had rated an eight.

"The next night, you was like playing darts so I went home. But on your third night ..."

Terry had no problem recalling her arrival for her second visit. Under her coat, she had been wearing a skimpy nurse's outfit with black stockings and crotchless red panties Several vodka and Red Bulls later, he had rated her a nine, nearly a ten. "Fun times. Great memories, Zoe."

"For me too," Zoe spoke wistfully. "You promised to take me to Paris."

"Not forgotten," Yates lied. "Maybe in October."

"Jess reckoned the night they was interested in was the middle night."

"When I was playing in a darts match?"

"That's what Jess told them. Then they asked about the next morning."

"Next morning?"

"Like, she showed them a booking. You and your mates were watching TV."

"You're right. The cricket. So what were the coppers interested in? I don't get it."

"Routine enquiries they said. From London, they was." She paused. "You in trouble Terry?"

He laughed. "Me? No. Just gobsmacked. Thanks for telling me. Great to hear from you. If you find out what this is all about, give us a bell."

"Let me know dates for Paris in October. We was great together."

"You naughty little Florence Nightingale!" Yates's throaty chuckle was genuine enough. "We'll take the Eurostar. First Class of course," he lied convincingly before blowing her a kiss and ending the call.

As he waited for the kettle to brew some English Breakfast Tea, he circled his kitchen. Head lowered, eyes fixed on the burnt-orange tiles, he struggled to understand.

That Detective Wansdyke.
Those questions about Yiannis Bakirtzis.
That had seemed kosher.
Back then.
But now?
Maybe not.
Those dates.
I confirmed King's Lynn.

He carried his tea in a mug bearing the MCC crest. On the way, he grabbed a couple of hobnobs. The postman had just delivered a clutch of mail. He picked it up and took it through to his office. A quick glance told him it was the usual crap – a letter from his bank, credit card bills and a couple of Final Demands. He slammed everything onto a spike with a dozen more.

Casting aside thoughts of the mail, he went to the conservatory. At noon on a sunny day, it was almost too hot. He opened a couple of windows before settling back in a well-padded Conran Chaise Longue. As he sipped his tea, he watched a couple of rabbits and a grey squirrel scamper and frolic on the immaculate lawn. Then, puzzled, he closed his eyes.

What did the cops think they knew?

Putney

"**You reckon it's** time to visit Terry Yates?" asked Carole Viment. She looked up to catch his eyes, intensively aware of his presence.

Ratso was perched on the corner of her desk, his suede jacket slung over his shoulder. "Tempting but we still have no evidence he owned any shares." He grinned. "That was a point you made rather forcefully as I recall. We've nothing to link Yates to the scene of any of the three murders. Five if you count those from abroad. I need your report pronto on Terry Yates's ex-SAS mates. How's that going?"

"Painful. Guys like them don't just settle down into cosy suburbia. I've eliminated several as useless. Major Tang at Hereford will give me no help because of Data Protection laws. Military Protocols, the usual bollocks."

"Right now, my bet is one of these mates owns an Audi A3. That's the guy you've gotta find for me."

"Boss, you've news on where the Audi had been parked."

"When Doyle was murdered, our latest info is that an Audi was parked at a B&B not far from Ladbroke Grove. It left there just after 4 a.m. The number-plate was false but different to the one on the M25. The B&B caters for sales reps or crew setting up events at Olympia. It had four bedrooms. It was full and no occupant had registered an Audi. All guests have been quizzed and cleared."

"Which way did it go?"

"South to the Bayswater Road. At Hyde Park Corner, it headed south again and into that mass of small streets behind Victoria Station. It did not cross the Thames at Vauxhall Bridge or any bridge near there. The trail went cold." Ratso's face showed his disappointment and Viment resisted an urge to place a comforting hand on his.

"Heading south? That's one-hundred percent wrong for King's Lynn."

"And flowery dress? Last seen in the crowds of Leicester Square. Still hitting the buffers, are we?"

"Inspector Strang told me twenty minutes ago. No change."

"For killing Dermot Doyle, in theory, Yates could have raced to London after darts. Murdered Doyle and been back for breakfast."

"But not in his Rapido. Not by Aston-Martin. And he had no Audi."

Ratso's stomach rumbled and they both laughed. "That's me looking enviously at your Cinnamon Slice." Viment cut it in half with a plastic knife and he helped himself. "Thanks! I'll repay."

A kiss would do nicely, she thought.

He wiped some pastry from his mouth. "This bribe, delicious and gratefully received, cuts no ice with the slow progress on the SAS mates. Tell me what you've got."

"I've in-depthed six of his mates. Two worked on the ships for Mbesa Security. They were both at sea during every murder."

"Could Yates discover you were checking? Finding out he's a suspect could be disastrous."

She leaned forward revealing more cleavage. "Sleep easy on that boss. No chance." She tapped her screen. "One was killed in Brunei. Two run a clay-pigeon shoot in Cornwall. They own an old van and a pair of Honda motorbikes. Another is in Singapore providing personal protection for a billionaire."

"Keep going – but quicker." Ratso eased himself off the corner of her desk and stretched as he yawned. A slimline Tosh Watson walked by, wearing a shirt and sleeveless waistcoat. Unusually, his cheery face was troubled. His forehead was crinkled by a frown and his broad shoulders were hunched and almost stooped. "Tosh, that shirt's louder than a plumber's radio!"

"Jealous? At least Caldwell appreciates a bit of high-fashion." Watson's face returned to hang-dog. "A word, boss?"

"Here?"

The sergeant shook his head. Ratso led Tosh to his corner office. "Getting into the swing again?"

"Feels like I've never been away. Loving it till this morning."

"And?"

"Look boss, I'm not a snitch. We all cock things up. Shit happens. But I feel I gotta tell you but I don't feel good about it."

"Go on." Ratso folded his arms across his chest as if protecting himself from an onslaught.

"It's about Valbona Jakupi."

"Yes."

"Yesterday evening, you and Jock instructed me to visit her in Roehampton."

"Yes. About her losses in WPCoin, the disappearance of Hanna Farkas and Goldie's murder."

"Here's my take." The look on Watson's face was intent. "A bitch like Valbona Jakupi? She wouldn't leave playing-cards. She's a mobster's daughter. Mobsters don't mess with that crap. They don't play mind-games. Don't leave no clues. Her thugs would kill to get a job done."

Ratso stared down through the darkened glass window at two red buses jammed in the traffic waiting near the bridge to cross the Thames. "You're right, Tosh. We more or less knew that. Even so, I wanted every possible line of enquiry closed off." Ratso offered

Watson a biscuit which he declined. "But that's not why you wanted to see me."

"Nah! I was going to Jakupi tomorrow. Anyway, I asked Danny Willison to come with me." Watson lowered his eyes and seemed more interested in an imaginary speck of dust on his colourful shirt than in continuing. Ratso remained silent. "Willison made excuse after excuse why he couldn't join me. They were bollocks, the lot of them. Y'know almost like he was too busy trimming his Gran's ingrown toenail. I told him straight – you're effing coming with me – end of."

"So he agreed?"

"He stormed off. Big-time huff. I cornered him later and banged down my foot. That's when he broke down, a gibbering bloody wreck he was. So I took him for a walk by the river."

"What's his problem besides being useless?"

"He fessed up. Those injuries? He never did trip. Never fell. He had been snooping round Valbona's place. Got caught and was beaten up by her bodyguards."

Ratso's face darkened. His entire face from hairline to chin looked fit to explode. His beaky nose seemed bigger, his eyes more prominent and the already narrowing chin, looked sharpened to a point. "I'll get him in," he growled.

Putney

Ratso looked at the list of names handed over by Bonkale. "So these are the top-twenty gay icons that could trigger the Ace." He showed the list to Tosh Watson who was still with him. "I'll pass this to Smart Alex. This is what he wanted but it's academic now. Least, I think so. Waste of time. It's subjective" He looked at the list. "Mine would be different." He pointed to a name. "Would you volunteer to tell a member of the Royal Family he's the likely Ace? He thinks his bi-sexuality is a secret. Probably, even his wife doesn't know. Anyway, we can't protect all twenty. Can't wrap them in cotton-wool. Shelve it. What else have you got?"

"We've tracked down twenty-eight bloggers who posted hate against Goldie. None could have murdered him. They all denied being in his pay. We haven't dug deeper on that. Not yet."

"Quite right. For now, a waste of resources."

"There's another seventeen as yet untraced."

"Thanks Bonkers." He waited for him to leave and then called Willison's number. "Come in. Now." He motioned to Watson to take a seat.

Ratso had barely put down the phone before the ginger-haired figure appeared, the area around his eye still yellow and blue. "Remain standing. What in hell's name were you doing? Disobeying Inspector Strang's specific orders."

"Using my initiative, boss. Didn't see no harm in sizing up the enemy." Willison hopped from foot to foot.

"You marched up to the front-entrance and asked to have a look round. Suggested you wanted cocktails with Jakupi?" The sarcasm was lost on Willison.

For the first time, he raised his eyes. "Never went near the entrance, boss. I was behind trees and shrubs in the park when two armed thugs pounced. It was impossible to see me."

"After your bullshit story about tripping and falling, how can I believe a single word you say? If it was impossible, how did they catch you?"

"Dunno."

"It was beyond stupid!" The words were spat out with contempt, months of frustration about Willison now surfacing. "There's your incompetence in not spotting the murders in Geneva and Bonnitor. Now, you may have screwed up everything with Valbona. *You* can't visit Jakupi. Neither can Sgt Watson. Not so soon after your so-called detective work." Ratso nodded at Watson "Tell him."

"Trying to nail Boris Zandro a few years back, I disobeyed the boss. The Albanians then tried a hit-and-run on me. I was lucky to live. So were you."

Willison never raised his eyes.

"Take his full statement." Ratso turned to the trembling Willison. "Now get out. Inspector Strang will consider what action is appropriate after reading the statement." After the door closed, he told Watson to keep the incident under-wraps. "Not a word to anybody about Willison. Except Jock." He nodded his head towards Caldwell's office." I don't want that sod having another stick to beat me with."

Even as he said it though, that stick was swinging perilously close.

Piccadilly Circus

It was a normal evening in the fast-food joint in Glasshouse Street, just off Piccadilly Circus. The mainly young crowd came and went, keeping the tables busy, filling the place with laughter and much chomping of burgers, chicken and fries. As if there was not enough noise, canned music thudded from a dozen speakers.

As usual mid-evening, at the table for eight near the door, a group of teenage boys were seated together, not laughing and joking like most of the diners around them. A couple were sipping bottled water; one had nothing and three were clutching disposable coffee cups.

In the large area, filled with over seventy tables and a long line of hungry customers, nobody took much notice of them. The staff, on zero-hours contracts, were constantly changing. There was little interest in this group who came and went. With a stream of consumers standing, sitting, queuing, arriving and leaving, nobody was much watching whatever else was going on.

Every so often, an older man, maybe mid-twenties or even the wrong side of fifty, would join the youngsters and chat for a few minutes, taking little interest in his food or drink. Typically, the conversation would get more intense before, with a smile and a cheery goodbye, the older man would leave closely followed by his chosen date.

Sir Hunter Bloor had rented a couple of these youngsters before. Tonight though, the very senior civil servant from HM Treasury, had eyes only for Marcel, a teenage black boy with soft and gentle eyes and a youthful innocence. Unlike the slightly older kids around him, Marcel showed no signs yet of boredom with his life-choice.

Outside, there was an unseasonal nip in the air as the unlikely couple headed for Piccadilly Circus. The eavesdropper at the next table had heard it all and knew how much the kid would charge; that his name was Marcel and that, sure, he was happy to take the Tube to Waterloo and walk to Aquinas Street. *No. I'm not staying the whole night. Not for that kind of money. Ninety minutes max. Yes, dear boy, there's plenty of buses to get you home afterwards.*

Putney

Ratso had been packed and ready to grab the morning flight to Geneva. Instead, he now had to update Caldwell. As he stood in front of the Superintendent's desk. As usual, it was free of any signs of activity. Neither did it reveal any human touch whether of family, friends or social life. Except for an apparent interest in classical music, Caldwell's life away from the Met, was a matter for speculation. "Yes?" Caldwell's tone was more resigned than interested.

"Overnight, the Ace was played."

"What?" Judging by the way Caldwell had straightened up in his chair to lean forward, Ratso took this exclamation to be outrage. Ratso faced down his glare. "Well-known poofter, was it?"

"Show some respect, boss – with respect. We now have four dead guys in the region. Until proved otherwise, all are innocent victims. Homophobes like you are a disgrace to the Met. You're lucky I have never made an official complaint."

"My personal views on poofters do not prevent me from wanting arrests and these murders to stop. That," he pointed with a sudden jab "is your job and not going well, not well at all." He then placed his hands across his chest, concealing the gold tiepin of an eagle. "The Ace? A celebrity, was it? One of the top-twenty I wanted identified?"

"Not exactly. The victim was a young black rent-boy. An orphan."

Caldwell said nothing, his hands still and his face impassive – not a muscle moving.

"You wanted high-profile gays warned. I said it was a waste of time."

Caldwell removed his new heavy-black-framed Buddy Holly glasses. "And?"

"Aged sixteen. His name was Marcel. He lived in a Southwark high-rise with an older cousin. Scarcely a chart-topping singer or Chelsea footballer."

Caldwell ignored his own misjudgement. "I warned you to arrest the killer before the Ace. Your career is going nowhere except down the shitter. Your cricketing pal was in King's Lynn. He's in the clear, yet you're still obsessed with being proved right. Tell me, when did you last achieve anything solid on *Footstool*. Remind me, *Chief Inspector*." Ratso could sense the contempt as he sneered at the rank. "I have the memory of an elephant but I can't remember that far back."

And the ignorance of a pig.
Don't rise to the bastard.
Play the long game.

As his lips curled, Caldwell's weasely thin face showed all the years of animosity since they had first fallen out. Ratso stared back, knowing that when *Footstool* was over, only one of them would remain standing. He said nothing.

"Where was the body found?"

"Aquinas Street SE1. Inner-city, ten minutes' walk from Waterloo Station."

"What was the kid doing in Aquinas Street? Apart from the obvious."

"There's a civil servant being questioned, a mandarin no less. His name is Sir Hunter Bloor. He rents an apartment there. He has a wife and three kids at home in Amersham. I'm told he's in meltdown. During door-to-door, when told of the body, he confirmed the kid had been with him. In theory, he's a suspect but I'd bet he's not our serial killer. DI Strang is there."

"Who found him?"

"An Uber driver starting his day around dawn."

Caldwell tapped his Rolex. "Why wasn't I informed earlier?" Caldwell loved nipping and yapping like a terrier.

"Because the Ace wasn't found for five hours. It was breezy. The card was only found later. It had blown away and was found in the gutter. Before that, the crime wasn't linked."

"Same killing method?"

"Nothing official. Looks like a yes. Quick, silent and deadly."

Caldwell adjusted the cuffs on his monogrammed shirt, revealing chunky gold cufflinks. Not for the first time, Ratso wondered how he could afford to dress like a Savile Row model. "You going to Aquinas Street or too busy packing your Bermuda shorts?" The contempt was as much in the downturned mouth as the voice.

"I'll check out the scene. I'm more interested in where Sir Hunter picked up the kid."

"Mavericks like you can't see the bleeding obvious. Four gays murdered. Four playing-cards." He waved his arm dismissively. "You logged there were no playing cards in Geneva or Bonnitor. But prima donnas like you would rather jet away chasing ludicrous scenarios. You'll find both destinations are irrelevant. Hours of wasted police time."

A variety of retorts sprang to mind.

Don't fight this war now.

You'll get your chance.

Win on your terms.

"The killer must have waited close by. Where? Was there an Audi in the area? How did he leave the scene." Ratso ignored Caldwell's unconcealed yawn before continuing. "As for the

Caribbean, during *my holiday*, I'm interviewing Olly Young and Molly Bishop, directors of Energy Management. I'm also going to interview Fergus Edwards in Barbados – all at no expense to the Met."

"Wild goose chase. You're letting your dick and that Florida woman overrule logic and common-sense."

"Ever wondered why I want to interview Olly and Molly?" Ratso was swift to answer his own question. "No. I doubt it." Ratso was rewarded with a sniff that could have meant anything. "Detective-Inspector Bastien Alleyne also wants me discuss the Kendall Campbell murder." Ratso forced a rare face-splitting grin. "Not much time for sand-castles, eh?"

"Not your job to bail out the Caribbean cops."

"Firstly, I know Alleyne."

"Learned bugger-all from you then."

Ratso shrugged dismissively. "Granted, I've seen torches without batteries that shone brighter than Alleyne." He debated and decided not to expand. "With respect, a great dollop of respect, your problem is you can't see the bleeding obvious." Ratso loved throwing Caldwell's words back at him.

Caldwell's double-take at the insolence was tempered by his brain fighting to join the dots. Ratso ignored the eyes blazing at him from across the desk. "I want an update on Aquinas Street before you pack the sun-lotion. Understood."

Ratso nodded yes and deliberately, as he exited, started whistling. That always pissed off Caldwell. Back at his desk, Ratso phoned Yorkshire. "Sprog! How's it going? Getting any cricket?"

"We've had several wash-outs. The forecast's better next week. You?"

"We've had cancellations but I've had no time to play anyway."

"Not arrested anyone then?"

Deadly Hush

"No. A fourth murder will hit the news later. Now listen. Terry Yates. Do you know where he was yesterday evening?"

"Sprog laughed. "Easy. No need to phone a friend to answer that. The team were at a plonk and pizza bash at his place."

"Started and finished when?"

"Seven till gone eleven. Maybe nearer midnight. Terry was in no state to drive."

Ratso doodled on his pad while he gathered his thoughts. "Does Terry do this often? Throw a party, I mean?"

"The last one was just after he moved here. Then, we drank unlimited champagne. There was a vodka luge. French wines. Oysters, clams, you name it. Tomahawk steaks, a side of salmon. Bit embarrassing really. Over the top for most of us used to pie, chips and beans."

"So when was last night arranged?"

"Impromptu, Terry called it. He messaged us yesterday morning. The boring lives we lead, most of us could make it."

"Cheers, mate." After opening a Chicken Tikka wrap, Ratso read the yellow sticker on his monitor. Not good. Whoever had phoned Goldie to fix the appointment had used a burner. Untraceable. As he munched, he scribbled some thoughts.

Yates not involved with Marcel.
Not directly.
Impromptu – interesting word?
The same guy may have killed all four – but not necessarily.
Foot sizes.
Did Yates have an accomplice?
Kick Viment's arse for progress.
The King's Lynn alibi?
This guy may be female.
Quiz Molly ... and Ollie.

Where were they in the UK yesterday?
Where was Jamie Fargher?
Can Tosh Watson's chis link Fergus Edwards's heavies?
Fergus an EMA shareholder?
Park Valbona Jakupi
Surrey – Audi update?
Geneva – get Swiss intel.
Full-bore on Marcel.

He wiped spicy sauce from his mouth before phoning Jock Strang. "You at the scene?"

"I left DC Naylor and the uniforms there. I've been observing the interview with Sir Hunter. He's got a toffee-nosed brief with him. A King's Counsel no less."

"Must be more worried than I expected. I reckoned his biggest problem would be telling his wife. Aquinas Street. What's it like?"

"It's a short wee street. Wee houses. Parking both sides. No real front gardens. Lined with trees."

"What's your impression?"

"Difficult for any non-resident to park. The killer could have hidden between wheelie-bins – they're grouped in clusters of four. The body was dumped between them."

"So now? Where are you?"

"Heading for Piccadilly. Big-Top Burgers in Glasshouse Street."

"Why?"

"Sir Hunter picked up the laddie in there. We're getting CCTV and street footage. He's admitted they took the Bakerloo Line and then walked. Plenty must have seen them. Unusual couple. A white male aged forty-three and a young black kid. Sir Hunter said someone in the Big-Top could have overheard his conversation. But he never noticed anybody listening or following."

"Could be a breakthrough – someone following them from the burger joint. Then waited for Sir Hunter to do his thing. Go for it Jock. We're going to get a clear image of any pursuer in Glasshouse Street."

Heathrow Airport

The Geneva trip now behind him. Ratso relished the recliner in the British Airways Lounge at Heathrow. By using his Air Miles, saved during Covid, he had treated himself to Barbados in First-Class. He ordered a glass of champagne with breakfast and felt decadent, convincing himself that he was not becoming an alcoholic. His thoughts turned to Kirsty-Ann.
Had she been reluctant to meet him?
Is she cooling on me?
Someone else in her life?
Overburdened in her new business?
We don't own each other.
We've been too long apart.
Grown apart maybe?
Thanks Covid!
Thanks Wuhan.

As he waited for his Eggs Benedict and champagne, he switched off the unwelcome thoughts. Breakfast TV was running and he swivelled his chair to watch. Marcel's murder was still big news. The media linked this as the fourth gay to be murdered but Sir Hunter's name was never mentioned. Moments later, he saw Aquinas Street followed by a photo of the fresh-faced innocence of Marcel. *What a sodding miserable existence the poor kid had endured. Never a chance in life.*

The picture changed and Jock Strang's cheerful but boozy features appeared. Ratso knew what was coming: cameras around Glasshouse Street showed an aerial shot of *a person of interest.*

A rather grainy picture also captured the same person leaving Waterloo concourse about forty metres behind Sir Hunter.

A woman.

Ratso's eyes crinkled and his fingers opened and closed with excitement.

It was a bloody sight more than interest.

A young Hungarian waitress from Big-Top had recalled a woman with mineral water seated just behind Marcel. She had left at about the same time as Sir Hunter, leaving her drink unfinished. Her hair had been almost invisible under a headscarf made into a turban. On the camera by the cash-till, her face had been rather obscured by over-sized tinted glasses. Her mouth was small, slightly pouting and her face had no pretensions to beauty.

Is this the same person captured on camera after Goldie's murder.

Yup!

Similar build and height.

But is this a man?

The woman was wearing a pale blue sleeveless shirt and black slacks. The walk was convincing – short steps with a slight hip swivel in what appeared to be clean white Reebok trainers.

Ratso had authorised the images to be released but only after a lively debate with Strang. As the steaming Eggs Benedict arrived, something was still nagging at him. There was something about this person that was familiar, as if he'd seen her before.

But I haven't.

Sure of that?

Yes.

No.

Not sure.

Am I missing something?

Barbados

Shortly after 2 p.m. local time, Ratso had cleared Customs and Immigration at Grantley Adams International. His ferry to Bonnitor was not for another six hours, ample time to meet Fergus Edwards in Rollo's Bar, a short walk from the Terminal. The location was easily spotted – a red, white and black shack with shaded outside seating. Ratso recognised Fergus Edwards at once. He was in a red T-shirt with a palm-tree on the front. As he stood up to greet Ratso, his pink baggy shorts emphasised the whiteness of his spindly legs. Yet his face was deep bronzed, as were his arms. "You must be Holtom." Edwards offered Ratso a seat, a beer but no handshake. The accent was full-bore London.

"You've done well since you left your manor in Deptford."

"Yeah! I've done good in me forty-two years. Bye-bye Deptford! Hello Sissinghurst. Couldn't resist buying this tasty little pad down in Kent."

"I was reading. Eighteen bedrooms – and a moat."

Edwards laughed. "That's to keep you lot out. No beer for you?"

"Mineral water. In this heat, I'm dehydrating." He did not volunteer that champagne, fine wines, port and brandy during the flight had left him with a thumping headache.

"You ain't here just to see me? Don't tell me that." Beneath the unrealistically black hair, his eyes were too narrowly set in his angular face. Momentarily, they hardened. Ratso could now spot the man who had rammed a broken bottle into his victim's throat.

Deadly Hush

Through Tosh Watson's chis, Ratso knew that Edwards still relied on heavies to sort out problems round his old stamping-ground. The chis had nothing linking Edwards to Logan Goldie's murder. "Boss," Watson had reported, "Edwards's enforcers – they're built like brick shithouses. None could have dressed as a woman. No way. Well maybe a pantomime dame."

Ratso placed an elbow on the metal table. "Bit unusual – being out here through the English summer?"

Edwards laughed. "You're right and wrong. The la-di-dah crowd, them rich Hooray Henries from the Cotswolds and Chelsea, all Gucci and Louis Vuitton. They jet in to escape the English winter." He paused. "That ain't my market. I'm keeping an eye on my timeshares. My punters are year-round. Can't be caught sleepin' on the job. No way, Holtom. If I go back for just a coupla weeks, the missus stays here. Trust nobody that's what I say. Except my two lads and maybe the missus, that is. The lads run our timeshares in the Canaries and Spain."

Edwards signalled for another beer. "Like my motor?" He pointed to an open-topped Ferrari. Beside it, a chauffeur was leaning against a tree, trying to escape the sun's glare.

"Done well for a street trader. Gotta give you that, Mr Edwards."

"Got lucky, didn't I? The first million's the hardest. After that, easy street. Anyway, why you here?"

"Charlestine Heights plc. Your timeshare and property empire. You're the majority shareholder?"

"Guilty as charged. Yes."

"The company had a lot of stick."

"That's timeshare. Goes with the territory, mate," he sighed. "Goes with the territory," he repeated. "You can't please thousands of owners all the time."

"Big troubles in 2020?"

"Bleedin' Covid. Ripped the guts out of us, that did. Defaulters everywhere. No travel equalled no stay equalled no pay. Under the contracts, they still had to pay their annual fees. Did they hell!" They screwed our cash-flow."

"You know Logan Goldie?"

"Goldie? Know him? Nah! But I'd enjoy meeting him one dark night. Bloody crucified us. That bastard crapped on our business. Him and his bleedin' rant. We was AIM-listed. Shares dropped quicker than a tart's knickers." He swigged beer from his bottle. "Anyway, what about Goldie? What's he doin'."

"He was murdered."

"You're kiddin' me?" His voice rose and his eyes bored into Ratso from across the small table. "Christ! Fuck me! Best bleedin' news I've had today." He thumped the table, his face alive with movement. "Best news all year come to that. The share price is still crawling along the bleedin' gutter thanks to that wanker. Cheers to that, Holtom."

"You didn't know?" Ratso's arched eyebrow showed disbelief.

"Nah! Me and the missus, we don't follow the news from Blighty. Bleedin' politicians, journalist scum. Bent coppers – if you'll excuse my French. Nah, we get cable news from the USA. Not much better neither but at least them Yanks don't steal all my money in taxes and then bleedin' waste it." He paused for a larger swig. "So who did him in? Painful was it?"

"Are you expecting me to believe your two lads didn't tell you Goldie was murdered. Front page news?"

"Like me, they're full on with the business. One lives in Tenerife all year. The younger kid, Errol, he's in Puerto Banus. I'm always tellin' them straight. Keep your bleedin' eyes on the shop. Timeshares is worse than rentin' villas. People nickin' plates, saucepans, even the effin' bog-brushes."

"So who runs the London end? Your offices – they're in Camberwell. Right?"

"My bean-counters is there. We've some dollies doing telesales. A marketing slicker. Our legal eagles – they're in Holborn."

"And none told you Logan Goldie was dead."

"Listen, my son, they know better than botherin' me with crap from back home. If I want info, I'll ask. I've got a tongue and a blower. Get it?"

Ratso made plain his disbelief with a roll of his eyes. "Goldie gave the owners a voice. Campaigned to get your company investigated. Wanted you prosecuted and struck-off as a company director. Crashed your shares."

"I don't need remindin' what that snivelling git did. What's your point?" An unpleasant grin split Edwards's face. "Goldie and his big mouth got nowhere. We're still trading. Doin' good." He belched beer-gas as he leaned forward. "And why? 'Cos it was bullshit. We ain't never did nothin' wrong. Just Covid. That's what done us. Cashflow problems."

Ratso wasn't buying that. "You behaved like muggers – reclaiming timeshare weeks from defaulters – poor out-of-work sods who couldn't pay their maintenance fees because of Covid."

"You can't let punters piss all over you. Read our contract me old cocker. Clause 71(4) as I do recall."

"Nobody reads the small-print, Mr Edwards. Certainly not to down to clause 71(4)."

"More fools them, me old sunshine," he grinned. "Me and the lads. We stick to the contract. We is men of our word. We play it straight. Play it hard. Like Millwall FC."

"Goldie had death threats. Going back eighteen months. You wanted revenge."

"Death threats? Do me a favour. Show some respect, Holtom."

He fiddled with his large medallion. "On the plus side, though it ain't sayin' much, you're smarter than you look." His grin was infectious but Ratso played dumb. "Look mate, I had over thirteen million reasons to stick it to Goldie." He swigged at his beer and signalled for another, waving a ringed finger at the barman. "We was gettin' death threats because of Goldie. We ignored them. Just sad loser wankers. If I believed every threat I'd had, I'd have locked meself in a padded cell. Nah. Bollocks, mate."

"Your guys still hammering on doors round Catford and Bexley? Terrifying widows and pensioners if they don't pay their rent?"

"I'm not a bleedin' charity." Edwards's voice rose with his indignation. "I own. Tenants pay rent. No pay, no stay. Like I said, read the contracts. Anyway, some of these old geezers are the biggest cheats around. They plead poverty and get out their violins. Y'know, the starvin' pensioner bit. Then my guys find out they've swanned off to Majorca for two weeks. Or gone on a cruise round the Med. Give us a break, Holtom."

"Tough life being rich then. A huge villa here. Thirty acres and a moat in Kent. A Bentley and two Ferraris. I wish I'd packed my violin to play you a lament. I can almost feel tears welling up."

"Right, Holtom. We're done. Goldie had it coming to him. I'm glad someone stuck it to him. Gun, was it? Knife?"

"Neither."

"Tortured, was he? I'd drink to that. Yeah, I can feel a cheeky Black Label comin' on. And Holtom – if you catch the geezer, give him a big wet kiss from me. Done us all a bleedin' favour."

Ratso stood up and before turning away threw in a final question. "Were you a shareholder in Energy Management?" Ratso watched for tell-tale giveaways.

"Energy Management? Should I have been?"

Ratso recognised Edwards was playing for time and said nothing.

"Energy Management? Me a shareholder? Nah. But the name's familiar. Maybe heard it in some bar. Can't think why." He watched Ratso trundle his case back towards the Terminal before picking up his phone. It was the start of a long conversation.

At Sea

Ratso could have taken the twin-engine flight for the short hop to Bonnitor but had opted for the ferry, reckoning it might be more fun.

An experience? Yes.

Fun? No.

As he sat in a packed lounge, heaving with passengers, the twenty-minute flight seemed much more appealing. Across the aisle on the ferry was an elderly woman, reading the National Enquirer with two goats tethered to her chair. She seemed oblivious to them crapping on the floor beside her. Just in front of him were two crates, one containing several chickens and the other a couple of ducks. The stink of shit and diesel from the aged engines, wafted around him.

"Not much more to report, boss," Strang had told him when Ratso had phoned from the airport before grabbing a taxi to the ferry-terminal. "Lot of callers after my call for witnesses and the CCTV. The usual timewasters, others well-meaning one or two useful, I'm still waiting for confirmation that Marcel and Goldie were both murdered by the same woman." The Scot paused. "You? Fergus Edwards?"

"Tried to pretend he didn't know Goldie was dead. Oh and he was evasive about Energy Management too. I've grilled enough villains to know he was telling porkies."

"Why lie?"

"Come on Jock! Dogs bark. Ducks quack. Spivs like Edwards

lie. They wouldn't know the truth if it bit them on the arse." He mopped his brow. "But I doubt he had Goldie murdered. As Tosh reported, his heavies could never look like a woman. He had no incentive, either."

"Why?"

"Okay, Goldie crashed the shares. Cost Edwards thirteen million but Viment's research showed he's still worth over eighty mill. Goldie pocketed maybe a couple of hundred grand as Edwards's shares fell. Then he moved on. Chose other targets including EMA. The noise against Edwards died down."

"Next stop the Olly and Molly Show, is it?"

"Tomorrow. Four-hours' time-difference."

Now, as the small vessel carved its way through the placid waters, Ratso revisited his notes of the Oxford meeting with Fargher. Against the laughter, shouting and the squawks, quacks and bleats, concentration was impossible. He gave up. Instead, he scribbled a reminder to read Energy Management's Annual Report.

But not immediately after checking in.

First – clean the shit off my loafers.

Second – a piping hot shower to wash away the journey.

He watched the twinkling lights of Torrington appear from the blackness. As the ferry manoeuvred to the dock, he stood up to look out of the picture window. If there were any high-rises, they had no lights on. Everything looked low-level, endless single-storey buildings – mainly wooden shacks that looked like easy pickings for a hurricane.

After a bump and a few thuds, the creaking old tub docked to the sounds and sights of excited locals waving to returning friends and relations. He saw several taxis. They looked as if they had passed their sell-by date in Barbados and been shipped across to continue belching fumes around Bonnitor.

Clutching his laptop-bag and towing his rollalong, he pushed and jostled his way among the hundreds of foot-passengers eager to be back home. A farmer towed a wobbly wheeled crate with a couple of young pigs in it, their squeals almost lost amid the noise from ghetto-blasters playing reggae. He joined the short line for a taxi, feeling swept up in the sheer joy and simplicity of his surroundings. The islanders, despite their poverty and a bust economy, showed no sign of discontent or misery.

When did I last see people so full of fun and cackling laughter?
Maybe after a big sporting win at Lord's or Wembley.
But in everyday life?
Not in London.
Not in the big cities.
Now, the default public mood was miserable.
Maybe these people in their multi-coloured bandanas, sweatshirts and grubby trainers had it right.

"The Grantchester Hotel," he told the driver as he wiped sweat from around his neck. The prospect of the air-conditioned suite with its oversized California king-bed and ocean views kept him going. With no sleep on the flight and his head still pounding, he felt knackered. Thank God Kirsty-Ann was not arriving till tomorrow. He wanted to be on top of his game by then.

But before that?
Oh yes.
EMA's Annual Report.

Torrington, Bonnitor

The suite was everything Ratso had hoped for, pastel shades, a work-space, a large terrace and plenty of room to relax. Now, having pushed aside the remains of his cheese and ham omelette, he booted up his laptop and opened Energy Management's Annual Report. It was seventy-eight pages long. The city jargon might as well have been in Chinese. There were countless pages of statutory guff and endless figures with footnotes and disclaimers. There were red and yellow pie-charts. The lines on the graphs sloped relentlessly downwards, consistent with the shares crashing to zilch.

No wonder fortunes had been lost and hopes dashed.

Over four pages, Oliver Young had summarised the challenging financial year. Ratso took in the key part of Young's report:

"As a responsible company, we acknowledge the genuine fears and concerns about climate change. We take no issue with the threatened lawsuit in which Mr Kendall Campbell KC had been retained by environmental activists. Although the timing was opportunistic and damaging to your company, we respect democracy. By the time the Bonnitor Supreme Court ultimately dismissed the attempt to stop us drilling, near terminal damage had been achieved.

This had followed the quite separate attack by Mr Logan Goldie which had undermined our Placing. In consequence, our institutional investors had lost confidence. Your board had to raise emergency finance on demanding terms from Laterre-Quercy Private Family Office in Geneva – terms that normally

your board would never have contemplated. Nor would such finance have been needed but for Mr Goldie's misconduct which we reported to the Regulators.

Although, to environmentalists, the increasing global demand for oil is an unwelcome fact, the global economy will depend on fossil-fuel for *at least* the next twenty years. Over 50% of oil produced is needed for production of medicine, animal feeds and dozens of purposes beyond transport. Under our Bonnitor licences, we are still entitled to exploit all opportunities and whatever resources we may discover over the next three years.

The failure to find oil in commercial quantities from a single exploratory well does not mean that our confidence has been irreparably damaged. We remain confident that we will find ways to monetise our assets in the most environmentally friendly way possible. Your directors still believe that shareholder value can be restored and that we will provide a massive benefit to the population of Bonnitor."

Ratso drained his glass of chilled Muscadet. The report had been written before the murders of Goldie, Kendall Campbell and Jules Quercy in Geneva. He turned to the Geology Report by Molly Bishop.

But he never read a word.

He sat mesmerised.

His only move was to grab the bottle.

Torrington, Bonnitor

It was maybe another minute before he jumped to his feet and punched the air.
Christ!
Nothing makes sense.
Yet everything makes sense.
He picked up his full glass of chilled dry wine. In seconds, he had downed it. Overhead, the twin fans swished. Then, head lowered, hand stroking his chin, he prowled the suite like a caged tiger.
Is Operation Footstool back to ground-zero?
Countless hours, endless meetings, debates, investigations and theories were now turned on their head. Hoping the night air would help, he slid open the doors and leaned over the latticed railings surrounding the terrace, savouring the dusk smells being carried on the sea-breeze. Overhead, the sky was inky black and no stars yet in sight. The nothingness and empty infinity of the Caribbean brought his pumping heart-rate down. As it slowed, he tried to make sense of what he had seen.
Molly Bishop the mystery woman?
Molly Bishop the murderer?
The woman following Marcel and Sir Hunter along Glasshouse Street morphed into Molly Bishop's photo in EMA's Annual Report. It was uncanny. It was unreal.
Am I meeting the murderer in the morning?
Where does that leave Oliver Young?

And Jamie Fargher?

He went back inside. After apologising to his liver, he opened a bottle of Dog Strangler and poured a tumbler of the Australian red. Then he messaged Strang for when he awoke. "URGENT – check out:

- Molly's picture in the EMA Annual Report.
- Contact Immigration – Were Molly or Olly in Europe when Jules Quercy was murdered?
- Were either of them in London when any of the murders occurred?
- Was Molly around Glasshouse Street this week?
- Does she or Olly own an Audi?
- I'm checking if Olly or Molly could have murdered Kendall Campbell.

Shrugging aside the 17-hour day, he set about rejigging his questions for Molly Bishop. Olly and Molly had an obvious motive. But murder? Could Molly steel herself to murder a youngster like Marcel with her bare hands?

How would Molly have learned to kill so professionally? Would she have enjoyed pulping the KC's head? Would she have stolen his cash and the jewellery?

He selected a handful of peanuts before pouring more Dog Strangler. *No point leaving it overnight.* It wouldn't improve. He emptied the bottle, fleetingly wondering how many units of alcohol he had sunk today. He settled down on a comfortable chair and sipped slowly.

Impromptu.

The word flashed across his mind.

He sent Jock another message.

- Check whether either of those women at the Merry Harriers tipped off Yates about your visit?
- Was the impromptu party because Yates KNEW he needed an alibi when the Ace was played?
- Check for an Audi at other caravan parks around King's Lynn.

Finally, his eyes drooping, he messaged Kirsty-Ann and got an immediate response – *can't wait for tomorrow – xxx*.

Torrington, Bonnitor

Strang had phoned just after seven a.m. local time. He had confirmed the striking resemblance between Molly Bishop and the woman who had followed Sir Hunter from Glasshouse Street. Even so, as he breakfasted from a bowl of fresh fruit on his terrace, Ratso was unconvinced. Women serial killers were rare, still less one who would kill a young boy with bare hands. He still fancied his bet that Goldie's killer was male.

In his shades and wearing a cap as protection from the power of the sun, he had then walked a couple of miles, to the small suite of offices used by Energy Management. The company shared a modern low-rise office block on West Ocean Avenue.

He was shown into Bishop's no-frills office. It was filled with utility furnishings and reminded him of the sparse simplicity of their Oxford HQ. A glance was enough for Ratso to form an instant impression that Molly Bishop was someone without pretension. Her features were unremarkable and she wore no make-up. *But was it the face of a cold-blooded killer?* She looked all of her forty-three years. Ratso reckoned her sun-damaged face was creased from working too long under cloudless skies and relentless sun in hot countries.

Her half-smile was curious, perfunctory and without warmth. Despite her watchful eyes, the overall image was of someone uninterested in impressing a male visitor – or probably anybody. Her hair was brown, shapeless and tinged with grey. Whilst not unkempt, it was certainly not well-groomed. Consistent with her overall image, in her open sandals, her bare feet were unmanicured.

As she stood beside him, he spotted the ring on her wedding finger but otherwise there was no sign of jewellery. She was wearing a shapeless, loose-fitting dark-grey shirt and a pair of khaki shorts big enough to make a two-man tent. Yet she was far from obese. "Chief Inspector. Welcome. Take a pew. Maree will fix coffee." The handshake was hearty but there was nothing manly about her surprisingly soft voice and Mancunian accent.

"Thanks. A double-espresso would work for me." Ratso seated himself on a metal-framed chair with a sagging canvas bottom. Together with the desk, it was ex-military surplus, just like Fargher's in Oxford. "It's Molly?"

"That works for me." Her wide-set eyes met his steady gaze. "You saw Jamie in Oxford?"

"He said you and Oliver Young had moved on from Morocco. To be clear, I'm not here because of you." Ratso downplayed his interest. "I'm meeting an old friend on the Bonnitor Constabulary and so decided to see you as well." He flicked open his notepad and produced a cheap pen. "Jamie told you about my meeting with him?"

"Couple of headlines. You think that Logan Goldie's murder may be related to him tanking our shares. Right?"

"It's one line of enquiry. Does that make sense?"

"Goldie wasn't the only cause of our problems. But yes, plenty of shareholders got hurt bad. Count us directors in on that too. But killing him?" Her strong eyebrows rose as her mouth downturned. "Look, I don't read or do blogsites, Twitter or Facebook. Those sites are full of sad losers. Jamie keeps an eye on that crap. He told me some anonymous tossers have even boasted they killed Goldie." She caught Ratso's eye and saw he already knew that.

"Not just our shareholders hated him. He corpsed a load of companies, many of them blameless. There are guys in jail because of him. Those wanting him silenced would form a long queue."

"But with EMA?"

"Goldie started the snowball. We never recovered., Right now, my share options are bloody worthless."

"How much did you lose?"

"The directors? Between us? Potentially eighty, maybe even one hundred million."

The word *MOTIVE* flashed before Ratso's eyes and was reluctant to disappear. "Will the shares bounce back?"

Ratso saw her turn away as if fascinated by the bare white wall to her left. "That's not for the directors to predict. Now we're strapped for cash. As Winston Churchill once said, *we just keep buggering on.*"

I believe you.
So far.
Like Jamie Fargher.
But what are you not telling me?

King's Lynn

Returning to the Merry Harriers had not been Jock Strang's idea of a fun day out. At least the weather was better than last time as DC Bonkale parked up close to Reception. Once inside, it was almost déjà vu with Jess Perkins rising to greet them and young Zoe on the phone. The mellow voice of Michael Bublé singing *Moondance* filled the air as they selected a window table in the café, the Duty Manager joining them.

"I never expected you back." Jess Perkins's tone was neutral.

Strang accepted the offer of a hot scone with strawberry jam. "Aye, Right enough. We never expected to be here." He glanced a prompt at Bonkale.

"Which is the nearest Leisure Park?" Bonkale asked.

For answer, she stood up and led them to a different view from another picture-window. "There. The other side of the hedge. That's the back end of Dunsdale Creek. Their entrance is a mile away."

"We went there. Do your guests go there for their music nights, karaoke?"

"Not many. Walking to their main building, that's near enough twenty-minutes using that gap in the hedge." She pointed further away. "We like the gap. For some of their visitors, our bar is just two or three minutes. Much closer than trogging off to their own Club-Lounge."

"Jess. Remember last time," Strang cleared his throat and rested his elbows on the table. "We spoke about Mr Yates. Terry Yates."

"Yes. That's right."

"We asked you to keep stumm about our enquiry."

"And I did. Never told anyone. Zoe knew of course."

Bonkale's dark eyes caught her full on. "Zoe, then?"

Perkins looked over her shoulder towards the front-desk. "Zoe? Why should she speak to him? That makes no sense."

"We may need your business and personal phones for checking."

Her face now screwed up, Jess Perkins blinked understanding. She hurried away to tell Zoe who then walked slowly towards them, as if heading for the gallows.

"Hello, Zoe! I'll get right to the point," Strang bluffed. "You've spoken to Terry Yates since our visit. Why?" Strang's tone was gentle, almost fatherly.

"I didn't. Not me."

Bonkale joined in. "In that case, we'll need your phone."

"Yeah. No prob. I'll fetch it." Her dreamy green eyes looked troubled but she sounded confident enough.

Strang and Bonkale shared a look as she walked away. "Which one is it, Bonkers?"

"Our boss didn't *know* it was either of them."

"That's not an answer. Which one?"

"The kid. To me, Jess was more convincing."

Zoe returned and plonked herself on the red plastic chair. Her voice defiant, she handed over her phone. "There you are."

"Listen Zoe," Bonkale twisted to ensure she saw him full face. "If I find Terry Yates's number on here, I'll charge you with obstructing justice and maybe something much, much worse. You don't want to go to jail, do you? Is Terry worth a criminal record?" His intense stare made her pink cheeks blush as she lowered her eyes. "Tell us everything. If Inspector Strang agrees, we might take no further action." He rotated her phone in his hands. "Leave your phone. Take a walk. Come back in two minutes."

They watched her exit via Reception without a word to Jess Perkins. Through the window, they were able to watch her, walking in a small circle on the gravelled courtyard, head down. "She's lying, otherwise she had no reason to think."

"Aye! She was lying right enough." Moments later, they saw her shoulders sag as she pulled out a tissue and started dabbing her eyes. "Bonkers, we'll need a private room." They went to the front-desk and Jess set them up in a cluttered sitting-room-come-back-office. "Bring Zoe in here when she comes back." It was gone five minutes before Zoe appeared, her face ashen and the dried tears still visible.

Bonkale pointed her to a three-legged stool on which she perched uncomfortably with her legs crossed but her defiance gone. "It was you, wasn't it?"

Zoe's false eyelashes closed. "I didn't mean no harm. Me and Terry, we was, like friends, y'know." With difficulty, she pulled a dry tissue from the pocket of her figure-hugging jeans.

"Ye chat often?" Strang fingered her phone as he spoke. "We'll know if we check on here."

"No. Just once. I thought kinda that he'd like to know you'd been here."

"You were lovers?"

Zoe's face, now looking haunted, showed her torment. She twisted the tissue in her hands before answering. "Like I mean not a big affair. So yes, I went to his motorhome. He's not married, not so as I know. Me neither. No crime, was it?" Her tears started to flow again.

Bonkale waited while she blew her nose. "We'll need to know when you stayed with him. Overnight, was it?"

"Twice, yes." She wriggled and re-crossed her legs. "Terry's lovely. Like I don't want to cause him no trouble."

After a moment's thought, Strang answered. "Aye! But Zoe," he lowered his voice to show he cared. "Look after number-one. This is your future. Tell us about your call. You phoned to tell him we were checking on him. Correct?"

"It was well, like, exciting."

"Zoe," Bonkale leaned towards her "you tipped him off. That is a serious criminal offence. So tell us everything."

"Everything? There's not much y'know."

Torrington, Bonnitor

With sitting for so long, Ratso's knees had stiffened. He rose and walked round Bishop's office, looking at odds and ends of geological equipment. There were labelled boxes and over a dozen jars containing stone chippings. On a side table was a microscope, a stack of blue notebooks and a strange looking yellow gadget, which Ratso picked up. "That's an Electronic Stratum Compass Clinometer," Molly Bishop volunteered.

"Beyond me." Ratso put it down and returned to his seat. "Each to his own." He paused and cocked his head. "The company's future?"

Molly shrugged and twirled her Bic biro. "After we drilled unsuccessfully, the piggy-bank was empty. We can't look down the back of the sofa. We've already pawned that. The oil is there though. We were so close. We could almost smell it." She adjusted her top before continuing. "Even without Kendall Campbell who was their lawyer, the environmentalists here are influential. We have the rights to drill again but no oil major finance would finance us. These Stop-Oil guys can be extreme and on Bonnitor, they are well connected – wealthy expats and Cabinet Ministers." She shook her head, her sadness obvious. "If we drilled, these activists would make life hell."

"Ever met Goldie?"

Bishop shook her head. "Till his photo was in the paper, I'd have walked past him in the street."

"Name Dermot Doyle mean anything?"

"Day-time TV, wasn't he? Not my scene." She spread her meaty hands in front of her chest as more coffee arrived. "His fame never spread to where I've worked."

Ratso debated whether to go big on Jules Quercy. For a moment, he flashed back to meeting Det. Insp. Albert Rougart from the Sûreté in Geneva. After a few minutes of meet-and-greet in their HQ, they had visited the murder scene in Rue du Puits-Saint Pierre. Then they had sat outside a café drinking weak beer and soaking up the sun.

Ratso had left after learning little of value. In contrast, Rougart had been gobsmacked as a whole new slant had been revealed. Apologetically, Rougart had confirmed the absence of CCTV. There had been no reliable witnesses, no fingerprints or other clues. The killer could have been male or female. Now, as Ratso sipped his coffee, he decided it was for her to volunteer something about Jules Quercy.

"So why are you still here on Bonnitor?"

For a long moment, Molly Bishop seemed to find a paperclip on her desk of great interest and twisted it out of shape. "We've not given up. The oil price has been rising. Now that Covid isn't wall-to-wall headlines, finance may be easier. We have a huge acreage of land and three years to exploit it." She spread her arms in an open-book gesture. "To drill another well, what we need is private finance and a way to beat the activists."

"You blame Kendall Campbell or his clients?"

She peered at Ratso over the rim of her mug. "Campbell was a good guy. A clever lawyer, he was never afraid to take on corruption." She gave a rueful smile. "He was a hired gun. Did his job and lost because our case was solid. Look," she spread her fingers flat on the desk as if in a seance. "It buggered us up big time. But he had a job. Drilling was our legal right and the judge in the Supreme

Deadly Hush

Court agreed. The world needs our oil." Her voice rose, showing her bitterness. "Some activists are Marxists or anarchists. They're sinister, dangerous even. Their agenda is to destroy capitalism. Blocking roads, smashing buildings, gluing themselves to trains. I've no respect for them."

"Who would have wanted Campbell dead?"

She paused for a moment of reflection and then rocked her head back in a hearty laugh. It came from deep in her stomach. "You mean besides us? I heard he was beaten up pretty bad. I'd assume drug-crazed thugs. Them apart?" This time it was the ceiling that seemed to fascinate her. "Perhaps a loony element among our shareholders? Tick! Members of the Government. Tick. His wife's lover. Tick." She shrugged. "If you're meeting the local cops, a dozy lot you ask me, they must know more than they say." She slapped her thighs as she laughed. "Least, I hope they do."

Ratso very much doubted that but let it pass. "You live in Robinson Cove?"

Her cackle filled the small room. "Me? Never been through the gates. Olly went there once, meeting some Canadian financier. Me?" Her eyes were now mocking. "I live in a rented apartment just off Main Street. At night, there's a constant risk of a home invasion. Not that there's anything worth stealing. Not even my body." Her laugh was self-deprecating. "Not that those hoodlums would care. When they're high, they'd screw the vicar's cat. Gang-bang time. I heard that the lawyer was sodomised."

"Sure of that?" It was Ratso's turn to sound surprised.

"Torn wide open, I'd heard."

Ratso decided to leave that image for his meeting with Det. Insp Alleyne. "If you drill, I assume the environmentalists will go to court again."

Bishop clenched her fists as she nodded. "Right now, outside our site, there'll be dozens of protesters with banners. When we drilled, there were several hundred, blocking our gates, hurling bricks and buckets of piss. Olly is on-site now. You could meet him up there. It's about forty minutes away."

"I'll wait till he's back. So how often are you in London?"

"The UK?" she corrected him. "Almost every month. At the moment, Oscar, my husband, he's on a rig offshore Namibia. We rent a cottage in Dinton about twenty miles outside Oxford. Handy for meeting Jamie at HQ."

"You're a geologist?"

"Mineral geology degree from Imperial College London. University of Miami for my degree in petroleum. I've worked in minerals in the Congo and the Australian outback before switching to petroleum in Borneo. Now I'm here."

"So here it's just you and Olly?"

"We hire in consultants as and when we need them. Lean and mean, that's EMA."

"When were you last in the UK?"

"Yesterday."

Ratso tried to hide his excitement. "Up in Dinton, were you?"

Bishop shook her head. "I stayed in London. Our cottage is having dry-rot eradicated."

"Routine question only but I need to know your movements in the UK."

Bishop said nothing but her face switched from surprise to concern to anger, her eyes burning into Ratso. "Why, may I ask?"

Ratso said nothing. Instead he opened his phone and showed Bishop a clip of the video from Glasshouse Street. She leaned across the desk, her brows now furrowed. He heard her sharp intake of breath. He froze the film to show the clearest view.

"Shit! That could pass for me."

"It was you."

"Where was it taken?"

Ratso judged that to be a dumb question. She should have said – wrong clothes, wrong height. Not my tinted glasses. Never wear a turban. But she had not. For now, no way was he telling her the time or location.

"When was this? Was that when Goldie was murdered?"

"This person was caught on camera when you were in London." As he spoke, Ratso was switching to the other CCTV image taken outside Goldie's apartment. He saw the familiar figure with a flowery dress. He watched her look at it and heard the snort.

"That ... is not me. Not that we can see the face. But the large feet? Not me. Take a look." She swivelled on her chair and plopped her feet on the desk. "My feet are average size, not above. She's wearing a flouncy frock. A swirly-girly thing. Like a 1950s cocoa advert. Yuck!"

"But the other picture? In the turban? That is you."

Bishop shook her head and spoke thoughtfully. "No."

"You do wear tinted glasses?"

"Sometimes, yes. Sunglasses."

"Hair tucked up inside a turban?"

She laughed and once again slapped her meaty thighs as she removed her feet from the desk. "Not as I recall. But as you can see, I don't do high-fashion."

Ratso produced the Annual Report. He turned to a series of photos. "These were taken on the drill-site. They're shots of you with some men in hard-hats and one of Jamie and Olly by an earth-mover."

"Show me." She leaned back in her chair and gave a theatrical yawn. "Jetlag still." She scanned the photos. "It's coming back to me." She drew the report closer. "Yes. That's me a while back."

"Dark red turban-scarf, oversized shades, pale-blue shirt and black slacks. Oh – and white Reeboks. Exactly the same as in this video."

"That turban was a one-off. It's coming back to me. I was on-site and working in the Portakabin. The PR guys turned up for a photoshoot. They wanted shots out in the blazing sun. I borrowed a scarf from one of the crew and made the turban. The shades? Okay, they look like mine."

"Where did you stay in London?"

"The Premier Inn at Waterloo. Beside the London-Eye."

Waterloo?

Marcel's body had been found less than a mile away.

Ratso wanted an update from Strang before digging deeper. "I'm expecting a call from London. Can we maybe take a couple of hours?"

Kings Lynn

After ham, egg and chips in Dunsdale Creek, Bonkale and Jock Strang returned to the car. "The boss should be on his recliner. Let's call him," Strang joked as he set the speakerphone. Ratso's familiar south London accent crossed the Atlantic.

"Snoozing in the sun? Sorry to disappoint you, Jock I'm having an early lunch watching a couple of pelicans diving for whatever they dive for. How did it go with the two women?"

"You were right. Zoe, the younger one did phone Terry Yates. She'd been bedded by him a couple of times. Ye ask me, she liked the drama of us being detectives. She's infatuated by him but none too bright. She couldn't see the harm in telling him. When she phoned, she was hoping he'd fix a Paris trip. I didna' tell her that Yates regards women as bedpost notches."

"How about this, Jock? Knowing he was a suspect, he had to play the Ace and set up set up Marcel's murder when he had a solid alibi – the impromptu party and it was another gay situation."

"Aye! Your theory stacks up. Whoever is the murderer, played the Ace. But if Marcel wisna' the intended Ace, then there's another to come."

"Good thought."

"There's more, boss."

"Go on."

"We revisited Dunsdale Creek checking on Audis. A solitary male in an Audi was booked in overnight when Dermot Doyle was murdered."

"Name? Address? Registration Number?"

"The guy paid cash. He gave a false address in Lowestoft, so I guess the name is also false." Jock's voice showed his mounting excitement. "No vehicle registration. but I've got the page the guy completed when checking in."

"Handwriting, That's good." Ratso shifted further under the sunshade. "Photo of the car?"

"No."

"Description of the driver?"

"White male. Medium height, maybe a bit more. Thirty-five to forty-five."

"Similar to Yates. Could be an SAS pal."

"Yates could have borrowed the Audi."

"Or his mate drove him there and back."

Ratso repeated the words slowly. "Or his mate drove him." There followed a long silence as Ratso watched a cormorant swoop low across the beach. Then he sipped his beer. " Let's assume one of them murdered Doyle. That's the TV presenter – high profile and gay."

"And picked for that reason."

"Then Yates may have murdered Logan Goldie but dressed as a woman. We have no evidence against him or for Lord Ongerton. We do know he didn't murder Marcel. So why be driven to London to murder Doyle? Makes no sense."

"Right enough but until now, he could not have been in Ladbroke Grove on the night of 16th into 17th July. Now, he had a motor or a driver."

"My take? Either Yates murdered Doyle and was back for breakfast or he briefed Mr Audi."

"What's news from Bonnitor? Molly and Olly?"

"I'm not finished with either. They were both in the UK when

Marcel was murdered. Her hotel was less than a mile from where Marcel was murdered but I agree with her – her feet look too small to match Goldie's killer."

"Anyroads, why would she kill Marcel?"

"Makes no sense but like Fargher in Oxford, she's holding something back."

"I checked martial arts clubs," said Bonkale. "In London, Manchester and Oxford. Molly is a black-belt in judo and also trained in karate in Manchester."

"Good thinking, Bonkers. Doesn't make her a trained killer but it helps."

"Viment has checked all Yates's SAS mates. She's interested in two or three, mainly two. One now lives in Barbados. The other worked for Mbesa on the ships. He was laid off after being injured in a piracy attack near Hong Kong."

"I need everything on the guy in Barbados. PDQ. Any advance on how the murderer reached the Big-Top Burger joint?"

"Work in progress."

"Were Molly & Olly in Europe when the Swiss guy was murdered?"

"Still not confirmed, boss."

"Yates's shareholding?"

"The Court Orders against the likely intermediaries, y'know banks or brokers who may have bought shares for him – all blanks."

"Disappointing." Ratso was not admitting it was much worse than that. "He must have owned shares. We just can't prove it." He checked the time. "I'm off to continue with Molly and Olly." Moments later, as he waited under the hotel's portico, a bleep on his phone attracted his attention. "Landed in Barbados, K.A xxx."

Torrington, Bonnitor

"Your purpose for your recent UK trip?" continued Ratso. He bit into a rum-based cup-cake from a selection that Molly Bishop had placed on the desk.

"Train to Oxford to brief Jamie for the AGM. When we'd done, we drove to Dinton. Checked on my builders. Had lunch in the Seven Stars. Then I trained it back from Haddenham."

"Why not Zoom or Teams? Save a fortune in travel."

"You think I was in London to murder somebody? Who? Where?"

"Where were you on Tuesday?"

"What time?"

"Any time." Ratso found himself being firmer with her than he had intended. Getting her explanations had been like chipping granite with a blunt knife.

"Was that the day it rained?" She was thinking aloud. *But is she playing for time?* "No That was Monday when I was down at the Kent Coast. Dover. I wore the wrong clothes. Got soaked. Wait one. Tuesday? Got it. Zoom call with Olly late morning. Then paperwork in the hotel. You can check. I paid extra for the premium Wi-Fi. Lunch was a sandwich and some wine from the supermarket. Snooze in the afternoon."

"Any alibi for the afternoon?" Ratso had no interest in the afternoon but was not revealing that.

"You mean with hubbie Oscar on an oil-rig, was I having wild nookie with some toy-boy? Me? With a face like a cracked brick

Deadly Hush

and my pubes going grey?" Her guffaw filled the room. "The answer is no. No alibi. I was alone."

Ratso shifted uneasily, uncertain how to react to her unflattering self-description. "After your siesta? What then?"

"Walking. I'm big on that."

"Route?"

"South Bank to Tower Bridge. A pint of lager in St Katherine's Dock. Then back through the City. Cheapside. St Paul's. Holborn. West End. Buck House. Birdcage Walk. Westminster Bridge. Hotel. About seven or eight miles."

"So back at the Premier Inn when?"

"I picked up a take-out from a Chinese place near Soho. Ate as I walked. Got back maybe between nine and ten."

"No toy-boy alibi for the evening either then." Ratso tried to lighten the mood and was rewarded with a wry smile and a shake of her head.

"Didn't get lucky, no."

"Know Glasshouse Street?"

"Should I?"

Ratso searched his photos. "There that's it, taken from Piccadilly Circus. Here's the reverse view. The way you appeared to be walking."

"Not me." She exaggerated a moment of deep thought. "I don't recall ever walking along there."

"Ever been into Big-Top Burger?" He pointed to the big sign.

Looking puzzled, she said no. "Like I said, I had crispy duck and noodles. Never walked along Glasshouse Street. Me? Eat a burger and fries? Do me a favour."

"You're a black-belt in judo?"

Bishop made no attempt to conceal her surprise. "Twenty years ago. My Dad insisted." She paused. "As a geologist in the

Australian Outback or the Congo, having no dick or balls, I was a freak. Reckoned to be open-season for the sex-crazed baboons I worked with. Mining then was male-only." Her style was matter-of-fact. "Dad was right about me becoming a Black-Belt."

"Yeah! I get it." Ratso then opened his laptop and showed her a photo of Terry Yates. "Recognise this man?"

"Should I?"

"Just look and think, please." Though the words were polite, Ratso's irritation was obvious. "Think carefully."

Bishop chewed thoughtfully on a slice of carrot cake. "I've seen him. Yes. But I can't think where or when. His name might help."

Ratso shook his head. "Not yet. No clues. I want *you* to place him. Airport lounge? A pub in Oxford? Checking into your hotel?"

"You don't think him and me were shagging in the Premier Inn, do you?"

"Just examples. I'm suggesting nothing."

"Oozes sex appeal, doesn't he? But no. The face isn't *that* familiar. He's never been on top or underneath me in bed." She stood up and walked to the window, staring at a couple of dogs scrapping across the street. Then she turned round and as she did so, she spotted the Energy Management Annual Report lying on the floor beside her desk. Her face lit up. "Got it. He attended an AGM."

Jamie told me he was never signed in as an attendee."

"Shouldn't happen. Could happen, especially last AGM. There was a huge attendance after the shares crashed."

"You reckon that's when you saw him?"

"Positive. He bumped into me as he came out of the gents. He apologised. I then spotted him way back in the crowd at the meeting."

"Did he speak?"

"No question from the floor. No and I never saw him again."

"Thanks. That's helpful." He played it down though he felt like dancing round the room, arms waving. "Just your diary now. Electronic I assume?"

For answer, she opened a drawer beside her desk and produced a slim black diary. "Habit from Africa. In the deepest darkest Congo, internet was bad or non-existent. This worked best. Help yourself."

Knowing the precise dates of each murder made Ratso's task simple. But he was not yet ready to show his hand. "Can you get every page copied please? I'll take them with me and we can chat again after I've met Mr Young. Does he usually travel with you?"

"Can't generalise. If you're specific, I can tell you. After that dreadful air-crash when the entire board of directors of Sundance was killed in Cameroon, we try to travel apart. I was working in Cameroon at the time. I knew some of the guys on that flight."

"Mr Young with you this last trip?"

"He did some City meetings. He trains it into London from Sevenoaks. I never saw him when I was in London."

"What cars do you and Mr Young drive?"

"I've an old Toyota RAV4. That's gathering dust in Dinton. Olly? Not sure. Maybe a VW or Audi. You'll need to ask him."

Ratso rose from his chair. He was not yet ready to talk about Geneva. Even so, he had seen and heard enough. Was Molly just interesting or a person of interest? Whatever, Yates had edged into pole-position.

Torrington, Bonnitor

Bishop ushered Ratso through to a less spartan office with a distant view of the port. Oliver Young rose to meet him. Ratso knew from DC Petrie's research that he was fifty-three. Except for the red veins on his puffy face, his tall and muscular physique made him look younger.

Ratso noticed a faint smell of stale alcohol as Young leaned forward to shake hands. *Was there a touch of a boozer's nose as well?* Ratso was unsure. Losing a share of one hundred mill was enough to make even a teetotaller sink brandies before breakfast.

"Oliver Young. Call me Olly. Everyone does." The accent was refined Home Counties. To Ratso, it pointed to a privileged upper-middle class background involving education at a fashionable public school.

"Thanks for seeing me. I guess you know what I'm interested in?"

"You don't need to be Sherlock Holmes." He walked to a fridge and swung open the door. "Local beer or a soft drink?"

"Beer sounds good." Ratso took in the displayed photos of men in hard hats with drilling equipment. On the desk was a photo of Young with two youngsters. "You were on site this morning. What's going on?"

Behind Young as he sat down, a pair of scented candles flickered in the draught from the overhead fans. The sickly-sweet smell reminded Ratso of buying a birthday card for K.A in a Fort Lauderdale gift store. "Groundwork. With the coffers near empty, we're trying to do a lot with a little." His laugh and sardonic shrug suggested *mission impossible*. "We're battling for the hearts and minds of the remaining shareholders. We can't over-egg it. We can't mislead them but can't let them feel our position is hopeless."

"Understood."

"Without the income from the Moroccan gas discovery we'd have gone belly-up. We've a few chaps down near Guercif in the Atlas Mountain trying to double or treble our production. Here?" He swilled down a generous mouthful of Banks Caribbean Lager before returning his hands to his pockets.

Ratso shifted on the rickety chair which creaked unpleasantly. "Your upcoming AGM. Is that hard-hat time?"

"Strictly, it's an EGM. Extraordinary General Meeting."

"Meaning?

"We have a Special Resolution, requiring 75% of votes cast in favour. The rest is Ordinary Business and just needs a simple majority to be nodded through."

"What's special then?"

Ratso spotted Young's tongue dart in and out. "Plotting EMA's better future after the previous drill. Last AGM, we had six security guys, four in front of the podium. There was a large crowd, pushing four hundred. Mainly loud-mouths yelling torrents of four-letter words. I've seen better behaved polecats. If just one person had rushed the podium, it would have started a stampede. Those security guys would have been trampled in the rush. Us too. The mood was *lynch-mob* – like when they strung up Mussolini in Italy."

"And this coming meeting?"

"Jamie says interest is low. Shareholders have lost heart and lost interest. Last year was their chance to rage at us. There won't be near four hundred." He drained his can and put it aside. "We expect some shit but nothing like before." He returned to the fridge and produced two more cans. "Fair enough. We didn't deliver."

"But the directors weren't to blame. Logan Goldie started the slippery slope to hell. Correct?"

"Mr Holtom, angry shareholders and logic don't march in step."

"This EGM?"

"We can seat sixty. Jamie expects about twenty, a few supporters but mainly hotheads. They can vote. Non-attenders can register to watch on-line but not speak. Most of our small shareholders, the poor bloody infantry, are past caring. Resigned to their fate. Disheartened."

"And broke?"

"Maybe. Most wouldn't attend even if it meant only paying a bus fare to cross London." A flicker of a wolfish smile seemed to play across Young's lips, something that puzzled Ratso.

"Has a Mr Terry Yates registered to watch on-line?"

"Jamie will know who's registered for the live-streaming link. I'll message him." Despite his large fingers, Young typed on his phone with enormous speed. Ratso was impressed. As he sat waiting, he took in the thinning hair but hairy ears. Before Ratso had even topped up his beer, he heard the ping of an arriving message. "Yes. Mr Terence Yates has registered for the live stream. Is he a person of interest for murdering that shit Logan Goldie?"

"He's one of many lines of enquiry." Ratso could see that Young was unimpressed with the answer. "What's your background, Mr Young?"

"After university, I joined a major oil and gas outfit operating from Perth, Western Australia. Back then, I was a suit, far from the sharp end. Since then, I've learned site operations on the hoof. Had to"

"You were a bean-counter then?"

Deadly Hush

"More than that," Young laughed. "I rose to one below mainboard, attending political meetings with Government Ministers, tyrants, oligarchs, African despots. We were never coy about who we dealt with. As our Aussie CEO used to say – *sod the ethics. Think of the bottom-line.* Then, after twenty-two years, I was head-hunted to join EMA. That was eight years back."

"Not many beans to count in EMA."

"Not right now."

"I can understand Molly, as a geologist being on site, digging and poking around. Why were you there?"

Ratso watched Young shift uneasily before he reached for his can. "Molly had to be here to meet you, so I went to show the flag. It means running the gauntlet between the demonstrators, wiping the spit from my shirt and face. Not pleasant."

"And what's happening? On your land, I mean."

"Just a few locals on groundwork supervised by Johan Bruyne. He's a Belgian consultant hired in as Chief of Operations."

"You're just back from the UK? Doing what?"

"I met our brokers in Leadenhall Street. Battled my way round the M25 to Oxford. A day at the cricket in Canterbury – incidentally, my idea of a perfect day out." He pointed to the photo. "I also took my twin sons to Whitstable for oysters. My wife and I live apart."

Ratso resisted an immediate conclusion that anybody who loved cricket could never be guilty of murder. *Hell, after all I'm trying to nail this on Terry Yates.* "What car do you drive?"

"Following our separation and the share crash, the old days of flashy Porsches have gone. Mundane really. Now it's a 2017 Audi."

"The model?" Ratso kept his question casual though he was intrigued.

"Audi A3."

"Just for the record, I'd better have the registration number and colour."

Young laughed, mouth wide open, no hint of nervousness. "Sounds like I'm a person of interest?" He waited for Ratso to comment but none came so he added that the car was black with four doors. He then fired off the registration number from memory.

Ratso jotted down the information. "You look very fit. The gym, is it?"

"Evergreen Health Club off Main Street. Expats' hideaway. Cardiovascular. Endurance. Swimming."

"I remember now! I read you got a Cambridge Blue for swimming. I'm impressed."

Young looked surprised. "You're well informed. That was a long time ago. The 1500 metres."

"I never liked water in my eyes," Ratso smiled ruefully. "Nor the thought of endless lengths."

"Valuable thinking time," Young laughed. "Or these days, *worrying where the next buck is coming from time*."

"I'll need your diary."

"No problem. Just this year's online diary?" He saw Ratso nod and turned to the laptop on his untidy desk. "Done. Email attachment now sent."

"Last Tuesday. Where were you from 6pm onwards?"

With no long pause for thought, Young answered. "That's about when I returned from Oxford. I had a meeting at the Rogerson Hotel by Blackfriars Bridge. Sorting the EGM arrangements – the podium, the seating layout, the sound-system. Selecting drinks and nibbles."

"And returning to Sevenoaks?"

"Left the Rogerson by say quarter past seven."

"Anyone to vouch for you at home?

"Sorry. No. I'm on my tod, Todd!" Young grinned from ear-to-ear. "Sorry about that awful pun."

"Like it! Any ideas about Kendall Campbell?"

"I met him not long before he was murdered. I was at Hiram G. Warrender's party in Robinson Cove. He's a billionaire. Made his money from Canadian oil and commodities."

"Is that the only time you've visited Robinson Cove?"

Young nodded, his eyes adding emphasis. "Robinson Cove is several million dollars out of my league."

"His address?" Ratso waited while Young checked his phone and then wrote the details. "So how come you were invited?"

"We'd touched base under an NDA about Energy Management."

"Was he a big shareholder?"

"Not one share." Ratso spotted Young's eyes narrowing before he looked at the ceiling – uneasy, just like Molly Bishop. After a pause while Young considered his answer, he clasped his hands together and leaned onto his desk. "I hoped he might fund us to drill a couple of wells. The answer was no." He shook his head ruefully. "No oil giant will invest in us now. Since Cop 26 in Glasgow, the Bonnitor Government is greener than a greengage. Warrender wasn't interested in a battle with Government and activist protesters. It was a terrific party though."

"Tell me about security to enter Robinson Cove."

"By reputation, pretty tight but I was surprised. My taxi drove in without any check. We just followed a pink Rolls Royce and were waved through."

"When leaving?"

"As I recall, the gates are triggered automatically as you approach."

"So Kendall Campbell was there?"

"We exchanged passing nods. If I'd got close, I would have

wanted to punch him on the nose – a right smacker." He chuckled. "Of course I wouldn't have – just in case you're wondering. He was a decent enough guy. Did a good job for the environmentalists by screwing our drilling plans. Even though he lost in the end."

"Any ideas who murdered him?"

"None. Look, Mr Holtom. His murder changed nothing. If we ever want to drill again, plenty of other attorneys will accept a juicy fee to stop us." He looked at his watch. "Are we done? I've a meeting at the Ministry."

"Pretty much. I'll see you at the AGM. Sorry, EGM."

"You'll be there?" Young's voice showed surprise and one eyebrow was raised.

"Low profile. Watching, listening, checking the attendees. Starts at eleven. Correct?"

"Coffee and biscuits only. No lavish spread I'm afraid."

Ratso rose to leave. "I'll need a few moments with Molly now."

Torrington, Bonnitor

After watching the twin-engine turbo-prop taxi to the gate, Ratso changed from foot-to-foot. Would Kirsty-Ann look the same? Would she *be* the same? Would she be bubbly, sharp as a tin-tack and as loving as before? He looked down. *I've changed.* Maybe over an inch around his midriff. Maybe a new wrinkle or two around his eyes -close to the scar down his cheek – his legacy of arresting Boris Zandro.

At least my hair isn't turning grey.

With Hysen Kola still on the prowl, maybe that's gonna change.

Most arrivals from Barbados had around thirty passengers. Apart from a few locals and a couple of taxi drivers, the airport was almost deserted. A smell of Starbucks coffee wafted across the small chair-less area. Then he saw her, dressed all in white with a striking red scarf. She was striding through from Customs, tall, willowy and swinging a single overnight grip. As soon she saw him, she broke into a trot, covering the distance between them in no time. Then, she was clinging to him, her bag dumped.

Ratso breathed in her perfume and nuzzled into her soft blonde hair. Nothing was said, both lost in the moment. He felt the entire length of her body quivering as she clung tighter than he had ever remembered. He sensed that perhaps her eyes were welling up. At last, they drew apart, eyes locked on each other, a prelude to a kiss before he wiped a tear from each of her cheeks. "Oh my God, how I've longed for this moment." Her voice was husky with emotion.

"Me too. I wondered whether normality would ever return." He picked up her brown leather bag which seemed almost weightless. "You'll love the suite. We'll catch the sunset on our terrace."

"I could slaughter a Bloody Mary." She grinned, showing her perfect teeth.

"I'm planning on a Zombie."

"Being?"

"The barman explained it was invented in Hollywood but Bonnitor has made it their speciality. Three types of rum, Pernod and Angostura Bitters and something secret." He laughed. "He warned me – three of them and you crash out."

She stroked his cheek. "Well, don't you go falling asleep on me tonight. But I'll try a Zombie or two as well."

He gave her backside a friendly tap as a taxi pulled up beside them. "You haven't changed at all. Just as beautiful as ever. How do you do it?"

"Hard work and clean living," she replied with a suggestive smile, her arms spread wide. He opened the door for her and followed her into the scented air of the ageing Mazda.

"Hard work and clean living? That's me too – except I'm ravaged and you're ravishing." Ratso turned his attention to the elderly driver in his green Che Guevara T-Shirt. "The Grantchester please." As they progressed along the narrow road heading for the coast, it was obvious that the Mazda's suspension had seen better days. Dozens of potholes and no servicing had taken their toll, "How your Mum? How's Leon?"

"Mom's turning seventy-three but she's become kinda frail. I'm so scared of her falling. I got her an Apple watch. If she falls, it calls an ambulance. Since her heart problem, she doesn't drive anymore. Most days, Leon's at kindergarten, so she gets by. They love being together but soon, I won't be able to leave Mom in charge of him."

Deadly Hush

"That's so sad." He leaned across the plastic seat covering to squeeze her elbow. She responded by moving closer where she remained the rest of the journey. Barely an hour later, Kirsty-Ann had showered and changed into a simple white tank-top and pink shorts. She had bare feet and her varnished toe-nails overhung the end of the navy-blue recliner. They clinked glasses, touching hands for a moment. "Here's to us," prompted Ratso. "I've dreamed of this. You. Me. Golden sunsets."

"Me too." She forked up some spicy conch salad. "You gonna tell me about your day, Chief Inspector Holtom?" She emphasised the word Chief.

Ratso shook his head. "Taboo this evening. This is about you, about me – about us. But tomorrow, let's take a ride to the south of the Island. I'm told it's very different. I want a look-see at Energy Management's operation. Then, maybe a snack in a friendly looking bar I spotted by the marina. For tomorrow evening, the restaurant downstairs has a five-star reputation."

"Sounds like a plan. My flight goes at ten the following morning. Far too soon."

Ratso's eyelids drooped. "That'll be tough. Mind, I'll be busy with the local police."

"The murder of that lawyer?"

Ratso nodded. "Enough of that. I just want to drink in all this." He waved a powerful arm in a wide arc. "You, me and the sun setting over the ocean."

Kirsty-Ann shifted slightly and reached over to stroke his chest. "For a tough London cop, you're quite a romantic. I like that." She was rewarded with the type of look that only lovers can share. He topped up their glasses of Zombie from the cocktail mixers provided by Room Service.

"In Fort Lauderdale, the sun's not a novelty. For us Brits, this is special." He stretched to stroke the back of her neck and she responded by clasping his hand and kissing each of his fingers. Ratso recalled her doing just that when she had stayed with him in London. He also knew precisely what it signalled. He felt a tingling sensation ripple through him and had to force himself not to sweep her inside to the California-King.

"Your English weather. I hear you," she drawled with something of Atlanta, Georgia still in her accent despite her years in Florida. "We take the sun pretty much as a given. But Florida is not paradise. The humidity. The crime. Seasonal plagues of lovebugs so you can barely step outside. The traffic on 95. Gridlocks. The hurricane-season. The junkies. Lying and cheating politicians. Poverty and vagrants. Extreme political activists. Deadly snakes, the gators, Black Widows, the Brown Recluse. Gun crime. Free speech is dying. Worst of all – there's no room for tolerance or respect." She sighed, looking wistful. "I could go on."

"Doesn't sound much like paradise after all," he said. Then he twisted to face her full on. "I was wrong about Florida. Perhaps it never was paradise – *that* was only you."

He was rewarded with a kiss. "You say the cutest things."

Then Kirsty-Ann's mood changed. Her eyes closed as if wrestling with an inner torment. "I'm getting busier every day. Always flying across state lines but for how long can I go on? If Mom can't cope, I gotta consider Leon. Mom too. My future, their future – that's a whole other thing." She downed her fork. "No. That's for some other time. Now is us." She clasped her drink and twirled the celery stick. "I could get too used to these Zombies."

"It should be renamed Mule-Kick. There's enough rum in this to keep a pirate crew happy for weeks." He was feeling more light-headed than he had expected. The bar-tender had been right about the strength. "Hey! Maybe we move here. Forget Florida. Forget

London. Bring your Mom and Leon. I'll cash in my chips with the Met and we'll run a detective agency. Here or Barbados."

"Live out here? You're not kidding, are you?" A dreamy look flitted across her oval face. "Hey, the sun's almost gone. Time to go in?" She squeezed his wrist.

"That thought had never crossed my mind," Ratso laughed. "But now you mention it …"

South End, Bonnitor

Addi, their taxi-driver, had ignored the faster route from their hotel to Energy Management's site. Instead, he had taken the winding coast road, pausing at beauty-spots so they could enjoy the views. Beyond the white sandy coves, the silhouette of Mount Hillaby, on the heights of Barbados, was visible across the shimmering calm sea. Small craft abounded – island hopping yachts, fishing boats, small cruisers and floating gin-palaces. Ratso pointed out the ferry chug-chugging back towards Bridgetown, creamy foam swishing from the stern. The sight prompted him to tell a subdued Kirsty-Ann about the goats and ducks on his crossing.

He half-twisted in the back seat to make eye-contact but her eyes were locked on a non-existent horizon, her mind uninterested in the here and now. He was puzzled – concerned too. Her mood was so different from the touchy-feely previous evening. Then it had been groans, moans, sighs, laughs and squeals. Now, she was locked in her own thoughts.

This is a first.
Locking me out.
What have I done?

Except for Addi in the front, Ratso would have asked what was bugging her. As it was, he said nothing. He stroked her arm but with no reaction. The taxi stopped so they could look at the rusting remains of a beached freighter that had smashed against a rocky headland. Then Addi drove on for a few minutes and announced they were nearly at EMA's site. "Sah, you goin' in?" Addi was waving towards an impenetrable chain-linked fence.

"Just looking, Addi." From what Molly Bishop had said, the company had the rights over the island's entire southern tip. Beyond the fence, the empty barren scrub stretched away into the distance. Of any previous drilling, there was nothing to be seen.

The Mazda shuddered to a halt. "Mon, you'se not gonna see much in there. Right here, this is the widest point of their land. Coast-to coast, their fence is over five miles. Inside there, their land narrows down to Devil's Point."

"Did people live down here? Did the company drive them out? Is that why people are protesting?"

The young driver shook his dreadlocks. "Nobody never did live there. Nobody, they did never go near Devil's Point. There ain't no sandy beaches down there, jess rocks. Dangerous currents. Nobody go swim or barbecue fish. Plenty fishermen drowned."

"What did you think about drilling?"

"Drillin' for sure wasn't doin' nobody no damned harm." Addi crunched the car into gear and continued driving slowly, parallel to the fence. "Bonnitor needs plenty big bucks. I don't see no alternative to findin' oil."

"You wanted the drill to succeed?"

"Sure did. Like most islanders but," he slowed to point out the protesters. "These guys, most are here every day. They been makin' noise, causin' trouble for mebbe three years." Addi's frustration showed in the way he slammed on the brakes to pull up a safe distance from about forty protesters, men, women and children, who surrounded the entrance. It was guarded by two men in khaki shirts and shorts, both seated on stools.

Addi turned to face his passengers. "Them interfering white protesters should go back to the US. They ain't wanted. Ain't a single islander protesting here. Us. We need oil, money, jobs. They don't give shit for us livin' on the breadline, too many unemployed. No future. No hope."

Ratso was reminded of a travellers' encampment he had once visited back in Essex. Along the perimeter fence, there was a mix of ageing caravans and early model motorhomes. A couple of mongrels were sniffing and yelping between a scattering of tents. Most protesters were wearing T-shirts with angry slogans. Their placards, scrawled on bed-sheets or pieces of cardboard, broadcast their hostility. For a moment, he imagined Oliver Young yesterday, facing the shouts and jeers and being spat on in his open-topped jeep.

"Sah, if we could vote tomorrow, who would be damn-fool enough to vote for unemployment, starving kids and murders. We want Mista Young do find that oil that belong to us, the people." As he spoke, the relentless breeze brought a smell of someone baking bread. Ratso stared through the chain-link fencing. There was little but endless barren land with a scattering of stunted trees and shrubs, all bent from the prevailing wind.

"No sign of activity," Ratso observed to nobody in particular. Kirsty-Ann was looking at her phone and busily tapping a message. "Where did they drill?"

"Mebbe two, three miles that way." Addi pointed towards the rising ground. "Out of sight beyond that hill. Nobody don't get in their compound. Me? I jess hope they raise big bucks and drill again. My four kid brothers ain't got no jobs. They jess driftin' around the docks, talkin' shit, mebbe kickin' a ball."

"I'm sorry." Ratso had to raise his voice against the shouting and jeering from the protesters. "That's tough. There's nothing to see here. Back to Torrington then."

"I kinda get what the protesters are doing," drawled Kirsty-Ann, her first words for too long. "Sure, we must save the planet for

Leon's generation. I buy that. But I respect the rights of the islanders to feed their families and preserve the fabric of their society. Poverty is not a human right. It's a blight on humanity. Oil may be their only chance."

Ratso pecked her cheek in agreement and squeezed her warm hand, hoping for that usual nerve-tingling reaction that had typified their relationship. He was disappointed. Right now, it just wasn't there but he carried on talking. "Yesterday, Molly Bishop said that Trinidad, Guyana and Suriname are exploiting their oil. Their kids, who once played in the gutter, now have schools, better health and a brighter future."

He glanced at K.A for a reaction but she had disappeared back into her own world again. "So Addi, what's happening in there? Out of sight?"

"Since the drill stopped, ain't nobody knows. I bring foreign guys jess to the gates. They ain't tellin' me nothin'. The gates open. They walk through. A jeep takes them over that hill."

As the Mazda rattled and bumped its way north to Torrington, Ratso also fell silent as he reflected on yesterday's meetings. Olly and Molly were hiding something. But was it murder? He was still wrestling with this when his phone vibrated.

"Hi Carole. All good?"

"Thanks, boss," DC Viment replied. "I've info on Yates's buddy in Barbados. He lives in Bridgetown." Rapidly, she explained. "His name is Zak Carter. He takes tourists on boat trips. Y'know an hour along the coast. Picnics and snorkelling off the boat. Sunset Cruises."

"You've done well."

"I'd been through all Yates's mates you'd listed. Got down to three of interest. That dropped to two when I found one was already in jail for GBH. I asked Major Tang about my final two. Both had seen plenty of action – *chasing down ragheads* as Tang had called it. Besides Zak Carter, there was a guy called Derek Foden, known as Degsy. I'm still working on him."

"Tell me about Carter."

"His parents were from Barbados. He was born there. Father was a Sergeant-Major in the British Army. Carter was brought up near Aldershot. Before acceptance into the SAS, Zak was a paratrooper. In the SAS, he was in the boat troop."

"You mean he was in the SBS – the Special Boat Service?"

"No. Like Yates, Carter was in the 22nd Regiment SAS. He had special training in amphibious action, some of it with the SBS."

"Other training?"

"Relevant to us – counter-terrorism and close-combat skills. Yates, Degsy Foden and Zak Carter all saw action together during the noughties."

"And?"

"I suggested to Tang they must have become blood-brothers. Like *The Three Musketeers – all for one, one for all*. He wasn't having that. He did say his men always had to rely on each other. *Life and Death*, he called it."

"Specifics? Their characters? Fields of operation?"

"You've met Major Tang. Sorry boss. He gave me nothing. I was left to join dots."

"Plucking teeth from a chicken would be easier. Next time, try pliers and water-boarding."

"I expect they're trained to cope with that, boss."

"I must meet Zak Carter. You've done well."

"Degsy Foden was harder to track down till I found a talkative guy who had worked for Mbesa on the ships. Some years back, Foden was injured fighting pirates in the South China Sea. They intended to toss him overboard but he crash-landed on the deck below. Smashed his thigh. Another guy, less lucky was left to drown. Foden crawled to till he was hidden. The pirates left after looting the safe at gunpoint and stealing the crew's valuables. I'm told that Degsy Foden, made a good recovery until he started having an irregular heartbeat. He was pensioned off. These pirate-busters have to be A1 fit."

"Was he bitter?"

"According to my informant, it seems not. He got a generous pay-out from Mbesa. He has an apartment overlooking the sea in Folkestone. I'm talking to local CID. There's no record of him owning an Audi – or any car come to that."

"Folkestone? That's south-east Kent." He stopped mid-tracks, remembering Molly Bishop had just been to Dover a few minutes' along the coast from Folkestone. "That's promising. Keep in touch. Oh yes – new idea. I've realised that Mbesa is registered at the Isle of Man Company Registry. I want court orders against bankers and brokers over there. Hopefully, his shares were bought through a Manx company."

Torrington Marina

After strolling round the marina, Ratso and Kirsty-Ann had settled for drinks and nibbles in the Lay-Zee Bar in Torrington. Their view was towards the fortified harbour wall and lighthouse. The bar was open-sided and a cooling breeze eased the relentless noonday heat. They settled onto thickly-padded seats beneath a striped sunshade. The ambiance was improved by the smell of grilled fish and hickory wood-smoke. Iced lagers had arrived, the glasses dripping with condensation. Thick creamy chowder then swiftly followed. Though Kirsty-Ann's smiles were friendly enough, Ratso knew she was preoccupied with whatever was troubling her. Her eyes showed she was somewhere else and what little conversation there was had little substance.

By the time Cobb Salads were served, Ratso could take it no longer. To his question about what was troubling her, she lowered her eyes sadly before clasping both his wrists. "Not here," was all she had said. "Let's talk on our terrace before dinner."

"Afternoon plans?"

"If you're thinking what I'm thinking, we should grab the first taxi."

Several hours later, they were seated on their terrace. The fierce heat had eased. Out to sea, beside the occasional pinprick of light from a fishing-boat, all was blackness. Room Service had delivered an ice-bucket with a bottle of champagne and a selection of canapés. They were both dressed in smart-casual gear, ready for dinner in the candlelit restaurant.

"You look just terrific," Ratso said. Kirsty-Ann was wearing a free-flowing wrap-around maxi-dress in coral pink. "Here's to us." Ratso leaned across with a kiss on Kirsty-Ann's cheek as he clinked her glass.

"I wish. Truly I do."

"Meaning?"

She sighed. "Todd, we've both known since way back. We had … we still have, something special. I still feel that today. Not just last night or this afternoon, although that was pretty amazing." She looked at him to see his reaction.

"But…"

"You've been promoted now. You love your Fulham FC and your crazy English cricket. You're married to the Met, to London and your English way of life. I've now realised that my hope, my big plan for us, was a no-no."

"Go on."

"When I arrived, I was going to ask you to quit the Met and join me in Florida. You'd be a co-owner of my agency. I wanted us to be together and for Leon to have the greatest dad. He needs a dad just like you. But now, being here and listening to you, I see it all – I can't expect you to give up everything you've lived and breathed." Her words had tumbled out but now she stopped to sip her champagne with a hesitant glance. "My dream is way too selfish."

"Your pitch about Florida yesterday? It sounded like the destination from hell." Ratso's laugh was genuine and was barely met with a smile. "Now, you've got your new agency, I've missed the chance of getting you to London."

"The UK's Immigration wouldn't let me, my Mom and Leon live there."

"Unless we were married."

"Unless we were married," she repeated the words as if in a daze.

"K.A, you know I love you. I always have. Maybe not written in neon. No love letters in the sand. That's not my way. Because of our situation. I hoped how I felt was clear from actions, not just words."

A dreamy, wistful look crossed K.A's face. "In the brief time we shared before he was killed on duty, I loved my husband, Andy. But I was younger then. My feelings about you are different, much stronger, more intense." Tears started to roll down her cheeks. "Then I messed up with that dumb one-nighter. That guy from Chicago." She sobbed and Ratso stroked her cheek before she continued. "Dumbest thing ever. If only Leon hadn't been born after a drunken grope with a guy I didn't know."

"He's got a terrific Mom. He's got plenty enough love."

"There's more, Todd."

Fearing the worst, Ratso braced himself by leaning back in his chair, his eyes fixed on the black horizon. "Go on then." He topped up their nearly empty glasses.

"There's a guy, three years younger than me. Divorced and no kids. He's a detective. He was flirting before I met you. I brushed him aside. I didn't want to screw up my career because of him."

"And now you're no longer a cop, he's…"

"Yes. He follows me around, like a puppy."

Ratso was silent for a long moment, wanting his words to be pitch-perfect. "I mean, have you gone out with him? We never owned each other."

"We've kinda dated. He's a regular guy. But we've never dated like the word now seems to mean. We've taken in a movie; we've held hands and he's kissed me goodnight. A big nothing else. But he wants more, wants everything. Marriage. Kids."

"Do you love him?"

"No." K.A's answer was immediate. "He's lovable ... so maybe I could learn to. Dirk, that's his name, he's hard not to like. Leon's not too sure. He told me he wants you to be his dad. Dirk's funny, hunky good looks. Smart too." She turned to face Ratso and then in an impulsive move, rose from her chair and eased onto his lap, flinging her arms round his neck. After a quiet moment or two, as he clung to her scented warm body, Ratso whispered softly in her ear. "You were right. I'm not ready to quit the Met. Not right now." He felt her shudder as he decided what to say next. "But I have an idea."

Grantchester Hotel, Bonnitor

Kirsty-Ann leaned across the curve of the dining-table to stroke Ratso's cheek. "This is insane. This is the craziest, maddest most ... wonderful, exciting moment of my life."

"So it's yes?"

Kirsty-Ann raised her glass of Chambolle Musigny which they were enjoying with a selection of French cheeses and purple grapes. "To us. United in love forever." She peered down at the *to-do list* that Ratso had been jotting down during the leisurely dinner. "Is it doable?"

"I checked with the Concièrge. You would have to delay returning to Florida for 24 hours. We'll know any time soon."

"But that Zak guy in Barbados? Your boat-trip. Meeting Inspector Alleyne?"

"I'll put them on hold for 24 hours. Getting married comes first. Married at noon. Fly to Barbados in the afternoon. A one-night honeymoon. You go back to Leon and your Mom. I'll become a copper again. Later, with Leon and your Mom, we can have a couple of weeks together – London, Paris, New York. Wherever."

"And you'll really quit the Met? Give up everything for me?"

"Promise. September next year. Then, I'll join your agency."

"Leon and Mom will be so excited." Her smile faded. "You'll miss your cricket."

"Can't deny that."

"You'll lose a lifetime of friendships." Kirsty-Ann reached out

to stroke his neck as she popped a grape into her small mouth.
"You'll do all this for me?"
"Real friendships never die. I'll still see my best buddies. I'll get to take Leon to Lord's." "You'll teach him the rules of cricket?"
"That would be ..." Ratso was about say *challenging* but he stopped in mid-flow. Clyde, the Concièrge, appeared followed by Miguel, the Sommelier. Both their faces were radiant, all big eyes and laughing smiles. "Mr Holtom. Everything is fixed. You pick up the marriage licence at the Ministry tomorrow at eight-thirty. Then, you'll meet the Reverend Carr to discuss the formalities. By your return, your terrace will be decorated with a floral arch for the service. The Hotel Manager and Miguel will be your witnesses."

"A privilege," Miguel bowed his head as he spoke. "And to enter into the spirit of the occasion, please accept this bottle of vintage 1991 Armagnac with our compliments."

Clyde smiled at the couple. "Sorry Ms Weber. One small thing. A certified copy of your husband's death certificate is essential. There are no other formalities. Outside of Las Vegas, Bonnitor has the most relaxed marriage laws."

"Not a problem. I'll also need a hairdresser and a boutique. Can you fix that?"

With an *of course*, Clyde and Miguel left Ratso to open the bottle and pour two glasses. alone to chink glasses. "I'll phone Mom now. Leon will be asleep. My Mom's dreamed of you and me getting together. You must say hi to her."

Bridgetown, Barbados

Still walking on air as if in a daze, Ratso jumped aboard *Mighty Meg*, ready for the boat trip skippered by Zak Carter. Though she was designed for eight passengers, there were only four when Carter set the powerful engine into reverse. Now that Kirsty-Ann was heading home, the last hour had proved difficult, much harder than he had expected.
I'm married!
I've got a step-son.
I'm retiring in just over a year.
Goodbye England!
Goodbye cricket!
Goodbye Fulham FC.
He watched a couple of kids on the quay with shrimping-nets. Regrets? None – just a stunned awareness of the bonfire of everything that had been his life. As he adjusted his seat cushion, he forced himself to forget K.A's tearful goodbye. Instead, as *Mighty Meg* chugged towards the open sea, he relived their moonlit kisses at the budget-busting Trade Winds Hotel. Then his attention turned to Zak Carter as he manoeuvred between the other moored pleasure craft.
Am I looking at Kendall Campbell's murderer?
Time to focus.
Time to find out.
Think like a copper.
But not be one.

Definitely not.
Don't raise suspicion.
The boat was comfortable enough but it stunk of diesel, dead fish and brine. Around the small seating area, there was a Japanese couple with phones on sticks. A surly looking American retiree had commandeered the stern, his bulk spreading across the bench-seat. He ignored Ratso's friendly nod and instead was scowling at the water swishing by.
Must be suffering from incurable piles and raging toothache.
Zak Carter though proved to be a cheery soul. His black face was as big as a medium pizza and just as round. His shoulders were broad and his arms had bulging biceps. Bare-chested, but wearing a peaked white cap with gold braid, he was below average height. Consistent with more overnight information from DC Viment, Ratso knew he was forty-two, divorced, paying off his ex-wife and buying *Mighty Meg* on the drip.

"Hi! I'm Captain Zak. Where yo' all from?" The skipper turned from the wheel and took in the muttered replies. "I'll fix drinks when we're out of harbour." His accent was English with little trace of Caribbean. The Japanese male said they were in from San Francisco. The American grunted something indecipherable which might have been *take a hike*. Ratso said he was from West London. "What you all do back home?" Carter asked.

Ratso guessed Carter went through this patter every trip, trying to get a bit of camaraderie between the passengers. *Mission impossible today,* Ratso decided as the American ignored the question. The Japanese volunteered ownership of a Japanese car importing franchise. "I'm Tom from London. I work for the Department of Transport," Ratso explained. "Traffic flow, curing gridlocks. Congestion Zones. Boring as hell but without it, I wouldn't be in Barbados. I'm not complaining."

Carter's face showed his interest at someone from the UK. "I was brought up in Hampshire before joining the Army."

"Which Regiment?" Ratso could see that the skipper was in peak condition. Below his navy shorts, the legs were muscular with not an ounce of fat. The bare stomach was flat. Even now, seven years since his SAS days, Ratso could imagine him yomping through mud, wind and hail on the Brecon Beacons or strangling a thirty-foot python during jungle training. *But could he really be the murderer who had sodomised Kendall Carter?*

"3 Paras. A Red Beret," Carter answered proudly. "I visited more places than I remember."

Ratso did not regard this as deception. Major Tang had explained that many ex-SAS never volunteered that they had been successful and joined the SAS. Others, though, wrote best-selling books. "Quiet this morning, Zak."

"Yeah, but the sunset cruise tonight is full." Listening to his accent, Ratso could have been in any pub round London.

"So for you, it's the same old, same old – day-in-day-out?"

"Pretty much. Some days we do deep-sea fishing-only – marlin and barracuda."

"Get back to the UK much?"

"Nah. My folks have passed on. Since Covid, business has been tough – but I get by. I support Chelsea and watch them on the box."

"Ever thought of island-hopping tours? I heard that was big business. Or maybe your boat's too small?"

"The fuel-tanks are plenty big enough. We go way out for deep-sea fishing. If it gets rough or there's a downpour, passengers can go below. Problem is we've no sleeping accommodation. If the goddamned bank would help, I would mebbe invest in something with cabins. You're right. There's big money in longer trips. Big tips too."

Deadly Hush

"How come you know about sailing? You're an ex-Para."

"I did some boat training." Carter laughed. "Yeah. Even that sounds effing crazy when I'd been trained to jump from 10,000 feet. Boat training even *seems crazy* when you find yourself dug into a sand-dune. Not much use knowing about landing-craft and dinghies there. But here in Barbados, man, that training's done me plenty good." After dishing out cans of beer and Pepsi, he pointed to the coast. "See over there. Starboard side. That's Sandy Lane, the best hotel in Barbados."

Ratso took in the view of the low-rise building surrounded by clumps of splendid trees. "I've heard all the celebs stay there. Unless I win the Premium Bonds, way out of my reach."

"Where are you staying, Tom?"

"I stopped near the Kensington Oval," Ratso winged it. "Just one night. I'm going over to Bonnitor. It's much cheaper."

"You get what you pay for. Barbados is the Rolls Royce. Bonnitor is a clapped-out Skoda. No offence, mate."

Ratso grinned. "None taken." He opened the beer and savoured the pleasure as the cold liquid hit the back of his throat. He looked across to the Japanese couple. The man was taking a selfie with a stupid grin on his face and his companion was asleep. *Not much point in paying for her, was there, mate.*

The sulky American was digging out a Kentucky Cheroot from a four-pack. Ratso shifted to watch the guy struggling to light it. He stretched out a hand to offer shelter but was ignored. "Great trip, huh? Call me Tom. I didn't catch your name."

The American patted down his bulging Hawaiian shirt and started to turn his fleshy back to Ratso. "Hey, pal, the politicians say we Brits have a special relationship with you Americans. You got a business-card? Maybe we could keep in touch?" Ratso was enjoying the wind-up and paused in case of a reply but expected nothing. He was not disappointed. "Another time, eh pal? Enjoy the trip."

Zak Carter had heard every word and his face was all white teeth and laughing eyes. He looked at the American's back and winked and shrugged as Ratso fired up the conversation. "It's not my job but one of my mates along the corridor, he handles marine registrations, all that boring crap. He drinks gallons of Red Bull just to stay awake! He was telling me about black boxes on ships. I never knew about them, only on aircraft. Is big brother watching you?"

"Yeah," Carter chuckled, deep and melodious. "Man! We're all being watched. Even in *Mighty Meg*. No law says my little tub must have AIS. She's mighty in name only! But AIS was on-board when I bought her. You know about AIS?"

"Sounds like a nasty disease but I guess it isn't."

"Automatic Identification System. The previous owner had bought a Class B-AIS Transponder. It's a small box of tricks packed with clever software."

"Collision avoidance then?"

"Yeah." He waved a muscled arm towards the horizon. "Duststorms, blinding rain, even fog, my little gadget warns vessels of my presence."

"I guess only so long as they use theirs?"

"Right on, Tom. Big vessels like cruise ships or tankers, they must use it constantly. They can turn it off only if that would be safer."

"Safer to turn it off? You're kidding? Right?'"

Carter handed Ratso another beer. "Nah! Straight up! Imagine sailing to Lagos, Wrest Africa. Pirates are ten-a-penny in the Gulf of Guinea. The master of a super-tanker might turn it off so those scum don't know his vessel is approaching. Me? Mine's on – except in port. Someone in London could locate *Mighty Meg* even now."

"Amazing! Can I make my mates jealous? Let them watch me swilling beer?"

Carter high-fived before shaking his head. "It's not that type of satellite. It's plotting position only." He pointed again. "See over there. That's the Trade Winds Hotel, another jet-setter place. It's my landmark for heading back. Excuse me." He placed both hands on the wheel and Ratso felt the boat rock and sway as it went about.

Ratso looked across the deep blue of the sea. So near, so far! He identified the room *they* had left, barely five hours before. He saw where *his wife* had stood on the balcony, her bronzed arms clinging to him.

But now? K.A would soon be landing at Fort Lauderdale, returning to Leon, for whom he was now Dad or Daddy ... or would it be Pop? He looked away and forced himself to concentrate on the genial skipper, who was humming Bob Marley's *I shot the Sheriff.*

No. Not the sheriff, Zak.
You seem a regular guy.
Did you murder Kendall Campbell KC?
Smash in his head and sodomise him?
It seemed implausible.
But with his questions answered, he'd get Tosh Watson onto it.

Grantchester Hotel, Bonnitor

"Welcome back Mr Holtom." The Concièrge left his desk to shake hands. "I'm so sorry that Mrs Holtom is not with you."

"Thanks, Clyde. That makes two of us."

"A dinner reservation?"

"Please. Two people at eight-thirty."

"Consider it done. And how was Barbados?"

"Your recommendation of the Trade Winds was perfect." Ratso picked up his overnight bag to head for his room. "I'm here for two nights and then back to cloudy old London."

From his suite, he had a long Zoom conversation with Kirsty-Ann. This had lifted his spirits as had bonding with Leon who had never stopped jumping up and down. Though K.A.'s Mom had been happy, Ratso couldn't miss her tired eyes. Her cheeks were more sunken than he remembered. Ratso was still mulling over the call when he went down to dinner.

He recognised Bastien Alleyne at once though it had been over four years since his training in London. Compensating for his receding hairline, Alleyne had cultivated generous sideburns and a stubbled whiskery appearance over his cleft chin. He also now walked with a noticeable limp, something Ratso did not recall. Alleyne pumped Ratso's hand, his eyes and voice demonstrating his enthusiasm. "Detective Chief Inspector Holtom! Welcome to our beautiful island."

"It's Todd. Great to catch up, Bastien. What's with the limp?"

"Knife wounds to the femoral. I was lucky to live but I've muscle weakness." He slapped Ratso on the back. "Alcohol kills the pain. Let's head for the bar." He led on and ordered a double Jack Daniels on the rocks. Ratso decided to have the same, though he would have preferred to have slung back a Zombie or two. "This evening, you're a dinner guest of the Royal Bonnitor Constabulary. If you solve the murder," he said, only half-joking, "I might even swing your hotel bill too."

"Dangling the carrot, Bastien? I might take a bite. But we've a load of catching up before talking about Campbell's murder."

"Suits me. Let's talk old times – those nights on the town."

"Can you remember them, Bastien?"

As Alleyne recalled being assisted back to his bedroom by Tosh Watson, he gave Ratso an apologetic but knowing look. "Them tuition mornings, staying awake, boy that was tough. So let's talk shit like back then."

"Agreed." Ratso gave Alleyne a sideways glance which was not lost on him. "Shall we go to the table?" It was only after more laughs about Alleyne's time in London that Ratso volunteered what he had been bursting to say all evening. "You're the first person to know. I got married here yesterday. No more wild nights for me, Bastien." He produced a photo of Mr & Mrs Holtom standing under a floral arch.

"She's a beauty. Lucky you." Alleyne clapped a hand on Ratso's shoulder. "You once told me you were married to the Met and cricket."

Ratso shrugged. "Then along came Kirsty-Ann. Now, there's all three in my marriage!"

Both men laughed. "This calls for champagne," Alleyne insisted.

Much later, after emptying the champagne, but still before

dessert, they had also sunk a bottle of Pouilly Fuisse with their flying-fish and cou-cou, a local speciality made from cornmeal and okra. With their T-Bones, a Russian River Pinot Noir had disappeared in a trice. Now, they were clinking glasses of Ruinart Brut Rosé as the Head Waiter flamed Crêpes Suzette at the table.

It was only after Ratso had declined the cheeseboard that Alleyne's eyes turned serious. "Okay, my friend. I hope you can help. I'm getting so much shit thrown at me by the Chief Superintendent. Let's talk Kendall Campbell."

The comment brought back unwanted memories of Smart Alex Caldwell. "Join the club! I get dumped on every day."

Alleyne leaned on the table and spoke softly, the mellow lilt of his accent even more striking than usual. "My investigation is going nowhere. You ... any ideas? You hinted ..."

"Don't get excited! Just a possible new line of enquiry. I may know more tomorrow." Ratso placed his champagne flute on the white table-cloth and paused to wipe up the last morsels of dessert. "Since I arrived here, I've picked up rumours that the KC was gang-banged or sodomised. That doesn't fit any scenario I'm thinking about."

In the hushed dining-room, Alleyne leaned back and let off a noisy cackle that attracted frowns and irritated stares from other diners. Ratso looked puzzled. "What's the joke? I've got a robust sense of humour. Being gang-raped isn't my idea of a fun night out."

"Todd, you been drinking in the wrong part of town?"

"Not guilty. No."

Alleyne rocked back again, still laughing. Then he pulled his chair up so close that Ratso could smell brilliantine. "On a small island like this, stories spread fast. I heard that rumour too. Todd, here's the truth. One of our young constables was in McDonalds. He was overheard saying the poor guy was buggered good and proper." Alleyne chuckled again. "He didn't mean sodomised. We've never revealed the injuries – we've just said it was a vicious attack."

Now Ratso laughed. "Buggered was just a figure of speech then?"

"Yes and no. Within minutes, the story spread and grew. *Good and proper* became gang-bang. Last week, in a downtown bar, someone told me, *as a fact*, that Campbell had been split open." He ran his hands over his head. "None of that was true. The killer *had* smashed Campbell's head real bad." Alleyne was surprised to see a growing satisfied look on Ratso's face. "Todd. You're looking relieved. Give."

"A gang-bang would have killed my line of enquiry."

"The attack looked drug-crazed. Tomorrow, I'll show you the pictures. My constable's description wasn't so wrong. One thing for sure – Campbell certainly wasn't set on fire." The twisted grin on Alleyne's whiskery face was not lost on Ratso but he let it pass.

"Any stolen property turning up?"

"Nothing. That's unusual."

Ratso gave a quiet smile. "That's good. I'd say Zombie-good. You up for that?"

Grantchester Hotel, Bonnitor

Ratso had just finished breakfast of fluffy scrambled eggs and Canadian bacon when his phone vibrated. He was alone on his terrace and about to pour more orange juice. He did not recognise the number. "Hello?"

"Reg Gastrell. Can we talk?"

Ratso looked right and left. The nearest terraces were empty. "You're good. You've arrested Hysen Kola?"

"Not yet. The day before you left, we spotted someone acting suspiciously near Jubilee House. It didn't look like him but he was a similar height and build. He approached Jubilee House going down the High Street towards he river. He walked slowly past the front entrance. At the Odeon Cinema, he doubled back. He again passed the front entrance. He then turned left and went along Putney Bridge Road."

"Down the side of our building. Got it."

"He then turned left again into Brewhouse Lane."

"Beside the rear of Jubilee House."

"Correct. He continued to beyond your car-park entrance."

Ratso was mentally tracing every step. "To near the Boathouse Restaurant?"

"Correct. He then retraced his steps and bought a ticket at the cinema."

"Go on."

"He never came out. At least, not looking like he did when he entered."

"How did he reach the High Street?"

"He took the tube to East Putney Station and then walked. But we don't know from where. The trail went cold."

"He's not been seen again around Jubilee House?"

"Not unless he looked different and didn't attract attention."

"Sounds like someone killing time before the movie." Even as he said it, Ratso was unconvinced. "Nah! Killing time, you'd hang about watching the river."

"And don't forget. He changed his appearance in the cinema bog. We checked. There wre no discarded clothes there or anywhere nearby." There was a pause before Gastrell continued. "Here's the thing." He hesitated. "Either this never was our guy or he disliked the location. We've not seen him again."

It was not what Ratso wanted to hear. He stood up and arched his shoulders back. Then he sucked in a deep breath and looked skywards. "Reg, it may be much worse. Perhaps there's been a leak and he's been tipped off I'm travelling."

Police HQ – Bonnitor

The moment he arrived at HQ, Ratso was aware of his VIP status. Not only was he greeted by both Bastien Alleyne and Det. Sgt Venables but he was ushered straight into the office of the Commissioner. "Good to meet you Mr Holtom," the impressive looking figure greeted him. He was dressed in a navy-blue uniform with silver crowns on the shoulders. Beside him was his cap with a red band and a gold braid peak. "I'm Winston Richards. Welcome to Bonnitor. I've heard great things about your track-record. I'm sure my officers learned a great deal in London."

Ratso saw no intent at humour in the Commissioner's face but his own imagination ran wild with images of pole-dancers' gyrating buttocks and spinning roulette wheels. "We did our best, sir."

"I know you're here privately but we would welcome any ideas about Kendall Campbell's murder. We've ruled out the obvious bad-ass locals. We can't link the widow Brenda or her lover to any hitman. Bastien told me you may have a new theory?"

"Yes … I may have something. You know how it is, sir – suspecting is one thing, proving is another."

"Venny, pour the coffee please." Venables did so. "Do continue."

"I am SIO of an investigation into a series of killings – all four victims were gay."

"Excuse me interrupting but our KC was far from that," Bastien Alleyne chipped in. "He was a devoted family man. His daughters have told us he worshipped Brenda. He would have been devastated if he'd known that she was poised to leave him for Morry Rolle."

"I don't see the deaths as homophobic." Ratso looked over his

Deadly Hush

coffee-cup with a sheepish grin. "Mind you, half my team think I'm hammering every fact to fit into the wrong jigsaw."

"My inspector thinks you somehow link the London murders with Bonnitor?"

"Still theory only. Mind you, my four-pip – that's Detective Chief Superintendent Caldwell disagrees."

"It happens." Commissioner Richards shrugged and shared a knowing look with his two officers. "What's the trans-Atlantic link?"

For nearly fifteen minutes, Ratso summarised everything starting with Quercy's murder in Geneva. "My take involves high-finance and crashed shares in Energy Management Associates. That's the link to Kendall Campbell."

Ratso was not surprised when Commissioner Richards was first to comment. His officers had both looked to him to speak first rather than say something foolish. "Todd, if I may call you that? Your entire scenario started with a drunken comment in a Yorkshire pub?" He waited for Ratso's acknowledgement. "This Terry Yates, so you guess, is like a spider in the middle orchestrating murders, maybe even murdering personally. Your guess is he's been using ex-SAS mates to help get revenge for his losses in Energy Management." He waved both hands in a dismissive *you're away-with-the-fairies* gesture. Oh yes and you can't prove that he owned lots of shares as a motive."

"Correct. Not even *any* shares but there's evidence he was seen at an AGM." Ratso's firmed up to add defiance. "Sir, he and his mates were trained to kill. All five deaths were similar."

"The lawyer here was different. You'd agree Todd?"

"Entirely, sir. It looked like a brutal assault with no finesse."

Ratso saw that none of three listeners were excited by his theory. "Without proving Yates had a big motive, I accept I'm flying on empty." He fixed each of the three seated listeners with a steady smile, his hands adding emphasis. "There's more though. Something just reached me this morning."

"You know who killed Campbell?" Alleyne's voice and raised eyebrows showed the incredulity of an under-ten watching a magician get a rabbit from a hat.

Ratso like Alleyne but his judgement was still as unbalanced as he remembered. "Don't get over-revved, Bastien. It's still inconclusive."

The Commissioner rose, spun his chair and then sat down again, all in a sudden movement. "Go on." He sounded impatient.

"What I'm about to tell you points one way. My interviews with the directors of Energy Management may point another. They were here when Campbell was murdered. They were in London when the black kid was murdered. All three EMA officers have been holding something back. I'd like to know why."

The Commissioner stroked his neat beard. Hie eyes messaged that he was still not buying Ratso's belief. He said nothing, leaving it to his inspector to continue after he had helped himself to a chocolate-topped macaroon. "The directors? You mean they killed all the victims? Or did they conspire with Terry Yates?"

Ratso avoided answering the speculation. "Kendall Campbell would have been high on Yates's revenge list – maybe top equal with Logan Goldie. A guy in Bridgetown, Zak Carter, is a good mate from Yates's SAS days. He owns a motorised yacht, called *Mighty Meg*. It is fitted with a satellite tracking system called AIS." He saw he had now captured their imagination. "That pinpoints the boat's position."

"Go on," enthused the Commissioner, his body now looking alert. "You can position it beside Campbell's jetty?"

Ratso pursed his lips. "I wish. On the evening of the murder,

Zak Carter's boat was tracked to under a mile from Robinson Cove. My theory is he then thought: *Holy Shit! I forgot to turn off the AIS.* This he then did. It was switched off for over two hours. I believe, he then chug-chugged into the next bay. Having weighed anchor, he swam to Campbell's jetty. Easy for him unless he bumped into a tiger shark. The lights would have been triggered but would have gone out long before Campbell returned. He then hid in the back yard waiting for Campbell and then followed him into the property."

"And left carrying the cash and jewels?"

"Carter had been trained in the marine sector of the SAS. He's super-fit. Swimming four hundred metres each way with a waterproof back-pack? No problem."

"So he switched on the AIS later?"

"It resumed when he was about three miles offshore for returning to Bridgetown."

"Anything else?" asked Winston Richards.

"The AIS records for *Mighty Meg* prove that, except when docked in Bridgetown, not once this year has Carter turned off AIS."

"Campbell's murder looked anything but professional."

Ratso's eyes dismissed the negative. "That doesn't faze me. Carter's smart. That's an SAS essential. He made it look like locals."

The Commissioner nodded slowly as he absorbed the news. "I'm impressed." The Commissioner waved his surprisingly short arms above his desk in an inclusive gesture. He then rose to his commanding height and shook Ratso's hand. "Todd, you're very welcome here. Come again."

Bastien Alleyne led them out. "I've cleared a desk for you."

"I was thinking. Yesterday you said Campbell hadn't caught fire. What did you mean?"

"I'll explain."

Police HQ - Bonnitor

Sitting at the L-shaped desk vacated by Sgt. Venables, Bastien Alleyne positioned a monitor so that both he and Ratso could see it. "These shots show Campbell's house – see the front-door smashed." He clicked again. "And these show the cause of death." On screen appeared the battered and bloodied head.

"The weapon?"

"Never found. The pathologist reckoned a long-reach spanner or more probably a crowbar."

"Dumped somewhere at sea."

"Agreed." Alleyne leaned forward and with a mouse-click revealed the lower half of Campbell's body. "We imagined our locals sniggering as they did this. It was a first for us though." Alleyne clicked again for a close-up view.

Lost for words, Ratso stared as he absorbed the picture. He shook his head. "A first for me too. Never seen anything like this." He was imagining yesterday's cruise with friendly, jovial Zak Carter. *Could he do this? Would he do this*? Lying beside the KC's bare buttocks was a fire-extinguisher. The nozzle at the end of the hose had been rammed into Campbell's anus and then activated. His buttocks were spattered with yellow fire-retardant powder.

"That's why my constable in McDonalds said he'd been buggered good and proper. His innards were full of the stuff." Alleyne clicked again to show pictures of the trashed kitchen.

"I can see why you suspected guys high on drugs." Ratso turned away to look down the street towards the offices of Energy

Deadly Hush

Management. "I can't imagine Olly Young or Molly Bishop doing this."

"Unless they hired someone."

Ratso remained silent as he weighed the possibility.

"Maybe hired Zak Carter?" Alleyne repeated his earlier suggestion.

Ratso was not enthused. "Open-mind." He saw a message appear on his phone. "I need to contact London."

"Pitch camp here." He watched Alleyne limp into the corridor and disappear. The message from Tosh Watson was typically brief. "Police in Vienna have arrested WPCoin's Hanna Farkas. Puts Valbona Jakupi in the clear? With Farkas alive, unlikely/less likely Jakupi had Goldie murdered. Jock will phone."

Ratso doodled on his empty pad as he waited. He found he had scribbled the word *motive* in bold black. He walked to the window, stroking his chin thoughtfully. Where was the magic bullet? The circumstantial evidence was impressive but still he lacked a noose to slip round Yates's neck. In the street below, everywhere was movement – old and rusted cars belching fumes, motor-bikes revving and swerving between delivery trucks, women with pushchairs, a couple of pensioners waving and shouting across the street. All the action was against a background of noise from a concrete-mixer churning its load before delivery. From a fast-food stall, a smell of jerk-chicken wafted through the open window. It smelled so good, Ratso decided to buy some before visiting Olly and Molly.

While waiting for Strang's call, he fired off a one-line text to Kirsty-Ann. "Thinking of you. Love you." Almost instantly, she replied *speak soon* and signed off with three kisses. His thoughts of a new life in Florida did not last long. His vibrating phone saw to that.

"Boss, all good?"

"If you've nailed Yates or traced a relevant Audi, that would be good." Ratso had no intention of volunteering his marriage to the Jubilee House team.

"There's a wee bittie news on them both. Bonkers got a result from the Isle of Man. The Deemster, that's like a High Court Judge in England …"

"I know what a Deemster is, Jock. I've even appeared before a Deemster on a banking fraud."

"Sorry, boss. I didna' ken that. Anyroads, the old beak gave the orders to examine the records of brokers and bankers. We hit paydirt."

"Searching for Yates's name?"

"Aye. Two broking companies had his name as the UBO – *ultimate beneficial owner* of two Manx companies. Both had owned millions of shares in Energy Management Associates. Way over 3% in total."

"Had?"

"Yates sold the lot when the shares crashed. He just kept a few in his own name."

"How much did he lose?"

"Ninety-eight percent of his money. Just under twelve million quid."

Clutching his phone to his ear, Ratso returned to the window to watch the colourful scene below. "That would have spoiled his day."

"Right enough – but does it make him a killer?"

"That depends on how damaging it was. Goldie's attack on Fergus Edwards's timeshare operation cost Fergus millions but he's still fabulously rich."

"Ye mean, Yates may have been almost wiped out.?"

"Get more evidence on his finances. In North Yorkshire, his mates think he's super-rich."

"There's more ye need to hear. Oliver Young?"

"Go on."

"The evening Marcel was murdered, he misled you. He didn't go home to Sevenoaks after visiting the Rogerson Hotel. CCTV tracked him to London Square, Bermondsey."

"That's no distance from where Marcel was murdered."

"Aye. Walking distance. He parked his Audi beneath an apartment block."

"Did he go out? Walk to Aquinas Street? Contact Molly? Contact Jamie Fargher"

"Pass. That's where the trail ends. So far." Strang paused to cope with a hacking cough. "Something else strange. The mystery guy who stayed at Dunsdale Creek caravan park."

"Yes, using a false address."

"ANPR picked up an Audi saloon about fourteen miles south of King's Lynn shortly before he checked in."

"And?"

"The DVLA in Cardiff has confirmed that the vehicle is registered to … Oliver Young." Strang knew he had lobbed a grenade. There was a long silence and Strang knew better than to say anything while the boss's brain recalibrated. He heard Ratso's sharp intake of breath followed by sounds of a desk-top being drummed.

"Recapping then. Olly Young told me porkies. He may have met Yates at King's Lynn." He doodled on the pad – a few loops and squiggles. "I just don't see Olly as a bare-hands murderer. He's got kids nearly Marcel's age. But he could have masterminded events around Aquinas Street. Set up the murder for Molly or a Molly lookalike."

Ratso continued the train of thought. "Olly and his Audi were within spitting distance of Yates in King's Lynn. He's controlling Yates."

"Maybe paying him," interrupted Strang.

"Yates races to London in the Audi and murders Dermot Doyle."

"How do we link Olly to Lord Ongerton?"

"Or Geneva come to that. Can we go for a working hypothesis that the directors paid a team of SAS guys to get revenge."

"Sorry, boss but I'm not buying it. Why dress up to look like Molly? That makes no sense."

"You're right, Jock. It doesn't." How would the directors know Yates to arrange murders for money? Nothing stacks up. Any news from Folkestone? Degsy somebody?"

"Tosh Watson and Nancy Petrie drove to the coast this morning."

"Thanks. Keep me posted." Concentration was difficult against a background of blaring reggae from somewhere below. After twenty minutes, he had no answer to the contradictions. Instead, he jotted down his questions for the afternoon before bounding down the stairs to grab jerk-chicken and fries."

Torrington, Bonnitor

"Been in Europe recently?" enquired Ratso as he clutched his tea in a chipped mug in EMA's offices.

Molly Bishop's eyes narrowed as if she were suspicious of the question "Recently meaning when?"

Ratso disliked prevarication. "This year will do."

"Anywhere in particular?"

"Europe will do."

"I was in Prague with Oscar, my hubbie. We also did Venice." She scratched her ear as if this would lead to inspiration. "In June, I was in France."

"Alone?"

She shook her head. "Cycling around Burgundy with Oscar."

Quercy had been murdered in June. Ratso sniffed a new line of questions but his French geography was woeful. "Tell me more."

"Train from London. Changed at Lille. We hired bikes in Dijon. We cycled to Chablis, Beaune and Macon."

"Were you there on 19th June?"

"In Burgundy?"

"Yes – where else?"

"We stayed in gîtes. – simple lodgings."

"Yes … but my question? The 19th." Ratso forced himself to be polite.

Bishop showed Ratso her diary entries simply showing the word France for each day. She then flicked on her phone and he watched her clumsy two-fingered typing. *Was she making mistakes*

-315-

because she was nervous? She opened her photos. "We were around Bourg-en-Bresse. Taken on the 20th. Here's a picture of us by the Cathedral."

Ratso studied Oscar for the first time. He looked ten years older than his wife and was both shorter and fatter with a comb-over. "Did you meet up with Olly?"

"We don't socialise."

"The day before the 20th?"

"You mean the 19th?"

Ratso's hackles were now raised. "Yes."

"I've no photos for that day. I think we must have been pedalling all day. Perhaps from Macon."

"So which day did you go to Geneva?"

Bishop frowned as if she was struggling to recollect something she could scarcely have forgotten. Her answer came, slow and thoughtful. "Geneva ?No. Not Geneva. We never went there."

"Not on the 19th?"

Bishop looked across her desk and shook her head like a dog in a car's rear window.

"How far were you from Geneva?"

"Let's look at a map." She switched to her laptop with a bigger screen. Moments later, she twisted it through forty-five degrees so they could both look. Ratso saw that Bourg-en-Bresse was about seventy miles from Geneva – easy cycling distance. He watched her unpainted nails thump on the keys. "Google reckons one hour-twenty-four minutes by car or over three hours by train. We had no car."

Had she added the last comment a shade too forcefully? Ratso was unsure.

"Five hours max by bike?" Ratso imagined Oscar's short legs pumping furiously up the hills.

"Bit less. Why are you asking about Geneva?"

"Olly dealt with Jules Quercy?"

"So did Jamie. They met him." Her face showed surprise, her mouth and eyes widening. "Oh! I get it! You think one of us three murdered Jules Quercy?"

"Not what I said or think." Ratso made a mental note to have Jamie's movements checked. "We'll need to speak to your husband. He's on an oil-rig?"

"He'll be on leave next week. He's coming to the EGM and then we're having a few days in a Health-Farm near Bath."

Ratso ticked a note in front of him and moved on. "And London. I'm still interested in your movements last week. Y'know – your long walk and after."

"Mr Holtom, we've covered this." Bishop sounded exasperated. "After my walk, I was alone. Sad person that I am, I sank a bottle of red *on my own*. Drowned my sorrows *on my own* in my room."

"So you never saw Olly that evening?"

"Olly?" The surprise sounded genuine, her puzzlement obvious. "No. Why would I? We're not an item. He was in Oxford and then checking out the Rogerson."

"Just asking." Hands on knees, Ratso pushed himself up. "I'll catch Olly now. See you at the EGM." After thanking her, Ratso went straight to Young's office. It was obvious Young had just returned from the barber's. His hair was much neater than earlier. Young saw Ratso's curious stare look as he sniffed the air. He answered the unasked question. "I had it trimmed for the EGM."

"Hopefully you won't smell quite so scented by then."

"The barber said the shampoo was Australian Desert Peach. Don't you like it?"

"I can get by without it."

"So what now, Mr Holtom?"

"Loose ends. I've read your online diary. You keep a paper one as well?"

"I do." Young took a leather-bound diary from a top drawer and took it to his assistant to copy. "How else can I help?" Ratso wanted to know why he had driven to King's Lynn but was not quite ready to ask that. "Let's start with your movements after leaving the Rogerson Hotel."

Folkestone, Kent

"I could retire to a spot like this." Watson and Nancy Petrie were on The Leas, the cliff-top promenade in Folkestone.

"Look! You can just see France," Petrie replied, pointing across the grey swell of the English Channel. Behind them was Degsy Foden's apartment. It was in a modern block overlooking the well-kept public lawns where they were standing. Overhead, were scudding purple clouds.

"That's his – the one with the red awning over the balcony. He must have great views."

"Let's go up. There's going to be some heavy rain."

"Bit different to the boss swanning round Bonnitor. Sun on his back and cool drinks served by dusky maidens." Petrie went first up the stairs, as nimble as a mountain goat. Despite, his weight loss, Watson was still breathless after the short flight of stairs up from the communal entrance. "After-effect of Covid," he explained as he pressed a buzzer. He was rewarded with ding-dong chimes followed by the smiling face of a woman aged mid-twenties. The officers produced their credentials. "Mr Foden is expecting us."

"Come in."

"And you are?" enquired Petrie.

"Sonya. Sonya Bird. I live with Degsy." She led them through a compact windowless hallway and into a long rectangular room. The quality of the easy-chairs, the dining-table and the plush carpet oozed a comfortable but not lavish lifestyle. Watson was thinking that Bird was a pretty good name for her. She had a small head, close-cut hair, a trim body and was on the small side of small. Even her head-shakes reminded him of a sparrow's darting movements.

Both visitors were immediately drawn to the window to enjoy the spectacular view. Of Foden there was no sign. "The kettle's boiled. Would you like tea or coffee?"

"Peppermint or any herb tea if you can manage that. Sgt Watson likes a black coffee."

"Mr Foden is at home, is he?"

"Oh yes. He's expecting you but he's in bed, resting up." She turned back towards the ultra-modern fitted kitchen. "Let me get the drinks first." She hurried behind a counter at the rear. Petrie followed her, leaving Watson to peer through a hefty brass telescope that he swivelled to focus on the curving sweep of the now derelict harbour far below.

Watson had been to Folkestone once before, retracing his great-grandfather's final steps on English soil. In 1915, after saying goodbye to his pregnant wife in Wandsworth, he had been one of thousands of young men who had marched down the Road of Remembrance from The Leas to Folkestone Harbour. Watson could still imagine him, kitbag over his shoulder, striding confidently, proud to do his bit for King and Country. He blinked back tears as he imagined the endless line of brave young men setting out on a one-way journey. Like too many, his great-grandfather had never returned – killed in October 1916. His body had never been found in the muddy carnage of the Somme trenches but Watson had seen his name, Alfred Benjamin Watson, recorded among the 72,000 victims at the Thiepval Memorial. Slowly, Watson turned the telescope to look at the Memorial Arch now cresting Remembrance Hill before swinging it south to the distant outline of the cliffs of France.

"Here's your coffee and a cookie if you want it." Petrie's voice brought him back from painful memories.

"Thanks." He kept his eyes lowered and stared out to sea until he had gathered his composure. Sonya Bird's chirpy voice and smile then invited them to come on through. Beyond the hall, they entered a room with the curtains closed and a bedside lamp casting shadows on the flower-patterned wallpaper. Although the room was spacious, it smelled of some type of Deep Heat rub.

Propped against a couple of yellow pillows was a man in striped blue and green pyjamas. His thinning brown hair had yet to be combed. Beside him was the Sun newspaper. Watson took in the sallow and unshaven grey features. With something between a sigh and a groan, Foden twisted on the bed and pointed to a chair. "I'm Degsy Foden. I'm not sure what you want but I'll help if I can." The voice was slightly throaty.

"Having a bad day, are you Mr Foden?"

"Comes and goes. I've never properly recovered from being attacked by pirates in the Far East."

"I think it's called PTSD," chipped in Sonya Bird from her perch at the foot of the bed. "You can get it after near-death experiences."

"Thanks, poppet. Call it what you like. To me it's an effing nightmare. That's apart from having a pacemaker for irregular heartbeat. For my age, I'm a bit of a wreck." He looked across to Sonya and smiled. "Would you believe I'm only forty-four? I'd be lost without her. Really, I would."

"I'm sorry. We could come back later," Petrie leaned forward from her chair beside the king-size.

"Let's carry on. See how we do." Foden popped a couple of Ibuprofens into his mouth and washed them down with Lucozade.

"You were hard to trace. After you left the SAS, you kept moving." Watson read from a note. "Wallasey, Hartlepool, Bracknell, Highbury and now Folkestone. Any particular reason?"

Foden's smile was self-deprecating. "I drew a line under part of my life best forgotten. Kept on moving from my bitch of a wife and ahead of her blood-sucking lawyers. Then," he slowly raised a hand to point at Sonya, "along came this little darling. Sometimes, I wonder how she puts up with me and my health."

"You *can* be Mister Grumpy," she laughed but without conviction.

"So you worked for Mbesa Security after leaving the military, right?"

"Happy days. Great job. Terry, that's Terry Yates my oppo at Credenhill. He'd set up Mbesa to protect shipping." Watson recognised Tulse Hill or Bermondsey in every word.

"We know all about piracy," Petrie joked. "We both saw the movie with Tom Hanks."

"I couldn't watch that. I still get flashbacks after being tied up, pistol-whipped round the chest and head and then hurled overboard – except I landed on the next deck. That finished me – stole my bleeding future. After near five exciting years working on the ships. I had to pack it in."

"Still see the old boss? Chat about memory lane, your missions?"

Foden closed his eyes and then pulled up the rose-coloured bed-cover. "Terry? Yeah. Last Christmas. Sort of annual piss-up in a pub in Islington. Saw some of the other SAS muckers from them days; others on shore-leave from Mbesa."

"Doing well, is it?"

The answer was delayed by Foden's bout of coughing. "Mbesa? Far as I know. But there's less demand for protection now. Them golden days are gone – least for now." Foden again coughed and spluttered into the back of his hand. "So what's this all about?"

"France is so near. You get over there? Take the car?"

"I wish. No passport, mate. It expired, ooh, twenty months

back. Anyroads, now I wouldn't want to be taken bad somewhere foreign."

"What sort of car do you own Mr Foden?" Petrie took up a new line of questions. She now knew from the local CID that Sonya Bird had been seen driving an Audi.

"I don't own one. Sonya has a car, don't you, love?"

"My pride and joy. An Audi saloon. We picked it up secondhand in 2019 from that garage in Canterbury, didn't we."

"Mr Foden, do you drive it?"

"I *can* drive," he emphasised the work *can*. "I've still got my DVLC licence from Swansea. I do the occasional trip to see my old mum. She lives with me sister in Basingstoke."

"Ever been to King's Lynn?"

Foden wiped a crumb of biscuit from his lip before answering. "Without a satnav thingie, I wouldn't even know where it was. Funny question. Why do you ask?"

Petrie looked at Watson and left him to reply. "We're interested in an Audi saloon seen in that area."

"Before you ask. I've never been there neither," added Sonya Bird. "Anyway, there must be millions of cars like ours."

"When was the last time you drove?"

"Cor, this is like bleeding Mastermind," Foden grinned. After much grunting and heaving, he pushed himself further up the pillows. "Last time? Do you remember love? Two, maybe three weeks back."

Bird shrugged indifference. "Margate, we went. Fish and chips at Dreamland. On the way back, we stopped to watch the ferries at Dover Harbour. Before that? Must've been when you drove to Basingstoke. That was, blimey, don't time fly. I'd say back in January."

"You're right Sonya. It was me mum's birthday. 4th January."

"No other trips since last January?"

"We went to the William Harvey Hospital in Ashford to get the pacemaker checked."

"Thanks, both of you." Watson eased himself up and edged to the door. He was keen to get away from the stifling heat and smell of embrocation. "I hope you feel better soon, Mr Foden. Just routine but we'd like to look at the car. A tick-box exercise for the boss."

"Is that necessary?"

Petrie was onto that in flash. "Is that a problem, Ms Bird?"

"No, no," she backtracked. "Look outside. It just means me going out in that pissing rain. The garage is about ten minutes away."

They regrouped in the hall. A line of five keys hung on a wooden souvenir plaque saying *Keys to My Heart*. Bird grabbed an umbrella and keys marked *front-door, Audi* and *11A*. "Let's go."

"No garages in this block?"

Bird shook her head. "We use a lock-up in Manor Road." After turning off The Leas and heading towards the town centre, the walk was no great distance. Even so, their waterproofs were dripping wet by the time they reached the garage, one in a long line. She unlocked 11A and lifted the up-and-over revealing a garage big enough for a much bigger car than the black Audi five-door saloon.

"Mind if we take pictures?" asked Petrie already lining up to do so.

"Help yourself. Want me to back it out?"

"Please."

Glad to avoid the rain, Watson used the passenger seat while she reversed. After Bird got out, he remained seated, looking round the interior. It was all unremarkable but Strang's instructions had been clear. "If he has an Audi, then Degsy Foden becomes *numero uno* on the guv's list."

Okay, boss, Watson told himself. *You got it. I'll photo everything.* In the glove-box he found hand-cream, a chamois leather, a shopping-list stuffed with food for vegans and a grubby Covid face-mask. He took several more pictures including the instrument display, the MOT certificate, the Audi servicing history and insurance certificate. Watson then ran his hands under each seat and found nothing more exciting than a Crunchie wrapper and a fifty-pence coin.

Meanwhile, Petrie, by now dripping wet, had taken pictures from all four sides before opening the spacious boot. Watson pulled up his collar to join her. In the boot, there was nothing but a toolkit. "Handy at car maintenance, are you? Changing wheels and sparkplugs?" Petrie was thinking of the Town & Country tyre tracks near Ongerton's body. Watson lifted the floor but beneath it, there was just a spare wheel.

"That kit came with the car," Bird laughed from under her umbrella. "Me? I'm hopeless. Any problem, I'd need the AA."

"We're done here," said Watson. "Thanks for your help."

"Any time."

Heads bowed against the driving rain, the two officers hurried back towards Sandgate Road and found a Trattoria with steamed-up windows. "Okay here?"

"Anywhere out of this rain," Petrie agreed.

"I could slaughter a pizza. Order me that," Watson asked before scurrying towards the Gents. Petrie took a seat and then waited for her boss to return. By then, she had ordered a barbecued chicken pizza for him and vegetable soup and avocado on toast for herself. Watson looked at her quizzically. "That guy Degsy? *Numero uno?* A frail guy like that. Nothing fits except for the Audi."

"But she's sticking with him." Petrie frowned. "Why? She's,

what, twenty years younger. With her looks, she could pick and choose. The local lads would form a queue."

"Money, then." Watson grinned. "Get this. Tucked beneath the bed I spotted her sexy Baby-Doll stuff, all black satin and frills. Her prancing about in that would blow a fuse in his pacemaker."

"You're suggesting he's not as frail as he appeared?" She curled up her mouth showing her doubt. "Good call though. Spot anything else?"

Watson's face was split by a huge grin. It wouldn't have been wider if someone had offered him a tomahawk steak and chips. "Perhaps."

"Me too."

Battersea SW11

Hysen Kola was bored rigid. It was late afternoon and he had switched off the TV – endless talking heads about buying properties on the cheap. Since the cryptic message that Todd Holtom was not even in the UK, he had avoided returning to Putney or Hammersmith. From his single visit to both locations, neither was perfect – day or night. After further thought, he had ruled out Jubilee House. Hammersmith Grove would be ideal for a drive-by but he didn't want to risk renting a car or powerful motor-bike. Somewhere else would be better.

Holtom had now been gone six days. Six long days. Six days killing time. Six days of eat, drink, walk, cinema, crap, repeat. He was just opening a bottle of Chianti when one of his burners buzzed. This was only his second message. Grabbing a pen and paper, he answered and scribbled down the instructions as he listened. **Target arrival 5-50 tomorrow morning. Terminal 5 Heathrow British Airways from Barbados. Uber pick-up at 6-45 at Row R in T5 Short-Term Car Park. Look for Silver Mercedes with driver in Row P. Take you to Farnborough Airport. Private jet to Le Touquet.**

Action at last!

He poured his wine to the brim and filled his plate with sliced serrano ham and strong goat's cheese. Action at last! After marking time for too long, the news electrified him. The release of so much pent-up energy made him want to leap around the room, shouting and laughing. That was impossible without attracting attention. But even though he was still eating, sitting still was impossible, so he stood up.

I'll eat standing up.

Better still, I'll eat on the move.

He spent the next few minutes circling the table, grabbing lumps of cheese or ham as he did so. This was just perfect – an unsuspecting Holtom meeting his Uber driver.

One shot should be enough, a second would make death certain.

Witnesses?

No problem.

With the Glock's rate of fire, and fifteen bullets in the magazine, he could fix them and still get away.

He checked journey times. In the Mercedes, 30 minutes max from Heathrow to Farnborough. 100 minutes at worst for the flight.

I'll be in the air with no chance of being stopped.

I'll be gone from Le Touquet before the French cops reach the airport.

Bonnitor

Det. Insp Alleyne fetched a couple of beers while Ratso waited for his flight. "The best brew on Bonnitor," Alleyne volunteered as he set the glasses on the table. "Hot news, Todd. I'm meeting Detective Inspector Dean Patterson in Bridgetown tomorrow. We'll discuss arresting Zak Carter."

"Good." Ratso was less enthusiastic than he sounded. He had wanted to brief Patterson personally but there had been no time. "Whatever you decide, take no action to alert Carter till you hear from me. Coordination is vital. I'll message you and Patterson at the same time."

"How did Yates communicate with Zak Carter?"

Ratso cut this throat in an exaggerated gesture. "Zilch. We'll need you and Patterson to link Zak Carter to Campbell's house. Maybe the jewels or cash?"

"And Olly Young?"

"He's been lying to us. His Audi was spotted near King's Lynn. The driver of the Audi used a false name and address. In London, Olly was close to where Marcel was murdered. As a Cambridge Blue for swimming, he could have swum to the KC's home." His downturned mouth showed his thoughts. "But I don't see him being a killer."

"You think Olly wanted revenge on Logan Goldie, Kendall Campbell and the Swiss financier?"

Ratso see-sawed his hands. "Great motive. But did he hire these SAS guys to fix it? And why get Molly framed by having her lookalike at the scene? None of this makes sense."

"Olly Young's excuse for lying?"

"You mean about going home to Sevenoaks when he was close to where Marcel was murdered?"

"Why lie about meeting a male lover? That's unconvincing. What's to be ashamed about?"

Ratso shook his head. "Olly wasn't *ashamed*. He was petrified. His voice was shaky. His hands were trembling. He was sweating like crazy. He told me he had lied because he can't tell his young lads their Dad wants to marry a twenty-five-year-old man. He's convinced their mother will turn the boys against him." Ratso shrugged. "That's plausible. I buy that."

Alleyne nodded. "Put like that, okay." He finished his beer and offered another which Ratso declined.

"This other guy down at the Kent coast?"

"Degsy Foden has a heart condition. He appeared to be frail. His woman friend, that's Sonya, drives an Audi. Apparently, he rarely travels. He told us he has no passport We checked with the Passport Office. That was true."

"Leaving the Geneva murder unexplained."

Ratso drained his glass and, with an exaggerated laugh, gave Alleyne a friendly punch on the shoulder. "That's what Degsy wanted us to believe."

"And?"

"Load of bollocks."

"Why?"

"Because a smart young detective, Nancy Petrie spotted his Audi had a UK sticker on the back."

"So?"

"Since September 2021, because of Brexit, to drive in Europe you must display a UK bumper-sticker. The old GB sticker we've used for years is dead. Foden and Sonya had

Deadly Hush

denied travelling anywhere – let alone into France." Ratso leaned closer.

"And?"

"Petrie checked Channel crossings in June. Sonya had booked to enter France by Eurotunnel. The Audi entered France the day the Swiss financier was murdered."

"You mean she was the killer? And was Marcel's killer too?"

"No. I believe Degsy entered France hidden in the car's trunk."

"So what next?"

"Degsy Foden is under surveillance."

A garbled metallic voice said something that Ratso could not decipher. He looked at Alleyne who nodded. "That was your final call, Todd."

Ratso stood up to leave. "Thanks Bastien. Remember. Do nothing about Zak Carter without hearing from me. We've a *Footstool* team just after ten tomorrow morning."

Battersea

When he left the White House in Battersea, the sun had not yet arisen. Hysen Kola needed his black windcheater in the chilly dawn air as he walked briskly towards Clapham Junction Station where he knew there would be taxis. The windcheater's deep pockets were ideal for concealing his lovingly checked Glock 19. At the rank, there were a couple of taxis waiting and moments later, he was being sped through the almost deserted streets of South London. Only once they reached the Chiswick Flyover did traffic start to back up.

"There's roadworks ahead, mate," said the cabbie. "We'll be twenty minutes longer than usual. We're down to a single lane."

Kola grunted, not wanting to get into a conversation. He checked the time. He had allowed for lack of taxis and the unexpected. He would be okay. Just. When he was dropped at Terminal 5 Departures, there was no time to waste and a little to spare. He was using his final disguise, one that added over twenty years to his age. This included silvery grey hair, a wispy grey goatee beard, grey sideburns and eyebrows to match, a pair of Harry Potter glasses and a black jockey-cap pulled tight over his head.

He looked across to the Arrivals Board and was pleased to see that the Barbados flight had landed just moments ago and five-minutes ahead of schedule. Unsure when he would get to eat in France, he bought a black coffee and a sausage bap at Costa and settled in sight of the Arrivals Board. From his rucksack, he removed both the full-face and profile pictures of Todd Holtom. As he had done so many times, he studied them carefully, trying to imagine how Holtom's appearance might have changed since the pictures had been taken.

Longer hair?
A beard maybe?
I won't be fooled.

He returned the photos to his rucksack and pushed aside the crumbs from the bap. He checked the Board again. *Have I missed something?* There was no sign the bags had yet reached the carousel. On his assumption that Holtom would travel light, that was his planned trigger.

Would he fly Economy?
Be slow coming through?
Or be up at the front and quick?
Play safe.
Assume he might be quick.

Slinging his rucksack over his shoulder, he followed the signs to Short-Term Parking. It was precisely 6-30 a.m.

At that same moment, Ratso was just clearing Immigration. After meal service, he had wanted to sleep but with so much on his mind and plotting the next moves on *Footstool*, that had been impossible. He had tried listening to his favourites on Spotify but even that did not relax him.

Nothing could.

Towing his Antler rollalong, he stopped off at the Gents. In front of the mirror, he doused cold water over the dark sagginess under both eyes. He felt and looked none the better for it.

Just about fit for the knackers yard.

He advanced the time four hours on his watch.

He exited the Gents.

It was now 6 -33 a.m.

Heathrow Airport

Kola had no problem following the yellow signs to the Short-Term Car Park. He took the elevator and seconds later was standing in the correct zone for Uber pick-ups. There were five people already waiting, some with suitcases beside them. Most were looking anxiously towards the ramp for their taxi to appear. None looked like Holtom. Hoping to seem like he was just killing time, he strolled, hands in pocket, to the next lane. He walked its length. Almost at once, he spotted the Mercedes and driver but made no eye contact. Satisfied, he again checked the time as he returned to stand near the other travellers. In three minutes max, Holtom should emerge. He watched an Uber arriving, a five-door Hyundai. The Asian driver helped a man and woman to load their six suitcases before they clambered in. Kola was amazed how much luggage travellers carried, even for short breaks. He wondered how many of their shirts, suits, jeans, shoes and the rest had never been worn during their travels.

Ninety seconds.

A Uber appeared, this time a Prius. A woman, travelling light, waved to the driver, climbed in and was swiftly gone. The final couple had three suitcases and a pair of small carry-ons. Downing them with the Glock would be no problem.

Sixty seconds.

Where are you, Holtom?

Kola positioned himself close to the elevator's sliding-door but still well positioned to watch the ramp, as if impatient for his taxi.

Right hand on his gun, he was ready. Another Uber appeared from the ramp and slowly circled the parking area in big loop and pulled up. The waiting couple checked the number and, looking irritated, shook their heads. "Not ours," said the woman leaning towards the open window.
Mr Holtom.
Your Uber is here.
You're cutting it fine, Holtom.
Slowly, the elevator door started to slide open.

Heathrow Airport

Creaking and hissing, the elevator door opened. Kola's hand was still clutching the Glock, ready to fire. He glanced to his side. His face flushed with irritation. It was not Holtom. Instead, a woman aged mid-twenties emerged. She was wearing a matching black two-piece suit with a white blouse and a small bag slung over her left shoulder. Deflated, he watched her move to join the line as the door slid shut.

With his focus on her and awaiting the next arrival, Kola never noticed a solitary figure exit from a parked Nissan. In a few strides, he casually approached the group awaiting pick-up. He came from behind Kola's line of sight. Only when he was close to Kola's back, did he speak. "Hysen! *Përshëndetje! Si jeni?*"

Instinctively, and startled at hearing his name and being asked *how are you* in Albanian, Kola spun one-eighty degrees. Instantly, the speaker, standing in a firing position sprayed him with PAVA. One, two and then a third short burst of the pepper-like substance jetted into Kola's face, filling both his eyes.

Shocked and feeling as if his eyes were on fire, Kola doubled over, his hands now rubbing them. The car-park resonated with his shouted obscenities and screams of pain. From an unmarked Transit van, six members of MO19 Specialist Firearms Command jumped out. Wearing baseball caps and protective chest-wear, their shouts of *Armed Police, Armed Police* drowned out Kola's curses. Suddenly, everywhere was noise and frantic movement as the armed officers formed a tight semi-circle surrounding Kola.

Their Heckler & Koch MP5 sub-machine-guns were all trained on him.

With Kola helpless as he rubbed his eyes, the couple who had apparently been waiting for their Uber also sprang into action. They pounced on him – one from behind and the other from the side. Their momentum crashed him into the wall beside the elevator, smashing his nose and forehead hard into the unforgiving concrete. Blood gushed, running down his face.

From across the car-park, there was a roar of revving engines and the sound of squealing tyres. A pair of flat-bed VW tow-trucks raced the few metres to block both the down and up ramps. The female detective sergeant, who had been observing Kola's every move, went straight to the right-hand pocket of the windcheater and removed the Glock. Her colleague continued to pat Kola down but found no other weapon. Only then did he rip the rucksack from Kola's shoulder and hurl it to the ground. As blood from Kola's nose and brow spattered onto and trickled down the wall, the detective sergeant handed the gun to the newly arrived detective constable in her black suit.

With the weight of two officers now pressing against Kola's shoulders and a large hand gripping the back of his head, his face continued to be squashed hard against the wall. As Kola continued to shout abuse, he kicked back and wriggled. He achieved nothing. The suited detective stepped forward and with the help of the officer who had first spoken to Kola in Albanian, they forced Kola's hands behind his back. After seizing his wrists they wrenched them together until the cuffs removed any final chance of resistance.

From the rear doors of a small red van parked immediately opposite the elevator, Det. Insp Reg Gastrell appeared. From in there, he had been directing operations. He spoke to the senior Firearms

Officer and pointed. "That silver Mercedes with the woman driver. We've just had confirmation. The owner is Albanian. Arrest her." The air was then filled with more shouts of *Armed Police, Armed Police* as the officers spread out and then closed in around the motionless Mercedes. Every weapon was now aimed at the driver. The MO19 sergeant ordered the woman to get out, hands on head.

Gastrell, from twenty-five metres away, held his breath. Was all hell about to break loose? For what seemed an age, there was no movement until he heard a door open. Then, the head and shoulders of a young woman appeared, her hands now high above her head. Gastrell hurried towards her. He watched from the next lane as she was pinned against her car and handcuffed.

After giving instructions for them both to be arrested, Gastrell then phoned Ratso. Reading a newspaper, he was seated in the Arrivals Hall with a black coffee in front of him. "It's over. Come on up." The coffee abandoned, Ratso hurried to the elevator. It seemed an age as it creaked, shuddered and rattled its journey. The door slid open and he emerged into a sea of action, shouting and flashing lights.

On seeing him standing hesitantly taking in the scene, Gastrell walked towards him to shake his hand. By now though, Ratso had seen Kola, half his face smeared with blood, his eyes streaming and his jacket torn. Ratso wanted to face-down the man who had wanted him dead.

Taking a few steps towards him and determined that Kola would see him, Ratso stared hard at the heavily disguised Albanian. His contemptuous smile came easily as he looked at the dishevelled and broken man. Unable to wipe the blood and wetness from his eyes, it took Kola a moment or two to realise who was now standing in front to him. Then, a snarl of hatred spread across his face as Ratso took in Kola's misshapen nose. It had a significant kink midway down its length. Blood was till dripping from both nostrils and staining his mouth and chin.

Seconds later, Ratso was met with a ball of jettisoned spit which struck the lapel of his jacket. This he ignored. For a moment, he wondered what to say and then he knew. "Who told you I would be here, Mr Kola? Who tipped you off?" He did not expect any reply and did not get one. Gastrell joined him to watch Kola being bundled into the back of a white BMW. Moments later, from across the car park, they watched the female accomplice being seated in the rear of another BMW. "That woman?" he asked Gastrell.

"When Kola appeared, he checked out the next line of parked cars. I could see the Mercedes had a woman driver. I radioed for a number-plate check and found it was registered to an Albanian."

"Great work, Reg."

"We don't know where she was taking him." Together they watched as a convoy of four vehicles moved towards the down-ramp, their sirens blaring and blue lights flashing.

"I gotta say, that didn't look like Kola."

"We assumed he would be disguised. I had an officer who spoke Albanian approach him. Kola gave himself away when he heard his name and a greeting in Albanian."

Ratso patted Gastrell on the back. "Brilliant! Absolute masterstroke. I owe you for that – well for everything."

Despite the stress he had been through, Gastrell's tired eyes and face showed he appreciated the compliment. "Thanks Todd but this was your idea. You stitched this bastard up. I just had to reel him in."

"I put that down to my second Zombie. You won't have tried that Bonnitor speciality. We'll hit a few when I take you out to celebrate." Ratso's face then turned serious. "Okay, we chalk this up as a success but ahead there's bad and even worse news." He looked at Gastrell who saw the bags under Ratso's eyes and the grey cheeks, not improved by the shadowy lights of the car-park.

"Tell me."

"We've suspected for too long that someone was leaking to Boris Zandro. My plan leading Kola into the trap has proved me right."

"How many of your team knew you'd be here?"

"My WhatsApp message went to eighty-two on the *Footloose* Group Chat. Of them, about sixty weren't involved back then before we arrested Zandro. That's when we first suspected a leak."

"So the mole is one of about twenty. That makes my task easier. What's even worse?"

"These are guys I've trusted for years Some I'd call friends."

Gastrell nodded in understanding. "Anything else?"

"Boris Zandro won't give up. Next time we may not be so lucky. We won't stumble on a tip from Tirana." Ratso forced a grin. "Until you nail the bastard, I'll have a cricked neck from looking over my shoulder."

"What about Zandro? You think we might be able to charge him?"

Ratso' shook his head slowly. "You'll never get the evidence. Kola won't admit anything. The best hope would be the woman but I doubt she knows who was pulling the strings."

Gastrell's sharp look showed agreement. "I fear you're right, Todd." He checked his watch. I'll be heading back shortly. Want a lift to Putney?"

"No need, Reg," Ratso laughed. "Don't forget I've an Uber booked. Just not at the time Hysen Kola was informed."

Putney

Within minutes of entering Jubilee House, Ratso felt he had never been away. The usual buzz and familiar smells greeted him as he trundled his rollalong through the narrow passage leading to the elevator at the rear of the building. Upstairs, he acknowledged a few friendly waves and greetings as he walked between the lines of desks to his office at the far end. The first to drop by was Jock Strang, beaming from ear to ear. "Welcome back, boss and I've great news."

Ratso looked puzzled as he leaned back in his chair, listening to the never-ending rumble of London's traffic. "And?"

"Smart Alex is no longer your four-pip. He told us thirty minutes ago. He's been assigned to Hendon. He's cleared his desk and is on his way there now."

"Best welcome back possible. It was his decision?"

"Nobody knows. Any thoughts?"

Ratso would have bet money on Wensley Hughes "Good question. And replacing him?"

Strang shrugged. "Anyroads, you wanted to meet at 10-15?"

"Change of plan. Stand everybody down except you, Tosh, Nancy, Bonkers and Viment. Oh and Willison if he's not too busy snooping round Jakupi's Roehampton pad."

"You're not looking tanned, boss."

"I saw precious little sunshine."

"Perhaps the new four-pip will wave through your expenses."

"See you in thirty."

Ratso's core team trooped in, mostly appearing expectant. Looking at Danny Willison, Ratso got straight to the point. "You're lucky, Danny. Time was when you'd have been for the big heave-ho for disobedience and incompetence. Under modern policing, Jock tells me you're being supported under a redemption policy. So be it. You've been working on whoever followed Marcel from Big Top Burgers. Anything?"

"Boss, Molly Bishop, or whoever, emerged from the rear entrance of the Golden Hotspur Casino on Lisle Street. From there, she took the short walk to Glasshouse Street and went into Big Top Burgers." He ruffled his ginger hair nervously. "But she never entered the casino."

"You mean she *did* enter it but not dressed like Molly Bishop. Front entrance is where?"

"Leicester Square."

"Boss, Molly Bishop told you she was walking near this area that evening," prompted Viment, clutching her cappuccino with both hands. "We've checked the CCTV and her story checks out. We picked her up at Tower Bridge, Shaftesbury Avenue and near her hotel. She could not be the murderer."

"What was she wearing?"

"Nothing like her lookalike. A pale pink shortie jacket and black jeans."

"Good work."

"Danny, I assume you've been through the casino's CCTV at both entrances?"

"Yes, sir. Carole and I studied the footage."

Viment, her face, as attractively hard-set as usual, continued. "Fourteen minutes earlier, a male of a similar build had arrived carrying a small bag. The internal shots no longer existed, so there are no full-frontal views."

From his rollalong, Ratso opened the Energy Management Annual Report. "That's Molly Bishop on site in Bonnitor. Room for a change of clothes in his bag?"

"Easily and there's a Unisex loo in the casino. I'd say he changed in there to emerge as Molly Bishop. Maybe like me, he also had a quick spin at the roulette table." She grinned. "I won ten quid betting on red."

When the laughter had died down Ratso continued. "This is our murderer then. He followed Marcel to Aquinas Street."

"But never returned to the casino to change."

"Did we check the trash-bins around Aquinas Street?"

"I don't believe so," Strang looked uncomfortable." We weren't looking for a weapon – or for clothes."

Ratso was not going to criticise his inspector in front of the team but Strang got the message from the penetrating stare. Instead, he said *number-plates*. Then, just as suddenly he stopped, half-standing up from his chair. "Got it! Forget Marcel. Think Logan Goldie. The woman who murdered Logan Goldie took a taxi. We lost her in Leicester Square. I bet she went into the Golden Hotspur and came out of the Lisle Street exit as a man."

"Guv, you're obviously not as jet-lagged as you look," laughed Watson.

"I suppose that might be a compliment, Tosh." He turned to Viment again. "Carole, Danny – visit the casino. After so long, it's probably too late but check for footage the night Goldie was murdered."

"Number-plates. You were about to say," Strang prompted.

"We have Oliver Young's Audi approaching King's Lynn." He looked round the group. "Anybody now thinking what I'm thinking?"

"Young was cooperating with Terry Yates?" Tosh Watson sounded hesitant.

Ratso's eyes quickly scanned the listeners. "No, Tosh. How about the killer used false plates to frame Olly. So far, the killer has used polycarbonate to obscure the plates and also false numberplates. At King's Lynn, he deliberately allowed the number to be read."

"Boss, as a shareholder, Yates would have seen her photo in the Annual Report but we know he didn't kill Marcel."

"Correct, Nancy. He didn't murder in Bonnitor either. He's recruited guys from his SAS days."

"Who murdered Doyle?"

"Nancy, my money's on Yates or maybe this Degsy from Folkestone."

Petrie was enthused. "Yates distanced himself from the Energy Management victims?"

Strang rubbed his hands together in satisfaction. "Right enough. Sounds good."

"Boss, I've been working on something different," said Bonkers. "I did a Land Registry search on Yates's house in Ravensworth. In the Charges Register, there was notice of bankruptcy proceedings registered a month before the first murder. He has a two million mortgage but he's in arrears with the Levenside Building Society. Once he's made bankrupt, he'll also be disqualified from being a director of Mbesa." His infectious grin was missed by nobody. "Yates was in financial freefall."

"Good work. What about Mbesa? Was that going belly-up? We know there's been less piracy and more competitors."

"The finances are not publicly available. We're getting another order from a Deemster for access to the Manx Tax Office."

Deadly Hush

"Thoughts on this?" Ratso aimed the question at Bonkers but it was Nancy that answered.

"Facing financial ruin, Yates was vindictive. Now he's gearing up to do a runner?"

"Let's keep that in mind." Ratso lobbed his empty cup across the room and straight into the bin.

"Can we take a quick break?" Watson was already pushing back his chair. "Too much coffee."

"Fifteen minutes. I'm famished anyway." Ratso looked round the group. "But before you go, I need to update you. Until now, I could say nothing. I've had a hit-man hired by Boris Zandro stalking me for several weeks. This morning, he was arrested just before he expected to execute me." Ratso spread out both arms in apology. "These past weeks haven't been easy."

Nobody said a word. In jaw-dropping silence, they trooped out, Tosh Watson accelerating with each stride.

Putney

"Mbesa uses a call-and-mail-handling centre in Old Gloucester Street, Holborn," explained Tosh Watson as the group settled down again in Ratso's office. "The staff there field everything for loads of different companies. I replied to an advert about a job with Mbesa." Watson saw he had rapt attention. "Yates interviews personally. He's in London on Friday and I'll be messaged about when and where I'm to meet him on Thursday."

"The nearest ye've been to the sea and ships is a pedalo in Benidorm." Strang was barely joking but he led the laughter.

"Not what my CV says," Tosh retorted. "Impressive to a fault."

Ratso shook his head in appreciation mixed with surprise. The Watson of old was not known for initiative or original thought. More often, he was only effective when pointed in the right direction. "Your idea?"

Watson unwrapped a granola bar as he grinned his reply. "I'll be a no-show or we'll be going in mob-handed."

"Nice work, Tosh. You're untraceable? Remember that previous incognito fiasco at the graveyard?"

Watson remembered only too well. "Lesson learned. Watertight this time, boss."

"Tosh, Nancy – tell us more about Degsy Foden in Folkestone."

Petrie looked at Watson and got the nod to answer. "Nothing from his phone. It's rarely used. Or Sonya Bird's come to that. If he's in touch with Yates, then there must be a burner."

"Or good old-fashioned hand-written snail-mail. That's hard to trace – if destroyed." Ratso's eyes seemed to bore right into both of them in turn. "Your gut reaction?"

"We know Sonya Bird went to France. Secondly, our application for Degsy's medical records was granted. They show Foden was invalided out of Mbesa. He does have a pacemaker but this year hasn't needed a GP. He saw his cardiac consultant last week at the William Harvey Hospital in Ashford."

"Sonya went to France alone?"

Nancy nodded yes. "If you believe the booking. Degsy has no passport. It was a driver-only booking. I'd say Degsy entered France in the boot. No passport is needed to enter Switzerland from France."

"He may have to prove he remained in England. Let's park that.," Ratso said. "Other thoughts?"

"On their key rack were four keys. She took ones for the front-door, the Audi and 11A. That's the garage we went into. Reliving it now, I'm positive there was an 11B. That lock-up might be full of broken washing machines and old sofas. On the other hand, it might be a treasure trove of evidence." She caught Ratso's eye. "Boss, I can smell Folkestone's bracing sea air."

"Photographs of Degsy. Get one of the forensics to test the new facial recognition software. Y'know, that programme human rights activists say infringes liberty. Well, sod them. We've got mugshots going back to his SAS days. Run them against the images from outside Big Top Burgers and in Curzon Street."

"Degsy was propped up in bed. He looked pretty sick," Watson explained. "His grip was weak. I doubt he could even strangle a rabbit. Nancy?"

"I wasn't convinced by his coughing fits. I never felt his grip. We never saw him out of bed. For me, an open mind. If he's that ill, why does Sonya stick with him?"

"Her Audi. Show me the pics."

Nancy projected external shots of the Audi onto the wall-screen. "These are the internal ones." Photos of the dashboard, footwells and glovebox. changed every few seconds.

"Stop. Go back." Ratso sounded excited. "Everybody, write down the mileage on the clock." Everybody scribbled down 73,164. "Tosh – scroll back to the Service Log. Now, write down the date of the last service and mileage then. He paused and saw the scribbling. "All agreed? I've got 68,639. That's over 4,000 miles since the service last February. Did neither of you do this simple maths?" He saw the sheepish looks. "Only been to Margate and local shopping, my arse."

Balling out his officers or shouting abuse and table-thumping, had never been Ratso's style, though he had endured plenty enough himself. Ratso's silence and glare at Petrie and Watson carried its own message. In the end it was Watson who spoke. "Guv, I guess that's why you're a Chief Inspector and I'm still a sergeant. My mistake."

"Mine too. Sorry, boss," added Nancy.

"Not Nancy. I take the blame," Tosh's tone and scolded puppy look showed his remorse. "I took the interior shots. We got side-tracked on the UK bumper sticker."

"Get the pics going again." The snapped command was icy. On screen appeared more from the glove-box. "Stop. The shopping-list?"

"They drank buckets of Campari and ate vegan."

"Okay but somebody has scribbled on it – *Buy Lottery Ticket*." Ratso twisted in his seat. "Bonkers. Split the screen. Put up the Dunsdale Creek page – where the Audi driver signed in with the Lowestoft address."

Everybody peered at the screen. Ratso continued. "Reactions?" He looked at each of the team in turn.

"Aye, there are simi-lar-ities" Strang commented speaking slowly "between the LO in lottery and the LO in Lowestoft."

"Agreed. We need that checked out by a forensic handwriting expert. I want Olly Young's writing compared to the Dunsdale Creek page as well. I want an opinion on both Olly and Degsy by 4pm."

"I'll sort it," Bonkers said.

"Listen up! With that daft young girl tipping him off, we must assume Yates suspects we are onto him. Degsy Foden must also be worried."

"And both do a runner?"

"Jock, that's one possibility."

"Would your Barbados guy be suspicious?"

"Zak Carter? Only if warned from England."

"We need to move soon then, boss."

"Fix surveillance on Yates and Foden and both garages. Foden could empty 11B. I'll ring Major Tang at Credenhill but first I'm going to phone Dublin. Call in a favour. Let's meet in one hour."

New Scotland Yard

For the past two hours, TV news channels and radio stations had been trailing a Media Briefing to be held at the Victoria Embankment HQ. This had followed Ratso's urgent discussion with Assistant Commissioner Wensley Hughes. Crime Correspondents had been alerted and already social media was rife with uninformed speculation. On the rostrum in front of the packed audience and the usual array of clicking cameras and microphones, Ratso sat beside Hughes who introduced himself and then passed the briefing over to Ratso.

"I am Detective Chief Inspector Todd Holtom and I am the SIO – senior investigating officer – on *Operation Footstool*. Understandably, the public is concerned that there have been no arrests following four murders. Over the past several weeks, we have had towards ninety personnel working on this complex investigation. The task has been painstaking, involving scouring thousands of hours of CCTV and other footage. The most significant development was the CCTV images of the woman walking down Glasshouse Street, near Piccadilly Circus and apparently following the young lad, soon to be murdered in Aquinas Street."

He turned over the page to continue.

"I can now tell you that we have opened up an important and significant line of enquiry in Dublin. We are working closely with the Garda following discussions between Assistant Commissioner Hughes and Assistant Commissioner O'Neill in Dublin. If any member of the public has any information that may assist with this new Irish development, they should contact us using the phone number on the wall behind me."

Ratso looked at the journalists and TV crews, all anxious to ask questions "I know that you'll want to ask questions but with an ongoing operation, I'm not able to share what has prompted this potential breakthrough. I will however take some questions."

"Dermot Doyle was born in Howth, just outside Dublin," shouted a reporter from the BBC. "Is that the link?"

"I cannot comment on that." Ratso shook his head while hoping to indicate that the journalist was onto something. Other questions concerned whether the killer was male or female and whether all the murders had been committed by the same person. Ratso batted them aside as if he were in his cricket gear and hitting bad bowling to the boundary.

"I must remind you about Stephen Port." A tabloid journalist raised his hand.

"No reminder needed."

"Some of his victims would have been alive but for homophobic prejudice which blinded the police to arresting Port much sooner."

"Your point?" Ratso's tone was both abrasive and dismissive in two words. He stared hard at the questioner and then shared that look across the entire gathering. "There is no similarity between what my team is doing to whatever went wrong in the Stephen Port investigation."

Hughes stood up. "Thanks for coming everyone. That concludes the briefing." Twenty minutes later, Hughes and Ratso were upstairs enjoying tea and biscuits. Hughes confirmed that Hysen Kola had already been charged with illegal entry and carrying a firearm with intent.

Their attention turned to the TV for news from Sky. As they had hoped, the Dublin connection had grabbed the headlines, pushing stories of a hurricane hitting Cuba and a row about fishing-rights down the running-order. They shared a look. "With luck, this Dublin sideshow has bought you a little time. For now, Yates and Foden may consider themselves off the hook."

"I'm waiting for a call from Credenhill. Major Tang is armour-plated. In case he breached the Official Secrets Act, Tang wouldn't tell you if your arse was on fire."

"But you're winning?"

"I persuaded Tang to get clearance from the top brass."

"Todd. We must track down who's been leaking to Boris Zandro."

"Not one for me, sir. I'm too close to guys that I thought I knew and trusted."

"Reg Gastrell will work with Anti-Corruption Command."

"Are they taking hints from Superintendent Ted Hastings?" Ratso had got hooked on the fictional *Line of Duty* TV series.

Hughes gave a quiet smile. "Even Hastings and DS Arnott wouldn't find it easy to find the traitor in your team. Now back to *Footstool*. You're expecting forensics on the handwriting."

"I wanted it by 4 pm but it'll be later. Staff shortages, all the cutbacks. Today though."

"The directors of Energy Management – likely in the clear?"

"I'm not getting the full story from them." Ratso raised his eyebrows in emphasis. "But it doesn't make them murderers. The shareholders meet tomorrow at the Rogerson Hotel."

"You'll attend?"

"I will. Yates won't be there. Like many shareholders, the Company Secretary told me he's registered for the live stream from the EGM."

"Why not get search warrants and bring Yates and Foden in for questioning?"

"I can't link Yates to the murder scenes or to orchestrating Carter or Foden. Someone trying to frame Olly and Molly is helpful but…"

"Not conclusive. I agree."

"The handwriting will be the clincher."

"Changing the subject," Hughes peered towards his own screen. "You'll want to know who the new Detective Chief Superintendent will be."

"My four-pipper?"

"Irene Boyd. Happy?"

"Ironballs Boyd!" She would not have been his first choice. "Big improvement on DCS Caldwell, sir. She's based in Barking, right?"

"True, she's a reputed ball-breaker but she respects initiative and hard work. She dislikes prima donnas. I pulled a few strings." Hughes maintained a poker-face as he prompted. "You've come across her?"

Ratso had no doubt that Wensley Hughes knew the answer. "Long ago, sir. I was a DC. Back in Lewisham." He could have added that Irene Boyd wore black stockings and suspenders and had been a right firecracker. "She was promoted just ahead of me. I was pretty angry at the time."

"She'll be in touch." Ratso rose to leave. "Todd, I doubt you'll be able to charm Irene – the way you used to." His eyes twinkled. "She's married now. To a woman doctor, so I'm told."

Ratso blinked at the news that his one-off with Boyd was no longer a secret. He knew Hughes would have spotted his hesitation. "I'll be happy to welcome her."

"Didn't Irene invent your nickname?"

Dumbstruck, Ratso nodded. For nearly eighteen years, he had assumed that what had happened between him and Boyd had remained their secret. Any doubt had now vanished. Only Irene Boyd knew the truth. They had pledged never to mention that night again. Irene must have blabbed.

"I gather you were quite a hero."

Ratso chewed his lip. Hughes was right. Irene Boyd had called him *my hero* and right there and then, his heroics had been rewarded up against the wall. Right there and then, while trapped in the half-light of a stinking basement abandoned by vagrants. In an impulsive move, she had flung her arms round his neck before stripping off. Right there and then, with a large dead rat lying among sodden bedding and rotted food, she had commanded: *Ratso the rat-killer! Now, right now. Hard, hard against the wall.*

For eighteen years, he had kept his silence. For eighteen years he had never explained his nickname, swatting aside speculation. "The nickname stuck." He wondered what else Boyd had volunteered of their eleven hours in the filth of the vagrant's den.

"I gather there was a huge rat sharing your small area."

Ratso could have said that when a large rat had jumped from a ledge and landed on her foot, Boyd had been a gibbering, hysterical wreck, screaming and sobbing. To protect her Ironballs image, he had promised secrecy about her meltdown. "She was a damsel in distress."

"You deliberately cornered the rat? Made it attack you?"

"You would have done the same."

Hughes's eyes showed uncertainty. "I hope I would. Bare hands, was it?"

"I used a broken broom-handle." He grinned. "My cricket experience came good. As it sprang at me, I played a hook shot and smashed it seven feet into a wall."

"No doubt, the crowd at Lord's would have appreciated your shot."

There was a moment's silence as Ratso demonstrated the shot and debated what next to say. but then he continued. "Sir, please don't broadcast this yet. Boyd is not the only person who is now married."

Hughes did a double-take and pushed his glasses up his nose. "I never thought you were the marrying kind."

"If you met Kirsty-Ann, you'd know why I am. She's special. You're the first to know here. I'm not telling the team till *Footstool* is over. We'd lose focus."

Hughes led him to the door. "Congratulations but back to business. With your record and experience, I barely need to say this. But I will." He placed a hand on Ratso's shoulder. "However much you plan, *there's always something else*. That's a lesson I learned the hard way. Never assume you have every duck lined up."

"Good advice, sir. You sound like Lieutenant Colombo."

"*Just one more thing*? Well, Colombo never failed, did he?"

Putney

"Holtom," Ratso answered the phone. "Yes – put her through."

"Hello! It's Molly Bishop. I'm at home in Dinton."

"All good for your EGM tomorrow?"

"Jamie's happy. Well done on the Dublin lead but here's why I'm calling. I've found the receipt for that red wine I bought the night the poor kid was murdered. It's timed at 21-35 p.m."

"Thanks. Send it through but I now know you were in your hotel. One of the team tracked your journey back there on CCTV. I'll see you tomorrow." He checked his watch. Major Tang's colleague was due in five minutes.

He went to a meeting-room, picking up Petrie on the way. "Handwriting report arrived, boss?" No sooner had she asked than she knew the answer from Ratso's jutted jaw and clenched teeth.

"Sometimes we're so third-world."

"Anything from Danny Willison and Carole about the Golden Hotspur?"

"Not yet." His phone buzzed and he read the text message. "I got my pal Sprog Booth to drop by on a pretext. There's been no sign of Terry Yates at home all day."

"And Folkestone?"

"Surveillance photographed Degsy Foden at his window using a telescope. Fully dressed and clutching a drink."

"How was he looking?"

"I'm told, pretty damned chipper. Sonya Bird walked to the

Deadly Hush

local newsagent. Otherwise, nothing." They entered the meeting-room. "Sergeant-Major Kreig thanks for coming down. I'm sorry for the inconvenience." Hypocritically, he added that he was sorry not to be seeing Major Tang.

Kreig ignored the offered handshake. Judging by the scowl on his face, he could have just swallowed a cockroach. "Very inconvenient but I'm here. A cup of strong coffee would be good." He spoke with raw military precision in a gruff voice that Ratso placed as a tough inner-London suburb like Holloway. "Sorting the files, getting clearance – all that involved a lot of midnight oil."

Petrie glanced at her boss who showed no reaction except to order drinks. Ratso, though, had felt like saying he had started his day in Bonnitor; changed flights; flown the Atlantic; been targeted for execution and had held a major Press Conference. Instead, he let it pass.

"I have these three files you asked for." Kreig removed the rather dog-eared and grubby sandy-coloured folders. "I hope they help after all this buggeration."

"Thanks, Sergeant-Major. Nancy, you read about Degsy Derek Foden. I'll start with Terry Yates." Ratso looked across to Kreig's sharp-featured face which was still twitching with irritation. "Seeing the thickness of these files, we're going to need at least an hour or more." He pulled out his wallet and handed over a tenner. "There's a Costa down below. Buy yourself a coffee and a toastie. Far better than sitting in here with us."

For the first time, Kreig looked less as if he had fire-ants devouring his bollocks. He took the note with a near smile. "I'll be back in seventy."

"Thank God he's gone.," Petrie laughed. "I didn't want him sitting there with a face like a wet Monday."

With military precision, Kreig reappeared seventy minutes later. "Finished?"

"We have. We need to keep every page we've flagged with a Post-it."

"My instructions were to leave nothing."

"Sergeant-Major, ring Major Tang, the Minister of Defence or the Chief of the General Staff if you want but if these documents leave with you, all hell will break loose." Ratso paused to let the warning sink in. "In fact, I can tell you straight. They are not leaving here. Your help today in rushing to London has proved invaluable. I can't explain why but when *Operation Footstool* is over, I will ensure that you will get commended for your help." Ratso produced one of his rare smiles. "Look. Let's start over. You and me, we both have our jobs to do, our superiors to satisfy. I have the media hounding me wanting results. I'm sure we are on the same side."

"I've read the files on the train. I heard you on the car radio. The Dublin connection. Four murders"

Ratso leaned across the table to shake hands and after a moment's hesitation, Kreig grinned and gripped Ratso's hand. "Look mate! If you're really worried," Ratso schmoozed "I'll speak to your C.O or whatever Field-Marshall needs to be appeased."

"Am I under orders from you that I must obey?"

"Ten years in the slammer if you don't," Ratso joked. "Facing a charge of obstructing justice. Does that help you?"

For answer, Kreig pushed the files closer to Ratso. "Keep the entire files. Less to lug back. Just sign for them." Kreig paused. "I don't know what this is about but I knew these three guys."

"You in touch?"

"Never since they moved on."

"What did you make of them?"

"They'd die for you. Die for the Regiment. Certainly die for each other. They had a strong bond."

"Any negatives?"

"Some reckoned Degsy Foden and Zak Carter enjoyed killing too much."

"Not Yates?"

"Less so. Much less so."

"For professionals like you, surely killing is part of the job."

"When essential. Not for fun."

After hasty pleasantries, Petrie ushered Kreig out leaving Ratso to revisit the Post-its.

Putney

Viment and Willison had joined Ratso, Tosh Watson and Petrie in his office. Ratso opened the meeting. "We now have photos from Credenhill dating back to 2005. At that time, there were no women in the SAS. There are now. After the 7th July 2005 terrorist attacks, some of the SAS men were deployed on London Transport. They roamed around on the Tube, watching for anything suspicious."

Momentarily, Ratso's confident delivery faltered. "I remember it so well. After the bombings, they sent me to Tavistock Square where the double-decker had been blown apart." Ratso's closed eyes showed he was reliving the sights and smells of unspeakable horror. He stopped, not close to tears but trapped by the unforgettable images. "Ironic when you think about it. In 2005, me, Yates and Foden were on the same side – trying to protect the public."

Nancy was keen to change the mood. "I'll show them what we found in the Credenhill files." She pushed across the photos.

"Some SAS are trained in use of disguises and accents." Ratso's voice showed a flash of anger. "Tang had never mentioned that. *Operational Reasons*, he said. Fortunately these pics were in their files." Yates was dressed in a grubby boiler-suit and cloth cap, looking every bit a plumber's mate with a small bag of tools. Degsy Foden was dressed like a female shop assistant. "They were among those safeguarding London Transport."

Viment studied each photo. "Impressive. For a hard bastard, trained to kill, Degsy Foden scrubbed up well." With a manicured finger, she pointed to the CCTV image of the Molly Bishop lookalike. "I couldn't see it before. Now, behind all the make-up, I can see Foden!"

Willison looked at Foden in 2005, all bouffant wig, blusher, eye-liner, lipstick and eyelashes. "She looked good enough to shag," he said with typical lack of taste.

"Looking like Degsy Foden does now, you might change your mind, Danny. Unless shagging apparently decrepit old men turns you on." Watson's comment lightened the moment.

"That's enough." Ratso waved his arm for quiet. "Here's the mega-plus. Here's why Foden didn't look like our Molly when murdering Goldie." He looked at each in turn. "The EMA Annual Report only reached Terry Yates after that."

"As Pink Floyd would say, that's another brick in the wall," said Tosh. "Links Yates."

"Working assumption – Degsy Foden was paid by Yates. With this photo, we've almost enough to bring in Foden and Sonya Bird for questioning. We just need the damned handwriting report."

"Proving Foden murdered Quercy won't be easy."

"Yes and no, Tosh." Ratso stifled a yawn as the last twenty-four hours caught up with him. "The Geneva police have no CCTV – bad. Lies about him not travelling – good. If we clinch the handwriting – bloody marvellous. Then we'll make Sonya Bird crack about driving him to Geneva."

"Then we can open up Degsy Foden like a can of beans. No need for thumbscrews," Tosh said.

"Any update on Yates's whereabouts, boss?"

"None. Carole, make sure Bonkers and the techies trace Yates when he logs in to watch the EGM. We may swoop to make an arrest."

Ratso was about to continue when Strang came in clutching a print-out. "From Forensics."

Ratso eagerly turned to the final page and read aloud: "I conclude beyond all reasonable doubt that the same person wrote the words on the shopping-list and the Dunsdale Creek Visitor's Page. The person who wrote the diary entries is unconnected." Ratso glanced away towards the river and rapped his fingers on the glass. "Olly's diary clears him."

"Boss, how about nabbing Foden, his woman and Zak Carter simultaneously," Strang asked.

Nancy looked cautious. "The Leas in Folkestone is pretty central. Loads of apartments. Let's involve no squad cars, sirens, flashing lights. Let's just quietly remove them. How about 11 p.m. tonight, 7 p.m. Barbados."

"I'm interested in garage 11B," said Ratso.

"Aye and let's raid Yates's home wherever he is. We can link him to Degsy. By the time he logs in for the EGM, mebbe we can link him to Zak Carter as well."

"Right! That's the plan." Ratso's exhaustion had gone. The forensic report had changed everything. Adrenaline was now pumping through him. "One quick point. All those who bet their fiver on Goldie's killer being male?"

Jock grinned. "Forty-seven were correct. Now we need the age to be confirmed. Danny, though, is disqualified."

"Why?"

"He voted twice, once for male and once for female."

"It was just a joke – an each-way bet." Willison did not sound or look convincing as he shifted his buttocks uneasily on his chair.

Ratso seized control. "Okay, moving on. Tosh and Nancy, get straight to Folkestone. Don't forget your buckets-and-spades. Carole, you and Danny, train it to North Yorkshire. I'll tee up Detective Sergeant Wansdyke. He'll sort the raid. Oh and by the way, our new four-pip is Detective Chief Superintendent Irene Boyd."

"Ironballs," groaned Watson. "Bring back Caldwell."

"Okay everybody, on your way."

In a few seconds, the room was empty leaving Ratso in the dry stale air. His thoughts were of Wensley Hughes's parting words. There was no escaping them. *However much you plan, there's always something else.*

He phoned Assistant Commissioner O'Neill in Dublin. "Sir, we're ready for that high profile presence at airports and sea-terminals. Link it to *Operation Footstool*."

Was that what I missed?

Or is there still something else?

He called Florida and for twenty minutes he and Kirsty-Ann relived memories of their wedding and he listened to chatterbox Leon. When K.A had got home after the wedding, she had been tearful. She still was. "Todd, I couldn't trust Mom to look after Leon again. Just in the few days when I was in Bonnitor, she's gone downhill." Now, as he listened to Mom's faltering voice, he could understand K.A's concern. She even seemed confused about who he was, asking how things were in New York. Saddened and worried, he ended the call.

Much as he wanted to be supportive, he had to return to *Footloose*.

What am I missing?

Is there something else?

He re-read Terry Yates's file but slower. He had been commended for courage, inventiveness and effectiveness. He had done ops in Africa, Ireland, the Middle East, Iraq, Afghanistan and South America. Like Zak Carter and Degsy Foden, he had been trained in close-combat and weaponry. He flicked through reports of what looked like deniable operations. Struggling to read the close-printed detail, he forced himself to continue beyond the easy stuff like photos and commendations. It was over thirty minutes before he spotted something at the foot of a page he had previously missed. He swallowed hard.

How the hell did I miss that?

The Rogerson Hotel

While Ratso sat at a table with empty porridge bowls and glasses of freshly-squeezed orange juice, Jock Strang was lined up by the self-service hot food counter picking up their full English. He returned with plates stacked with a mountain of carbohydrates and cholesterol. "Looks good, Jock. Not my preferred brekkie but I never got to eat properly last night. Never even got home."

"You got some kip though?"

"I was being updated about the three raids. At some time after four, I took a nap at my desk but then K-A texted me!" At least the message had been worth being woken for. *Great news. That Montreal investigation? In six weeks, I'm giving evidence at your High Court. All expenses paid. I'll bring Leon. We three will stay in a suite at the Connaught. My little sis is going to take care of Mom. Can't wait. Love u lots xxx.*"

Fully awake now, he had replied. *"Wow! Amazing news. The Connaught! Out of my price-range! Do I need a new suit? Should I buy brogues? Love you all. xxx"*

"Sorry Jock! I was miles away. You were saying?"

"Barbados? You were worried."

"Went well. One of Paterson's youngsters found the jewels including the Pomellato chain. They were hidden under a pile of rags and engine-spares in a locker on *Mighty Meg*. Hopefully Luminol will find blood traces linking him to Campbell." Ratso flourished his fork. "Amazing, isn't it! On that boat trip, I was almost in touching distance of the jewels."

"Has Zak Carter named names?"

Ratso exhaled a sharp outflow of breath. "The SAS are trained to give away nothing during interrogation – even under torture. I don't expect anything." He topped up more black coffee. "The search at Yates's place is still going on. He still hasn't surfaced."

"Bonkers is with the techies behind Reception. He'll know where Yates is when he logs in."

Ratso pushed his black pudding to one side and Jock immediately forked it. "From what Tosh was told, Yates is not in London till Friday."

"Maybe he's with that Zoe girl for a spot of leg-over?"

"His van's at his home. So's the Aston Martin. Nothing incriminating found so far. Stacks of papers about his debts. Financially, he's in shitsville. The bank in Richmond have just closed his account. Mbesa owes wages, National Insurance and VAT. The house is being repossessed."

"Degsy and his woman?"

"Arriving in London later for interrogation," Ratso nodded agreement. "The directors till expect no angry mob attending the EGM this year. That's in the Bartlett Suite on the third floor. Make sure the surveillance team capture all hotel arrivals and departures."

"You expecting any bother?"

Ratso thought of Wensley Hughes's warning. "No but we must be ready for the unexpected."

"Such as?"

"If I knew that, it would not be unexpected."

"Energy Management's two security guys have arrived."

"There's still 38 minutes till the EGM. The sniffer-dog team arrive in five minutes."

"Sniffer-dogs?"

"I found a footnote in Yates's file. He'd been trained in explosives. In Colombia, he made and used two IEDs – Improvised Explosive Devices. He blew up a bridge used by drug cartels. If the dogs find anything, we'll sound the Fire Alarm."

The Bartlett Suite

Up in the meeting-room, Ratso chatted to the security guards, quickly establishing their credentials. "We both did last year's meeting. A brown-trouser day, that was," explained the taller of the two big men. "If the meeting hadn't ended when it did, some of the hotheads would have ripped the directors to shreds."

"That bad, was it?"

"Like, it was okay and then whoosh – a few jeering guys whipped up a storm."

"Like animals, they was," agreed the other guard. "Shouting, booing, chucking coffee-cups. This year, Mr Fargher has said the mood is different. I effing well hope he's correct."

Ratso said nothing.

The guards looked to the door where two German Shepherds and their handlers from the Met's Dog Support Unit had appeared. "Jeez! Fargher didn't tell us we'd have the effing bomb squad here."

"Blame me for that. Excuse me. I've got to speak to our new arrivals." Ratso chatted to the handlers before leaving them to their task. The two officers, both wearing stab-vests, worked through every row of seats from the rear to the front. Ratso followed and then bounded up the four steps to join them on the rostrum. Centred on it was a long table with four chairs, note-pads, freebie Rogerson pens, a bowl of mints, jugs of water and four microphones. A youngster in well-pressed jeans and a check-shirt was adjusting a tripod camera aimed at the stage. "I'm DCI Holtom and you are?"

Deadly Hush

"Melvin Grant, in charge of live-streaming. What's with the dogs? Expecting trouble?"

Ratso shook his head. "Routine precautions. If the dogs give the all-clear, then we're good to go. If they find something, don't hang about." Ratso looked back down the room over the lines of chairs. At the far end, beyond the back row, was the only entrance. Beside it was a white-clothed table where a young waitress was setting out cups and plates of biscuits. Ratso knew better than to interrupt the handlers. Instead, he checked for messages on his phone. Nothing. Yates had still not been located. Would he log in from Vietnam? From Brazil? Or was he somewhere in London?

Wensley Hughes's words continued to make him uneasy.

There's always something else.

The two dogs had now finished. Ratso joined the handlers by the coffee-table. "All clear, sir," he was informed.

"Good job. Thanks." He watched the dogs head for the escalators, passing Strang who was coming towards him. "All okay downstairs?"

"Aye! Bonkers is like a pig in shit watching the CCTV monitors and fiddling around with something techie. The dogs gave the all-clear?"

"Yes." Ratso sounded reassuring but then, like a kick in the gut, it hit him. He knew what he had missed. His tone changed. "Yates is entitled to attend the EGM. He's bust. Going to lose everything. Suppose he's a suicide-bomber, maybe in disguise .A bomb strapped to his midriff."

Strang said nothing, just swallowed hard.

"Here's the plan. Nobody enters the meeting-room without I.D. All bags to be double-checked. Thorough pat-downs. All the uniforms in the lobby must be ready to prevent Yates getting to the Bartlett Suite, whatever his disguise. There'll be abuse from the but sod them. Got it?" Strang was already on the starting-blocks when Ratso had another thought. "Bring back the handlers. Let's keep the dogs at the hotel entrance. It's a pity you ate my black pudding. The dogs might have loved that."

Strang exited like a man with his pants on fire.

The Rogerson Hotel

Bonkers had commandeered a corner desk. He saw Ratso enter, balancing a white cup-and-saucer. He pointed to three young nerds, their eyes locked on their monitors. "When Yates logs in, those three guys can trace him."

Ratso watched the two men and a young woman. In their torn jeans, and sloganned T-Shirts, they looked dressed for a very casual night out. *Perhaps they had just had one.* He was about to brief Bonkers when a text arrived from K.A. "*Mom just passed.*" He replied at once. "*That's awful. I am running a major Op. Will call xxx.*" He turned to Bonkale. "The moment Yates signs in, let me know. Understood." Ratso was rewarded with a broad toothy smile. For a youngster, Bonkale was impressively calm. "Where are the directors?"

"The Albion Room. boss. Third Floor. Room 377. That's the opposite wing to the Bartlett Suite." After dumping his cup, Ratso hurried up the stairs and along the blue-carpeted corridor. At the second knock, Jamie Fargher peered suspiciously round the door. "Chief Inspector, come in. Thank God you're not a shareholder about to give us grief." The rectangular table was set for four and the remains of breakfast had been pushed to one end. "Coffee, tea or juice?"

"I'm good." Ratso nodded a hello to Young and Bishop. Also seated at the table, with papers in front of him, was a suited man with no tie. He was young, maybe mid-thirties and alert with watchful eyes. He said nothing and nobody introduced him. "A quick update. We have arrested a man from Kent on suspicion of murdering Jules Quercy. I'll be questioning him later about other murders. In a joint operation with the police in Bonnitor and Barbados, there's a suspect in custody for murdering Kendall Campbell."

"Excellent," said Olly Young. "But Yates? Any developments?"

"We expect him to log-in just before the EGM. The Bartlett Suite has the all-clear." He turned to go. "Oh and the other good news is that…" Ratso was interrupted as his phone buzzed. It was Bonkers. He stopped in mid-track. His face showed much more than surprise and he did a double-take. "No. No fire-alarm yet. No panic. 277 you said? Do not enter. I'll join you."

Ratso turned to the seated group. They looked spooked by the words *fire-alarm*. "You've gotta leave. Get out now." His voice rose. " Go, go, go."

"But…"

"Go. Get Out," Ratso shouted, gesticulating towards the door. "Leave the building." Ratso stood back from the door. Arms waving, he shooed them into the corridor. Fargher was last to leave, carrying his laptop and papers.

"You're not coming?" he enquired.

"I'm staying." After closing the door, he lifted the tablecloth and knelt down to look under the table.

The Rogerson Hotel

On all fours, Ratso crawled along the carpet to look beneath the table. Half-twisted on his back, he used the torch on his phone. He pointed it to all four corners and along each side. There was nothing. He scrambled out and took a few hurried steps to the sideboard. He checked it, drawer by drawer, sliding each one out with a slow and steady movement.

Nothing.

Ratso dashed into the corridor and, after turning left, ran along it, dodging a young couple with a pushchair. He saw an emergency exit and, on impulse, selected it. He could save twenty metres in each direction using the short-cut. One floor down, he emerged into an identical corridor. He turned right and squeezed past a housekeeper's trolley before he saw Bonkale further along the corridor.

Bonkale pointed to the next room. "Yates checked into room 277 yesterday. Directly below the Albion Suite."

"How do we get in?"

For answer, Bonkale flourished a plastic key. "A Master."

"Taser ready?"

Bonkale nodded as they edged closer to the white door with brass numbering beside it. "As soon as the fire-alarm sounds, use the key. Yates will be momentarily confused." Ratso dialled the Front of House Manager. "DCI Holtom here. Fire-alarm immediate. Evacuate the building."

The Rogerson Hotel

Very few police in the UK carry guns. Most don't want to, knowing that a wrong split-second decision might kill an innocent civilian The small percentage who do are specially trained. But at this moment, uncertain whether Yates might be inside Room 277, Ratso wished they had more than tasers. If he was in the room, Yates could be armed and dangerous.

Still panting from his exertion, Ratso felt his fried breakfast doing cartwheels in his stomach. Breathing heavily, they stood close to the door, tasers ready and the key poised by the slot.

It seemed an eternity but was less than seven seconds before the penetrating shriek of the alarm filled the corridor. It blared out from the overhead sounders. Strobe-lights flashed as Bonkale slid in the key and turned the handle. Shouting *police*, they careered into the bedroom. It was spacious and similar in size to the Albion Suite immediately below. The curtains were shut and only a single bedside lamp provided some light. There was a king-size bed, a narrow but long desk, bedside units, a closet with sliding-doors and two easy-chairs pointing towards a large-screen TV. To the left of the bed was the bathroom. Of Yates, there was no sign. A large open suitcase lay on the unmade bed.

There was no hiding-place under the bed or elsewhere. Ratso saw the suitcase at the same moment as they both heard the sound of movement. It was coming from inside the bathroom, perhaps from a floorboard or perhaps a shoe squeaking on a damp floor.

Before Ratso could stop him, Bonkale had kicked open the

Deadly Hush

bathroom door, taser ready for action. The door swung back with a violent bang. It hit the side of the bath and started to rebound as Bonkale rushed in. Almost instantly, with a deafening roar that almost drowned the alarm, a figure came from nowhere and jumped on him, seizing Bonkale by the neck. With the force of the impact, Bonkers crashed backwards into the basin, his taser being knocked from his hand.

Ratso saw his colleague toppling from the violent impetus, Tery Yates almost smothering his body. Bonkale hit the floor, half in and half-out of the bathroom, Yates's hands clamped around his throat. As Bonkale struggled to free himself, his torso arching and knees and feet thrashing around, Yates's grip never wavered.

Ratso saw Yates's familiar profile, the one he had seen so often on the cricket-field and at sing-along nights in Kirby Hill with Sprog. Right now, Yates's eyes were manic, his face contorted, his mouth dribbling like a rabid dog. Ratso took careful aim and squeezed the trigger. Instantaneously, as 50,000 volts slammed into him, Yates's grip was gone. His body writhed and wriggled as it slithered sideways and off Bonkale. For a second, Ratso watched his futile attempts to take control of his body as he lay writhing on the damp floor.

With no time to lose, Ratso went straight to the suitcase. He saw its contents. No shirts, no underwear and no washing-kit. Instead, he saw an initiator, switch, main charge, batteries, the wiring and a large eerie-looking container. Worst of all, he saw the green flashing quartz crystal timer, ticking down even as he stared at it.

1 minutes 35 seconds.

1 minutes 34 seconds

If I run, I may not even escape the collapsing building.

His mind raced back nearly twenty years when he had been selected to learn about bomb-disposal. His training had been at Chattenden Military Camp in North Kent. Since then, he had never had cause to remember what "Tank" Ormsby, a giant broad-shouldered Ammunition Technical Officer had taught him. Ratso remembered enough to wonder about the explosive mixture.

Was ammonium nitrate the oxidiser – that plus fuel oil?
Had Yates packed the container with shipyard confetti?
Thousands of nails, bolts and other shrapnel?
Of more concern was what activated the device.
A wave of nausea swept through him.

Momentarily, he was transfixed, fighting to regain his professionalism.

This is one helluva bomb.
Big enough to bring down this side of the building.
The flashing quartz.
Taunting me.
One minute 28 seconds.
What did I learn at Chattenden?
What can I remember?
Please don't be too sophisticated.
He studied the device.
A damned sight easier during training when an error didn't mean your body-parts would be scattered all over London.

"I got him cuffed, boss." The voice startled Ratso, lost in his battle to remember his training.

"This is a monster. Get out. Go on Bonkers. Run. That's an order. You can't help me." His eyes focussed on the hypnotic rhythm of the flashes of the green quartz crystal display.

One minute 11 seconds.

Vaguely aware of Bonkers leaving, he struggled to remember what he had learned. Ormsby, built like a tank but with nerveless long, slender fingers, had made it seem so straightforward. He had exuded calm, had urged Ratso stay calm.

Like fuck!
One minute 7 seconds.
What had "Tank" Ormsby said?
Breathe normally.
That was it.
Keep your heart rate in check.
Keep your hands steady.
Shut out the noise, the chaos, the flashing quartz.
Ignore the Fire Alarm.
Shut out the incessant instructions to leave the building.
Fuck that!

Trying to ignore the flashing green numbers, he removed his Swiss Army knife from his pocket.

Last chance.
You could run now.
Might get clear of the collapse.
Probably would.
But I'm trained.
I can do it.

As he fought for composure, the components of the device looked familiar and pleasingly low tech. There was one big difference from Chattenden. Right now there was no bell and no light bulb. In training, the bell and bulb proved whether the device had been successfully defused or he had screwed up and had blown himself apart.

For fuck's sake, stop blinking.
And someone turn off that bloody fire-alarm.
I'm trying to concentrate.
There it is.
The anti-handling device.
Looks like a typical mercury tilt switch.

Remember Airey Neave at the House of Commons.
Don't go tilting anything.
Don't move it.
No bell and light bulb if you cock this up.
He fiddled and fumbled trying to open the knife.
37 seconds
From somewhere, now adding to the noise, he heard the wails of approaching sirens.
What would Tank Ormsby be saying?
Relax.
There's more time than you think.
Breathe slowly.
At last, he had the knife open, converting the internal arms to a small pair of pliers. As the nose of the pliers came into focus with the bomb as its background, Ratso could see the tips moving in sync with his shaking fingers.
Relax
There's more time than you think.
Twenty seconds.
Is that the correct wire to cut?
That one there.
The red one?
9 seconds.
Come on Tank – give me a clue.
Remind me!
He moved the pliers towards it.
If I'm wrong – so what.
I'm fucked anyway.
Go for it.
The red wire.
Is this my last ever decision?

Ratso's eyes flicked a glance at the timer.
Have I guts to squeeze now?
His face was screwed up, his mouth clamped tight shut.
As if that would make a difference.
6 seconds.
He squeezed the metal handles of the pliers, a bead of sweat splashing onto the timer.
The flashing stopped.
5 seconds remaining.
He sat on the bed shaking, thanking God and Tank in equal measure. After a long moment, he tried to stand but his legs were shaking. He was forced to sit on the edge of the bed. Yates was lying face down, hands clamped against his spine and still twitching. Ratso grabbed his phone. His voice sounded cracked and distorted from his dry mouth and throat. "All clear, Jock. Bomb disarmed. Yates will soon be able to walk. Get him removed. Yes. Perhaps an ambulance crew. No. Not for me. I'm fine. Nothing a pint of Guinness won't fix."

Ratso looked down at Yates who was regaining control of his limbs. He leaned over him "Terry, whatever money you lost, this was never the answer. You've chucked everything for revenge. You'll never come out of jail."

The Rogerson Hotel

It was 12-30 p.m. before the Energy Management meeting could commence. Oliver Young stood up to absorb the cold or sullen looks from the thirty or so shareholders. Besides having lost so much of their personal wealth, they had resented being corralled outside because of the Fire Alarm. Up on the rostrum, despite being shaken by their experience, all three directors somehow managed to look confident as the routine items on the agenda were quickly passed.

Ratso had been standing close to the rostrum, next to Strang. He signalled to Olly Young who came over and crouched down. Ratso handed him a typed note, hot off the press. After glancing at it, he returned to behind the microphone and read from it.

"I apologise for the lack of information about the 90-minute delay. This was on instructions from the Metropolitan Police. This note allows me to tell you more." He looked down at Ratso for reassurance and waited for the nod. Then, he read it slowly, pausing often for emphasis.

"The Metropolitan Police have confirmed that a person, a shareholder, has been arrested and charged with intended murder of your three directors this morning." Young turned and looked along the desk to Bishop and Fargher. "A large bomb designed to kill us and perhaps dozens more, was neutralised with just seconds to spare." Young put down the note. "I want to say two things. Firstly, I would like to congratulate and thank the police for disarming the bomb.

Secondly, I hope none of you consider that your regrettable heavy losses can ever justify such behaviour."

At first, Ratso noticed the total silence and then he saw neighbour turn to neighbour as sporadic conversation broke out. Someone clapped and moments later the entire room was standing and applauding. Olly Young let it ride for a few moments before waving for everyone to be seated. He reached again for a glass of water which trembled in his hand as he took a few sips. His tall figure rocked back and forward on his heels while he gathered his thoughts. "I now return to the implications of the Special Resolution which was passed with 92% approval." He milked the moment, looking at row on row of still shocked faces. "I am now passing you over to our geologist, Molly Bishop."

She rose to muted applause. "Under this Special Resolution, you have authorised your board to exploit the Bonnitor land in the optimum way. That includes further drilling for oil. We could not include in the Special Resolution just what we had in mind. We were waiting for the Government to approve our plan. Approval was received less than 48 hours ago."

A voice from somewhere in the room *yelled get on with it*. Molly Bishop took this in her stride. "In the course of the unsuccessful drill, I found preliminary evidence of rare earth minerals. Despite its name, rare earth is *not* that rare. What is rare is to find it in commercial quantities. Your board has obtained an independent Competent Person's Report. This confirmed the presence of lithium in commercial quantities." Excited murmurs and puzzled frowns spread through the audience. "The Bonnitor Government had hoped to improve their dire economy with an oil-strike. That was not to be. Now, following top-secret discussions, and subject to this Special Resolution being passed, the Government has moved with unusual speed and granted us a licence to exploit rare earth rights.

This will be a game-changer for the welfare of the island's citizens and for you as our shareholders."

A suited pensioner stood up. "Is this a green project or will the activists again cause trouble?"

Bishop's face was suddenly a flashing smile. "It is green, sir, indeed yes, it is. Lithium is an exit route from fossil-fuels. It is essential in mobile-phones, laptops, cars and aircraft. Lithium-ion batteries power the electric vehicle sector. Some of you may drive an electric car. Its battery probably contains 12 kg of lithium. There is a global race to find and exploit this rare earth. We have it." She folded her large arms across her ample chest in an image of defiance. "We do not expect hostility as we move forward." She sat down.

"So how will we pay for this?" shouted a suited middle-aged man with a bristling moustache and florid face. "The company has no money. We're tired of your optimistic jam tomorrow bollocks." He turned to look at the audience, expecting to have captured the mood. He had not. With only one or two muttered hear-hears, he sat down, his face redder than ever.

Young looked over the heads of the attendees and waved to a man who had been sitting quietly in the back row. "Come on up, Hiram." Ratso immediately recognised him as the man who had been in the Albion Suite. The lithe young man rose and then mounted the rostrum. "Let me introduce Hiram G. Warrender. Hiram, over to you."

"Thank you, Oliver. I'm from Toronto but I also have a home in Robinson's Cove, Bonnitor. By reputation, I am a commodity billionaire. That may even be true," he grinned. "In the fourteen years since I was twenty-one, I have achieved my wealth through rare earths. I have spent considerable time exploiting them in Chile, Calgary and Vancouver." He produced a single sheet of paper from his leather case and flourished it. "Subject to shareholder approval, this is my agreement, to invest up to seven hundred million pounds in your company. This will involve another Shareholders Meeting. The value of your current shares will be devalued." He let the mutterings die down. "My investment will open the door for eye-watering profits for your company."

Young chipped in. "Hiram, give the shareholders your projections."

"The cost of lithium is rising. I am expecting yearly production of 21,000 tons. At $40,000 per ton, that's a top line of 840 million US dollars every year." He bounced across the platform, grinning from ear to ear. "Is that enough?"

Putney

Five days had passed since the Energy Management EGM and it was turning 3 p.m. when Ratso was ready to speak. The room was hot and smelled of yesterday's burgers and stale sweat. Two nights before, he had celebrated his wedding announcement in the Drum & Flute and his sore head had just about recovered. The night had ended with rounds of Zombies. At the time, to noisy shouts, some enthusiastic singing and hoots of laughter, the rum had slipped away, no trouble. The trouble had only come next morning. Except Nancy Petrie, nobody lining up in the canteen had been chipper. Even Jock Strang had brushed aside an offer of his usual full English.

Ratso's new boss, Irene Boyd, had stayed at the party only to down a few bites of Tandoori Chicken and a glass of Prosecco. Ratso had been amazed she had come at all and was relieved when she quietly slipped away. Party-Animal she was not.

Since her arrival at Jubilee House, three days earlier, few of the gathered crowd had seen much of her as she had got up to speed. Now, at the final full meeting of *Footloose*, Ratso fought to ignore memories of their night trapped in the stinking basement. He introduced Boyd *as someone he had known and always respected. Someone who he knew, even back in their Lewisham days, was going to deserve fast-tracking to the top."*

As Boyd thanked Todd for his welcome, and he looked her in the eye, flashbacks of suspenders and the sound of her fingernails scratching on the wall flooded his mind. Now though, she was

Deadly Hush

brusque and efficient – very much a Det. Chief Superintendent with the words *Future Commissioner* stamped on her forehead. With her delicate but deliberate arm moves, she commanded the room. He could see why she had raced through the ranks with all the relentless power of an advancing steamroller.

Nothing and nobody will stand in my way.

Across the room, he took in her blonde hair, immaculately coiffured, and now tinged with grey. Despite the hard knocks of over twenty years of policing, her face barely needed make-up. From the tips of her delicately shaded fingernails to the pointed toes of her black slingbacks, everything yelled class-act. The slender heels increased her height and added to an already imperious *don't mess* image.

Her eyes were restless and watchful as she encouraged the listeners to apply the highest standards. Although she had been friendly to the small group at Ratso's party, her face, with her Slavic-high cheekbones, had confirmed an aloof and haughty image. Ratso could almost see the words *do you think that's wise* written on her face as she had heard the mindless banter at his party.

DCS Boyd sat down, eyes intent on Ratso as she nodded for him to report. "This will be the last full meeting of *Operation Footstool*. Thank you all for your long hours and determination. You have delivered. This has been an amazing team effort. It will not surprise most of you to know that a certain very *smart* Detective Chief Superintendent," he paused for effect "is now telling everyone he never thought *Footstool* involved gay-hate."

He waited for the mutterings of *well-*do*ne Smart* and the sarcastic applause to subside. "I'm seeing Terry Yates later in Belmarsh Prison. But first, DC Bonkale will update you about Logan Goldie."

"Goldie was paying guys to slag-off companies like Energy

Management." He picked up a note. "They were paid to write garbage like *EMA's going down the bog to join its shitty directors. Hope the directors' families die horribly. Thieving bastards. Sell! Sell! Sell! Don't say tomorrow I didn't warn you.*"

"Were there many like that?" asked Petrie.

"Dozens. Some were even more unpleasant. Like *EMA's bust and buggered. Let's hope the directors die slowly in a cement-mixer or burn in sulphuric acid.* Every time they put this stuff on blogsites and chat-boards, Goldie paid them, driving down the share price. Easy money for the bloggers while Goldie made his fortune from trading the falling shares. Back to you, boss."

Ratso clapped his hands for attention. "Good news now from the Caribbean. We already had Zak Carter slam-dunk for the stolen jewellery. Today, he's been charged with murder."

"How come, guv?" enquired Carole Viment.

"D.I Bastien Alleyne came good."

"I thought he learned his policing at that girlie club in Soho." Tosh Watson's comment brought a burst of laughter and a sniff of disapproval from Boyd.

"I'm surprised ye remember even being there, Tosh," Strang said.

More laughter.

"Carter used a bin-liner bag when he swam back to his boat. Alleyne got D.I Patterson in Barbados to go big on the fire-retardant. Traces of yellow powder have been found in three places on his boat and inside the bin-liner."

"Did Terry Yates pay Carter?"

"Working assumption is he could keep whatever he stole."

"How did Yates communicate?" asked Petrie.

"We had assumed burners but first, I want to update you on Degsy Foden."

"And that little raver he was shacked up with," added Tosh Watson.

"Sonya Bird? She's one tough cookie but we've got her for smuggling Degsy Foden into France. She cracked, didn't want to be charged with being an accessory to murder. At that point," he grinned, "we hadn't a prayer of a case against Foden for murdering Quercy. The Audi wasn't tracking its journeys. Neither was Degsy's phone or his watch. He thought he was untraceable." Ratso almost bounced along the aisle between the listeners. "Not so."

"Degsy's now been charged. How did we nail him?" Ratso slapped his right hand just below his left shoulder. "There's your clue. Anybody?" He looked round the upturned faces of old timer constables, the youngsters, the civilians who worked with Holmes 2 and the rising stars. Nobody volunteered anything. "Tell them, Jock."

"Foden had a pacemaker. The boss got me to check with Foden's heart consultant. His heart is remotely monitored. The doctor can check the transmitted messages. The records showed that, right enough, Degsy Foden's heart-rate had peaked at dawn when Lord Ongerton was murdered and again when Goldie, Quercy and Marcel were murdered. With the other evidence – that's game set and match."

Ratso stopped pacing and stood very still. As he looked at the expectant faces, his blood ran cold. Someone in the room, one of the listeners was the mole who had wanted him dead. Looking at them. it seemed scarcely credible but Kola knowing of his Heathrow arrival had proved it.

You're the people I trusted.
One of you.
Wanted me dead for money.
And you'll do it again.

Leak to Boris Zandro.

All eyes were still on him, waiting for his lead. He forced himself to continue and turned to DC Petrie. "Nancy will tell you about Degsy's garage in Folkestone."

"Garage 11B was like Santa's Grotto or an Aladdin's Cave. We found several false number-plates including the ones identical to Olly Young's car. There was a canister of liquid polycarbonate used for masking number-plates. There was a marked-up street-map of Geneva."

"Aye, faced with that lot, Foden cracked – spilled the lot."

"Thanks, Jock. Thanks, Nancy."

"Including Dermot Doyle too?" asked Viment.

"No. Terry Yates killed him," Ratso replied. "Degsy Foden has now been charged with being an accessory to Doyle's murder. He drove Yates from King's Lynn to Notting Hill and back."

"Why didn't Yates get Foden to kill Doyle?"

"Good question, Carole. I'll be asking him. Foden said Yates didn't like close-quarter killing. Besides adding confusion about foot size, Terry Yates wanted to keep his distance from anything EMA."

"Was Foden paid?"

"Fifteen grand a time but he said he would have done it for nothing. Yates had saved his life during an op in Syria. Tosh found over thirty-thousand hidden in their bread bin." Ratso eased himself onto the edge of desk and swung his long legs. "Jock, tell them about playing the Ace."

"Degsy admitted the bomb was to be the Ace but when that Zoe girl in King's Lynn tipped off Terry Yates, there had to be a murder when he had an alibi. Marcel was never part of the plan. The kid was picked at random and his murder bought time for Yates to carry out the bombing. That's why Degsy dressed as Molly Bishop."

Deadly Hush

Ratso got off the desk and waved a Joker. "It's just arrived in the mail at the Yard. Terry Yates had sent it as his calling-card from hell. He knew that no playing-card would be found after the bomb. He mailed this the day before the EGM."

"Boss, how did Yates communicate?"

"Burners with Degsy. Only Degsy communicated with Zak Carter. He would call from hotel bedrooms or he used small-ads to conceal coded messages in Private Eye magazine."

He turned to Strang. "Now to something more important. Who won the jackpot?"

Jock Strang looked at his scribbles. "Bonkers. He was right about Degsy's age and sex."

It was a popular win. Ratso waited while Bonkers collected the cash to cheers and laughter amid shouts of *mine's a pint*. "That's it. Thanks again everyone." Once again, he looked round the sea of faces.

Which of you is the bastard who tipped off Hysen Kola?

I thought you were my friends.

One of you isn't.

Belmarsh Prison

The journey from Putney to Belmarsh Prison meant crossing south London. Progress was slow and it was nearly 90 minutes before they reached the intimidating exterior of the Thamesmead site. Because Bonkers had never been before, Ratso had asked him to drive and assist with the interview. For Ratso, it was his first return to Belmarsh since he had interviewed Boris Zandro.

Who's his mole?
A friend.?
Jock, Tosh, Nancy, Carole?
Surely not.
Not a friend.
But Terry Yates had been a friend.
A drinking buddy at the Shoulder of Mutton.

"Boris Zandro was here before they moved him up north," Ratso said.

"What did it feel like having a killer stalking you?"

"I was never scared but I can't pretend I wasn't concerned." Ratso unbuckled his seatbelt. "That's not me being all Arnold Schwarzenegger or Bruce Willis. I hope it never happens to you but here's my take. If we hadn't tricked Kola, I would have walked up to my Uber and bang, bang. Two bullets. I'm gone. *Goodnight Irene.* Hopefully, with a professional killer, you won't see it coming."

"You just get on with life, business as usual?"

"Business as usual? Not quite that easy, Bonkers. But something like that. Let's go see this callous bastard."

Consistent with its Category A status and top-security, it was another twenty minutes before Terry Yates was escorted into the interview room. Dressed in his drab prison clothes, already Yates looked a shadow of the cocky cricketer who used to stride up to the wicket expecting to smash the ball into the next county.

During moments of silence on the journey, Ratso had weighed up how to start the interview. The recording started and Ratso introduced Bonkale. "Terry, this a bit different to supping pints with Sprog in the Shoulder of Mutton. You won't be doing that again. You've destroyed your life and six others have been murdered. And for what? Do you feel better for it?"

For a long minute, Yates looked at the table-top and remained silent. "You'll never understand, Toddy. I was a born soldier. Loved living on the edge. Suddenly ... nothing. Just mooching on Civvy Street. Then I saw an opportunity! I got into ship security. Perfect timing. I was back in the game. Chucking scum pirates overboard. Making sure they never fathered no more kids. I was back living on the edge and becoming filthy rich."

Ratso nodded but said nothing. This was not the moment.

"Mbesa grew like crazy. Bleeding pirates – killing, kidnapping, looting, blackmailing. I made a fortune. Moved to Yorkshire. Then I read about Energy Management."

"Oil exploration. You went in too big?"

"I've taken risks all me life. The risk was finding no oil. Big deal. I didn't expect to be taking that risk. I was gonna sell just before spud, making megabucks. No risk."

"But Quercy, Goldie, the lawyer?"

"Them bastards torpedoed everything. My shares crashed to chicken-shit. Selling before spud became pointless. I had to cling on. If they'd found oil, then I was back to multi-megabucks."

Ratso shook his head. "But they didn't."

"Correct. I sold almost every share."

"Why murder them?"

"Toddy. You'll never understand gut-wrenching hatred. You've never seen your mates slaughtered on ops. Can't know what it feels like to want revenge from wake-up till bedtime? That's how I felt about EMA. Them bastards ruined my life. Then the bleedin' ship security industry changed. There was more competition. Sentiment turned against shipowners using armed personnel. Insurers required owners to adopt different measures – razor wire, citadels, new procedures. Suddenly, Mbesa was going tits-up and I had no cash to inject to save it. And why?" Yates thumped the table, his voice barking out the words. "Because of Quercy, Goldie and the KC getting even richer at my expense. Them and the directors."

Ratso permitted a long pause to let the rage cool. "You've seen the Financial Times?"

Yates looked up, suddenly interested. "Nah. Not in here." His brow furrowed. "Why? Why should I be interested?"

"Because the directors you planned to murder have hit paydirt."

Yates tapped the side of his nose. "Did they vote themselves a huge bonus at the EGM?"

"No, Terry." Ratso was enjoying himself. "You haven't seen EMA's share price?"

"Me? I've only got two hundred shares. Not interested, Toddy. They ain't worth shit. Worth a coupla quid maybe."

"Pity you sold. How many shares did you sell?"

"Telephone numbers, mate. I lost about eleven million quid." His face flashed hatred, his mouth was twisted and his eyes became slits. "All down to them greaseballs – specially that Logan Goldie and that pompous fat prick of a lawyer in Bonnitor."

"Okay, Terry. You're facing several life sentences. If you're ever released, it'll be with a Zimmer. I'd say that's pretty bad. But

Deadly Hush

can things get worse?" Ratso turned to Bonkale. "You want to tell him, or shall I?"

"I don't want to steal your moment, boss."

"Eleven million invested before the EGM is expected to be worth over one hundred million pounds – one hundred million quid, one hundred million smackeroos. Enough to travel the world watching cricket every day. Enough to clear your debts. Chase skirt. Save Mbesa and still have plenty left for solid gold-taps in your Rapido."

Ratso tilted his head to one side and raised an eyebrow as he waited for a reaction. There was none, so he continued. "Think about that every morning for the next thirty years. That's if you can sleep at all after the murders of Dermot Doyle, Lord Ongerton and young Marcel – all picked at random."

In the stillness of the room, the silence was stifling. At first, Ratso saw disbelief, then shock, a frown, confusion and then burning inner rage contort Yates's features. His lips whitened. His fists clenched and unclenched. "Toddy, you're not kidding me?" The words came slowly and in a hushed tone.

"Show him."

Bonkale produced the Financial Times and laid it in front of Yates. The headline alone was enough. After a few moments, he looked up. It was as if he had aged years. His eyes were dead, his cheeks had turned ashen. No sound came from his open mouth.

"I'm adjourning the interview for an hour. I'll let you think about what you've done before we take your statement." Ratso rose and Bonkale stood up with him. As they reached the door, Yates spoke.

"The bomb was meant for me too. You stole that from me."

The Connaught Hotel

After a day in the Family Division of the High Court in London, Kirsty-Ann had been happy to be flopping round in the Connaught's Library Suite, in a cosy blue onesie. Although her client's litigation had been going well, ever since the funeral she had felt below par. Even the excitement of being married and staying in a top hotel with Leon had not kept her tears away. During quiet moments when she was alone, she had sat on one of the comfy chairs, staring at old photos of her Mom and dabbing her eyes with endless tissues.

Ratso had managed to get to the funeral. In Florida, he had done what he could to support Kirsty-Ann who had wept uncontrollably throughout the service. Leon had been almost as inconsolable, howling on his bed and covering his head with a pillow. But after the funeral, Ratso had gradually brought him round with promises of what they would do together in London.

Now, in the splendour of the hotel, Ratso had just settled Leon down on his king-size. The little lad was happier now, asleep in his Fulham FC pyjamas and with his new cricket-bat lying beside him. Meanwhile, in the comfort of the spacious living-room, Kirsty-Ann and Ratso curled up on a sofa, awaiting room-service. "Mom had so wanted to take Leon to Hamleys, Buckingham Palace and the Changing of the Guard." Kirsty-Ann's eyes welled up as she rested her head on Ratso's shoulder.

"I'll do all that and more. The cricket season's finished but I'll take Leon to Craven Cottage to watch Fulham. And maybe this weekend, the three of us can take a boat up-river to Hampton Court where King Henry the Eighth feasted."

"I said you'd be a terrific Dad." She kissed him full on the mouth. "He loved lunch with you at the Jungle Cave today."

"We had such fun. Afterwards at Piccadilly Circus, he asked why there were no clowns and elephants." He stroked her ear. "Sheer magic being a Dad. Pity you had to be in court."

There was a knock on the door and Ratso let in the server. Rapidly, she set up their dinner and they fell silent while everything was laid out. When the young woman had gone, they settled down to crushed avocados, followed by lamb chops. Ratso started to pour a glass of red.

"Thanks but I won't have any wine."

Ratso looked across the table. "You won't? It's Gevrey-Chambertin, courtesy of your paymaster. You love Burgundy."

"I do ... but I checked just an hour ago." She broke into the biggest smile Ratso had ever seen. "I said you'd be a great Dad. Now you can prove it – twice over."

Ratso left his chair and circled the table to stand behind her. He placed a hand on each shoulder before leaning over her. "That's just so, so wonderful. Amazing! You are so adorable. I love you rotten."

"And me you."

After a lingering hug, Ratso returned to his chair. "If it's a girl, let's name her after your Mom."

"That would be so neat, so thoughtful. Thank you." She munched on her brown toast before continuing. "Ever since you promised in Bonnitor to give up your career – well ... everything for me, I knew I'd found someone truly special." She fought to control her emotions. "That was quite some sacrifice." She pushed aside the remains of her avocado. "I could never move to London while Mom was alive. Her roots had been in Florida for over forty years. Now, with her passed on, the position is different." She faltered. "We have a new little person to consider. Remember in Bonnitor, I listed so many bad things about Florida."

Ratso laughed. "Yes. Not approved by the Florida Tourist Board."

"Now with me, well us, expecting a new arrival, I'm ready to quit Florida. I'll run my agency from London. Until I take maternity leave, that is."

Ratso looked down, concentrating on his starter, his mind adjusting to what he had just heard. Once again, a different life-path was unfolding. "Well, if you're sure."

"I won't hold you to retiring in two years. You're a terrific detective. You love the job still. Stay on with the Met – if you want to."

Ratso was lost for words.

He said nothing.

****

DEADLINE VEGAS
In this standalone crime thriller, after his sister dies horribly, Dex vows revenge on a casino group which has cheated her at high-stakes roulette. The trail takes him from London to Panama and Las Vegas where he discovers his sister was not the only violent death. At whatever personal risk, he must achieve the unthinkable and destroy a multi-billion casino empire who will stop at nothing.

BUY DEADLINE VEGAS ON AMAZON
Just Copy and Paste this link: amzn.to/3UmNs8W

Did you enjoy DEADLY HUSH?

I would love you to leave a review on Amazon

Enjoying the Ratso Series?
Want to know what happened on the French Riviera involving Ratso and Boris Zandro before *Hard Place*?

- SIGN UP here to receive your FREE copy of *Hard Place -THE PREQUEL* and news of other exclusive offers. Just Copy and Paste this link: bit.ly/dshppoin

FIND ME ONLINE
Facebook: bit.ly/fbdsauthor
Website: bit.ly/dsauthorsite
Instagram: bit.ly/douginsta
Email: doug@douglasstewartbooks.com

COMING SOON

Deadly Shadows – Ratso Book 4
Ratso, his team and Kirsty-Ann Webber return after a young woman is home alone in London and a brutal murder follows. Her family is not all it seems as Ratso unravels an international conspiracy and a global scam.

BOOKS BY DOUGLAS STEWART

Fiction
The Ratso Series
Hard Place
Dead Fix
Deadly Hush

Other Mystery Thrillers
Deadline Vegas
Undercurrent
The Dallas Dilemma
Cellars' Market
The Scaffold
Villa Plot, Counterplot
Case for Compensation

Contributions
M.O. – a compendium
Capital Crimes – a compendium
Death Toll – a compendium

Non-Fiction
Terror at Sea
Piraten (German Language market)
Insult to Injury
A Family at Law

ABOUT DOUGLAS STEWART

I was born in Scotland but raised in England. I have lived and worked as a lawyer and writer in London, Las Vegas, Cyprus and the Isle of Man. **Deadly Hush** is my sixteenth book and the third in the Ratso series, **Undercurrent** was a WH Smith Paperback of the Week. An earlier book topped the charts for 24 weeks as did a Compendium to which I contributed. Whether fiction or non-fiction, my books reflect my legal background and my love of interesting and interesting locations, whether distant or closer to home.

Copyright © Chewton Limited, Douglas Stewart

This novel, although inspired by some true events, is entirely a work of fiction. In particular, the names, characters and incidents portrayed in it are the work of the author's imagination. Any resemblance to actual persons, living or dead or to events is entirely coincidental and unintentional.

The right of Douglas Stewart to be identified as the author of this work has been asserted by him in accordance with the Copyright, Designs and Patents Act 1988 and all other current legislation.

You may not copy, store, distribute, transmit, reproduce or otherwise make available this publication (or any part of it) in any form or by any means (electronic, digital, optical, mechanical, photocopying, recording or by any other manner whatsoever) without the prior written consent of the author and of Chewton Limited. Any person or body who does any unauthorised act in relation to this publication may be liable to criminal prosecution and civil claims for damages.

All rights reserved under International Copyright Conventions. You have been granted the nonexclusive, non-transferable right to access and read the text of this e-book on screen. No part of this text may be reproduced, transmitted, downloaded, decompiled, reverse engineered or stored in or introduced into any information storage and retrieval system in any formal by any means, whether electronic or mechanical, now known or hereinafter invented without the express written consent of Chewton Ltd. Without written consent, no part of this book may be used or adapted for any purpose whatsoever (including for any visual or audio media) by use of what is generically known as Artificial Intelligence (A I).

Chewton Publications, an imprint of Chewton Limited

Printed in Great Britain
by Amazon